Praise for *The Bone Witch*

★ "Mesmerizing. Chupeco does a magnificent job of balancing an intimate narrative perspective with sweeping worldbuilding, crafting her tale within a multicultural melting pot of influences as she presses toward a powerful cliffhanger."

—*Publishers Weekly*, Starred Review

★ "Fantasy worldbuilding at its best, and Rin Chupeco has created a strong and colorful cast of characters to inhabit that realm."

—*Shelf Awareness*, Starred Review

"Readers who enjoy immersing themselves in detail will revel in Chupeco's finely wrought tale. *Game of Thrones* fans may see shades of Daenerys Targaryen in Tea, as she gathers a daeva army to unleash upon the world. Whether she is in the right remains a question unanswered, but the ending makes it clear her story is only beginning."

—*Booklist*

"Chupeco delights. Exceptionally written from beginning to end."

—*BuzzFeed*

"Chupeco craftily weaves magic, intrigue, and mystery into a captivating tale that will leave readers begging for the promised sequel."

—*School Library Journal*

"A fantasy lover's fantasy, with a rich history and hierarchy of its own. The secrets and workings of its magic are revealed slowly in a suspenseful novel that is sure to appeal to those with a love of serious, dark fairy tales."

—*Foreword Reviews*

"Fans of high fantasy looking for diverse representation will be eager to get their hands on this book. A series to be reckoned with."

—*School Library Connection*

"A high-fantasy *Memoirs of a Geisha*, Chupeco's latest excels in originality… Chupeco is a writer to watch."

—*Kirkus Reviews*

The

HEART
FORGER

The

HEART
FORGER

RIN
CHUPECO

sourcebooks
fire

Published by Sourcebooks Fire, an imprint of Sourcebooks, Inc.
P.O. Box 4410, Naperville, Illinois 60567-4410
(630) 961-3900
Fax: (630) 961-2168
sourcebooks.com

Library of Congress Cataloging-in-Publication Data

Names: Chupeco, Rin, author.
Title: The heart forger / Rin Chupeco.
Description: Naperville, Illinois : Sourcebooks Fire, [2018] | Sequel to: The
bone witch. | Summary: Armed with the ability to tame and control the
monstrous daeva, Tea enacts her revenge against the royals who wronged
her, but she is hampered by her disapproving brother and pursued by
enemies wishing to use her dark magic for themselves.
Identifiers: LCCN 2017037532 | (13 : alk. paper)
Subjects: | CYAC: Magic--Fiction. | Witches--Fiction. | Monsters--Fiction. |
Fantasy.
Classification: LCC PZ7.C4594 He 2018 | DDC [Fic]--dc23 LC record available at https://
lccn.loc.gov/2017037532

Printed and bound in the United States of America.
BVG 10 9 8 7 6 5 4 3 2 1

This is for Momofuku Ando, the creator of instant ramen, which sustained me for many a long night as I struggled with both words and self-doubt. Nothing but respect for my president.

THE FAR SEA
DAANORIAN SEA
SWIFT SEA
SEA OF SKULLS

Stranger's Peak
Srevny Fjord
Bayevik
Grezel
Farsun
The Ice Falls
ZARICH
ISTERA
Gorvekan Stepps
Heartsbane Islands
River of Peace
Runeswood
The Vigil
Setras
Deavasteeth
Freydin
Mogredin
AKVAN
TRESEA
HIGHGAARD
Tuadan
Gregior River
Santiang
Haitsa Mountains
Lake Kaal
DAANORIS
Leiksha
Laepsang
Miekong

THE WORLD
OF THE BONE WITCH:
THE EIGHT KINGDOMS

*S*HE WORE THE CORPSES FOR *show. They trailed behind her, grotesque fabrics of writhing flesh and bone, spreading across the plain for miles around us. Those bereft of legs and feet used hands and elbows; those lacking jaws and tongues moaned from the hollows of their throats. Those onlookers who drew close grasped at the train of her gown until I was no longer certain where her dress ended and they began.*

"Intimidation," she told me, amused by my repulsion. "Men abandon battle when they see their own fates in these ruined faces."

I could not argue with her results: resistance crumbled as soldiers disobeyed their commanders and ran rather than face her horrors.

She plundered every graveyard we found, no headstone left unturned, since entering Daanoris. Her strength had grown since leaving the Sea of Skulls. When she first resurrected her daeva, each summon had sapped such strength and life from her that by the time she had raised the last, she was nearly dead herself. Yet she brought back these unfortunate ghouls from their graves with relative ease.

Asha reached their limit after raising five or six corpses, I remembered. Even the strongest bone witches could not manage more than a dozen at best. I knew the girl's immense power had everything to do with her heartsglass, as black as the darkest night when other ashas' would shine silver.

I was appalled by her disrespect for these innocent dead, beseeched her not to interrupt their rest. To this, she only laughed. "The dead do not need rest," she told me, "only the living believe the grave can bring you peace."

There was no reason to raise these armies of undead, and she knew it. The daeva that surrounded her were enough to ruin kingdoms. Strangely docile, all seven plodded beside their mistress, each more terrifying than the next. In ages past, they had the reputation for violence, capable of supping on whole armies with little effort. Yet throughout our journey to Daanoris, they paid no heed to the men and women who fled from their approach. Stragglers were shown mercy and ignored.

I understood the people's fear. For many nights, I had broken camp with these demons, wondering each time if I would live to see morning. Only the presence of the Deathseeker, Lord Kalen, calmed me, though he was no more alive than the throng of cadavers that followed his lover. His chest rose and fell like mine, his face bore none of the pallor associated with death, and his brown eyes were sharp with the spark of life, even if the absence of true breath in him disproved this.

"It is necessary that they flee," he said quietly one night. "In time, you will understand."

"Then tell me her intentions now," I challenged him. "I promised to tell her story. Why leave me in the dark?"

"Conquer one fear at a time," he responded with a pointed glance at the daeva frolicking with its master in the near darkness. "Accustom yourself to one type of fiend before we introduce you to another."

The words filled me with foreboding. What did the asha intend when we reached Daanoris's capital?

I watched them, the necromancer and her familiar. I watched her cast quick secret glances at Kalen when she thought he did not see.

"Am I distasteful now?" he asked without looking away from the fire. "Am I that much different?"

"Never," she said quietly.

"How did you raise me? Silver heartsglass can't…"

"I didn't." She looked down. Her hands trembled. "I was…so full of the Dark. I felt powerful enough to believe I could stop the sun. And so I did."

He knelt before her then, taking her heart-shaped face in his large hands.

"Are you angry at me?"

For the first time, I saw her afraid.

"Do you resent me for bringing you back to this chaos?"

"I promised you with my dying breath, with my blood and your heart in my hands. I promised that I would crawl out of my grave and kill everything that stands between us." He bent closer, kissed her hard.

She kissed him back, hungry, her hands stroking his neck. He drew her tightly against him, as if holding her could never be enough. I turned away.

There were faint marks on the bone witch's neck when we left the next day, and her eyes were very bright. The Deathseeker sported no injuries, and his gaze was gentle whenever he looked at her.

The Daanorian capital, Santiang, lay before us. I took in its high walls and fortified towers. I saw the bobbing torches of the men who manned its garrisons. Even from this distance, I saw their fear rising, higher than any flag they could wave.

I watched the familiar reach forward to wrap her in his arms. I watched the Dark asha relax, leaning back against him with a vulnerability she rarely allowed herself to show.

"The Daanorians will not surrender easily, Tea," Lord Kalen said.

"That will not matter. Their gates shall fall anyway. We rest here tonight and begin on the morrow. It will give them time to send their women and children away and the rest to put their affairs in order."

"It is not too late. We can go—anywhere. They won't find us."

For a moment, I saw the temptation in her eyes, the longing his words sowed. "You know they will do the same to the next bone witch after me, and the next, and the next. You know this will never end."

The Deathseeker pressed his forehead against hers. "Then we will fight."

The girl turned back to her throng of faithful undead. "Thank you," she told them softly, the way one might tell a bedtime story to children. "Sleep and wait."

The corpses sighed in unison, a frightening sound that echoed from the nearest ghoul that clawed at her skirts to, as I imagined, the farthest of her carrion, many miles away.

And as one, they fell. They sank down like groundwater, the land swallowing them whole until no trace of them remained. What was once a company of thousands of corpses became a fellowship of three and seven, and the daeva bayed their good-byes.

The asha sat by a fallen log, gathering stones. The Deathseeker gestured, and fire sputtered from the pile. She gestured at me to sit, and I complied.

"You have more to tell me," I said, knowing this was far from the end of her tale.

"Yes." She gazed thoughtfully at the fire, at the flames licking through the stone. Then, like it was the most normal thing in the world, she said, "I suppose the trouble began again when I tried raising a king from the dead."

I

*H*E DOES NOT LOOK SO *formidable*, I lied to myself, staring at the warped, decaying body before me. *I can defeat his will. I will break him. It is a wonder what Mykkie had ever seen in him.*

It was not the first time I had deceived myself in this manner. Neither was this the first time I had raised King Vanor from the grave. But if I repeated that mantra enough times, I thought I could finally believe my words.

The dead king refused to look at me, his eyes distant. The royal crypts were built to strike both fear and awe in those who visited, but I had grown accustomed to the stone faces looking down at me with quiet scrutiny from their high precipices. But King Vanor's continued silence unnerved me every time—more than I cared to admit.

"A wise philosopher once said," Fox drawled from the

shadows, "that doing the same thing over and over again while expecting a different result is the mark of a fool."

"Why do I bring you along?"

"Well, a wise philosopher once said—"

"Shut up." My brother had no need to tell me my quest was hopeless. Numerous Dark asha, all more experienced than me, had made the attempt. But I had to do *something*.

"You're in a worse mood than usual. Did Kalen chew you out at practice again?"

"If you don't like it here, why not find some women in the city to flirt with instead?"

"Not in Oda—" He caught himself. "None of your business. Can we get this over with?"

I turned back to the corpse. "Where are you keeping Mykaela's heartsglass?"

No answer. The colossi statues guarding the catacombs were likelier to respond than this infernal sod of a king.

"Answer me! What have you done to her heartsglass? Where did you keep it? Why do you hate her so much?" My headache worsened. Somewhere in the back of my head, I was aware of a shadow thrashing about, sensing my anger. I saw a vision of water, green and murky, before it faded out of view.

I took a deep breath and let it out carefully. The ache lightened and the shadow retreated as I recovered my calm.

"This is a waste of time." Fox folded his arms across his chest. My brother looked to be in peak physical health, though he was no more alive than the royal noble standing before us.

Their similarities ended there; there was barely enough skin and sinew clinging to Vanor to pass for human. That was my doing. The first few times I resurrected him, I had been respectful, taking great pains to restore his body to how it appeared when he was alive.

Now I allowed him only enough muscle and flesh to move his jaw.

"He's not going to talk, Tea. You know that, I know that, and he definitely knows that."

"I will *make* him talk." Many years ago, my sister-asha had fallen in love with this wretched excuse of a ruler. In exchange for her unwavering devotion, he had taken her heartsglass and hidden it so well that no one had been able to find it.

And now, more than a decade later, Mykaela was dying. She could no longer return to Kion. Her health had deteriorated to the point where she had to remain near her heartsglass, still hidden somewhere within Odalia, here in the city of Kneave. It was hard enough to be a bone witch; that she'd survived for this long was a miracle in itself.

I grabbed what was left of the king's shoulders, pulling him toward me. He reeked of death and obstinacy. "Answer me!" My voice echoed off the columns. "Didn't you love her even a little? Or are you so petty that you'd allow her to suffer for the rest of her years? She's *dying*. What grudge do you harbor to hate her this much?"

"Tea."

I froze. So did Fox.

I had told no one else about my weekly excursions to the

royal crypts. Not my friend Polaire, who would have boxed my ears if she'd known, nor Mistress Parmina, who would doom me to a life cleaning outhouses. Only Fox was privy to my secret, which he had agreed to keep despite his own misgivings. And Mykaela was the last person I wanted to find out.

She had aged more rapidly during the last few years since she had taken me under her wing. There was more gray in her golden hair, more lines on her face. Her back stooped slightly, like she struggled under a heavy burden. She had taken to using a cane everywhere she went, unsure of her own feet.

"Mykaela," I stammered, "you're not supposed to be here."

"I could say the same for you," she answered, but her eyes were fixed on King Vanor, her pain obvious. He watched her gravely, without shame or guilt, and my anger rose again. How many raisings had my sister-asha endured, forced to watch while this king refused to speak?

I raised my finger to sketch out the rune that would send Vanor back to the world of the dead, but Mykaela lifted a hand. "Vanor," she said quietly, "it's been a while."

The decaying figure said nothing. His eyes studied her, savage and hungry and ill suited for such an impassive face.

"I apologize for my wayward apprentice. She has been willful and intractable since her admission to my asha-ka and has shown little improvement since. Please return to your rest. Tea, let him go."

Mykaela's words were a steel knife through my heart. Stuttering apologies, I completed the spell and watched as King

Vanor's body crumbled back into dust in his open coffin. Even as his features dissolved, King Vanor never once looked away from Mykaela's face.

"Close the lid and move the stone back in place," she said. I could detect the anger behind her calm. "I would tell King Telemaine to seal his coffin, but even that might not stop you. Whatever possessed you to let her do this, Fox?"

Fox shrugged, grinning like an abashed schoolboy. "I'm her familiar. It comes with the territory."

"Being her familiar is no excuse for being an imbecile! And you! What possessed you to summon dead royalty in the middle of the night?"

"I wanted to help." The excuse sounded weaker when made to Mykaela than to Fox. "I thought that I could control daeva now! You said no Dark asha's ever done that before! That's why…why I…"

Mykaela sighed. "And so by that logic, you think you are different from Dark asha of the past? What you have in ability, Tea, you lack in wisdom. You cannot compel the dead if they are not willing. Wasn't that the first lesson I taught you after you raised Fox from his grave? Arrogance is not a virtue, sister."

I looked down, blinking back tears. Was I arrogant to want to save her? Unlike Fox, Dark asha and all those with a silver heartsglass cannot be raised from the dead, and that permanence frightened me. "I'm sorry. I want to help. But I feel so powerless."

I heard her move closer, felt her hand on my head, stroking my hair.

"It's not such a bad thing, to feel powerless sometimes. It teaches us that some situations are inevitable and that we should spend what little time we have in the company of the people that matter most. Do you understand me, Tea?"

"Yes." I wept.

"Tea, I'm not dead yet." A finger nudged at my chin. "I would appreciate it if you stopped acting like I was. I do not give up so easily, but we must adopt other means."

"I'm sorry."

"It is only an apology if you mean it. This is the last time you will be summoning anyone in the royal crypts, no matter how noble you think your actions are. Promise me."

"I promise," I mumbled.

"The same is true for you too, Fox."

"I promise, milady."

"Good. Now help me up the stairs. My legs aren't what they used to be."

Fox reached down and scooped Mykaela into his arms. "It's the fastest way," he explained. "You've expended enough energy yelling at us."

The older asha chuckled. "Yes, that's always been rather tiresome now that I think about it. Perhaps you should direct your energies toward more productive tasks so I can tire less."

"How did you know we were here?" I asked.

"I've taken to wandering at night. I looked in on Tea, but her room was empty. I detected a shifting of runes nearby and merely followed it to its source."

"I didn't mean to make you worry." The staircase led back to the Odalian palace gardens. For the past two months, Fox and I had been King Telemaine's guests, traveling the kingdom and tending to the sickly. Most of the people here fear and dislike bone witches, though with lesser fervor than before. It is not easy to hold a grudge against someone who has nursed you back to health.

At the king's invitation, Mykaela had taken up residence in the castle indefinitely. But every day finds her weaker, and I feared the palace would serve as her hospice.

"There are many other concerns, Tea. Likh has a new case pending, hasn't he?"

The asha association had rejected Likh's appeal to join, but Polaire had dredged up an obscure law that permitted Deathseekers to train in the Willows until they turned fifteen, which was Likh's current age.

Mykaela glanced over Fox's shoulder, back at the catacombs, then turned away.

She still loves him, I thought, and fury burned through me like a fever. "I'm really sorry, Mykkie."

She smiled. "As I said, only if you mean it, Tea. Get some rest. We've got a busy day ahead."

.. ⎯⎬⎰⎯ ..

I listened until my brother's footsteps faded before sneaking out of my room a second time. I opened the doors of my mind to welcome the hidden shadows; they wrapped around my core, creating a barrier that had for many months prevented Fox from discovering the other sentience I hoarded away, like a sweet vintage I had no intentions of sharing. I couldn't. Not yet.

Chief waited for me at the stables. A lone woman on a horse caused no outcry, and we rode undisturbed out of the city, into a copse of trees that hid us further from view. I climbed off my stallion, told him to await my return, and moved deeper into the forest, into a small clearing that served as a rendezvous point.

I reached out once more to the moving darkness. The scar on my right thigh was hot to the touch. It burned in the cold air, but I felt no pain.

Despite its size, the beast was made of stealth and shadows. Where there was once nothing, it now stood beside me, as if summoned from the air. Three pairs of hooded eyes gazed down at me, forked tongues dancing. Its wings extended, and twilight rolled over me, soothing and pleasant.

Master? It was a voice but not in the manner we think of voices. Our bond gave us an understanding that went beyond language.

I reached out. Its scaly hide was a combination of coarse bark and rough sandpaper.

Play? It sat, unmoving, as I climbed up its back.

Yes.

In the blink of an eye, we were soaring across the sky, rolling meadows and fields of green passing below us. *Turn,* I thought, testing the limits of my control, as I have over the last several months. The *azi* complied, wings curving toward the horizon.

I laughed, the sound joyous and free against the wind, and one head dipped briefly to nuzzle at my cheek, purring.

This is not selfishness, I told myself, *but a responsibility.* Mykaela was partly right; I was arrogant and overconfident, but I was not like other Dark asha. No other Dark asha had been able to tame the *azi.* And riding with it on quiet nights meant it was not rampaging through cities.

But I also knew I had to keep my companion a secret. Raising a dead king was a far lesser sin than taking a daeva as a familiar. *I shall conquer this,* I thought and, in doing so, sealed my fate.

*W*HY ARE WE AT DAANORIS?" *I asked again when she paused.
"Why won't you tell me?"

"Because I need you as a witness as well as a storyteller, Bard.
You will not remain unbiased for long if I supply you with foresight."

"You summoned me. I travel with you. My opinions will make
little difference."

"You have a reputation for impartiality, Bard. I trust your
judgment and my prudence. And here in Santiang, there is someone I
would like you to meet."

"Who?"

"They call him the Heartforger." She flashed me a quick
mischievous grin. "I find it difficult to believe you will be so eager to
rule in my favor after the endless stretch of corpses I summoned in my
wake. Or after informing you of my intentions to take Daanoris. It
is not easy to mask your repugnance. Why have I come to Daanoris?
Perhaps simply because I can. Has that not crossed your mind?"

"Tea," Kalen admonished, his voice low and amused.

She laughed. "Let me continue my story while we still have the
luxury."

The shadows grew across the trees. The daeva melted slowly into
the forest, moving silently despite their sizes. No other sound passed
through the woods—no chirping of birds nor chatter of squirrels.

There was only the wind whispering through the leaves, the crackling of fire, and the sound of the asha's voice.

2

"Have you gotten around to kissing a boy yet?" Councilor Ludvig asked, and I choked on my tea.

We were sitting in one of the rooms at the Gentle Oaks in Kneave, one of the rare teahouses in Odalia where asha were acknowledged. It was a far cry from the more elaborate *cha-khana* found in Kion, but I liked the fewer formalities required here. Fox had gone off to train with the Odalian soldiers and I'd attended a few functions that day, choosing to spend the rest of my free time with the councilor, a veritable Isteran leader in his own right. I had expected more history lessons from him or a sharp critique on current politics. I had not expected this.

"And why, pray tell," I managed, after wiping the spill on the table and clearing my throat, "should that be any of your business?"

Councilor Ludvig grinned, making him look younger

than his seventy-odd years. "Is it wrong to inquire after my favorite student? Asha much younger than you have had more experience in romance, despite having done much less for Kion. I've kissed a pretty asha a time or two myself back in my prime."

"I'm…far too busy to be thinking about that."

"Poppycock." The councilor tore off a piece of *tanūr* bread. "Balance must be struck. You are still so young, my dear, and in danger of being overworked if it were up to your asha-ka mistress. Enjoy your youth. Do not let harridans like Parmina convince you otherwise. And also," he added, chewing thoughtfully, "I have a wonderful nephew. He is only a couple of years older than you…"

I groaned. "Thank you, Councilor, but I already have my hands full juggling relationships with people I know without adding anyone new to the mix."

"So I presume there has been progress between you and the prince?"

"Absolutely not!" My cheeks colored. "He's a prince! And I'm just…I'm a…"

A bone witch. Feared and hated everywhere but in Kion. And even in Kion, I frequently felt that we were entertainment first and people second.

The councilor only nodded. He'd been in politics longer than I had been alive and knew the lay of the land, so to speak. "Yet you are drawn to Prince Kance."

"Well, he's kind. He's the first person besides Mykaela and

my brother who does not care that I am a bone witch. And he cares for his people. *Really* cares, not just parrots what will appease his subjects. He's sincere about what he believes in. And he's very…" This was harder to admit. "He's very nice looking in the face. But not just in the face—overall. I mean—"

He chuckled. "I get the point. But marriages between asha and royalty have happened before. Even with Dark asha. It is not so uncommon."

"It doesn't matter. He has enough trouble helping his father run Odalia as it is." *And there's an azi inside my head, milord,* I added silently. *Everyone knows daeva are a weapon of the Faceless, and I am wielding the most dangerous of them all. I don't want the prince involved.* The shadows in my head shifted, agreeing.

"How are your friendships with the other boys in court then? Prince Khalad?"

Only Councilor Ludvig would still refer to Kance's brother as a prince, though his heartforging abilities had put an end to his claim to the throne. Khalad and I had grown close the year I became a full-fledged asha, and no other asha had his unique ability to forge memories into heartsglass. "Pretty good," I said, "though Khalad's even busier with work than I am."

"And what about Kalen?"

I stared at him, then started to laugh. "Kalen? He still hates me."

"*Hate* is a strong word, Tea."

"He does. He ignores me whenever he can, and when he can't, he talks down to me in that infuriatingly passive-aggressive way he has. I can never do anything right, if you listened to him, and if he could sever my ties to Prince Kance, he'd do it, then expect me to kowtow to his demands without protest."

"Have you done anything to arouse his enmity?"

"I haven't kept my resentment hidden exactly," I admitted sourly. "And I might have ignored his orders on occasion, on account of him being a jerk with no redeeming qualities."

I paused. Councilor Ludvig was staring at something behind me, his expression bemused. I took a deep breath. "I suppose he's behind me."

"Right on the first try." Kalen leaned against the door, hands folded across his chest. As was customary for Deathseekers, he was dressed all in black, like that was supposed to make him look more impressive. His heartsglass swung from his neck, a bright silver. He gave the Isteran politician a small, respectful nod. "Lord Ludvig, it's good to see you again."

"Likewise, Kalen."

"How is King Rendorvik?"

"Refusing my advice, as he is wont to do nowadays. How are the prince and his father?"

"Doing well. Please send our regards to his Highness." Kalen turned to me. "Kance wants to see you now," he said shortly, then walked back out.

"I'd advise you not to get on his bad side," Councilor Ludvig said as I rose to my feet, careful not to trip over my dress. "Kalen is Prince Kance's closest confidante after all. Perhaps if you opened up to him, he'd relent."

I sighed, then leaned over to give the councilor a hug and a quick kiss on the cheek. "Given that his point of contention is *me*, I believe the point is moot."

.. ❧ ..

"Wait up!" I yelled, hurrying after Kalen as he stalked back to the castle, attracting more than a few curious stares. "I'm sorry for what I said, but I'm not the only one at fault. You've been nothing but rude to me since we met."

"I have no need to explain myself to you," he said stiffly.

"I thought we'd reached some kind of understanding." Which was true. He'd been almost friendly in the weeks after we'd fought the *azi* at Lake Strypnyk, but that fragile amiability disappeared and he was back to criticizing how I fought, what I did, and what I said.

"You thought wrong."

I glared at him. "Out with it."

"Out with what?"

"You heard me listing what I don't like about you. It's not very sporting of me, I know. So now it's your turn. Say something about me that you don't like."

"This is not the place or the time—"

"If you had your way, there will never be the place or the time for it because you're as dense as a rock on Mithra's Wall, with the immovability to match. See? It's not that hard to share your feelings. Let it all out. Give me just three things—"

He glowered but took the bait. "You're overconfident. It always gets you in trouble. And you're irresponsible. You don't think through your actions and then expect someone else to bail you out—your brother, usually. You have this annoying way of scrunching up your nose when you don't like what you're being told to do, which makes you look even more ridiculous."

I clapped a hand over the bridge of my nose, suddenly aware I was doing exactly that. "Fine, you've said your—"

"You never listen. To anyone. You're slow to take advice, especially at sword practice. You always think life will turn out for the better, although it never does, but that doesn't stop you from making the same mistakes again—"

"I said *three* things, you lout!"

He stopped. For a moment, I thought he was going to smile. A spectrum of colors spread across his heartsglass; his initial anger was abating, giving way to amusement and grudging acceptance—and something else. But when he saw where my gaze lingered, his heartsglass turned back to its unblemished silver.

"And you're still a danger to Kance," he added quietly. "You can just as easily lure a daeva to him as kill it."

"But I haven't."

"That doesn't matter. I've seen more Dark asha than you, and they've all burned out sooner or later. Mykaela had to kill a fellow bone witch once because she was too far gone in the Dark. You may not have stepped over the line, but you sure as hell enjoy having the magic, and that's even worse." His expression was unreadable—I preferred it when he was angry. "My job is to protect Prince Kance. I train you only at Kance's request and against my better judgment. I am not your friend. And I can't be in a position where I treat you as one."

So that was it. With Kalen, it would always be about his duty to the king and the prince. Which still hurt. "Fine. And I'm sorry about my previous outburst. Like you said, I don't think things through. And whether you believe me or not, I have no intentions of harming the prince. But if we can't be friends, can't we at least be civil?"

His shoulders relaxed. "If that's what you want."

That wasn't what I wanted at all, but I gritted my teeth and swallowed my retort. "Swell."

"Good. Let's move. Kance is waiting."

I slunk quietly after him. His words stung—but I couldn't blame him. My words probably had too.

Prince Kance was up to his ears in paperwork when we entered the room. My asha-sisters Polaire and Zoya were beside him, and all three looked up as we approached. Though Prince Kance looked tired, his features brightened. I hurriedly tucked a few stray hairs back in place, my mood lifting. While seeing Polaire hard at work came as no surprise, Zoya avoided grunt work whenever possible.

Prince Kance apologized. "I asked Kalen not to bother you if you were busy."

"Yes, he made that very clear to me." I glared at Kalen, who showed no shame at this concealment.

"As you know, there were reports of a daeva sighted along

Odalia's borders this week," he began, his bright-green eyes on me. I was wrong; *nice* didn't even begin to describe his face.

"An *aeshma*, yes," I said.

"We've finally tracked it to the Kingswoods. My father gives his leave for you to hunt it down."

"I'll get right on it."

"I wouldn't think of underestimating you or any other asha, but I can bring an army. More catapults perhaps. Fortifications. It isn't safe."

"Your High—"

"Kance."

"Kance." I was pleased by his concern—for me?—but I also took in his pallor. "We'll be fine. I've done this before. And you need rest. I'm sure Lady Zoya and Lady Polaire can assist you in the meantime."

"Lady Zoya is not so sure about that," Zoya chirped and was swiftly silenced by a stern look from Polaire.

Prince Kance smiled wanly. "Is it starting to show? I've been having trouble sleeping. Lady Altaecia's made me an herbal potion for it."

"All the more reason not to overexert yourself," I said.

He shook his head. "I've been working on a new form of taxation that will lower land taxes and cut out unnecessary intermediaries. The sooner we can put that into law, the better for Odalia."

"Shouldn't the finance minister be overseeing that?"

"The finance minister is good at what he does, but he is also part of the problem. Most officials make concessions and exemptions to curry favor with the nobility, so their reforms impose a heavier tax burden on the poor. I convinced Father that we had to lay the groundwork ourselves to weed out claims of favoritism. With my plan, we can both help our citizens and generate more revenue in under two years. Polaire and Zoya are working with me on the details."

Kance was perfect—intelligent, compassionate, empathic. How could anyone *not* like him? I snuck a glance at Kalen. He had said nothing since we'd arrived and lounged by the door like a statue ready to come to life at the first sign of danger.

"And it's a good plan," Polaire said with a smile, though she looked tired herself. "Our young prince is quite the genius with numbers. But Tea is right, Kance. That's enough work for today."

The prince made a rueful face but nodded, moving to organize his papers. I stepped closer to Polaire, remembering something Kalen had said earlier.

"Mykaela killed a Dark asha before," I said softly and urgently, not wanting the others to hear. She had told me about that once before when she had taken me to see her raise a daeva for the first time.

Polaire raised an eyebrow. "And what of it?"

"I need to know more about what had happened."

She sniffed. "Illara was a good girl and one of Mykaela's charges, but she was far too ambitious for her own good. She was eager to learn of the Dark, but she didn't realize it would burn her out. She craved the Dark beyond her own limits. She called a daeva and sought to control it instead of killing it. The daeva drove her mad—and Illara became almost like a daeva herself. Mykaela had no choice. To wield anything that the Faceless would, from the most terrible of daeva to their innocent-seeming runes…there must be no compromise."

"Oh" was all I could say.

"To be headstrong is not a flaw, Tea. Mykaela was quite impulsive when she was younger. We all were. Why do you ask this now?"

"I was only wondering, Polaire." *Because there is an* azi *nesting in my brain.* Did that mean I was taking in more of the Dark than I should? Would I be another bone witch casualty, another Illara?

I almost told Polaire my secret. I *wanted* to tell her.

But if I did, would they kill me too?

Polaire shook her head, having read the sputtering strings of color lining my heartsglass and mistaking them for lesser worries. "There is nothing to concern yourself over."

"Is something wrong?" Prince Kance approached us, a quizzical look on his face.

"It's nothing, Your H—Kance," I said, moving the conversation away from my morbid thoughts. "But what does this taxation have to do with me? I have no experience with drafting laws."

The prince blinked. "Oh. No. I asked you here for something else entirely. It's about the *aeshma*. I intend to accompany you when you confront it."

"Absolutely not!" Kalen and I exclaimed at the same time.

The prince was still smiling, but he had a determined tilt to his chin that I recognized from both his older brother and their cousin. "That's not a request, I'm afraid. To be a ruler goes beyond lawmaking, and if there is a creature terrorizing my land, then I will not hide behind my throne like a coward. Does a departure at seven tomorrow morning sound good to you?"

There was no other choice but to agree. For all Kance's merits, stubbornness always did run in that family.

SURRENDER," SHE CALLED OUT. THE *walls were no barrier to the* zarich's *claws. Stone and granite tumbled down like they were made of sand, and armed men were sent screaming. The* akvan *sang and battered at the gate walls with its massive tusks and trunk until, with a loud splinter, they disintegrated.*

"Surrender," she called out. From above, the indar *struck, raking its terrible claws into wood and masts until every catapult and weapon of war splayed before us was rendered useless. The* aeshma *hissed and curled itself into a ball, using its spikes as a battering ram to break through the last wall. The cries of the fleeing soldiers and the groans of the injured carried louder than the sounds of battle.*

"Surrender," she called one last time, and the nanghait *strode forward, its two faces in full view for all to see. The daeva stood proudly in the open, and no manner of sword or cannon or pitch could pierce its hide, until, finally, even the bravest of the soldiers were forced to retreat from the nightmare staring back at them.*

But it was the azi *that posed the greatest threat. From the skies, it swept down and bathed the roofs in fire and ashes until the city writhed from within a great bonfire. The beast screamed its defiance into the clouds, heralding death to the people below. But even then, Lord Kalen was quick to act; he raised his hand and water poured from the heavens, quickly extinguishing the inferno before it could do more damage.*

I cowered behind the savul, *the only one among his brethren ordered to remain for my sake. It rested placidly beside me. With the scales of a large lizard and bulging yellow eyes, the* savul *was reptilian in appearance, yet this twenty feet of monster ended in sharp talons. Whenever a stray arrow or fireball drew too close, it lifted a hideous limb to snatch it out of the air. The fire did little to singe it, and arrows caused it no harm.*

I clutched at the zivar the asha had given me; it prevented compulsion against my will but did not protect from physical harm. Without any other armor, I clung to it desperately, the way a drowning man clings to driftwood.

In the space of an hour, every line of defense from the city of Santiang had been demolished. At Tea's signal, the beasts lumbered on, stepping past the gates and into the now-deserted streets of Daanoris's capital.

"Make for the palace," the asha said and then added with a touch of steel in her voice, "Harm no one else."

Quietly, I wept. I heard the wails of the injured, of those searching for loved ones. The bone witch had tried to stem the casualties, but...

"I had no choice," the asha said quietly, her face drawn and tired. She repeated the words a few seconds later, like a mantra.

The Daanorian palace stood before us, the ivory gleam of its curved towers shining brighter as we approach. Soldiers still manned the palace walls, the tips of arrows quenched in fire pointed at us as we drew nearer. Beyond them, heavy catapults mired in pitch waited for the signal to burn.

The asha stopped, her face suddenly wreathed in smiles.

"So it is the hanjian,*" she called out pleasantly, her voice carrying through the distance. "How nice to see you again."*

From atop the highest wall, a man in gilded armor came into view. He called out to her in Daanorian in a shaking voice, but she responded with laughter. "You know as well as I that you understand the common tongue, hanjian. It was the language you spoke when you betrayed your emperor."

The man staggered back, his fear palpable. He turned toward his soldiers and issued a harsh command. At his shout, they released the fire-tipped arrows. At the same time, the catapults flung flames into the air.

The savul *faced them with imperturbability, shielding me from the incoming storm. The arrows did no damage, but the fiery boulders produced better results. The* savul's *scaled hide caught fire, and the beast began to burn.*

Alarmed, I backed away, but the asha took hold of my arm before I could step out from the daeva's shadow. "Do not be frightened, and do not move if you wish to survive."

"You called him a hanjian.*" The Daanorian word for traitor.*

"There is only one punishment for traitors." She seated herself beside the savul's *webbed talons, heedless of the growing heat. Already the fires on the daeva's hide were dying out, leaving no wounds. "We shall wait until the bulk of their arrows are exhausted, their stores of pitch and rocks depleted. It is the only way to save those soldiers' lives." She glanced back up at the wall, where the man in bright armor had revealed himself. A strange, terrible eagerness came into her voice.*

"That man, on the other hand, is a different matter. Shall I continue the tale as we wait, Bard?"

I stared at her in shock, but already she was calmly resuming her story, even as fire and fear were all around us.

3

THERE IS NO TRAINING ADEQUATE to prepare one for fighting daeva, and I speak as one who has faced them all. Of these beasts, the *aeshma* is easily the most intimidating. Its body is an armorer's dream, with spikes and talons of everlasting sharpness. It was two dozen feet high but still fast on its feet, scampering from view long before the soldiers' arrows could find their mark.

I had protested the presence of the king's army, of Prince Kance coming to watch me. A daeva raising is not a cherry blossom viewing. It is not a kingdom festival that requires royal approval. A daeva is a creature that makes no distinction between noble and common flesh, and even all the armies of the world in attendance—and they were—will not improve anyone's chances of survival.

"Hold your fire!" I barked at the royal soldiers. "Make no sudden moves, and leave the fighting to Fox!" Brave as they were to stand their ground, the soldiers' swords and bows were as useless to the fight as silk ribbons and dresses.

The *aeshma* bellowed, but Fox dodged its attack, his own sword meant to distract rather than deliver a killing blow. Over the course of a year, Fox had had as much experience baiting daeva as I had had in putting them down.

The monster charged, and my brother vaulted over its massive head, the *aeshma's* spikes missing him by inches. He landed, then swatted tauntingly at its nose. Even Fox was not above theatrics when there was an audience.

Pain blistered, an ache ripening behind my ears, but I fought through the hurt. I braided the wind around me, and a *binding* rune shone. The *aeshma* froze in its tracks as tendrils of my magic covered its form.

"*Die*," I growled, and the creature fell, paralyzed. But it was not vanquished yet; it took strength to kill, and my headache was proving a hindrance.

A collective sigh of relief rose from the army. Prince Kance, his eyes unnaturally bright and his movements strangely stilted, stepped closer.

In my head, the shadows shifted. I had another vision of water and wings folded back behind me as I sped quickly through the depths of the sea...

I forced the image out of my head, but in that short, broken moment of concentration, the creature had gathered itself for one last desperate lunge. Kalen was already moving, grabbing Prince Kance by his robes and dragging him back as Fox jumped to shield him. One of the *aeshma*'s spikes caught my brother squarely in the chest, sliding out through his back.

"*Die!*" I shouted again, and the spell tore into the *aeshma*, straight to its heart. The hideous monster fell backward, dragging Fox along on top of it. Its stubby, furred legs kicked out involuntary before it shuddered and went still.

"Fox!" I'd seen him with far worse injuries, but an impaled brother was a vision no sister could grow accustomed to.

From atop the unmoving beast, Fox rose to his feet, still skewered. With a faint grimace, he set his boot against the creature's ridged hide and ripped himself free with a wet tearing sound.

Around us, people retched. Prince Kance shook, averting his gaze, and Kalen was grim, his glare accusatory.

"I'm fine," Fox said. "A little heartache never killed anyone."

"You're a moron," I said, breathing easier now that I could see he was OK, and drove my knife deep into the fallen *aeshma*, ignoring the stench of entrails and blood as I probed deeper until I heard the telltale click of my blade against something stronger than bone.

I plunged my hand in and pulled out the violet-hued bezoar. The *aeshma*'s corpse immediately crumbled to dust. All that was left of it was the gem that gleamed brightly in my hand. *It is odd*, I thought, *how something so beautiful can come out of something so grotesque.*

•• ⊰⊱ ••

Back in the palace, Prince Kance trembled. He rubbed his forehead. "I don't know what came over me, Lady Tea. I was foolish enough to think it was safe. I didn't know how close I was until you shouted."

"A daeva killing is not something you see every day, Your Highness," Fox pointed out. "In all the excitement, it's easy to act impulsively."

The prince smiled weakly. "I wouldn't have called getting stabbed by a two-foot spike 'excitement,' Fox."

"If the Dark asha had put the *aeshma* down completely the first time," came the frosty rejoinder from the palace window, where Kalen had taken up residence, "then additional 'excitement' might have been avoided."

"Perhaps if the prince's bodyguard had been more vigilant," I snapped back, "I might not have been so distracted."

Kalen opened his mouth again, but Prince Kance beat him to it. "It's nobody's fault but my own, Kalen. I was careless, and if it wasn't for your presence of mind, I might have met a disastrous end. In my haste to learn more about how asha do their work, I was careless."

"I could have told you that in the safety of the castle, Your Highness," I said, and Kalen made a small sputtering noise, and in my mind, Fox snickered. "Wh-what I meant was there was no need for you to view the daeva yourself!"

"For far too long, I have been sheltered from the realities of my own kingdom, Tea. I cannot rely on books and advisors to tell me how to rule. How can I govern wisely if I have none of my own experiences to fall back on?"

"The common people don't exactly experience Daeva on a daily basis, Your Highness."

"But you do as a Dark asha, don't you? Lady Mykaela is still convalescing, so that responsibility falls to you. I wanted to see you in action, to help me understand how I might lighten your burden. Instead, it seems I have only added to it."

I could feel my ears turning red and prayed that my cheeks did not follow suit. "Any burden you give will be light enough to carry. Your Highness's safety is most important."

"I cannot be protected from all dangers, Tea. But I shall strive to be more careful next time."

"Next time?" I echoed as Kalen exploded with, "There'll be no next time, Kance!"

"You cannot tell me what to do anymore, Kalen," the prince said. "I must know what lies beyond my borders and within them. In fact, I had hoped that I could accompany you when you return to Kion."

"Really?" My mood brightened almost immediately. Kalen's glower spoke volumes.

"I believe we can make it in time for the upcoming *darashi oyun*. I hear that Zoya and Shadi are dancing the lead roles again this year. Are you leaving for Ankyo after Lady Mykaela's Heartsrune ceremony?"

"A week or so after, Your Highness."

"Khalad shall be attending too. I offered him a room at the palace, but Father thought it best for him to take up lodgings at the Kingshead instead."

A shadow crossed Prince Kance's face, and I knew why. Khalad had long since embraced his apprenticeship to the old Heartforger, but Prince Kance had never gotten over the guilt of inheriting the throne in his place.

"The old forger probably insisted," Fox remarked. "He's not a fan of the king or most nobles in Odalia."

"I think it's more than that. Khalad and Father had never been on the best of terms."

"No, we haven't," King Telemaine agreed, entering the room. As always, I had to tilt my head to look at him; he was tall, but he would have been a towering presence even without his extraordinary height. "For the longest time, he blamed the asha and me for your mother's death, though time with the forger has tempered his anger. But son or not, to welcome a Heartforger under our roof foments more distrust and suspicion. That Mykaela already resides here has not set well with many."

"He's my brother, and it is a ridiculous superstition."

"I had not wished a silver heartsglass on Khalad, Kance, but even kings must follow custom. Even if I would have wanted otherwise. Lady Tea, Sir Fox, you have my thanks once again."

My hands disappeared, engulfed within the king's. Gratitude shone through his heartsglass, and I was embarrassed. "It's nothing, Your Majesty."

"'It's nothing,' she says. Saving my son and putting down the terrible beast plaguing my kingdom is everything to me, Lady Tea, and I vow to do everything in my power to repay you for your service." He paused, unusually hesitant. "Is—is Khalad doing well?"

"He is. He does a lot of good work, Your Majesty, and he takes pride in it."

"Good, good. If only…" The king sighed, his eyes distant.

Bezoars found within kingdoms were customarily entrusted to their rulers, but I couldn't move my hands to gift the gem. Fox solved my dilemma by fishing it out of my pocket and handing it over.

King Telemaine shook his head in wonder, staring down at the purple stone. "So many wars won and fought over such a small stone. Lady Tea, Sir Fox, please excuse us. There are certain matters Kance and I need to finalize before his birthday celebration."

"I told you that we have no need for such lavishness, Father."

"You are my son and my heir. How is that not reason for lavishness?" The king's laugh boomed. "Kalen, I shall need your advice as well."

Prince Kance bowed to us and followed his father out of the room, Kalen half a step behind.

"Are you all right, Tea?" Fox asked.

"I think my fingers are dead."

Fox's tone shifted to one of concern. "Are you in pain? Did the *aeshma* hurt you?"

Familiar or not, I wished Fox couldn't decipher my moods so easily. "It's nothing, just another headache."

"You've been having a lot of those recently."

"I'm tired. I didn't get to sleep much last night." That was true enough. "I'll rest once we visit Khalad. I want to ask him about his progress on Mykaela's new heartsglass."

"If he'd made further headway, he would have contacted us."

"Well"—I cleared my throat—"I was also thinking about getting Prince Kance something for his birthday, and I have an idea I wanted to run by Khalad."

For someone who no longer needed breath, my brother's sigh was loud and exasperated. "Tea."

"It's only a gift! I can go without you if you've got other things to do."

"Oh, I'll come with. But mark my words, little sister. Getting your hopes up will bring you nothing but misery."

Looking back, I suppose I should have wondered why he seemed so bitter, like personal experiences had inspired the remark more than sound advice.

.. ＼╿╱ ..

"It won't need much," Khalad said. "A few happy thoughts and nostalgia. This is the easiest glass I've been asked to make in years. Did you kill the *aeshma*?" He paused. "Did you give the bezoar to Fa...the king?"

The Heartforger apprentice's room at the Kingshead was filled to overflowing with books, papers, strangely shaped glass containers, and bottles upon bottles of flickering lights and hues. I wondered how much the innkeeper had been charging Khalad to keep them all stored here. "I did."

"Did he say what he planned to do with it?"

"He didn't say. He asked about you though."

A frown marred Khalad's face. "I don't care. Fox, I'm going to extract a happy memory from Tea, so you might feel some tugging on your end."

"Thanks for the warning."

"Khalad, how long has it been since you've talked to your father?" I asked.

"Not long enough." Khalad slid a finger across my forehead, a gesture he had done many times before. There was a familiar tingling as Khalad turned the pages of my memories, searching.

"Ever thought about visiting?" I ventured.

"Tea."

"Sorry."

"There's a good reason we don't talk anymore. Let's leave it at that." He withdrew his hand, and a few stray wisps of blue and yellow clung to his fingers. In those colored strings, I could see memories of me running across a field with my brothers and sisters and of a younger Fox giving me a piggyback ride through a shallow stream. Asha retain their memories even when a Heartforger takes them, but their removal never stops feeling odd. "How is Lady Mykaela?"

"In bed, resting. Polaire is taking care of her."

"If 'taking care of her' means bullying Mykaela into submitting, then I agree," Fox said.

"Says the guy who bullies me as frequently."

"Lady Mykaela is nice enough to listen when she has to. You don't."

"Children," Khalad said mildly, his skilled hands forming a

small lump of clay in front of him. Sparks flew from his fingers, and the small mound twisted and turned, trapped by magic not even I could see. He kneaded the strings of memories into the clay until the thick mixture absorbed them and hardened. The mound made a tinkling noise and split open, revealing a spherical glass crystal where blue, red, and yellow lobbied for dominance, shifting from one color to the other.

"I don't know what to call it," Khalad admitted, handing it to me. "It's the first of its kind. It'll boost his mood, keep him calm whenever he tires. I can only imagine what he has to deal with every day. That's one thing I don't miss. As a ruler, you never have time to yourself."

"Do you miss any of it?" Fox wanted to know.

Khalad gestured at the bottles lining his shelves. "I got a rare memory today. The old man who had it escaped death by hanging in Drycht. In one of these boxes, I have a heartsglass for a woman who forgets everything she's done the day before. Ironic that I take a memory from a man who does not wish to remember for a woman who would give her all not to forget. I've helped more people in the last two weeks than I ever helped people in the last three years as the crown prince.

"The only thing I regret is turning over those duties to Kance with little warning. I used to blame my father—and Dark asha, if I must be honest—for killing my mother. But now that the anger has gone, my dislike for my father remains. He holds many views I do not agree with, and I have always rebelled against him with my temper. He always saw me as an heir more than a son. He favored Kance long before my hearts-glass turned silver."

He paused and frowned. "Have you been feeling unwell lately, Tea?"

"She's been having headaches," Fox reported.

"When I was looking through your memories, I felt something unusual."

"Unusual?" Khalad was as good at reading heartsglass as I was, so I tried to keep my calm.

"I don't know how else to define it. It felt like there was something that wasn't a part of you but somehow still is. Is Aenah still in Kneave?"

"She's warded as closely as the asha can. She has no control over me, Khalad—quite the opposite actually."

Khalad didn't look convinced.

"I just put down an *aeshma*, Khalad. Controlling daeva, even for a short time, doesn't leave one feeling clean."

"Take the rest of the day off."

"I see you don't take your own advice."

He smiled. "Heartforgers don't have to deal with daeva. Although Master likes to say they'd probably be better company than the people we deal with."

"How is the old man?"

"Traveling." Never idle, Khalad was building a pyramid of pebbles on the table. "He visited Istera last month, and he's now in Daanoris. He's on the hunt for rare memories, and there are a few strange illnesses he wanted a closer look at. There have been some cases of a sleeping disease that turns its victims' heartsglass gray. He's been working on an antidote. Said it was promising." He looked at me and then glanced back at the small glass case he had made. "We haven't been able to find the rest of the ingredients for Lady Mykaela yet. I'm sorry."

"Don't be." Dark asha cannot regenerate heartsglass, though new ones can be forged. But finding the memories needed for Mykaela's had been difficult: a memory of love and sacrifice, a memory of a heinous act committed, and a memory of surviving dire odds. Khalad had already extracted that last one from my battle against Aenah and the *azi*.

"Master told me something about King Vanor," Khalad began, hesitant. "He had met with the king shortly before he was assassinated. Master wasn't fond of Odalian nobles, but he was fond of my uncle. Master says he isn't as bad as you think he is—"

I covered my heart with both my hands, glaring. "You saw me raise Vanor!" I accused.

Khalad blushed. "I don't get to choose what I see in heartsglass. You know that." His hand jerked, and the pyramid he was building tumbled. "Sorry."

"Well, you're wrong on one count. He's a horrible bastard, and I can understand why he was killed."

"Tea!" Fox warned.

"You know I'm right. Why would Vador hide Mykaela heartsglass if he loved her?"

Khalad exhaled noisily. "I don't know. But Master was adamant about Vanor's innocence. He was sure of it."

"You don't have to feel guilty because you were related to Vanor, you know. It's not like you were responsible. You feel things too much."

"My master has said that on many occasions. He's not wrong, but it helps me forge better." Khalad was suddenly eager to change the subject. I made no complaints. "We still need those two memories for Lady Mykaela's new heartsglass. I've looked through several possibilities, but none are of the potency I need."

"How about a heinous act committed by a Faceless?"

"That would probably work. They're not known for doing things half..." He trailed off, shocked. "Tea, you don't mean that!"

"Why not? We have her imprisoned and then she's in no position to refuse us."

"I have to side with Khalad on this one," Fox said. "Aenah's crafty enough even when she's powerless. Don't drag Khalad into a battle he hasn't volunteered for."

Khalad's eyes lit up from behind his spectacles. He tugged at his hair, which was white, like most Heartforgers'. "You misunderstand me, Sir Fox. I'm not turning it down. I can't extract any memory from a Faceless if she's not willing, but I'm curious about the other notions I might find in her head."

Fox groaned. "I'm surrounded by idiots."

"It's worth a shot, I think." Khalad paused and added after a sidelong glance at my heartsglass, "But don't tire yourself for Kance. He wouldn't want that. He can be a little...oblivious sometimes. Even more so nowadays."

Was my crush really that obvious to everyone but the prince himself?

Yes, Fox said in my head. *Yes, it is.*

*T*HERE IS SOMETHING STRANGE ABOUT the soldiers, Tea," Kalen said.

That was true. When the arrows and fiery pitch had failed, soldiers streamed out of the Daanorian palace. It was a suicide mission, and they struggled forward as if every step was agony. It was obvious they were terrified, their eyes rolling back in fright. But despite their reluctance, they continued, drawn onward to their impending deaths by some unseen force.

"Compulsion, and a poor one at that," the bone witch noted. "He is unskilled and desperate, barely able to control his army."

Shock tore through me. "But only Dark asha can use such magic."

"And Faceless. Most likely he wields a seeking stone, modified to channel magic. But the darkrot comes quicker, and to allow him to use compulsion unfettered suggests that his master has already marked him for death."

The monstrous three-headed azi swept down, and the asha climbed on its back with ease. "You say I have kept you in the dark. I offer you the chance to see with your own eyes. If you are not afraid, come with me."

But I was afraid. I feared her pet dragon as much as I feared the one who could compel these poor soldiers against their wishes, but after my earlier protest, there was only one choice to make.

I scrambled up the azi's *back, white-knuckled and bathed in sweat, and held on as it flew swifter than any wind. It made for the castle with all haste, the asha sitting beside me as serene as if she were on an excursion to the countryside.*

We found the hanjian *atop their highest tower. The changes in him horrified me. Only a few hours ago he had stood in golden armor, issuing orders. Now he lay wizened, like some unknown creature had drained him of blood and sustenance, then left him crouched on the floor like an emaciated monkey. He clutched at a round black stone in his hands, gibbering nonsense. A growing shadow surrounded him, lashing at the air like a whip. His heartsglass pulsed silver.*

"He is lost," the asha said calmly. "A pity. I would have liked him to be sane before the end."

The man saw us and shrunk away.

"Your masters doomed you the instant they gave you that stone, hanjian.*" There was no warmth in the asha's voice. "Soon, the darkrot will consume you until there is nothing left. Release your hold on the soldiers."*

The man howled his impotent fury, barking out something unintelligible before making a cutting motion with his hands.

The shadows around the stone grew. The man's limbs stiffened, turning black as we watched. His face grew more elongated, eyes bulging from his face. He opened his mouth, and I saw fangs sprouting.

The bone witch did not wait. All three of the azi's *heads lurched forward, and I succumbed to my cowardice, covering my eyes. Even then, I heard the snarls of the beast and the shrieks of the doomed* man, the tearing of flesh and the snapping of bone. When the silence returned, I fought the urge to throw up.

"You murdered him," I whispered.

"I saved those soldiers." She stood, the man's heartsglass in her hands. She watched the light from it fade, lips twisted in grim satisfaction. "It is all a matter of perspective."

4

I RESENTED KING TELEMAINE FOR HIS humanity. His dungeon was damp but well kept, bare but with minimal discomfort. For a prisoner who had done her best not only to rob me of my mind and will as well as kill Fox, this was a luxury she did not deserve.

The orders I gave were simple: I went in alone—always. Even Fox was barred from entering, resigned to standing on the other side of the cell door, listening for signs of trouble through our bond.

Not for the first time, I wished the Faceless woman had not been interred to Odalia from Kion. Except Empress Alyx wanted little to do with her, and Telemaine had offered to shoulder the Faceless's imprisonment, which made Aenah's proximity to Prince Kance a source of worry. If a Faceless leader could pose as a servant at the Valerian—as my very own asha-ka!—then what other devilry could she devise, even while imprisoned?

I hated her. The Faceless would wield daeva and destroy kingdoms in their quest for power, but Aenah had made it personal. Every injury I suffered since first entering Kion was from her schemes—the damage at the Falling Leaf teahouse, through the seeking stone she had placed to amplify my abilities beyond my control. The *azi* she had commanded before me, killing several asha at the *darashi oyun*. The deaths of the Deathseekers who pursued her, and my own near-fatal battle at Lake Strypnyk. I have good reasons to kill her, and it infuriates me that I cannot simply because she has set other schemes in motion that we require knowledge of.

My interrogations over the past several months had borne fruit: an attempt by Usij's followers to attack the Isteran palace; a move to blow up a diplomat's residence in Kion; a threat against King Telemaine's life. Despite these successes, I was always left feeling that—given her notoriety and high ranking among the Faceless—there were bigger plans she was leaving unsaid.

"Be careful," Fox told me, as he often did. I nodded, and the heavy metal doors swung shut with a loud clang behind me.

"Hello, Tea." Aenah was chained to the wall, the links allowing only five inches of movement in either direction. I knew this, having measured them myself. It permitted her only enough distance to the bucket she relieved herself in and to the meals that were pushed through a slot in the wall by the Deathseeker on duty.

I felt the strength of the Runic wards crisscrossing the room, blocking the magic and leaving a strange, gaping emptiness, a feeling of incompleteness. In that room, she could use no spells.

The only elegance left about her was the black heartsglass she still wore, for there is no magic that could pry it away without her consent.

"How long has it been, child? Two months now? Three?"

"You know what I'm here for."

"What you say you are here for never changes," she laughed. "And yet, you have never asked the one question you have been dying to since we began."

"I am not interested."

"How unkind of you to say so, Tea. Do you think so little of Mykaela's life that you would be quick to throw her away?"

"Leave Mykaela out of this."

"You know as well as I that is impossible. Mykaela's well-being is what drives you to accept her responsibilities without complaint, though once upon a time, you feared to serve as her replacement. And now you are here, dooming her to an early death by refusing to listen—"

The words ended in a startled shriek. Aenah sank back against the wall and thrashed, head tossing from side to side as her whole body stiffened in pain. I waited a few seconds more and then stopped, leaving her gasping for breath. There was no room for gentleness here.

"I've told you many times before. You will leave Mykaela out of our conversations."

Aenah coughed weakly, then laughed. "You are persistent. What an ally you would have made."

"Tell me what I need to know."

Aenah's lips twisted into a smirk. "What would that be, I wonder? Should I tell you about the strange illnesses flitting about the nobility in the upper kingdoms? That Usij is behind it perhaps? Or that Druj intends to wreak havoc within the Yadosha city-states next? Perhaps I should tell you what you have always been afraid to ask: Can Mykaela be saved? Do the elder asha prevent her from finding her heartsglass? Or"—Aenah leaned forward, shaking off my attack like it was but a shower of water—"that there might be a way to bring the dead back to true life, unfettered by runes and bonds? What would you choose, Tea?"

The silence that followed was the quiet of the tombs. I clenched my fists, refusing myself any emotion. It was always like this. While I could use *Compulsion* to command her physically, I could not compel her to speak any secrets she had no desire to say. A strange barrier to them lay in her mind, one I could not yet batter down.

"Tell me more about Yadosha and about this strange sickness."

Aenah sighed, disappointed. "Usij and I do not always see eye to eye in how to lead the Faceless, but I kept myself abreast of his comings and goings to ensure his schemes do not interfere with mine. I know he intended to poison a few royals as the first step to achieving shadowglass."

"And what does shadowglass do?"

"This has been a fixation with you as of late. Why so curious about shadowglass?"

I said nothing, only waited.

"Perhaps I shall tell you this time." Aenah grinned. "It is the prize we all seek, Lady Tea. Did you not wonder at the color of my heartsglass that fateful night I revealed myself to you?"

"That fateful night we *caught you*," I corrected her.

"However it happened, black heartsglass is the ultimate fate of bone witches like us, Tea. Dark asha do not live long lives. But when they do, it is only a matter of time before their hearts become corrupted."

The air turned hot, took on a spiteful edge. She smiled again, with a mouth full of secrets. "How long will it take for yours to turn as black as mine, Tea? A year? A month? A day? I have been inside your mind. I know of the shadow that makes its home there. Do the others know? Does your brother know? Perhaps not—they would not grant you this much freedom if they did."

"Enough!" My fingers itched for more runes. If only I had full control of her heart, I could use it to wring every drop from it until it bled knowledge—but no asha would permit such torture, even on the worst of criminals. And so I put aside my anger because if there is one thing I am, it is that I am not her.

"If you will not provide information about Yadosha and this sickness you speak of, I will leave. What does the illness have to do with black heartsglass? What does Druj intend to do in the city-states?"

"Druj is a fool who plays the same old tricks but crows like they were new. The target is Lord Besserly this time, at his residence two days from now. And as for the royal illnesses…" She smiled again, but this time, her mouth was bitter at the corners. "The old Heartforger and his apprentice. How sad of the young lad to be stripped of his titles to serve a crotchety old man with little humor to his name."

I remained silent.

"They praise Blade that Soars, the first forger, and Dancing Wind, the first asha." She snickered. "Blade that Soars and Dancing Wind doomed us from the beginning. When Hollow Knife was close to finding the key to immortality, they united to kill him. The prince would have saved us all—no death, no diseases. But you are gullible fools to believe Dancing Wind's lies, that she would do it simply out of love. Love! Ha!

"Well, we all diseased in our own way, sweet Tea—our heartsglass tainted by mortality. Whatever our wars and petty quarrels, in time, it will matter little. Riches and glory do not matter when our bodies rot.

"There is a way, or so it is said, to achieve immortality. But the ingredients we require are not as trite as happy or sad memories. Lineage is important. We require royal memories." She chuckled at my confusion. "The legends talk of the five Great Heroes, descendants of Blade that Soars and Dancing Wind, who put down the first Great Daeva who roamed the land. But their slaying was incomplete, so the Great Daeva was split into seven lesser daeva instead."

"I do not wish to sit here and listen to children's tales, Aenah," I said, fuming.

"This is far more than myth, Tea. For the Great Daeva's

bezoar granted immortality. Surely you do not go about collecting bezoars and still not believe that such a possibility exists?"

"But what does that have to do with nobles falling sick?" I asked impatiently.

"Not just any nobles—nobles who can trace their lineage back to the Five Great Heroes."

I stared at her.

"Must I spell the rest out for you? I would take good care of your Odalian king if I were you. His family belongs to the house of Wyath, of the Great Hero Anahita's line. A pity if that family should fall sick under unusual circumstances. Quite ominous circumstances for a betrothal, I'd think."

"I require a memory from you," I interrupted, refusing to rise to the bait.

"Oh? Does the young Heartforger have need of my assistance?"

"He requires a memory of an atrocity committed."

"I can provide enough of those with more to spare." She smiled. "But I would like something in exchange."

"This is not a request. There will be no exchange."

"Then I refuse. Perhaps when we have more to bargain with."

"I could compel you." That was not true. And heartforgers could not draw memories from the unwilling.

Oddly enough, she grinned. "Perhaps. There is nothing more exhilarating than the ability to impose your will on others. Do it, Tea. Compel my mind. I do not need to cast spells to know you wish to test your strength against mine, to see if you could make a better Faceless than me."

I banged on the door, my signal that the interview was at an end, her morbid eagerness unsettling me. Aenah's laughter rang through the halls before the doors slammed shut. My angry thoughts swimming out to Fox were the only answer he needed about the productivity of our session.

It was easy enough to find Polaire and Mykaela for consult. They were in the latter's rooms, curtains half-drawn to allow in afternoon light, which surrounded Mykaela's yellow locks in a golden haze. Polaire, whose short, dark hair had no patience for sunlight, arched an eyebrow at us.

"A plot against the king?" she asked. "What proof does she have?"

"What little she reveals has always proven true," I pointed out. "It would be good to alert the Yadoshans in any case."

"Did she say anything else about shadowglass?"

"A little. The Faceless believe it will bring them immortality and that it requires the bloodlines of the Five Great Heroes. There may be a connection to a few sleeping sicknesses in other kingdoms."

Polaire frowned at me. "You must keep pushing, Tea. Compel words from her mouth if you have to."

"Why do you think this is important?"

"Because the elders believe so, because she seems to think so, and because she is being deliberately ambiguous about it, which makes me uneasy," Polaire responded.

"Aenah told me that the elder asha might know something about…" I paused, glancing back at Mykaela. "About Mykkie's heartsglass. She insinuates that they might know where it is."

Both asha stared at me.

"Impossible!" Polaire scoffed. "Aenah is not to be trusted, Tea."

"You trust her enough when it comes to providing information on everything else," Fox pointed out.

"Information we can verify. This smacks of an attempt to sow discord."

Mykaela tapped a finger against her lips, looking thoughtful. "King Telemaine is not a descendant of House Wyath."

"What do you mean?" Polaire asked.

Fox's eyes widened. "King Randrall the Quiet, the dead king Tea raised by accident two years ago."

"The one who declared that King Telemaine's ancestor was the offspring of the queen and the commander of his army and therefore *not* of his lineage. We went through great lengths to have that confirmed," I said.

"Doesn't that affect King Telemaine's claims to the throne?" Fox asked.

Mykaela shook her head. "King Randrall had no other surviving kin. He claimed the queen's son as his own, so his legitimacy holds. Even so, Prince Kance and Khalad can still trace their line to House Wyath through their mother."

"Politics are confusing," my brother complained.

Polaire frowned. "We should launch our own investigation into that strange illness—which kingdoms have been affected and so forth. I'm surprised we have heard so little about it."

"Kingdoms would not boast of it," Mykaela said. "And they might not be aware of the connection."

The shadows flitted through my mind again, and I saw wings beating on either side of me as the *azi* soared high into mountaintops that no human had ever scaled. The cold wind felt good on my face, but I closed my eyes, unprepared for the sun's bright glare. I felt the *azi* nudge my mind affectionately. *Master?* it queried. *Play?*

"Tea? Are you OK?"

I felt a hand against my forehead. The mountains and the crisp air disappeared, leaving only the others looking back at me.

"She's had a tiring day," Fox said.

"You're to return to your room and not leave it until dinnertime, Tea," Polaire commanded. "We'll look into the plot against the Yadoshans and these sicknesses."

"But—"

"No buts, Tea! Go! And I'll check up on you shortly to confirm you're in bed as prescribed!"

Polaire always made me feel like I was a child of six, and I said as much to Fox as we left the room. "It was still *my* information. I would have appreciated a thank you at least."

"She orders me about in much the same way. I haven't met anyone who hasn't gone through the same treatment when it comes to Polaire."

But my mind remained ill at ease. The thought of having a black heartsglass like Aenah's weighed heavily on my mind. How long did it take for silver to change? A month? A year? What other effects would it have on me?

Aenah was right about one thing: I had kept my links to the

azi hidden from all, even my brother. I did not want to spend the rest of my life in the dungeons like her, left with a rotting heartsglass and no future to look forward to.

*H*E WAS BLIGHTED." S*HE WAS* angry. *Her fists clenched and unclenched. "I thought we'd found them all."*

"Blighted?"

"Spells that turn men into daeva-like creatures, most against their will. It is a consequence of darkrot—but this is different. Deliberate. I devoted nearly a year to hunting them down. Apparently, I did not find them all."

I remembered the hanjian's bulging eyes, his monstrous transformation before the azi ended his life. I knew it would haunt me for the rest of mine. What vile magic could have caused such a horrifying change?

"He knew he'd been Blighted. He completed the spell himself, to spite me..." She shook her head, almost admiring. "Silver-blighted are stronger than red, with far more frightening deviations. They kill even familiars, it is said. Slaughter them before they turn or rip out their heartsglass after they do. Perhaps he thought he would make a better opponent cursed than human." Her lip curled. "He was wrong."

Even here, the bone witch showed no respect for the deceased; her azi had carried the monstrous carcass away in its jaws, and now it lay on the ground before us. I was grateful for the heavy cloak spread over it to spare the others from the grisly sight.

"Are you still angry?" She sounded amused. *"Despite your travels, you are unseasoned by war."*

Blighted or not, she intended to kill that man and for me to watch him die. *"You talk like a recipe exists to accustom one to death,"* I said, bitter.

"Oh, but there is," she responded. *"Take a girl and remove her heart. Add a touch of tragedy and a thirst for vengeance. Divide her into equal parts of grief and rage, then serve her cold. This is not the worst deed you will see before the week is out. If you have changed your mind about our mission, then leave. I am not yet done."*

"I will stay," I said shortly, rising to my feet. *"I will see this through, for good or ill."*

Most of the soldiers had fled, and those who remained were too injured to follow. Kalen saw to their wounds, moving from one to another to offer aid, though they shrunk from him in fear.

The asha signaled to me. I heard the crunch of marble behind me as the aeshma, the smallest among the daeva, followed closely behind, only barely able to fit through the palace doors, dragging the blighted corpse along with it.

The palace had long been deserted, servants and nobles having fled at the castle's breaching. No bodies lay strewn along the corridors and hallways, which was some consolation. The asha did not waver and moved confidently from one room to the next until we arrived before the throne.

I was mistaken. The castle was not completely deserted. Someone sat on the golden chair.

I had always seen him from a distance, as one face in a sea of many, looking on when parades and processions brought the emperor through the busy streets of Santiang. I heard that most who throng those crowds were carefully selected, trained to kneel at a command, spurring the rest to follow suit. Dissenters were carefully culled from the herd by his loyal guards, sometimes never to be seen again.

But even guards can be goaded into betrayal, and the sycophants had long since abandoned the emperor of Daanoris. Without heralds to sing of his fine looks and proud form, he lost much of his appeal. His brows sagged underneath a face puffy from vice and arrogance. There was a lack of symmetry in his cheekbones and shadows over his dark eyes. It was an attractive face but one eroded by years of pride and avarice.

He awaited the asha's approach, unmoving and unyielding. She stopped before him, so close that her skirts brushed against his bright throne. The aeshma padded after her, dropping the corpse before the emperor.

"My people will not suffer this indignity." I was surprised to hear the emperor speak the common tongue. His still-powerful voice boomed, echoing across the chamber. "Whatever monstrosities you wield, you will fall. My allies will—"

The asha's hand slammed across the emperor's face, depriving him of both breath and strength. He crumpled against his throne, and my stunned cry bounced off the marbled walls.

"'Your people,' Your Majesty?" On her lips, his title sounded like a mockery. Her fingers moved through the air, and the emperor froze. "Your people are scattered, unburdened from the yoke you impose on their necks and call freedom. Your allies? The madman sniveling on *the throne of Drycht tolerates you only for the money you exchange for their runeberry cloth and their soldiers. Even now, he has broken your treaty and allies himself with Druj. You are alone. Send him here then if you please. I shall cut out his heart and sup on it and leave the dregs for my daeva."*

Kalen stepped forward and grasped the emperor of Daanoris by the hems of his robe. The man's struggles were futile; the Deathseeker dragged him to a corner of the room with little effort, discarding him there like a sack of old clothes.

The asha settled herself on the gilded throne of Daanoris.

"Where did I leave off, Bard?"

5

A HEARTSRUNE CEREMONY WAS ALSO A celebration: children received their first heartsglass in their thirteenth year. Nobles and commoners alike looked on while asha summoned runes to fill heartscases with various colors of red. Occasionally, a lucky child would see their hearts turn purple, singling them out for the artisan's life, inexorably entwined with those of an asha's. They would become apothecaries who create beauty, accessory makers who churn out zivar, and ateliers to cloth asha in the latest fashions—even village witches, like my sisters.

The unluckiest of the bunch would find their heartsglass shine silver and would be required to turn themselves over to the asha-ka association the following day, an asha's apprenticeship awaiting the girls and a Deathseeker's novitiate for the boys.

Drawing Heartsrune was a relatively easy task even for someone with Mykaela's poor health. I would have preferred that she remained in bed, but I understood her need to be useful. Polaire had been just as hesitant. The brunette hovered close by like a mother hen in case Mykaela should falter. She did not.

Odalians were suspicious of asha but tolerated them for the historical ties Odalian royalty shares with the spellbinders. But Dark asha are a separate category altogether, and for them, the people's hatred runs deep. Attuned as I was to heartsglass, I felt the differing emotions running through the audience. Their contempt for bone witches like Mykaela and me—the only two surviving in all the kingdoms—was plain to see, and they felt secure in the knowledge that, in crowds, it was safe to hate without repercussions. Not for the first time, I wondered how Mykaela managed to do this year after year.

Four hundred and twenty-six children turned up for the event, and as we neared the end of the line, my sister-asha had found seven purple heartsglass and three silver. It was not those children I worried for. All the silvers were girls. My trepidation was for Likh, who was among the last of those waiting. There was no need for Mykaela to trace Heartsrune for him; his was already a blinding silver. But due to his unusual circumstances, he had yet to hold his own Heartsrune ceremony, and it could no longer be delayed.

Deathseekers were even rarer than asha, bone witches the only sect more limited in number. Likh was the only Deathseeker found in the last two years, and that realization was not lost on our audience. Heads craned in his direction, their expressions a mixture of derision and confusion. Likh served as an apprentice for Chesh, the popular zivarmaker, and was dressed in his apprentice robes. And yet, looking at his graceful features and slender frame, one would find it difficult to see him as male.

Mykaela's pace did not slow. She bowed gravely to the young boy, and Likh returned her gesture with solemnity. His resigned expression turned to one of amazement when other asha stepped forward: first Polaire and Zoya, then Shadi and Zoya's friends Yonca, Sveta, and Tami. And then to my surprise, Altaecia stepped forward from the crowd; as Princess Inessa's bodyguard, I thought she was in Kion, looking after her ward.

As much as I wanted to, I made no move to join them. The Odalians will not treat a bone witch's opinion with the same merits they would an asha's. I watched my sisters surround the startled Likh. Lady Mykaela moved back, quietly losing herself in the crowd of courtiers and nobles, as Polaire slid a beautiful diamond-studded zivar out of her short brown hair and gently tucked it behind the boy's ear.

The other asha followed suit, taking off their beautiful hairpieces and placing them on Likh. There were gasps from the crowd, the implication obvious. We had lodged numerous appeals to the asha-ka association to admit Likh to the asha, with little success. Now Polaire and the others were making their protests public for all to see.

Likh trembled. His gaze turned in my direction, and I responded with a tiny, supportive wave.

Prince Kance stepped forward. He was dressed in the Odalian royal uniform, ceremonial clothes of golden buttons and silver embroidery worn only for coronations or royal weddings. He bowed low to the awestruck boy.

If that is not approval enough, then nothing else will sway the association to our side, Fox murmured in my head.

The prince turned toward King Telemaine. I glanced back at the crowd and saw Khalad among those watching, his face set and angry as he stared at his father.

Mykaela had quietly resurfaced beside us. I tugged at her sleeve. "Why is Althy here?" I whispered.

"The First Daughter arrived from Kion a few hours ago," she whispered back. "Althy was quite keen to take part in the festivities. Given her position, her actions carry the empress's support as well."

"Nobody told me about this." I felt a little hurt.

It was her turn to look startled. "Didn't Polaire tell you?"

"No. And Prince Kance too?"

"He offered. This will lend more credence to our petition. The association will want the prince's support on other issues and may be more amenable as a result."

"And so ends our Heartsrune day," King Telemaine announced in a grave voice. "Younglings: use your heartsglass well, and choose your paths wisely. Let today be the first day of the rest of your lives. I know that it will be the first day of the rest of mine."

A faint murmur ran through the crowd, unsure of what he meant.

"Today is a day for celebrations," he continued. "It is only fitting that I announce another. Kance."

Obediently, the crown prince stepped forward, his confusion was obvious. "Father? You still haven't—"

"I am honored to have the lovely Princess Inessa here in Odalia to celebrate Heartsrune Day with us. Kion has always been our staunchest ally, and together we have worked to bring peace and prosperity to our respective kingdoms. Today, we will officially cement our long alliance."

A beautiful young woman joined the prince and his father. She wore a magnificent *hua* of amber and white, with sleeves that trailed past her arms the way royal princesses from Kion wore them, and her train flared out several yards behind her. The lower half of her face was veiled, as was customary, though the sheer lace was transparent enough for her delicate features to be seen. I heard Fox draw in a sharp breath beside me. Shock flared through the bond we shared before he swiftly hauled it back.

"It is my honor today," King Telemaine said, "to officially declare the engagement of my son, Crown Prince Kance, to the beautiful Princess Inessa, the First Daughter of Kion!"

The crowd cheered. Kance's eyes widened, and he turned pale for a moment before swiftly recovering. I stumbled back.

"Steady," Fox instructed, though the faint tremor in his voice painted his own words shaky. He could not look away from Princess Inessa, who spotted him but averted her gaze.

The next couple of hours passed in a daze. I was barely cognizant of what I was doing, like I was watching myself through some other person's eyes. I looked on as I smiled and shook the hand of the beaming King Telemaine. "I must commend Polaire for helping me bring this all together," he said with his customary near-deafening laugh. "She is a treasure, your Polaire."

"Is she, Your Majesty?" I heard myself murmur, struggling to make small talk.

"She broke up a plot of the Faceless against the Yadoshans—an attempt on Lord Besserly's life, their Grand Duke. Endeared them to us in the process, so we're in talks for a better trade route. And she was most supportive regarding my son's engagement. I cannot thank her and you, asha, enough."

I barely had time to congratulate Princess Inessa before a bevy of handmaidens swept her away to the next group of well-wishers.

Then Prince Kance's hand grasped mine. With as much sincerity as I could muster, I found myself mouthing platitudes, wishing him all the best in his forthcoming marriage.

He smiled back, and I wondered if I only imagined the faint melancholy lingering at the edges of his mouth. "Thank you, Tea," he said, "I'm glad you approve." His kind words dug deeper into my gut. "I only wish that…" He stopped, staring over my shoulder with a puzzled frown.

I turned but saw no one. "Prince Kance?"

He blinked and shook his head. "I'm sorry. I've been having headaches for the last few days."

"You must not work yourself too hard, Your Highness."

"I know, but I've had little time to rest, and Lady Altaecia's herbal teas don't seem to be working." His green eyes, worried, met mine. Then he said, "I wanted to tell you sooner. About the engagement. I *should* have told you sooner. I don't understand why I didn't."

"I thought you didn't know," I said, bewildered. "You looked fairly shocked at the announcement."

"I knew. I just wasn't expecting Father to issue the proclamation today. And he didn't…" He stopped, frowning, almost seeming to forget I was there.

"Are you all right, Your Highness?"

"Kance," Kalen said, materializing behind the prince, "your father wishes to speak to you."

The prince shook his head and smiled weakly at me again. "I have to go. Thank you again, Lady Tea. Kalen, keep her company for me."

"I have better things to do."

"No, you don't." The prince's voice was unnaturally stern. "See to her concerns. I want you to watch over Lady Tea the same way you watch over me. I have some important matters I need to discuss with Father."

"She can handle herself just fine."

"Please, Kalen."

Kalen scowled. Together, we watched the prince leave, but as soon as he was out of sight, I spun around.

"And where do you think you're going?" Kalen demanded.

"Away." Kalen was the last person I wanted to see me cry. I took a step toward the door, and he grabbed my hand.

"Listen here, Tea. I know that you're—"

I whirled back, my eyes glistening. "I thought you had better things to do," I hissed.

Kalen hesitated, staring at my face. After a moment, he let go.

Fox was waiting for me by the doorway. His face was grim, as he was eager to be off himself. But Polaire caught me as we were leaving. "Come here, Tea," she commanded. "Stay. Their royal majesties would be offended by you slinking away like this."

Perhaps it was the events of the day compounded by my vulnerability, but I chose to be snippy. "I don't want to."

Polaire frowned. "Immaturity isn't becoming of an asha, Tea."

"Maybe if you didn't persist in treating me like a child, I might be more motivated to act like an adult!"

She scowled, displeased by the furtive looks being thrown our way. "Is this because I neglected to tell you about our plan with Likh? Come now, Tea. You shouldn't fuss over such a trivial matter."

"Yes, I should. I suppose your taking credit for rescuing Lord Besserly shouldn't be held against you either. Or the prince's own engagement, which I had no inkling of until the announcement an hour ago."

"Tea, that's not fair."

Tea, Fox warned me. *This is not the time.*

I knew I had to leave. To lose my temper in a roomful of nobles would not be to anyone's advantage, least of all my own. But I couldn't resist one last dig.

"Or perhaps it would suit you better if I shut my mouth and did as you wish, like a little toy dog performing tricks for no purpose other than to please you. Perhaps it shouldn't matter that

I risk life and limb to put down daeva, risk sanity to confront a Faceless you are too cowardly to interrogate yourself. But *I'm* the immature one, aren't I?"

I didn't wait for Polaire's response. I turned on my heel and strode off, glad she realized her hypocrisy enough not to pursue.

The celebrations continued for the rest of the night until, I was told later, the early hours of the morning. Fox and I said little, looking out from my window into the world below, at the expanse of the city. "What are we doing?" I finally asked. "How ridiculous are we to be depressed about two people who are engaged to one other?"

"At least we're still doing things together."

I started giggling, and it caught on. Fox and I laughed at our absurdity, laughed until we had exhausted our surplus, until the lights winked out, one after the other, as the twenty thousand eyes of the city closed to dream.

Fox stayed with me until I fell asleep. When I woke sometime later, he was gone. I could feel him somewhere within Kneave, aimless. Beyond him, the shadows stirred and sighed, the *azi* sensing my melancholy and commiserating.

Alone in my room, I held up my heartsglass. Framed against the moonlight, it sparkled back at me. Resigned sadness occasionally marred the surface, but to my credit, neither resentment nor anger clouded its glass. It would take much more than this, I knew, to break my heart.

I HEARD OF THE ENGAGEMENT," *I said, intrigued despite myself.* "I had always wondered what brought it about." *Kion rarely made arranged marriages. Possessions and titles were passed down through the matriarchal line, so their women often had a say in who they married.*

The bone witch closed her eyes, as if done with the conversation. "I can feel him, Kalen," she said after a moment. "He's here in the palace." She strode to the still-cowering emperor, and her voice rose. "Where do you keep him, maggot? If you have shorn so much as a strand of white hair from his head, you will regret it for days."

The Daanorian noble cringed. The Dark asha's hand whipped through the air, and he sank back, crying out in pain.

"The prisons," he gasped. "The prisons!"

The asha's eyes hardened. She stepped toward the fallen man and crouched. "You will stay here until I return," she said. "You will not move or blink from the moment I step out of the throne room until the moment I step back in. If you so much as twitch, I shall twist your insides and roll out your entrails like a royal carpet, and you will die as you choke on your own liver, your heart in my fist."

The emperor said nothing and remained stock-still, his eyes round with fear.

And then, inexplicably, the asha began to laugh. "You are

powerless. *You* are *powerless! You are nothing more than an illusion. Oh, the irony!" She pushed him, sending him sprawling back to his corner. "If I find him harmed in any way,* Your Majesty, *I shall make good on my promise to gut you."*

The aeshma *plodded nearer, settled itself at the base of the throne, keeping a languid, lazy eye on the dethroned noble.*

Kalen rose as well. "I will search for the princess, and I will ask the soldiers about the blight. There might have been more sightings."

The asha nodded. "Follow me, Bard. There is someone I would like you to meet."

I followed her down the hallway and into an unused wing of the palace. The asha knew the way; she drew a sword and a locked wooden door shattered under its blow. Darkness beckoned us in. She led me down to the dungeons, and I shuddered to think of what we might find there.

But only one of the cells was occupied. Its prisoner sat, unblinking, as the asha moved closer. Even in the gloom, his heartsglass shone a blinding silver that was a light all on its own.

"This is Khalad, Bard," the asha said. "The first-born son of Odalia, the former crown prince of House Wyath, and Heartforger to the Eight Kingdoms."

Khalad stared up at us from underneath a shock of white hair— though he was still a young man, no older than Lord Kalen—with eyes almost the same shade as his heartsglass.

"What took you so long?" he asked quietly.

6

A ND TO WHAT DO I owe this honor?" Aenah drawled. "Two
visits in two days! What a wonderful surpri—"

The rest of her words were cut off as she sagged back against
the wall, coughing uncontrollably, her hands clutching at her
throat. I hated being in her head, even when forcing her to do as
I wanted. But I had all of the anger and none of the patience, and
this was the fastest way to find my answers.

"Tea!" Fox had never followed me inside the cell before.
Khalad was close on my brother's heels, looking nervous.

"How did you know?" I nearly snarled.

"How did I know what?" Aenah gasped, struggling for breath.

"*Quite ominous circumstances for a betrothal, I'd think.*" I
echoed her words from my last visit. "How did you know about
the prince's engagement to the Kion princess?" I ignored Fox's
startle of surprise. The thought that someone within the prince's

inner circle worked for this Faceless scum was terrifying enough. "Who are your spies? Tell me!"

The woman laughed weakly. "You have nothing to fear, Tea. I compel no one from the Odalian nobility. I simply found a flaw in your wards."

I applied more pressure—not enough to rob her of speech but enough for her to realize I was willing to do worse. "This room is warded with enough magic to stop a daeva!"

Aenah smiled. "You exaggerate. The magic here is impressive, that is true. It prevents me from escaping. The wards can cloud your bond with your brave older brother here and, to a lesser extent, with the *azi* you share your innermost thoughts with."

"What?" Fox exclaimed, but I refused to let go.

"Are you saying you can overcome these wards?"

"Not in the way you believe." She tapped her forehead. "When you were but an asha apprentice, I was foolish enough to think I could compel you. I could plant suggestions in your mind and you would believe them as your own. All that changed, however, when the *azi* chose you. And now it is I who, embarrassingly enough, must dance to your tune."

"That's not an answer," I said, seething.

"It is called a *Scrying* rune."

"There is no such thing as a *Scrying* rune."

"Do you require a demonstration?" Aenah closed her eyes, and a strange rune flickered across my mind, one I had never seen before.

Fox tensed, ready and watchful.

The *Compulsion* rune flared brighter as I plunged into her head, commanding her to *remain still*, to *do nothing*. And yet I could sense her thoughts drifting where I could not reach.

"There is a guard stationed outside my door named Garveth. His wife is nine months with child and due for labor any day. But he worries his duties at his post prevent him from being with her should her water break."

Fox left the room before she had even finished her thought.

"He must be a joy to have around," Aenah said cheerfully. "Aren't you glad you could spend more time with your brother than fate originally intended?"

I tightened her hold, and her smug grin vanished. "Explain yourself."

"I imagine it would be a difficult to teach you the *Scrying* rune in this small cell, all the wards being what they are. Perhaps a small compensation for my assistance—a larger room, perhaps an actual bed—"

"No."

"You wanted a memory. Why not ask the young Heartforger to extract it now from my mind? He can see for himself that I do not lie."

I glanced at Khalad, who nodded. "If this is another trick…" I warned.

Khalad laid a finger against the Faceless woman's heartsglass. His eyes widened, and his hand trembled.

"Don't be shy," Aenah cooed. "Do not let my unusual memories color your judgment of me."

With a violent jerk, Khalad stepped back. Violet-hued smoke clung to his fingers. "I got it," he said hoarsely.

"Are you all right, Khalad?"

"Yes. It's just…her mind…"

"I should have warned you," the Faceless said cheerfully. "I have quite the checkered past."

"She's telling the truth." Khalad placed the purple smoke inside a glass vial. "But scrying is the extent of what she can do."

Fox returned, scowling. "The guard's name *is* Garveth. It's true, every word she says. Damn her. He swore he never talked to her, much less entered this room."

"He could be lying," I insisted.

"I can give you more examples if you wish," Aenah offered. "The prince was here. I brushed against a royal mind some days ago. He worried that his sheltered upbringing prevents him from ruling Odalia. He wished to see more of the land beyond its borders, to allow him a better understanding of his people. Incidentally, it was in his mind where I first gleaned knowledge of his impending engagement—"

I increased my hold on her, and her eyes rolled back in her head, her body twisting in agony as the grip tightened.

"Tea!" Fox's arms circled me, shaking me out of my rage. "Tea, stop it!"

I let go. Aenah collapsed. Only the manacles chained to her wrists kept her upright, and those just barely. Her head drooped. I thought she had lost consciousness until she made a soft wheeze.

"I must...congratulate you...Tea. You have only...gotten stronger in...the year since..."

"Whatever possessed you, Tea?" Fox was furious and rightfully so. I didn't answer, focusing on reining in my anger, aware that I could not lose control of myself like that again.

Aenah lifted her head. A tiny smile hovered on her lips. "Very well. I swear to never enter your beloved prince's mind again. I swear it on my daughter's grave. But I have been very forthcoming today. I only have one boon to ask of you in return."

"No."

"It's only a book, Tea, passed down to those like me for centuries. Many have killed for it, yet I give it to you freely and ask you to protect it."

"And what book is this?"

"A book of hidden runes, Lady Tea. Hidden runes wielded by Dark spellbinders, lost over time—deliberately—by the asha, to prevent Dark witches like us from rising too high. I learned of the *Scrying* rune there and of many others. Your own elder asha possess a copy."

"You lie."

"It's all about control, my dear Tea. They only teach you the necessary runes to put down daeva and risk your life for their cause. Why would they teach you the very runes that would allow you to rise above them?"

"Then why are you giving this to me?" I asked.

"Because I have not given up on you." Now recovered, she leaned back against the wall and stretched. "Your anger is promising, my bone witch. We have need of your fury. Once you have decided to take my claims seriously—about the effectiveness of these runes and about your asha elders' treachery—then come back to me, and I will tell you everything."

"I need none of your help."

"Ah, but this knowledge will eat at you. We have shared minds, Tea. I know a little more about you than others do. I know of your hunger for strange books and stranger learnings. I know you worry constantly over Mykaela's fate, your concern that one day the *azi* that lodges in your mind might overwhelm you—that your mind will be corrupted and overwhelmed by the darkrot that your elders frighten you with.

"There are many spells in my book that hold the answers to your troubles. Once you acquire such tastes for power and appreciate its sweetness, you shall stop playing asha and come to us, the Faceless, where your skills will be put to better use."

"Never," I spat.

"Never is such a long time to promise, Tea. We live too short of lives to consign ourselves to an eternity you may regret. And it is not terrible to have a black heartsglass. We are stronger with it, more steeped in the Dark, less vulnerable to darkrot. Ah, but the elders will not allow you to think that."

"I don't believe you."

"Black heartsglass will never be taken from you the way Mykaela's heartsglass was taken from her. Black heartsglass will always return to you regardless of anyone's control, whether you wish it to or not. Is that not temptation enough to take my book?"

"The process makes it less than appealing."

She laughed. "A little corruption is good for the soul, Tea. The book I speak of lies within the Odalian cemetery. Where lies poor forgotten Millicent Tread of Istera, there you shall find your true calling."

I said nothing and headed for the door.

"Until we meet again," Aenah called after us before the heavy metal doors slid shut.

"Tell the commander that Garveth is to have time off until his wife gives birth," I instructed one of the passing soldiers. "And I want all guards keeping watch over this cell, standing at least twenty feet away. No one but the Deathseeker who delivers her meals may approach." I knew it would probably be ineffective, but I had to do something.

"What did she mean about an *azi* lodged in your mind?" Fox demanded as we left the prison. "You killed it two years ago, didn't you? Has it been resurrected?"

I swallowed. "No. I never killed it."

"This sounds like a private conversation between you two," Khalad said nervously from behind us. "I should be going."

"Stay, Khalad," Fox commanded. "You've been taking memories from Tea all this time. Did you not know about this?"

The forger swallowed. "Well…"

Fox gaped at him. "You *knew*?"

"It's part of our oath as Heartforgers—memories are no one else's business but their owner's."

"It didn't want to fight!" I protested. "The *azi* was under

Aenah's influence. It fought her as much as I did. But now I'm in its mind and it's in mine, and I know it meant no harm."

"Break your bond with it, Tea! It's too dangerous!"

"I don't know how even if I wanted to. But it knows I'm not the threat Aenah was. It's made no move to attack since I took control."

Slowly, Fox shook his head. "That doesn't make it harmless."

"Harmless or not, it hasn't done anything to me. There's something about this bond that makes us aware of each other's presence. And...and it gives me control of it when I ask."

"Tea!"

"What do you expect me to do, Fox? Tell the asha elders? Khalad, tell him what would happen if I did."

Khalad swallowed. "You'd be locked up just like Aenah. You'd be considered a source of danger to everyone, and neither Mykaela nor even Altaecia has that much authority to protect you."

"Tea, don't you think Mykaela ought to know at least?" my brother persisted, though much of his irritation was gone, knowing Khalad had spoken the truth.

"She won't know how to break the bond any more than I do. At this point, I know more about handling daeva than she does. And as for the others..." Telling Mykaela meant telling Polaire, and after my blowup at Polaire the other day, telling her would be tantamount to telling the association. "That I'm a bone witch makes it worse. There'll be people crying for my head soon enough. King Telemaine and Prince Kance could even be accused of conspiring with me. I won't let that happen."

"I really should be going," Khalad said nervously, backing away. "I really should put this memory in a safer place."

"Khalad, come back here. I'm not done with—ah, hells. He's gone." Fox turned back to me. "I'm not 'other people,' Tea. I'm your brother. You should have told me."

"I know about your dislike for daeva, Fox. I knew you wouldn't approve."

"Not approving doesn't mean I'm not going to stick by you. Your problems are my own." He paused. "At least that explains the disorienting sensations I get from you sometimes."

"I'm sorry. I'll try my best not to keep anything from you again," I said, reaching out to squeeze his hand.

"I like how you say 'try,' like you would do it again if you thought it would spare me the trouble." My brother sighed. "I guess we have no choice then."

"No choice in what?"

"We have no choice but to find that blasted book that harpy's been yapping about. If there is guarded magic in it that might break your bond, that warrants a look."

I REMEMBER THAT DAY," THE HEARTFORGER said. "*Your heartsglass shone so brightly, Tea. There was anger and frustration and sorrow, an unhealthy combination. I remembered Aenah's too. She was afraid of you, no matter how she tried to hide that. She was adept enough at disguising it, but I could still see the flecks of blue.*"

"*I'm surprised how much you recall, considering how quickly you fled.*"

The Heartforger actually laughed. He was everything she described and, at the same time, everything she had not. He was dark from his travels, and his eyes were a light gray, nearly as colorless as his hair, which hung long past his shoulders. He looked stronger than I expected—shoulders broad but hunched, arms heavily built. He narrowed his eyes as he focused on me, a habit I recognize, having poor sight myself. His heartsglass was a masterpiece—a dizzying crystal of fractured colors, of a finer cut than the best diamonds. "*Who is he?*" the Heartforger asked.

"*My chronicler, of a sort.*"

The Heartforger frowned, but his final impression was of sadness rather than of anger. "*This is a dangerous thing you do, Tea.*"

"*No more dangerous than other choices you have made, Khalad. And you know as well as I that I am running out of options as quickly as Daanoris is emptying of people.*"

"*How did you know to find me here? You were still in exile when I left Ankyo.*"

She smiled at him. "*I didn't. But I knew you wouldn't stay in Kion for long. Ankyo and Odalia disgust you now as much as they disgust me. During my exile, I scried my way down the coast and followed the minds leading into Santiang. Imagine my surprise to find this man in charge.*" She nodded at the emperor, who had made good on his promise not to move while we were gone. "*I knew he would seek you out and that you would be in danger.*"

"*You were able to scry over that distance? Your powers are stronger than even before you were...*" His eyes met hers, and she nodded. "*I had little time to do much forging for him,*" he continued. "*I've barely been in prison two days. Is that why you came to Daanoris with all the daeva in your heartsglass?*"

"*Can you see them?*"

"*Their hearts are intertwined with yours, and only your death can pull them apart.*" He looked troubled. "*I am afraid, Tea.*"

The asha knelt before him, her hands clasped around his. "*Will you stop me then?*" she whispered, and for a moment, she sounded very young. "*Is there any other alternative, Khalad?*"

"*No,*" the boy said heavily. "*There isn't. That is the problem.*"

"*Do you approve then?*"

"*No. But I understand why you do it.*" He glanced at me again. "*How much does he know?*"

"*As little as possible,*" the asha replied.

"*I found the princess, and the rest of the soldiers are tending to their wounded,*" Lord Kalen said, entering the room.

The Heartforger's jaw grew slack, and he rose to his feet as Lord Kalen approached.

He continued, "They surrendered swiftly, and I do not think they will cause more trouble, not with the daeva waiting outside. Hello, Khalad."

Lord Khalad's mouth worked uselessly, and tears of both shock and joy filled his eyes. His heartsglass wept, a shining star.

"I am glad to see that I can still hide things from you, Khalad," the bone witch said, smiling.

"We saw you die," the Heartforger finally croaked, clutching the other boy's shoulders. "Tea tried to raise you. We couldn't bring you back. We saw you die."

"I got better," Lord Kalen said. A strange smile played on his lips, and his heartsglass burned as brightly as the Heartforger's.

7

MILLICENT TREAD'S GRAVE WAS A neglected tangle of grass and dandelions. The small headstone that marked her final repose was obscured by the tall weeds and heavy stones. It lay the farthest from the graveyard entrance, relegated to a plot near forgotten folk who had died in the last century and were, therefore, of little use to the current one. I could see why Aenah would plant secrets along its periphery; few people had reason to go this deep into the boneyard, and Millicent Tread was difficult to find unless you knew she was there to begin with.

Despite the overabundance of vegetation, the earth around the tomb had been recently disturbed.

It had taken us nearly two hours of searching to locate poor Millicent, and by the time we unearthed her small, crumbling coffin, the sky had lightened into softer gradients of grays, the hours moving toward dawn. I hoped that some force would prevent Lady Mykaela from wandering out of bed again; it would be far more difficult to explain trespassing at this grave than at King Vanor's tomb.

"If she lied, I'll strangle her myself," Fox grumbled. He did most of the digging, though I did the sweating for the two of us. My brother lowered himself gingerly into the hole he dug, clearing away the splinters of wood and prying off what was left of the coffin lid.

An unknown rune of intricate markings suddenly blazed forth in front of me, shining brightly. There was a strange yapping sound, then a withered hand shot out to grasp Fox by the sleeve. Fox's blade swung, shining in the dim light, and took the skeletal hand off cleanly at the wrist. "I knew it," he growled. "She set us up!"

Millicent Tread's corpse was not the only body rising from the ground. Other gravestones shuddered and broke apart around us, their occupants struggling out of their graves, decayed jaws snapping.

Fox spun in a circle, taking two heads with one clean swipe. Yet even as the skulls dropped to the ground, their bodies lumbered forward. Every arm or leg Fox chopped off became an additional appendage to defend against, and my brother soon traded his blade for its hilt, driving the heavy, blunt end to crush their bones.

I drew *Compulsion* in the air and was immediately assaulted by a barrage of personalities. None of the corpses were intent on fighting off my control; if anything, they were eager to embrace me, to lay bare all that was left of their minds. The mishmash of thoughts made my head spin.

—*my little boy Achmed, to take the time to lay flowers by my grave—*

—*good-for-nothing husband, always carousing till the break of dawn! Would a visit every so often kill him?—*

—*my daughter! Have you heard news of her? I've been waiting years and years—*

The *azi's* thoughts crept in amid the chaos. Instinctively, I latched on to it and embraced the familiar magic that flowed freely through our link.

"*Return to your graves!*" The *Compulsion* rune flared brighter than I had ever seen it, and the corpses froze. Like marionettes being jerked on invisible strings, they collapsed back into the holes they had clawed out of, moaning piteously all the while. Only after the last disappeared back into its soil did I let go of the *azi*, sinking down from the effort it had taken me.

Fox was by my side in moments, worried. "Was that the *azi*?"

I grinned weakly. "It…helped. I just need to catch my breath. As horrifying as the corpses were, they posed no real threat."

"I inferred as much. I caught the tail end of their thoughts." He glanced back at Millicent's grave. "This one seems peaceful again too. But what did that Faceless woman hope to achieve from this if not to attack?"

"She was showing off—one of the many unknown runes her book holds, I think."

"Why tell her secrets? She'd lose the advantage."

"I'm not sure what her plan is. But if that book exists, then I'm going to find it. If there's any means to better control the *azi*—"

But my brother shook his head. "Absolutely not. You swore you'd get rid of the daeva, remember?"

I hesitated, then nodded. "Yes, I know what I promised."

"Good, because I'll be holding you to that." Fox returned to Millicent's grave, his every movement laced with caution. He nudged away the rest of the debris with a foot, used the tip of his blade to prod the woman's remains out of the way, and peered inside.

"So she can speak the truth after all!" he exclaimed, producing a small rectangular package carefully wrapped in twine and waxed paper. "I'm surprised it lasted this long, buried under all this dirt."

I remembered the churned earth around the grave. "Unless it's been buried recently."

Fox frowned. "True. Though the idea that Aenah might have an ally running loose in Kion is worrying."

He handed the package to me. I removed the twine holding it together.

It was a leather-bound book of some age but in good shape. An upside-down crown was embossed onto the leather, and my heart leaped to my throat. "This is the False Prince's crest, Fox."

I turned to a page at random and saw unfamiliar runes. The text was archaic, like the book was written in an era when speech required more formality. "This rune shows you how to control a hundred corpses at once."

"Isn't that impossible? Aren't asha able to control only a dozen at most?"

"Unless you use a seeking stone, and using that will overwhelm you quickly with darkrot if you're not strong enough." I winced, remembering my first encounter with one. "I'll need to see if the magic is as effective as this book claims."

"No."

I looked at him. "Fox, I have to. If any of these spells work, we can use them to our advantage. If we can't tell the asha-ka association about the *azi*, then we definitely can't tell them about this. The only people who could manage these spells are Mykaela and me, and she's in no shape to handle these runes."

"And once the association discovers your secret, you're going to be hauled to prison for having this book in your possession—just as you would be for your bond with the daeva." Fox rubbed the side of his head. "Can you not even share with Polaire or Altaecia?"

I hesitated. I remembered Polaire's intimation that I was not relevant to the decisions the association makes, even when they involve me. "No," I decided. "Polaire's too close to the elder asha. I...seriously don't know how Althy would react to this."

Fox scowled. "Fine—for now. But you cannot experiment without me around." And then, for the first time, he grudgingly addressed the shadow that had quietly been eavesdropping in my head. *And the same goes for you too. Do you hear me, you overgrown snake?*

That was so typically Fox that I had to smile, and the *azi* rumbled cheerfully in my head in response.

·· ⌇⃰ ··

At Fox's insistence, we started with the simplest of the book's spells—*Scrying*. Its rune resembled a distorted tree branch climbing upward, limbs twisted and splayed. To commit it to memory required practice. Like all spells, I was to trace the rune, to let my will bleed into its shape, and then direct it into another's mind and wrap the rune around its presence.

"This is not secretly an *Exploding* rune or something that will send a thousand dead people climbing in through the window, right?"

"At this point, I know as much about this as you do, Fox." I took a deep breath. "Let's do this. We can spend all day arguing until we're blue in the face, but that won't change anything."

Fox's hand strayed to the hilt of his sword, as if swinging a blade at a spell would make all the difference. "*One* decaying head popping up from *anywhere* and I'm sending it back to whatever hell it crawled out from."

I studied the rune again, committing as much of it to memory as I was able. As I drew it in the air, I let my mind settle on its form until it felt as solid as I was, and then I guided it toward Fox. We already shared a bond, but finding another volunteer was not an option at this point.

I felt a spurt of dizziness, which quickly abated. I stared at Fox but had the oddest sensation of staring back at myself.

I squeezed my eyes shut and watched myself close my eyes at the same time.

"Fox, turn around."

My perspective swiveled. I disappeared from view, replaced by the small dresser in my room and the small chair beside it.

"Is something wrong, Tea?" My bond with Fox was even stronger now, his worry and concern felt like they were my own. In the past, I could always sense his emotions without necessarily feeling them myself. Now I was experiencing the world through him.

Fox was puzzled; I felt puzzled. "I don't feel any different. Is it working?"

"A little too well." I dispelled the rune and felt Fox's thoughts vanish, weariness taking its place. "This is the spell Aenah used."

"That's enough for one day." Fox decided. "And don't argue—I'm getting tired just sensing your exhaustion. Between this and the graveyard, it's been a long day."

I tried to protest, but it came out as a yawn.

Fox tucked me into bed, something he hadn't done since we were kids. "Stop pushing yourself," I heard him say affectionately before I fell asleep. "The world will turn even when you are not awake to busy yourself in it."

•• ⌇ ••

I was fresh and rejuvenated when I opened my eyes again—exceptionally so. Marveling at my sudden energy, I sat up in bed and spotted the Faceless's book, half-hidden underneath a dozen other volumes on my table. It would have been better if Fox had kept it with him and prevented me the mischief, but I remembered that the soldiers' barracks had little privacy.

I promised Fox I wouldn't experiment, but that didn't mean I couldn't look through the rest of the spells.

I climbed back into bed, taking the book with me.

The Puppet Rune, I read, *requires great concentration. Wrap the spell around your victim to command as you may. The cadaver performs its last command unless dispelled or until its master's death. Till then, it takes on the artifice of life, moving and acting independently of other forces. Sufficient strength can raise hundreds, even tens of thousands.*

I stared at the symbol. With some imagination, it did resemble a marionette being jerked on its strings by a dark blob in the background. This must have been the spell Aenah used at the graveyard. But how? Didn't Mykkie say I cannot control the dead if they aren't willing? Already the book was breaking rules I'd always believed sancrosanct.

The next page showed a rune of two intertwined hearts. The *Heartshare* rune, it said, bolstered a fading heartsglass with a second healthier one to delay death until medical attention is administered. It could even control one's mind to an extent, but where the *Compulsion* rune used force, *Heartshare* used trust and claimed much better results. It also seemed to be the only spell in the book that asha and Deathseekers alike could use.

It was probably not a rune the Faceless preferred, given their mutual distrust. When the *azi* had attacked the *darashi oyun* years ago, asha and Deathseekers withstood their attack by linking runes together. When I had confronted Aenah at the Valerian, Mykaela, Polaire, and Altaecia had lent me their strength in much the same way, similar to how I could take strength from the *azi* to add to my own. But sharing heartsglass appeared to be a much more intimate spell than even that.

I turned the page. The *Illusion* rune was a series of whorls and loops. Rather than cast the image into one's mind as most other runes would, this one cast the illusion *around* the target, to disguise it instead, a deception of sight rather than of mind. When done right, it was capable of hiding structures, people, even thoughts.

Another rune dealt with controlling multiple *living* minds at the same time. *The* Dominion *rune is a constant battle*, I read, *of pitting one's will against many others. Use at your own peril.* It sounded like almost every rune in the book should be used at one's own peril.

Next was a rune patterned after a chokehold of vines or perhaps a nest of intertwined snakes. *The* Strangle *rune targets the seeking stones of your enemy. Weave and direct the flow into its center to disperse its source.*

There were no runes on the next page but a sketch of a silver heartsglass.

To you, seeking Blade that Soars's path: take that which came from Five Great Heroes long past and distill into a heart of silver to shine anew.

I turned to the last page and found a sketch of another heartsglass, this one as dark as the first was bright.

To you, seeking Hollow Knife's path: present yourself with a heartsglass of black, where love's blood has been shed and seven daeva's bezoars. Boil the stones separately, and drink a vial's worth of their waters. Weave Compulsion *in the air; its heart shall reveal itself to you. Take it into your heartsglass.*

The process is not gentle.

Each daeva increases the darkrot. The sacrifice is great, but the rewards are priceless. The unity of seven into darksglass and five into lightsglass is the key. Merge both with the First Harvest to achieve shadowglass and rise as the Great Prince once did, to rule as you see fit.

I couldn't see how Aenah and the other Faceless would be willing to give up so much for immortality if they might die in the attempt anyway. Take five into lightsglass? Boil bezoars? First Harvest? It read more like a recipe for those suspicious "cure-alls" sold in the shadier parts of Ankyo. And yet…

None of the spells talked about severing links with *azi* either, and with the unexpected relief came guilt.

I browsed through the rest of the book and discovered some pages were torn out. Aenah might claim to help me, but it was apparent some spells weren't meant for my eyes.

I turned back to the *Scrying* spell. My promise to Fox held; I had only sworn not to use spells I had not yet tried.

Faint flickers of thought surrounded me, an unexpected smorgasbord of stray minds. I soon realized just how complex the rune was; without a specific target, its magic harnessed all nearby thoughts for sampling. Aenah had not needed to know of Garveth the guard to have access to him.

I followed the path back to Fox and found him at the training grounds, attacking one of several straw dummies in the field. His mind felt warm and familiar—a calm clear pool that suggested more depth than it presented.

He was quicker, stronger than I remembered. His body spun and whipped about in ways my clumsier form could never perfect, and his sword blurred, crackling like lightning as he scored decisive blows until he struck his straw opponent's head off its shoulders with one final stroke of the blade.

Not bad, I heard him think, *but still not enough.*

Cheers rose from the onlookers at the sidelines, and I watched embarrassment march through my brother's thoughts.

"Three dummies in a week. Ten minutes in your care and they are demolished, when they would have lasted months with others. Your blows are deadly, Sir Fox." Commander Lode of the Odalian army came into my view, smiling.

I am still not strong enough to protect Tea, my brother thought but only said, "I do so under your excellent tutelage, milord."

"Modesty is well and good, but acknowledging improvements to one's skills is as necessary as acknowledging improvements to one's character." The man clapped him on his back. "Though I must admit, you're faster and stronger now than when you were on patrol. We will find that damned daeva and get revenge, Fox."

"Looking forward to it, Commander."

"Good work. You'd be a match for even Lord Kalen, and that's saying something."

The men feared Fox, his ability to withstand injuries that

would kill others, when we had first arrived. Many were old comrades he'd known before the *savul* killed him. But Prince Kance told me how the soldiers of the Odalian army were the best in the world, that skill and courage were lauded above all else, and that Fox would be welcomed despite his ties to bone witches.

Thinking about Prince Kance sent a lump to my throat. I closed my eyes, willing away my own emotions before I alerted Fox to my presence.

As the commander moved on, I caught a sudden flash of gold and a whisper of silk. A veiled girl stood half-hidden behind a pillar, staring at me. Our gazes met.

In the next instant, she was gone, darting through an open door leading back to the palace. Within Fox's mind rose memories of lavender and perfume.

"Is this for me?" She held up a simple silver pin, a silhouette of a fox dotted with small crystals.

"I'm sorry. It's not much." The tiniest of the turquoise gems in her hair had probably cost twenty times more than the trinket. A soldier's paycheck did not offer many options.

The princess of Kion laughed and hugged it to her chest. "Don't be ridiculous. I'll wear this forever."

Fox blinked and looked up into the sky. "Tea?"

I flushed at the private memory. *I'm here, Fox. Sorry. I woke up and saw you were gone.*

I'm training with the guys. Want some company?

No, just checking up on you. I paused. *I think I should get more rest anyway.*

Good. Don't overexert yourself.

Gently, he nudged me away from his mind, and I retreated guiltily back into my own head, focusing on my bed, my room, the book on my lap. The *Scrying* rune had opened up a new link between us—I had better access to Fox's thoughts, which made it easy to stumble into his mind without meaning to.

I thought about my brother and the Kion princess. I thought about how our laughter sounded that night after the engagement announcement. My infatuation with the prince was a one-sided affair. I imagined promises the prince never whispered, knew enough of myself to understand that I could catch him no more than I could catch a shadow on the wall.

But without selfishness clouding my judgment, I saw how Fox mourned a relationship with the princess. His grief was sharp, and it sliced him deeper than any *aeshma*'s spike could, in places my magic could not heal.

Khalad had said memories were no one else's business but their owners'. And as close as Fox and I were, some memories *were* too private to be shared.

Trembling, I stared at my hands. Learning these runes was surely a lesser transgression than hiding and abetting an *azi*. I could tell Mykaela at least. I could…

I paused. Mykaela was too weak, and she didn't need this stress right now. Polaire then? Altaecia?

Polaire's words drifted to memory. *To wield anything that the Faceless would, from the most terrible of daeva to the most innocent-seeming runes…there must be no compromise.*

Did Mykaela care for Illara as much as she had cared for me? Did my mentor hesitate before delivering the killing blow? Would she hesitate with me? Surely Polaire was exaggerating. There is so much power in this book that could be harnessed in Kion's favor. So what if they had been the runes of the False Prince, guarded by his Faceless? A rune by itself did not define the righteousness or the immorality of the magic they cast—its user did…

No, telling anyone about this magic would be premature, I decided. I should study the runes first, give myself more time to assess how harmful they could be. I laugh now at how foolish I had been then, thinking I knew enough to tell the difference.

But fear is a powerful motivator. I had already compromised myself by taking in the *azi*. If I was to be condemned anyway, then I may as well be hanged for a sheep as a lamb.

I turned the book over. The inverted crown stared back at me.

"I will master you," I told it. "I will protect everyone from you." If only I were as confident as I had sounded.

*A*ND WHAT SPELL FROM THE *book did you learn to raise Kalen?"*
the Heartforger asked.

The bone witch grinned, suddenly impish. "It was not a spell
from that book."

"May I?" Lord Khalad inspected her heartsglass, placing a finger
against the dark surface. There was a faint spark as his finger met the
glass, but the forger did not react. He watched the colors of her heart
swirl and ebb before removing his hand.

"You raised him from the force of your own heartsglass, channeled
by the strength of all seven daeva. Did you know it would succeed?"

"No. But they promised I could achieve everything with shadowglass. So why not this?"

"I don't understand," I interrupted. "It is no secret that Dark
asha can raise the dead. What is so different this time?"

"Those with silver heartsglass cannot be brought back to life. But
Kalen should never have died." Anger was a potent venom sustaining
her determination.

"If you raised Kalen," the Heartforger began, a sudden wild
hope in his eyes, "then can you... Would you...?"

The bone witch bowed her head. "I don't know. But I will try.
I can promise you that."

"Thank you," Lord Khalad whispered, still trembling, and

turned to the corpse, unfazed by the eviscerated remains. "Blighted?"
he asked.

She nodded. "We must be vigilant."

"I will inspect every soldier for symptoms," the Heartforger
promised, turning to the wounded. At Lord Kalen's command, the
injured had been carried in, and the room soon filled with groans and
cries. Those who'd survived the daeva unscathed hurried in, lugging
heavy pots of water behind them.

"Set them up at the end," the asha instructed. "Keep them
boiling hot."

The men obeyed. The aeshma watching them curiously coupled
with the thought of the other daeva waiting outside made them
compliant. They barely spared a glance at their former emperor, still
under the beast's watchful eye.

"You're going to treat them?" The bone witch had talked about
laying waste to Daanoris, to bring the kingdom to ruin. Yet she
bade her monsters not to kill, to allow most of the population to flee
unharmed. And now she treated the wounded.

"The Heartforger will think less of me if I do not at least try,"
the asha said even as she pulled up the sleeves of her hua, folding
them up her arm like a fisherman's wife might before she took in the
daily catch.

"I have never thought less of you, Tea. No matter what anyone
said. And the sooner we are done with these men, the sooner I can
finish the heartsglass I promised you."

"L-Lady Tea?" It was a stuttered whisper, an unfamiliar
voice. A frightened young Daanorian girl stood, hiding behind

Lord Kalen's back. The asha smiled. "It is good to see you looking well, Princess Yansheo. I am sorry to meet again under unfavorable circumstances."

"But the kingdom! My people—gone! The monsters at our doors! Lady Tea, what have you done?"

"Upheavals come with every new ruler. Your people have fled, but they shall return. Your army will heal. I have come only to rid Daanoris of a malignancy, and chaos was the quickest way to bring it festering to the surface."

"But what malignancy do you speak of?"

"Do you need to ask? Who confined you to your rooms these long months? Who made you a prisoner in your own palace?"

The princess glanced at the emperor and looked away.

The bone witch's voice gentled. "Do you miss him still?"

The young noblewoman trembled. "Yes."

The Dark asha sighed. She wrapped a poultice made from herbs around a wounded soldier's side and rose to her feet. She walked toward the girl and took the girl's hands in her own.

"Yansheo. Some days will be better than others. Some days you will wake up crying, his name the first to fall from your lips. Some days, you will look up at the stars in the sky from a lonely beach and know none of them look down on him." Her eyes slid briefly to the Deathseeker, who had taken his place among the injured, and then returned to the princess. "That is the nature of grief. But to grieve means you have loved. To love opens up the possibility for grief. There cannot be one without the other."

"But, milady," the princess choked, "it isn't fair. He died so terribly—and for me."

"Life isn't fair, dear one. And sometimes, neither is death."

8

"TEA! ARE YOU IN THERE? Tea!"

I shoved the book underneath my pillow and scrambled out of bed. I cursed the time, myself, even Kalen at my door, bellowing for blood, and then myself again for good measure. I had forgotten about practice!

"There is no excuse for being this tardy!" Kalen exploded the instant I opened the door. His brown hair was tied back from his face and his hand was raised, ready to punch the door again had I been a second slower to respond. "Spare me your explanations. If you've enough time to slack off, then you've enough time to spar. Let's go!"

"I'm sorry!"

"Sorry doesn't cut it," he growled but said little else as he all but dragged me to the practice field. Normally, he would have blistered the air around him with remonstrations, so my apology must have startled him, my character typically being one that has few reasons to give him apologies.

The fields were empty. A quick poke at my bond told me Fox and the other soldiers had moved to the archery grounds, and Kalen wasted no time beginning. Despite his earlier threats, he assumed the defensive, giving me the first chance to strike.

My reflexes were slower, clumsier than usual. I was no master at swordsmanship, though Kalen had been training me for many long months. Regardless, the Deathseeker had never been one to give up on lost causes, even if that lost cause was me.

Kalen's blade blocked my first blow. I could hear his orders—"Bring your arm up! Keep your feet moving!"—but my body refused to comply.

The Scrying *spell*, I realized. I'd used it before Kalen had come stomping in, and now that my initial burst of adrenaline was gone, I had no second wind to fall back on.

I ducked low, using my smaller height to my advantage, and swung my sword up. He sidestepped the move, and I managed to parry his next attack. He backed away and waited again, but I never knew if I could have followed through with another blow.

My knees buckled, and I must have blacked out, though I had no memory of hitting the ground.

When I came to, I was sitting propped against a tree, a cloak bunched behind my head. Kalen was beside me, a combination of annoyance and concern.

"You OK, Lady Tea?"

Kalen never called me that before. "Didn't you tell me that

honorifics had no place in battle?" I croaked, strangely light-headed. I felt something cold and soothing pressing against my forehead.

"The battle was over as soon as you passed out. Why didn't you tell me you were exhausted?"

"There wasn't time," I mumbled, though that was only partly true. "You dragged me out of my room like the palace was on fire. But I'm better now."

"Don't lie." The Deathseeker gave the green flickers in my heartsglass a pointed glance. Sometimes I forgot that Kalen could read them as well as I could. "I should have known something was wrong. Your sword techniques are terrible, you leave your defenses so open that any expert swordsman could stab you through several times and run before you recovered, and you always try to overextend your reach—but tardiness has never been one of your bad habits."

Only Kalen could insult and praise me all in the same breath. "I'm glad you think so highly of me," I said, but my sarcasm missed him by miles.

"I know I'm not the first person you'd choose to divulge your secrets to, and I'm sure you have other friends in the asha-ka you can confide in. Share your worries with your brother. It isn't good to keep them bottled up inside so you start losing sleep over them."

Was he trying to be nice? I was accustomed to a contrary, belligerent Kalen. A kind Kalen was a strange animal I had little experience with. "What are you going on about?"

Was I imagining it or did pink touch his cheeks? Kalen was a master at concealing his emotions, so his heartsglass only showed obvious irritation. "Prince Kance, of course!" he shot back testily. "Stop feeling sorry for yourself!"

I gaped at him. It had not occurred to me that Kalen was trying to cheer me up.

His tone softened. "His impending marriage isn't something he has control over. Neither of them do. This was an arrangement between Empress Alyx and King Telemaine, an alliance between Kion and Odalia. Prince Kance has nothing but the highest esteem for Princess Inessa, but he isn't happy. Polaire and Mykaela were aware of the engagement, but I didn't know they hadn't told you."

I was sure my face burned, and my embarrassment made Kalen even more formal, more awkward in his attempts to soothe me. "It came as a surprise to all of us. Princess Inessa is furious at both Kance and King Telemaine, though she can't appear so in public."

"She has no reason to be!" I exclaimed despite myself. "It isn't fair that Prince Kance should have to shoulder her anger for his father's…"

I trailed off. Kalen was smiling, a rarity. "Kance could declare war on an innocent village and you'd find a way to defend him still, wouldn't you?"

"Their engagement shouldn't begin with a misunderstanding," I mumbled. I tried to stand, but Kalen placed both his hands on my shoulders—gently but with enough pressure to keep me where I was. "I said I'm fine."

"No, you're not." He sounded annoyed again, more like the Kalen I knew. "Stop being so stubborn. Rely on others more often."

Anger burst from my lips. "But I can't! Do you know what it's like to have no control over who people think you are? To be feared and hated, even when you protect them, help them? To be deemed unimportant by your friends, the very people you look up to? It isn't fair!"

There was a pause before the Deathseeker responded. "You're right," he said, and his voice made me look at him more closely. "It isn't fair at all. But you live with it and accept it. There isn't much use to complain when there is little you can do." Kalen set his jaw.

"What's wrong?"

"It's nothing."

"A few seconds ago, you told me to rely on other people, to not be so stubborn."

He sighed. "The official engagement ceremony will take place in a week. King Telemaine has temporarily released the Duke of Holsrath so he can attend both the official betrothal and the wedding."

"The Duke of Holsrath? But…" The king's brother had been languishing in prison for years. Arrested after an attempted uprising against his own sibling, his noble blood had spared him from the gallows but not from life imprisonment.

And Kalen was his son.

"Blood ties are stronger than treason." Kalen laughed

bitterly. "Perhaps King Telemaine wishes to reconcile with his brother despite all he's done. Whatever the reason, my father shall be present for the betrothal, whatever the rumors may say."

"What rumors?"

"They're not important."

"Kalen!"

He glared but gave in. "People have been talking. They think the duke still plots to take the throne. That I insinuated myself with the royal family to gain the influence needed for his reprieve."

I understood and was ashamed. Kalen had been judged far longer than I had. To be a traitor's son was hard enough; to be believed a traitor yourself, despite dedicating your life to serving the very people who despise you, was even worse. I had been an object of derision for more than two years. Kalen had been subjected to it since childhood.

"I'm sorry." I was horrified by my lack of empathy, at having dismissed his personal experiences for my own. "All my talk about being hated—I had no right to say that to you."

"People need someone to hate. And it's easier to see that in others than to find it in themselves. I should know," Kalen added in a strangely calm voice. "I've hated my father nearly all my life."

"Was he cruel?" I asked hesitantly, then cursed myself. "I apologize. You don't need to answer that."

"Three apologies in one day? That's promising." Then, before I could argue, he continued. "No, he was always kind, as warm as a father could be. My mother's death changed him. It was a daeva assault, the same attack that killed Khalad and Kance's mother." Kalen smiled grimly. "It made us all blood brothers of a sort. Three months after they died, my father rebelled against the crown. He and the king had been on good terms till then. He was barely an adult when Vanor died and Telemaine assumed the throne, and he had never once expressed any desire to take power. He bade me good-bye one day and then went missing for months. The next time I saw him, he was in chains.

"The king felt sorry for me and took me in—first as Kance's companion and then as his bodyguard. And when I learned I could channel runes, it almost felt like a blessing. It gave me purpose, a better chance to protect the royal family. The people's hatred didn't matter after that."

"That's not true at all!" I said hotly. "They don't hate you. The soldiers have nothing but the highest regard for you, including Commander Lode! You are well liked, and I have never heard you spoken of with contempt. If there are those who refuse to acknowledge your loyalty, then—then they aren't worth a second thought anyway!"

Kalen stared back at me, startled, and it occurred to me that in my zeal, I was leaning far too close to him, which he noticed as I did. A stray thought passed through my head: *If he smiled as much as Kance, he could be just as appealing.* I reared back, coloring, and tried to think of something offensive to say to make up for the ludicrousness of what I didn't. "If—if they find your ugly face offensive though, then that's a different matter entirely."

It was obviously an untrue statement and a poor comeback at that, and he started laughing, which made it worse. *He really is as good-looking as Prince Kance when he laughed.* "I was trying to make you feel better. When had our situations become reversed?"

I racked my brain for a better repartee, but he bopped me lightly on my head before I could get anything out. "That is enough practice for today. I expect you to be well rested for tomorrow's spar—even if I have little faith there will be much improvement."

I glowered at him as he stood. He ignored my glare, more concerned with choosing his words carefully. "Kance and I are as close as two brothers can be. We have both known Princess Inessa since we were children, but he never told me if he thinks of her as someone more than a friend. I also know that he considers you one of his closest and most trusted confidantes. While he has never been one to voice his feelings aloud, I suspect his decision for a more personal approach in ruling the kingdom was motivated by his desire to see you safe. I don't know if that helps."

I had to smile. "Thank you, Kalen."

"You're welcome. It's good to see Kance take his duties as the crown prince seriously, although I now have you to blame for the additional responsibilities he assigned me—including the training of someone who cannot be trained."

"You're horrible!" My protest was loud in the empty field, but he only laughed again and walked on.

I KNEW OF TEA'S INFATUATION WITH the prince from the moment we met," Lord Kalen said quietly, watching as the asha moved down the rows of injured. "My knowledge of it has commanded every meeting, every conversation with her since. I suppose I was disposed to dislike her long before we had ever been properly introduced."

The men no longer shrunk from the asha's touch. When Lady Tea moved to assist them, they relaxed, submitting to her treatment. More people had been brought in, this time civilians who had been caught in the crossfire. They cried out at the sight of the aeshma, who made a strange rumbling noise and laid down on the ground with its head tucked between its paws, the picture of docility if not for the terrible spikes along its form.

"But why?" I asked. Throughout the asha's telling of her own story, the Deathseeker had been silent, content to listen with few objections. Of his own life he had said very little, and save for his earlier proposal to his lover—to abandon this enterprise and flee—I knew little of his thoughts during this mad invasion. That he spoke to me now with little prompting was encouraging.

"The oracle told me so." He smirked at the shock on my face. "Deathseekers are just as much spellbinders as asha, though we do not train in their refined arts. We are slaves to many of the customs of the

Willows and also present ourselves to the oracle after ending our own novitiates. I was never one to believe in her myself."

"But what did the oracle tell you?"

The bone witch stood and murmured something to Princess Yansheo, who still stared with terror at the aeshma. From the window, I could see smoke rising from the fields outside the city, a testament to the previous battle. Below us, the rest of the daeva were at attention. Bored, the taurvi and the savul yowled and nuzzled and swiped mischievously at each other like lion cubs at play. The nanghait stood proudly; to my horror, I see more visages creep out from underneath the sags and folds above its neck so it could scan more of the horizon. From above, I could hear the song of the azi as it circled the city.

"The oracle told me that she would kill the prince."

I gasped.

He smiled again. "At least, that was what I thought. My first instinct was to reject her predictions. Magic and runes can be explained. But to my way of thinking, prophecy falls under the realm of con artists and charlatans. My duty was to protect the prince, and to my eyes, Tea was as much a threat as any other."

"Her predictions were wrong then?" I asked.

A small child, too young to understand the danger, approached the aeshma. The spiked daeva turned and regarded the child thoughtfully. It sniffed the boy's fingers and rumbled, a monstrous giggle. The child laughed along with it. His hand stroked at the furred face.

His mother turned and cried out in alarm. Immediately, the child abandoned its play, dashing back to her. The aeshma whined and drew its head down, bereft of companionship.

"No. The oracle was right. Only my interpretation of the words was inaccurate. The oracle bade me to be vigilant, for the next Dark asha to come to Kion would bring about the death of the person she loved. For many years, I assumed the prophetess referred to the prince." He raised an eyebrow. *"Funny, isn't it, how that turned out?"*

9

Y OU WOULD THINK AFTER THE exhaustion that came with *Scrying*, I would have been deterred from using it. Fox thought I was insane. "You can't expect this will get better," he said as I pored through the pages of the book.

"It barely fazes Aenah. I can train till I get to that point too." If the Faceless thought I could become a powerful spellbinder, that was her one message I was willing to believe. "Here, listen to this." I waved the book in my brother's face. "It talks about a *Veiling* rune."

"That makes as much sense to me as Drychtan."

"If done right, it can stop anyone from accessing your thoughts and prevent them from using *Compulsion* on you."

That got his attention. "What do you need for it?"

My fingers ran down the page, tracing the rune inscribed in dark red ink, trying to commit the complicated pattern to memory. "After the invocation, I am to formulate an image in my mind like a shield."

"A shield?"

"Or a door, it says. Anything that best represents shutting yourself away from the rest of the world. I don't know if it would affect any bonded familiars."

"Can't hurt to try. How long does this spell last?"

"For as long as you hold the shield in place. It requires some conscious effort at first, but the book says that with enough practice, you can learn to keep those defenses in place even when asleep." I wove the rune in the air and found the image of a closed door worked better for me. I could sense Fox's touch drifting over my mind, carefully testing for weaknesses. "I can't sense anything from you," he reported.

"Really?" I asked. In that moment, I lost my concentration, and his presence once more flowed easily into mine. "This is harder than it looks," I complained.

"You think it'll work on me?" Fox asked.

I obliged, weaving the rune around him this time. I probed cautiously into his head but encountered an unbreakable barrier separating our thoughts. I tried pushing forward to no avail.

"I guess it works with familiars too." I felt the door he was holding in place shift but remain strong. "It would be a good way to keep you and your three-headed pet out of my head for a change."

"Can you sense him?"

"Just around the edges. It gives me some mild discomfort, like shoes that are getting a little too tight."

"How are you not distracted enough to let go of your wall?"

Fox grinned. "Might have something to do with being dead. You're not too prone to stray thoughts, and it's easier to concern yourself with the bigger picture. It's always been easy for me to compartmentalize."

"You would have made a fairly good Deathseeker, Fox."

"Perish the thought. Let's see how long I can hold this up. Any other rune we can take a stab at?"

We tried the *Heartshare* rune next, to little effect. "Only for spellbinders, I suppose," Fox conceded. "Or for the living anyway. What's next?"

I cleared my throat, trying not to act too excited. "Well, there was this one spell I've been meaning to talk to you about…"

He glared at me. "We agreed you wouldn't snoop without me around."

"I made no promises about *reading* them." I placed the book on his lap. "See for yourself."

"You know I don't understand half the gobbledygook in this."

"This one's straightforward enough."

I was impressed. His face turned pale as he read, but he never once let the shield in his head lapse. Finally, he looked up. "What does this mean, Tea?"

"Exactly what you think it means." It was one of the most complicated runes I'd ever seen, a tangle of crisscrossed lines and convoluted angles that made it resemble a thornbush run amok or a spiderweb caught in an inkblot.

While other runes were spelled out in diminutive cursive, this was sprawled across the page in heavy block letters, as if the writer himself was aware of its importance.

Resurrecting Rune, it said. A rune capable of bringing familiars back from the dead in the truest way possible.

I didn't care if the rune had twenty times the complexity of Yadoshan architecture, if I were worth my salt as a bone witch, I was going to learn that spell, whatever it took.

Fox shared neither my enthusiasm nor my excitement. He read the page again with furrowed eyebrows and a clenched jaw. "This is too dangerous, Tea."

"The chance of it succeeding is worth the potential risk."

"No, it isn't!" He stabbed at the page with one finger. "Have you read what this requires?"

I knew. I had spent many hours that morning staring at the page, as if looking long enough could make the task easier on my conscience. *Distill the juices of the First Harvest into a familiar's heart to take back what death had decreed. Beware, for the First Harvest is poison and kills all it touches, asha and familiar, save for those who possess the black. Reap its fruit and suffer death.*

"We can ask Khalad to help. It's possible that—"

"It says it kills everyone who tries to take it, Tea! It's implying that whoever uses it would require their own life as a sacrifice!"

"Well, we don't know what a First Harvest is yet. I've been looking everywhere, but there's been no mention of it in the books here. But like I said, I'm sure we can find a loophole—"

Fox slammed his hand on the table with enough force that

the wood splintered. "Don't play semantics with me, Tea! Willing or not, you're asking someone to die, and I know exactly who you're volunteering. You are under no circumstances allowed to risk your life for me, Tea. Do you understand?"

"I wasn't…" That was a lie, and he knew it. But the *Veiling* barrier slipped, and I sensed a hodgepodge of his emotions: shock, worry, determination, anger—more anger than I had ever felt from him. And fear—crippling fear, which I had never felt from him so keenly.

Impulsively, I reached over and hugged his middle. "I won't. I promise. It's not like we're pressed for time or that you're in any danger. Hey, I'm protecting you too, right? I can't do that if I'm dead."

There was a pause. Fox's fist unclenched slowly, and he sighed but returned my hug. "Remember that, brat. You know I'd be lost without you."

·· ＞|＜ ··

I was a fast learner and soon committed most of the runes to memory. For six days, we practiced; when we weren't testing the extent of the book's magic, I was fast asleep. But the more I experimented, the less exhaustion I felt.

Eventually, we learned to prolong the effects of the *Veiling* rune, finding it easier to enforce the same shield in our minds instead of creating our own individual barriers. It became a game of sorts, figuring out how long we could maintain it and which of us could do so the longest. Sometimes, I felt the *azi*'s presence, though it showed only curiosity at our magic.

There was no way we could use the *Puppet* rune on actual corpses, so we made do with rat bones instead. I knotted the threads of magic together like the book instructed, commanded the rats to run from one corner of the room to the next, and let go. We watched as the skeletal rodents scuttled on their own without any further influence on my end.

The *Illusion* rune was more complicated. After I learned to bend the spell around an object instead of pouring magic into its essence, I was able to successfully hide it from view. I tried it on Fox.

"I don't feel any different," his disembodied voice reported. "Although it's disconcerting to see that I have no reflection in the mirror."

"Stop moving around or you'll be invisible forever." The spell was a little too good. It took me a dozen tries to draw it right, and I got it just as Fox was beginning to worry.

"The next time we practice this," he growled as he finally came into view, "we're going to use a blasted potted plant instead."

We couldn't practice the *Dominion* and *Strangle* runes given their implications, but I studied them regardless. I also found myself going back to the lightsglass and shadowglass spells, though I knew we couldn't—*shouldn't*—do anything with them. The same held true with the *Resurrection* rune. "We need to find another way, Tea," Fox said curtly, and that was that.

Spell practice was a good means to keep me distracted from Prince Kance's impending engagement. Fox never spoke of Inessa, but every now and then, I would catch a thought, a vision of him and the princess walking down Kion's market district at night or sharing mint-seasoned *doogh* at a teashop. I also sensed he would much rather not talk and so kept my silence. Because of all the preparations leading up to the engagement party, Polaire and Althy were constantly busy, much to my relief. I wasn't quite ready to talk to Polaire after our fight.

Fox had returned to the barracks after our last practice, still keeping a firm hold over the *Veiling* barrier I'd drawn. I went through Aenah's book again, but every time I became too engrossed, I felt the barrier starting to slip from my grasp, much to my irritation. It's odd how the spells that seemed easiest were always the ones that required the most discipline.

I switched to *Scrying*, determined to master that one. I was still leery of spying on anyone else in the palace, but I finally decided on a target that wouldn't affect my conscience.

I was wondering when you'd try this on me, Aenah's voice drawled in my head, speaking from her dungeon. For all her bravado, I could feel her discomfort. That gave me satisfaction.

Why tell me about this book? I asked her. *There was nothing for you to gain.*

She chuckled. *I suppose it was my last card to play. Oddly enough, I like you. You're clever and resourceful and not yet set in the ways of the asha, though several more years in Kion will surely erode your independence. There are many things asha cannot do that I can, and your problems will not be solved by the paltry runes your asha-ka teaches.*

There is more to you sharing this than you taking a liking to me.

True, Aenah replied. *I know now that I cannot win you over by guile—that mistake is the reason I am imprisoned here. So I turn to truth where deception has failed. I ask for nothing, Tea. Not for my release from this prison and not for you to join my cause. All I desire is to show you how the asha have deceived you. I have done many terrible things in my life, sweet child. But your asha have done worse, and it is time you look at them with new eyes. If you are willing to listen to me, then I will tell you more about the elder asha, their machinations, and the more powerful of the runes in my book.*

What have the elder asha done that make your transgressions pale in comparison?

It was your asha elders who conspired to hide your sister's heartsglass.

You lie!

And for what reason? The truth should be easy enough to ascertain. Ask them why they abandoned the search so easily. Ask them why the young King Vanor refuses to speak, even in death. Ask them why shadowglass interests them so. Ask how Blade that Soars and Dancing Wind's story truly ends. What secrets can you find when you step into Mistress Hestia's study?

I quickly broke off the link, more shaken than I want to admit. That wasn't possible. She was lying. Why would the elders withhold Mykaela's heartsglass?

A sudden barrage of emotions that were not my own flooded into my mind, at once unexpected and familiar. The *Veiling* dissipated; Fox had broken his barrier.

I scried again and reached out to him, prepared to tease him for the sudden lapse, but it was not the practice fields or straw dummies I saw when my vision refocused. It was the angry, teary-eyed face of Princess Inessa.

She was exceptionally lovely, beautiful from her delicately curved nose to her high cheekbones and smooth flawless skin. Her bright-blue eyes were perhaps her most arresting feature, a rarity for a Kion, proof of the royal house's ancient ties to the old kingdom of Arhen-Kosho, and a devastating contrast to her chestnut-colored hair.

"I can do whatever I want, now can I?" I'd never heard the princess speak like this; her normally pleasant alto was loud and harsh. "You have no say over where I go and who I marry!"

"But it's not your decision, is it?" Fox sounded different too. His voice was too even from holding back his anger with great effort. "Why can't you be honest for once in your life?"

"You are the last person to talk to me about honesty!" She shot back. "We have nothing! We *had* nothing!"

I hunched over, the pain in my chest catching me by surprise. The jolt soon passed. Fox responded without any change in expression. "And that's why you've been watching me at practice for the last three weeks."

She reeled back this time, and I could see her heartsglass mist over into blue. She clutched at the collar of her dress. "I don't… I haven't—"

"And now you're to wed the Odalian prince," my brother continued ruthlessly, much to my dismay. "It's nice to see you free to make your own choices."

The princess lifted her chin. "It was never my decision. But I'm prepared to honor my promises, unlike other people who come to mind."

"Honoring your promise to a stranger one moment, honoring it to a prince in the next. And in between, honoring it to every Ahmed, Farshid, and Hamid who so much as looks at—"

Her slap knocked me to the ground. I blinked up at the ceiling with my cheek burning, but Fox remained upright, watching the princess stomp away. Once she was gone he said, very quietly, "Tea?"

I'm sorry, I squeaked, scrambling to my feet. *I wasn't intending to pry. I felt you loosen the barrier, and I wanted to—*

It's fine. We can talk about it later.

A quiet Fox was the saddest thing I'd ever felt. Gently, I disengaged from his mind but not before his melancholy washed over me, aimless and drifting.

Deliberately, I reached out and sketched the *Resurrecting* rune. I cast no spell, summoned no magic.

The elders couldn't have worked this sorcery. Polaire was right. They would never have compromised themselves this way. But if I acknowledged that Aenah could be telling the truth, let her tell me more…

I sat and watched the rune glittering before me, light as air yet like a millstone around my neck, before I raised my hand again and watched it disappear.

*I*T WAS LORD KHALAD WHO *sounded the warning cry. He grabbed three injured Daanorian soldiers from the line of wounded and dragged them out of the room, one after another, with a ferocity I had not expected of him. Stunned, I followed Lord Kalen and the bone witch as they rushed out after him. Princess Yansheo attempted to do the same, but the Deathseeker admonished, "Stay inside, and do not come out until we tell you to. You too, Bard."*

Still, I lingered by the doorway, ready in my ignorance to protest in the Daanorians' defense.

"Stay back," the Dark asha commanded, and the servants loitering in the corridor turned away without another sound.

Choking, the soldiers dropped to their knees. One of them cried out, his face contorted in pain. Then his face lengthened, elongating in a way no human face had ever been shaped. With a harsh curse, Lord Kalen drew his sword, as did the bone witch.

Limbs burst out of the poor man's back, as the soldier morphed before our very eyes. His body jerked haplessly, bones cracking, until it was as tall as a horse, an emaciated, horrifying creature with yellow, bulbous eyes and foot-long teeth. I backed away in fright. Something close to recognition flared in its lidless eyes as it turned to the Dark asha, and she was the first person it chose to attack.

Her blade swung true; a stroke severed a twitching limb and the monster dropped, snarling.

A second soldier fell to the ground as a human but soon rose to its feet a beast, pincers taking the place of a mouth, terrible eyes glowing with a diaphanous sheen. Unlike its brethren, it leaped for the Heartforger.

Ice crackled and slid up its arm. The monster staggered, and Lord Kalen brought his sword down upon it, shattering the frozen appendage. The beast screamed, but just as quickly, another arm iced over and another arm was pulverized.

The bone witch sank her sword into the monster's side. Its hide proved tough, the blade cutting in but not deeply enough to kill it. The creature swiped at her with its claws, and she spun, switching targets and driving the steel deep into the back of its head. It shuddered once, twitching, and collapsed. Lord Kalen finished off his opponent, bringing his sword down on its neck.

The final soldier remained in agony on the floor, still in human form. The asha knelt beside him. Her hands found his, squeezing comfortingly.

The man cried a high-pitched plea in Daanorian.

"I am sorry," the bone witch told him, and from behind, Lord Kalen's sword struck one final blow. Death came quickly, mercifully.

The Dark asha didn't move for some time, staring down at the body before she gently disengaged her hand from his.

Back in the throne room, I suspected that the emperor would've cowered if wasn't already cornered by the aeshma. *She punched him, hard, in full view of his subjects. His head whipped back, and she slammed another fist into his stomach.*

"Tea!" Princess Yansheo screamed.

"Did you do this?" The Dark asha grabbed the man's hair, pulling his head from the ground. "Did you blight them?"

"No," the emperor gasped, his mouth full of blood.

"I killed your lieutenant when he was on the cusp of transforming. My azi devoured him before the blight could be completed. You're lying if you claim to know nothing of this."

"Then kill me, witch," the emperor rasped. "Take your revenge once and for all."

"I've been inside your mind, you old crone. A quick death is the least you deserve."

"Then what is it that you think I deserve, bone witch?"

"Here is a small sampling."

The emperor screamed. It was a long, drawn-out screech, like a soul shattering, ripping away from its body. His head thrashed, but even that was all the movement he could afford with the bone witch standing there, her dark eyes aglow. But she showed no sign that she enjoyed this man's suffering.

"Remember our last meeting? You belittled me for my lack of spine. You said I should not hesitate to dirty my hands if it was the only way."

Her lip curled.

"You must be proud now. Did you choose the blighted because you knew bone witches have no access to their minds?"

"Lady Tea!" Princess Yansheo's face was pale.

"Tea," the Heartforger said, his face strained. "Stop it."

"You told me once that the emperor deserved to die, Khalad. What makes this moment any different?"

"Whether my death changes anything is not important," the man said, almost in a whisper, "but whether you allow my death to change you is another matter entirely."

There was a momentary pause as the asha released her hold on the emperor, who fell to his knees before her, still gasping. "Did you cause the blight in these men?" she asked again.

"No," the emperor wheezed, still fighting for breath. "I swear."

"Your vows mean nothing to me. Khalad, monitor the rest of the Daanorians for any additional changes. Take this filth from my sight."

"You're different, Tea," the Heartforger told her, still troubled.

She grinned. "And it does my heart good, Khalad, to know that you will never change."

10

THAT EVENING, THE PEOPLE OF Odalia gathered to witness the formal betrothal of the crown prince and the First Daughter of Kion. My voice rose over the din of the festivities without much effort.

"That was a low blow you took with the princess," I told Fox. "Even for you."

"No. Maybe." Fox rubbed his nose. "I wasn't thinking."

"You were nicer to whatshername. That girl from Tresea you liked who preferred that other jerk, Maharven—"

"Her name's Gisabelle. I don't know why you remembered that ass's name and not hers. And I didn't know she was a princess when we first met." Fox's voice was testy; he was clearly eager to end the conversation.

"How could you not know she was a princess?!" Several people turned to look at us, and I lowered my voice.

He colored. "I never paid much attention to royalty."

"That's a terrible excuse, and you know it. You're my *familiar*. How did I not know any of this?"

"I don't have to tell you everything about my life, Tea."

I wanted to argue that further but relented. Hadn't I done the same thing regarding the *azi*? "At least tell me how you met Princess Inessa."

He paused. "A public teahouse. She was dancing."

"Dancing?"

He fixed his eyes on something in the distance. I could feel the emotions he often kept at bay, how raw they felt.

"Even veiled, she held the eyes of every man in the room. She said she had an overbearing mother and that night was the first time she'd snuck out. I thought she was a merchant's daughter."

I remembered finding Fox in a heated argument with a girl at the palace while I was a novice. I hadn't known her identity to be Princess Inessa until later, and that was over two years ago. "And you've been…seeing each other since then?"

"Not after this engagement." Bitterness seeped into him, lodging in my own throat. "Can we talk about something else? Or get away from all this?" He gestured at the revelers. "All this noise is giving me a headache."

A hand landed on my shoulder. "And here's our errant asha!" Zoya's voice boomed. Uncaring of the widening circle around us by the crowd wary of asha, Zoya smoothed the wrinkles on the sleeve of my *hua* as a smiling Althy appeared beside her. "We've been looking all over for you!"

"Where's Mykaela?" I asked.

"Resting, on Polaire's orders. She'll be here once the ceremony starts, but she needs to relax until then."

Another figure beside them caught my attention, and my eyes widened. "Likh?" I asked disbelievingly. Unlike the other asha, who were dressed in elaborate *hua* and beautiful zivar, he was dressed in the black clothes more typical of Deathseekers. His long hair was pulled back, and despite his attire, he still looked exceedingly pretty.

I bounded over to give him a fierce hug, and he made a soft, little squeak at my exuberance. "Have the asha-ka made their decision?" I demanded. "If you're wearing that because they're forcing you to become a Deathseeker, then I am going to rip—"

Likh shook his head, waving his hand as if that could dissuade my bloodlust. "They'll make their ruling next week. But I thought I ought to get comfortable, just in case." Though he smiled, his silver heartsglass was an erratic display of blue and silver.

"We're not going to give up on you that easily," Fox told him.

Althy nodded. "We're on good terms with the head of the Deathseekers. Zahid's more flexible than the association when it comes to rules. If the prince and Zahid's support is not enough, then we'll figure out some other way."

"You always do, Althy."

We turned to find Mykaela standing before us, smiling, her hand on Polaire's elbow and Kalen following close behind them.

Polaire nodded at me, our previous fight still rankling in the air between us. "You are not to wander around on your own in this crowd," she lectured her best friend.

"I think Lady Mykaela can make her own decisions," I said before thinking.

Polaire's eyes flashed fire, but Althy stepped in. "We have other duties to attend to, such as the forming of the guards and seeing to the security."

"Polaire's been more domineering lately," I noted sourly after the two had moved off.

Mykaela seemed amused. "Many of my old tasks she has since claimed responsibility for. Her nose has been in every nook and cranny of the palace, ensuring things run according to plan."

"That's a terrifying thought."

"It keeps her occupied. She enjoys it, for all her complaints."

"But how have you been?" I felt guilty. I had been so busy with my responsibilities that I barely had time to talk to Mykaela beyond a few minutes each day. "I don't want you pushing yourself, Mykkie."

She ruffled my hair. "I never do. I trust you've been sleeping well yourself?"

I made a face. "I haven't gone back to the prisons. As much as I want to."

"Thank you, Tea. I know that was hard for you to agree to."

I sighed. "Can't I—not even one more night so I can—"

"Tea."

"Fine."

She laughed. "Shall we go? There're some people I'd like you to meet."

"Ah, Lady Mykaela," Kalen began, faltering slightly. "Lady Polaire told us to stay here."

"And I am telling you that I have a small matter to attend to elsewhere." It was easy to dismiss Lady Mykaela's frail condition and forget her forceful character. Her voice took on the tenacity of steel. "It would be a shame to leave you behind, Kalen."

It didn't take much for him to give in. "But of course, Lady Mykaela."

"Pushover," I murmured in a voice that wasn't as soft as I thought it was, for Kalen shot an irritated look my way.

Zoya grinned. "Waiting is boring anyway."

"And Likh?"

Smiling, the young boy nodded.

"Excellent."

I fell into step beside Likh. "How are you holding up?" I whispered.

Likh shrugged. "As well as can be expected. Kalen and the others are nice. Many of the Deathseekers support my appeal. I'm not used to the attention." His ears colored.

"The asha-ka are going to see things our way, even if I have to box them around the ears until they do."

Likh giggled. "That's a terrible image, Tea."

"Tea! Fox!"

Our family stood several yards away, waving. My parents looked unchanged, though my dad stooped a little more than I remembered. Wolf and Hawk had gone from chasing each other around my father's forge to becoming bearded blacksmiths like my father. Wolf was even starting his own family, which made my head spin. Beside them, Marigold, Violet, and Lily bloomed like their namesakes. Rose and Lilac, not quite asha but my sister-witches still, were the same as always, but Daisy had become even more beautiful. My heart ached, knowing how fast they had grown. Was this how Fox felt whenever he had come home on leave from the army?

Yes, my brother murmured.

We were swept up in a sea of hugs and kisses, my siblings surrounding us. "You rarely write!" Hawk complained, clapping his oldest brother on the shoulder. "You used to write enough to fill a book when you were in the army but then practically nothing after you and Tea left for Kion!" He turned to grin at me then—they all did, a little awed as I stood in my *hua* with its delicately embroidered waist wrap. What money Fox or I could save, we always sent their way, but I was self-conscious that my outfit cost more than what my family normally made in a year.

"Lady Mykaela was kind enough to invite us for the ceremony," Marigold said happily. "So many people! It's like solstice back at home, only the dresses are prettier."

"I got a new heart for the occasion," Daisy informed me proudly, displaying a gorgeously intricate heartsglass around her neck, gleaming red.

I groaned. "Daisy."

"What? I dumped him because he was a louse. I wish I had

a pretty silver heartsglass of my own." Ever the opportunist, she turned to smile brightly at Kalen. "Aren't you going to introduce me to your friend, Tea bunny?"

Growing older hadn't altered who my family was. Had I changed to them? Did they still see me as the twelve-year-old with her head constantly in a book or did they see me as an asha?

Because I *had* changed. I wasn't the girl they remembered. Would they be afraid of me if they knew the runes I wove, if they knew the monsters I'd raised? Would the girl they knew have hidden an *azi* in her mind and told no one? I knew the answer to that, and it hurt. I was a puzzle piece that no longer conformed to the shape of their lives.

"Thank you, Mykaela," I whispered as my family joined the rest of the asha.

She smiled. "I know how difficult it is to be away from family."

I had no time to voice more of my gratitude when my parents descended upon me.

"You're not eating right," my mother fretted. "Have they been feeding you well? Are you working too much?"

"Please, Mama," I mumbled.

My father was a man of few words. "We've missed you, Tea," he said in his low rumble, and I blinked back tears.

"I'm sorry I haven't been able to visit."

"We heard about you putting down daeva." Worry colored my father's heartsglass.

"I'm protected. The Deathseekers and the king's soldiers

make it a point to accompany me…and Fox, of course. The prince even accompanied me once."

"The prince!" My mother clapped a hand over her heart. "Lady Mykaela told me she would introduce us to him today. Imagine that! Never in my lifetime did I think we would meet the king and his son!"

"Everyone's excited." My father cast a glance back at Daisy and Kalen and added dryly, "Even your oldest sister, although I suspect it's for a different reason."

To set Daisy loose in a roomful of eligible noblemen was always a bad idea. I hesitated. On one hand, it was amusing to see Kalen looking out of sorts. On the other, he had been nicer to me as of late.

Fox approached, knowing the plan that ran through my mind. My parents turned delightedly to him as he began introducing the other asha.

"Perhaps one of the king's soldiers can show you around the city," Kalen said as I headed for Daisy.

"But I'd feel much safer with you," Daisy persisted, her hand tightening on his Kalen's arm. I felt a twinge of irritation. This was moving too fast, even for her.

"He's right, Daisy," I said cheerfully, worming my way between the two, taking great care to remove my sister's hand from Kalen's as I did. My sister glared daggers at me. "Lord Kalen is a high-ranking member of the Deathseekers. What little time he can spare, he spends with me."

"With you?" It was my turn to grab Kalen's arm, pulling

him away. "You can have your pick of suitors in Kneave, Daisy, but it would be nice if you could leave mine alone."

Kalen's mouth was working soundlessly. I stepped on his foot, warning him not to speak.

"Goodness!" Daisy's hand flew to her mouth, looking both surprised and pleased. "Really? You never mentioned—"

I looped Kalen's arm around my neck and snuggled closer to him. "It's not like we *want* to announce it to everyone, but our relationship is not forbidden. Right, my love?" I poked Kalen in the ribs.

The Deathseeker coughed. "Yes. I, uh…"

"Oh, Tea! My little sister is growing up so fast!" Daisy clapped her hands in delight. She'd gone from flirt to doting sister in less than a second. "My apologies, Lord Kalen. I haven't seen Tea bunny in such a long time, and I still see her as the shy girl she always was. So you really do love him, Tea?"

I planted as genuine a smile on my face as I could muster. "Of course! I've never been so sure of anything in my life." I tugged hard at his sleeve. Kalen was selling this poorly, and Daisy would be sharp enough to figure it out.

"Agreed." Kalen's voice sounded so strange that I had to peek up at him to see if he was all right. The next thing I knew, his grip around my shoulders tightened, and he pressed his lips against my cheek.

It was like a jolt of lightning lanced through my skin. I jumped, though it was not an entirely unpleasant shock, and Daisy looked satisfied.

"My apologies, Lord Kalen. Tea bunny, I can see he's quite smitten. Ooh, Marigold and Lily will be so thrilled to hear!"

"Wait!" I shouted, to no avail. Daisy was already dashing over to my sisters.

"Tea bunny?"

"Shut up," I hissed. "What did you do that for?"

"I thought you wanted me to be convincing," he hissed back. "And whatever possessed *you* to say we were in a relationship?"

"Daisy has a lot of bad habits, but she would never chase after a guy who's already taken." I stepped out of his reach. "Look, since you're clearly uncomfortable, let's just pretend this never happened. I'll deal with my sister."

I was spared from making a further fool of myself by the trumpets sounding as the ceremony began.

My family looked on in awe as both Prince Kance and Princess Inessa stepped into view. I could feel a faint tightening in the corners of Fox's thoughts, his heartsglass gleaming too brightly to be natural. I reached for his hand and squeezed lightly. After a moment, he squeezed back.

Together, we watched them formalize their betrothal. They exchanged heartsglass, as was the custom, a symbol of their commitment to one another, and I felt my own heartsglass flicker when the prince leaned over and kissed the princess, concluding the celebrations.

The party was in full swing by the time I entered the throne room, where dignitaries from most of the kingdoms mingled. Prince Kance smiled, catching sight of me as I entered.

"I've been looking for you all evening," he said, folding his hands over mine, as was his habit.

"Are you feeling all right, Your Highness?" His face looked pale again.

"Kance," he corrected me.

"Not today—a formal engagement in a public setting. Calling you by your first name wouldn't be appropriate."

"Then at least let me apologize."

"That's not necessary, Your Highness."

"It is to me," he said earnestly. "I wanted to tell you personally about the engagement, but I didn't quite know where to begin. After all my talk about taking command of my own life, this reeks of the worst hypocrisy."

"That doesn't matter, Your Highness."

The prince shook his head, and his heartsglass shone a somber blue. "It does. First Drycht and then this situation with Likh and now my engagement... Father's been impossible all week." He stopped, his eyes unfocused.

"Your Highness?"

He snapped out of his strange reverie, blinking rapidly. "What was I saying?"

"I think you need to excuse yourself from the celebrations, Your Majesty. You're not well. You haven't been well since before the *aeshma* hunt."

"You're right. Perhaps after greeting the rest of the guests." He sighed. "I haven't even talked to Inessa tonight."

"Do you love her, Your Highness?" I asked softly, fearing what he might answer.

He hesitated. "I think I could *grow* to love her."

That was a consolation. "If you truly believe that she can make you happy, talk to her about your engagement. You owe each other that much."

Prince Kance smiled wryly. "I agree. I should."

"And I have something that could help you with your exhaustion. Khalad made it." I reached into the folds of my robe. The prince's birthday was in three days but now seemed as good a time as any.

The prince brightened at the sight of the small glass pendant sparkling under the bright lights of the throne room. "I'll keep it with me at all times." He bent his head and pressed his lips against the back of my hand. "Thank you, Tea. You helped me understand that there's more to a kingship than sitting on a throne."

"It's nothing, Your Highness." My throat constricted. "And my best wishes on your engagement, Prince Kance. I hope you and the princess will be happy together."

A melancholic smile appeared on his face. "Thank you. I wish I could—"

"Your Highness?" A courtier materialized by his elbow. "The king wishes to speak to you."

"Let's talk later, Lady Tea," Prince Kance said, exhaling. "Please excuse me…"

I watched him stride to where King Telemaine and Princess Inessa waited and turned away. Polaire and the others were busy entertaining, something I was also supposed to be doing. This was a nobles-only event, so Fox was somewhere else in the palace with the rest of my family. I was on my own.

"You look like a little thundercloud hovering in the middle of a field of sunshine."

I bit back a sigh and faced Kalen. "I'm flattered you made all this effort to keep the thundercloud company."

"I was in the middle of a boring conversation with the Earl of Heides. You were an escape."

"There's something else eating at you." I nodded at his heartsglass. "Do you want to talk about it?"

He paused, nodded.

I followed his gaze to his father, the Duke of Holsrath, who sat at the farthest table from the crowd, a drink in one hand and a small smirk on his face. Everyone pointedly ignored him, and the large coterie of guards around him was proof he was still a prisoner. He looked gaunt, undoubtedly from his time in the dungeons, though his hair and beard were freshly trimmed. He resembled Kalen on a superficial level, but I disliked him at first sight.

"I want him out of here," Kalen said stiffly. "If it wasn't in direct conflict with the king's orders, I would have—"

He stopped at the sound of breaking glass. Heads turned toward the throne.

A glass had slipped from Prince Kance's hand. He was ashen.

He took two steps forward, his mouth forming my name before he collapsed on the floor.

I rushed forward, but Kalen was quicker, reaching his side before King Telemaine. "Send for a doctor!" the king roared.

Prince Kance took a deep, shuddering breath. His eyes met mine, then Kalen's.

"Protect her," he whispered.

Helpless to do anything else, the Deathseeker could only nod.

The prince smiled at him and then at me before the light in his heartsglass went out.

I T WAS CHAOS," THE ASHA said, reminiscing. "I remembered little else of that night—only faces hovering over us, Kalen yelling at them to stay back. It was terrifying to feel so helpless. I knew there was nothing I could do, yet I was convinced I'd overlooked some danger at the party."

"You did everything you could, Tea."

The Heartforger's equipment had been sent for, and it was a strange collection of tools. Different glass containers of miscellaneous sizes and shapes stood on a row before the throne. Oddly colored liquid sloshed in many of these vials, bubbling and hissing and resembling no form of water I was familiar with. There was also an apparatus built like a pottery wheel but with more spikes and pedals than seemed necessary. The Heartforger ran his hands lovingly over it, inspecting every hollowed nook.

A cooing noise came from by the window—the taurvi's giant eye peered quizzically down at us, and it sang a few short notes.

"Lady Tea," I whispered. "You cannot treat the Daanorian emperor this way."

"He is a horrible emperor, Bard." Disdain marked her voice. "He did many terrible things."

"Lady Tea." This time it was Princess Yansheo pleading. "I do not know what impels you to treat my kinsman so poorly, but I *beg of you. Whatever your quarrel with him, he is still the ruler of this kingdom, and he is my liege, however badly he has treated me. Daanoris does not deserve such punishment."*

But the asha shook her head. "Kings and emperors need the people more than the people need them, princess. Kings are kings only because one ancestor was quicker than another to place a crown on his own head. Bravery and courage are not passed down through blood. Kings and emperors do not require valor or good works; all they require is submission."

"But there is no one else fit to rule, milady."

"In Odalia, they tell us that all men are made in Blade that Soars's image, and all women in Dancing Wind's. What claim would he possess to hold the crown better than yours, princess?"

I I

For TWO DAYS, A LINE of worried doctors traipsed into the prince's bedchamber and traipsed back out again armed with conflicting diagnoses. King Telemaine held a vigil by his bedside, but not even Princess Inessa or Lady Mykaela was allowed entry.

I divided my time between waiting anxiously in the hallway and sitting in my room, desperately searching for something, *anything*, within Aenah's Faceless book that could help the prince. "What good are you?" I finally sobbed, flinging it in a brief fit of rage. What was the use of *Scrying* and puppets when they couldn't save the prince?

Kalen had taken the events worse than I had and was reduced to pacing Kance's hallway, rejecting food and rest. "I can't think about eating at a time like this, Tea." He looked like he hadn't slept since the prince collapsed.

"You'll become as sick as His Highness without anything in your stomach." I shoved bread into his hands. "Do they even know what's happened to Prince Kance?"

Giving in to my bullying, Kalen accepted a piece. "Nothing yet."

"Why not ask Althy to help? She's the best healer among the asha."

Kalen sighed. "Politics. Lady Altaecia is a Kion asha, and as friendly as they are, to ask for help from a neighboring kingdom is a sign of weakness."

"But not at the cost of the prince's life!" I insisted.

"I wouldn't put my son's life over the needs of the kingdom." For all his bulk, King Telemaine could walk silently when he wished to. Kalen jerked to attention. "Lady Mykaela, however, has taken a look at him, even she was at a loss."

"Can't we do anything?" I pleaded.

He smiled kindly at me, though his eyes were heavy with fatigue. "It warms my heart to know that Kance has friends he can trust. But his illness is beyond our understanding. The doctors can find nothing wrong with him, save for his heartsglass turning an unusual gray. All he does is sleep."

Dread seized my gut. "Gray? He won't wake up?"

"So they say. The best doctors in the kingdom and they have no idea. Lady Tea?"

I was already backing away. "I'm sorry, Your Highness. I have to go." I tore down the hallway, heart pounding. *A sleeping sickness.* Where had I heard that before?

Kalen caught up to me easily as I reached the gate. Fox, so attuned to my emotions, was already there astride Chief. My horse-familiar pawed at the ground, eager to be off.

"Where are you going, Tea?" Kalen yelled behind me.

"To see Khalad!" I vaulted onto Chief, who was intelligent enough to pick up on my thoughts. Soon, we were cantering into the city, leaving the Deathseeker staring after us.

Khalad was hunched over another one of his creations when we burst into the room. He started but deftly caught the delicate heartsglass before it fell. "Please knock next time, Lady Tea," he said sternly. "This new heart has a very rare memory. It's not every day you find one over a hundred years old—"

"Prince Kance is ill, Khalad," I gasped out. "They say it's a sleeping sickness!"

Khalad's eyes widened, his expression suddenly stricken. "Kance is sick?"

"He has been for two days! His heartsglass turned gray right before my eyes! Wasn't that a symptom of the sleeping sickness the old forger was investigating?"

He flushed. "But that's impossible! The master was certain there would be no such cases in Odalia."

"That's not how illnesses work," my brother objected.

Khalad rummaged through a pile of books in one corner of the room, returning with several parchments.

"Master conducted a thorough investigation," he explained, unrolling one of the parchments. "There have been four known incidents so far. Baron Cyran of Istera: age twenty-three. He went to bed one night and couldn't be woken the next morning." He uncovered another. "The Earl of Mancer, from Arhen-Kosho: age thirty-eight. He was out hunting boar when he suddenly toppled off his horse. Here's another: a royal princess from the house of Weixu, of Daanoris: age sixteen. She fell unconscious in the middle of a ball."

Khalad swiftly unfurled the last parchment. "The Marquise of Thanh, one of the smaller city-states of Yadosha. The marquise was sixty-seven, though still in good health. He drifted off while giving a speech. None could be roused, their heartsglass a muted gray."

"Different ages, all of noble blood. Physically healthy," I said, scanning through the reports. "But they don't seem to have anything else in common."

"There is one attribute." Khalad sounded grim. "Master said they were all descendants of the Five Great Heroes."

"That's…" I opened my mouth and closed it again, remembering. *To you, seeking Blade that Soars's path: take that which came from Five Great Heroes long past and distill into a heart of silver to shine anew.*

"Mithra the Protector." Fox ticked them off with his fingers. "Ashi the Swift. Anahita the Mighty. Rashnu the Just. And Sraosha the Obedient. But how can the Heartforger be so sure?"

"Because he can see their bloodlines in their heartsglass." Khalad touched his. "So can I. It's difficult but not impossible. Master had long suspected that someone was targeting their descendants, but he didn't know why. The only Great

Hero descendant left untouched by the sickness is Anahita the Mighty." Khalad sighed. "My father, King Telemaine, isn't a direct descendant however. Neither was Vanor or Lance, the Duke of Holsrath."

"But Prince Kance is!" I burst out, remembering. "And so are you!"

Khalad blinked. "My master had reason to examine both Vanor's and Telemaine's heartsglass in the past. They—"

"Do not have your mother's ancestry," Fox broke in. "Remember when Tea accidentally resurrected King Randrall? Randrall claimed that the crown prince was not his son but the son of the commander of the Odalian army. Vanor's and Telemaine's lines did not spring from his, but your mother was also a descendant of Anahita."

"I hadn't thought about my mother's line," Khalad muttered, looking embarrassed. "But surely that would not have escaped my master's notice."

"Could it be that he said nothing to spare you the worry?" I asked.

"It's possible. He was terribly secretive about his conclusions until I pestered him." Khalad leaped to his feet and began stuffing papers and other equipment into a large sack. "But I have to be sure. I need to take a look at my brother's heartsglass!"

"Can you cure him?"

Khalad shook his head, despairing. "Master talked about having tested one, but he gave few specifics."

"Do you know where he is?"

"He'd gone to Daanoris to take another look at the sleeping princess. He found her death the most suspicious of the lot."

"Why?"

"Daanorians don't wear heartsglass. They've always been suspicious of magic, although their current emperor is quite keen on asha and has been infatuated with Inessa for years. Someone would have needed to draw Heartsrune for the Daanorian to fall sick in the same way the others had."

"For now, let's return to the castle to ensure Khalad's safety as well," Fox decided.

"Me?"

"Might I remind his Lordship," Fox told him quietly, laying stress on the last word, "that though you have officially abdicated from the royal succession, you are still Kance's brother, so you can still be reinstated. Should anything happen to the prince, I doubt that your father will allow you to remain the Heartforger's apprentice for much longer."

.. ⫫ ..

I was shocked to see the throne room full of soldiers as we entered. It felt like the whole Odalian army was waiting for us.

"Tea!" Kalen's voice rang out. He was being restrained by some of the soldiers. "Get out of here!"

I took a step back but found my path barred by swords. Two men stepped forward to place their hands on my shoulders. Two more took hold of my wrists.

"What's going on?" Fox asked, stunned. "Albie? Parviz? Why are you doing this?" I felt his anger, felt him struggling behind me. His eyes flicked to his commander. "General Lode?"

The older man shook his head. His heartsglass showed me his reluctance, his implacability. Good soldiers obeyed orders.

The Duke of Holsrath stepped forward. He was smiling, and his heartsglass glittered a bright, malicious red.

"We haven't been properly introduced have we, Lady Tea?" He bowed to me. "King Telemaine has elected to remain by his son's side. He left me in charge of the palace while Kance recuperates."

"I don't believe you!" It was inconceivable to think that the king would willingly turn over the reins of his kingdom to a brother he had imprisoned for conspiring to take it from him. "I demand to see him!"

"You are not in a position to demand anything, milady. Telemaine made the announcement in full view of the soldiers. Kalen himself witnessed it. Didn't you, Kalen?"

The boy gritted his teeth. "Go to hell."

The duke regarded his son carefully and then casually punched him.

I lunged forward, white-hot rage searing my vision. I felt Fox leap after me. Hands pulled us back, and I heard more swords being drawn from scabbards as the tip of one rested against my throat.

"You may hate me, Kalen," the duke said coldly, "but I am still your father. I will not tolerate such disrespect."

My fingers twitched, *Compulsion* already half-formed.

"Would you really do that, Lady Tea?" There was a slickness to the duke's voice that repulsed me, like grease that clung to skin. "Would you compel all these soldiers, your brother's own comrades? Will you force these soldiers to commit treason against their will, a crime punishable by death? How very little you must think of life, milady. After all, you have always dealt in death."

Trembling and angry, I let the rune slip away.

"Tea Pahlavi, I hereby arrest you in the king's name for the attempted murder of His Highness, Prince Kance. Fox Pahlavi, I arrest you in the king's name for being complicit to the same crime."

"Are you mad?" Kalen shouted. "They did no such thing!"

The duke lifted his hand, and I saw the pendant I had given Prince Kance dangling from his fingers.

"It is easy to conceal a malevolent spell inside this trinket, and there were witnesses who saw my nephew take sick shortly after receiving your gift. Lady Tea, you are to be confined until your trial. Do not worry. I am not so cruel as to keep you in the dungeons. Your prison will be a warded room at the farthest wing of the palace. Armed guards and Deathseekers will prevent further incidents.

"And as for the Heartforger's apprentice." The duke turned to Khalad, who was still pale. "While there are no charges to bring against the former prince, you are to be detained indefinitely for questioning. Your previous royal status will not exempt you, Khalad. You are a practitioner of the Dark arts and must therefore come under scrutiny. Assist us in our investigations and it will be easier on you. You may be my nephew, but that will not save you—I do the same to my own son."

Behind my back, I sketched *Compulsion* again, this time directed toward the Duke of Holsrath's mind. But what I encountered was a thick wall of resistance as strong as steel.

The duke laughed. His heartsglass glittered, and I noticed a lapel pin on his shirt, shining bright gold as the zivar repelled my attempt. "A good try, Lady Tea. But I have not come unarmed. Perhaps I should mention that Lady Mykaela has also been detained and charged."

I leaped toward him again, heedless of the blade at my neck, my hands curled into claws that were prepared to do what my magic could not, but I was dragged back.

"She's resting well, given the circumstances. However, her comfort, I think, shall be dependent on your actions. If you are innocent of the charges, as you claim, then you will be released as soon as that is established. Conversely, if you admit your guilt, we can overlook other...*unpleasantness* necessary for interrogation. What is your answer, milady?"

"I did nothing to Prince Kance," I snarled.

"As you wish." The duke turned to the soldiers. "Kindly escort our dear asha to her quarters. Look at any of my men the wrong way, Lady Tea, and it will be Lady Mykaela who suffers the consequences. It's getting late, and there are many other pressing duties to attend to before the morrow, including your cross-examination."

THE ASHA TALKED LITTLE THAT *night. While the Heartforger bent over his task, shaping lumps of mud and clay on the strange potter's wheel, and while the emperor remained unconscious, trussed and bound behind the throne, the girl stared out the window into the city. Her daeva, obedient to a fault, kept a watchful guard. Occasionally, one would draw close to the window and purr, seeking her attention. She would lay a distracted hand on their rough hides and smile, but she never once looked away from the horizon. I wondered what she could see that I could not.*

Lord Kalen approached, and her hand sought his. Side by side, they watched the setting sun, and I wondered at their thoughts, at the bond they shared.

I marveled at the Heartforger's concentration. For two hours, he worked on the dismal lump of clay. No breathtaking design came to life in his hands, no bowls or sculptures deserving of fire or of glaze. I have seen potters craft masterpieces in half the time.

"Name?"

It took me a while to realize he was talking to me.

"Tea never asked for your name." The Heartforger did not look up from his work. "She wouldn't."

"She calls me 'Bard,'" I said, surprised by how vinegary the words came out.

"Don't take it personally. This is how she reminds you of your purpose. She has no need for friends—she has lost enough of those over the last year." He selected a small tool from his collection. "It must be frustrating to see very little results in the time I have spent on this."

"I have no knowledge of a Heartforger's art," I responded, immediately ashamed of myself. "I have had no opportunity to watch one at work before."

"It's not worth an audience, as you can see. Unfortunately, I cannot make a living conducting demonstrations in exchange for payment. I remember my own impatience as an apprentice, watching my old master spin for hours without result. I was hot tempered and headstrong, and those are not the best virtues to be found in a forger." He smiled down at his work. "Patience is the long pause between action and its consequences. Lengthier silences open you up to intro-spection, and I've known a lot of solitude."

There was no sound, no flaring of light that often accompanied the magic. The pathetic-looking chunk of clay hardened, cracked, and fell away. What remained was not a heartsglass but a strange sliver of a line, a frozen thunderbolt that sparkled like crystal.

"My master called it an urvan, from the old Avestan languages," the Heartforger said, "one's 'soul,' so to speak."

"But whose soul is it?"

"Imagine an empty flask. I give it to you, and you fill it with water. I give another to Kalen, and perhaps he would fill it with wine. The flasks are simply vessels that hold the liquid you add to it. It is the same with urvan. It is nothing on its own until I add it to someone's heartsglass. It serves as a vessel to recreate their souls. I remember every memory that comes through my hands. I can replicate a soul very easily with this." He stopped for a minute. When he returned to his work, his hands were careful and gentle. "And I thank every god there is that only I know the secrets. There are far too many people who would kill for such an ability, and sometimes, I regret that my master taught me this skill. It makes me a target."

"They are here," Tea said abruptly, turning away from the window.

I looked out and saw at a distance, much to my horror, a mass of soldiers converging on the city.

"I see the blue flags of Kion," Lord Kalen said, "and the greens of Arhen-Kosho, but none from Odalia."

"But why?" It was a ridiculous question. The answer looked back at me, her smile grim, so I asked another. "How did news of Daanoris's fall travel so fast? Surely a week is not enough to raise this army."

"They have had weeks to plan. They must have known the very night I ended my exile." She stared back out into the throng of soldiers, as if straining to seek out one particular face among them. "It would appear," she mused, "that the bond I share with my brother is stronger than even I realized."

12

THE DUKE HAD DONE HIS research; I regretted telling Polaire about the weaknesses in Aenah's wards, for they had been quick enough to strengthen them in mine. The asha association relied heavily on the Royal House of Odalia for unfettered access to their kingdom. They might not like the duke, but they wouldn't go out of their way to offend him.

I paced the windowless room, past the one small cot they afforded me. I cast my mind out again but couldn't detect Fox's presence. Despite all his threats, Holsrath would most likely keep Mykaela and I unharmed. But my brother, though my familiar, may not fare as well. I was worried too for Khalad and Kalen.

I examined the walls and floor and gave the door a good kicking, with little result. "This is useless," I growled.

I wouldn't be too sure about that, child.

I gasped. Had Aenah escaped?

I am gratified by your faith in my abilities, Lady Tea. But you called for me, not the other way around.

An image came unbidden to my mind: Aenah sitting in her cell, still bound by her wards but in better spirits than I.

Who are you working with in Odalia, Aenah?

Me? Would I be sitting in this old dank dungeon if I had an accomplice working for me? I assure you, my dear, no one in the Odalian palace answers to me. In fact, it's the exact opposite.

You gave me an offer. I'm taking it now. Tell me about shadowglass.

Threats are all well and good, but not even you and your pet azi *can conjure enough runes to force me. But I will help you. I have my own grudges against Usij that need repaying...*

Quick flashes of memory cross my mind—a burning town, the edges of it sweeping out to sea. A younger Aenah, her face tearstained and grieving, holding a still baby in her arms as she watches her world burn.

I'll have that back, thank you. Just as swiftly, the image was gone and Aenah's presence returned, angry and melancholy and cold. *You have had practice to eavesdrop on my memories so easily.*

I'm sure you can understand why.

I will tell you more about shadowglass. The book I gave you was deliberately vague on the matter. The Great Prince had many reasons to keep his secrets.

Are you saying Hollow Knife himself wrote this book?!

My book is a descendant of the original, which has since been lost to time. The shadowglass is his promise to us for immortality, but its ingredients come at a price.

The sleeping sickness? You're dooming these people to death!

Death? They sleep, peaceful and happy, surrounded by memories of loved ones and better times until the end of their natural lives. I would call it a gift, Aenah said.

I drew on *Compulsion* without thinking, but nothing happened. Her throaty chuckle was proof of my failure.

Did I strike a nerve, Tea? Perhaps Prince Kance prefers endless sleep over the stress of ruling a kingdom. Who knows? Mayhap he dreams of you. I presume Usij has the pieces of their heartsglass. It has been a stalemate between us for the better part of ten years—we all strive for the same goal, but the shadowglass can only accommodate one, and we have always found it difficult to share among ourselves.

Get to the point.

It is a simple recipe. Blade that Soars and Hollow Knife were two halves of the Great Creator's heart. When he formed the world, it was necessary for him to divide his heart to bring a balance of light and dark into it. That is why Hollow Knife needed to take Blade that Soars's heartsglass for his own, to become truly immortal. To create a facsimile of Blade that Soars's heart, we gather the Five Great Heroes from where his blood flows down and forge it anew into a pure heartsglass. But to achieve Hollow Knife's heart, it is necessary to turn one's own silver heartsglass black.

And how is that possible?

There are many paths that lead to a black heartsglass. Hollow Knife's requires a corruption of self. I have found killing to be the easiest method. And not simple commonplace murder—one must delight in it.

Quick visions blurred through my mind: blood and desires, deaths and unholy rites. She laughed when I reeled back from her, my disgust clear. *It gets better with every killing, I assure you.*

You vile, disgusting—

That may be so. I make no pretense of sainthood. Unlike your fellow asha, I do not claim to be what I am not. It is a shame, really, that you fled Odalia so quickly that you had little time to conduct a thorough investigation of your own elders. Oh, the atrocities you can find there!

Tell me more about what they did.

But her thoughts were already fading. Try as I might, I was too weak to wrest them back.

Thwarted for now, I took stock of what I knew. If Aenah was right, then the sleeping sicknesses were Usij's doing. The other Faceless leader either knew of Aenah's book or had his own copy and sought to create the lightsglass spell himself. But was this endless sleep a permanent consequence? Nothing in the book talked of a cure.

But to create the lightsglass, Usij would also need a Heartforger. And only two came to mind. Kance wasn't the only one in danger. Khalad and the old Forger were too.

I tried again, but all my attempts at *Scrying* failed. How had I gotten past the barrier to Aenah? I reached out desperately and found nothing but darkness—a darkness that slithered, waiting.

Visions of forests and streams burned into my head. The *azi* was somewhere upriver, circling the sky. Even with the strongest wards keeping me in place, even across the long miles, it could find me.

Something curled along the edges of my thoughts. The *azi* did not think the way humans do, but there was a faint question in its mind, one I understood.

I could bind no spells in this room, but the *azi* was here. How could I use it? How could I control it? The thought of merging minds with a creature so grotesque, a daeva whose kind caused my own brother's death, once horrified me.

I took a deep breath and plunged willingly into the *azi*'s mind.

It was thick and cloying; if I could have breathed in the abscesses of its soul, I would have suffocated. Consciousness slid around me like thick molasses, and its thoughts were primal, simple. It desired freedom. People hunted it, so it hunted them. It yearned for solitude, food and sunlight its only pleasures. The old scar on my thigh burned.

Master?

Yes!

There was a rush of wings, and my stomach plummeted as the *azi* swooped down, so low that its tail grazed the ground. With a loud cry, it soared back up, picking up speed as it shot through the air, a new destination in mind.

The walls of my room shook. It was close, far closer than I realized. I had a bird's-eye view of rooftops, roads, and the familiar towers of the Odalian palace before the world shifted again. The *azi* dove down, straight into the heart of the city.

No! I yelled, grabbing at the shadows, and the beast rose at the last second, nearly missing a house. Its three heads screamed at the sky, tongues weaving, and somewhere in the palace, I could hear glass shattering.

I pulled again, and the *azi* complied, goaded into circling the city. At that distance, it had little chance for mischief, though I suspected that made little difference to the fears of the people below.

I tried to pierce through the wards around the room again. How could I remain linked to the daeva yet still be unable to channel the smallest spells?

On impulse, I drew *Scrying* and burrowed back into the *azi*'s mind, guiding my magic through it like a culvert so the rune poured out through it instead of through me. It purred its assent, and then Fox's voice broke through, faint but clear.

Tea?

"Fox!" I sank to my knees, relief making the room spin. *Where are you? Are you hurt?*

Nothing I won't survive. I thought they warded your room.

I found a loophole. Already shouts were coming from outside the door along with the sounds of running feet. *Where are you?*

There was a heavy thump outside, like someone ran into a brick wall, followed by several hard thuds. There was a quick choking sound that was abruptly cut off. And then came a tap on the door.

"Right outside. Stand back."

The door was no obstacle for Fox's sword. The air crackled with energy as the wards in the room were forcibly drawn back like curtains and quickly dispatched.

Men littered the hallway, Deathseekers and soldiers alike. Zoya and Likh were laying an unconscious man on the floor. "Govan's a friend," Zoya said ruefully. "I hope Zahid will forgive us for knocking out some of his Deathseekers. Good work on the wards, Likh."

"You can dispel wards?" I asked.

The boy asha grinned. "I guess I have a knack for it."

"We need to get out of here." My brother's shirt was torn, and painful-looking lashes along his back and shoulders were testament to his "interrogation."

"I am going to kill Holsrath," I snarled, taking Fox's hand and making a small nick on my finger with his sword before he could stop me. The *Bloodletting* rune shone, settling around Fox like a warm blanket. The wounds along his chest thinned into white lines before disappearing completely, leaving only the horrible scars inflicted by the *savul*.

"I don't feel pain, Tea," Fox reminded me, flexing his left foot experimentally. "The only thing I wasted was their time. I could have managed without healing until we were out of the city."

"We're leaving?"

"Was there any doubt? There's a daeva flying overhead, and the army is busy with it." Fox's glance was quizzical, and I could feel the question forming in his mind.

I nodded, and he frowned.

"Polaire and Althy are taking Mykaela," Likh reported. "And Kalen is breaking Khalad out. We're to meet by the stables."

"Where are we going?"

"Away from Odalia, but Kion seems the best choice. Daeva or not, none of us are welcome here."

"But what of my parents? My brothers and sisters?" Concern rang in my voice.

"They're safe," Fox assured me. "Polaire spirited them out of the city yesterday when she learned of our arrest."

"We can't leave!" The thought of abandoning Kance, alone and defenseless, preyed on my mind.

"We can do nothing for him right now, Tea," Fox reminded me gently. "You and Khalad will be of more use where they aren't accusing us of murdering him."

"Wait!" I grabbed at his sleeve. "We can't leave the book behind either."

Fox opened his mouth but didn't have the words to disagree.

"This is no time to be salvaging a favorite novel or zivar, Tea," Zoya said impatiently. "The king's men may have their hands full with the daeva, but we don't know for how long."

"You have my word that the *azi* won't destroy the city." The less they knew, the better. *Bloodletting* left me feeling light-headed so soon after *Scrying*, but I could feel strength leaching through my link with the *azi*, and I latched on gratefully. "We must make the time. It's too important to leave this book behind."

Zoya and Likh exchanged worried looks, but before they could react, a band of soldiers rushed in, a dozen in all...and were immediately buffeted by a gust of wind that slammed them against the wall, knocking them out.

I stared at Likh, whose forehead was creased and beaded with sweat from the strain. "You are marvelous, Likh!"

The boy grinned bashfully. "Zoya and Kalen have been teaching me runes. I don't think the association will approve though."

"I doubt the association will approve of anything we do today." Zoya gestured, and another burst of air divested the soldiers of their weapons, sending swords clanking to the ground. "Be quick about it."

I had little time to consider anyone unfortunate enough to get in my way. Advancing soldiers, scurrying courtiers, and fleeing maids all dropped, fast asleep almost as soon as *Compulsion* flared up. There were obvious signs of my room having been rifled through, and I could see many of my most powerful zivars and potions were missing. But my relief was palpable when I saw the familiar leather binding underneath the pile of books where I hid it.

Kalen and Khalad waited for us by the entrance to the stables. Beside them were Althy and another person, whose face was obscured by a heavy cloak. Fox froze, recognition pervading our bond even before the stranger drew back the hood. It was the First Daughter of Kion.

"What took you so long?" Althy asked me crossly, ignoring Fox completely. "All exits to the city will be under heavy guard by now."

"What is she doing here?" Zoya asked Althy, gesturing to the princess.

The plump asha shrugged. "She insisted."

"We're in the company of several wanted felons, and the alarm *will* be raised once they realize she's gone. This is not a good idea."

"I think it's a pretty good idea," Princess Inessa said shortly. "I must return to Kion immediately."

"You're leaving Prince Kance?" I gasped.

"I have the most important part of him here with me." Inessa opened her cloak. Twin heartsglass gleamed red, Prince Kance's beside her own. "Althy says this is what they're after, and Ankyo is the safest place for us."

"We must sneak out while the duke's men still engage the daeva," Althy cautioned.

"The gates are heavily defended," Likh pointed out.

"But wooden," Fox added thoughtfully.

"We'll worry about that once we're there," Inessa insisted.

"I cannot leave Odalia," Mykaela whispered. She was thinner and frailer than before, leaning heavily on Polaire. Her horse familiar, Kismet, stood beside her, calm and placid. With her were three other Drychtan stallions, the best of the royal stables.

"Yes you can, Mykkie," Polaire encouraged.

While I could understand Mykaela's frail health, I was taken aback by Polaire's gaunt appearance. Her cheeks were sunken, with dark circles ringing her eyes, and her dark hair had lost most of its luster. She had lost considerable weight and looked only slightly better off than Mykaela.

"What happened to you?" At my wordless command, Chief cantered out with his ears pricked, already eager to run.

The brunette only shook her head. "Don't worry about me. Mykkie, you know as well as I do that we have no choice."

"But—"

"It's final, Mykkie." Polaire's heartsglass bore flecks of green similar to Mykaela's. I took a closer look, saw a familiar rune spinning in the air around them, and gasped. "*Heartshare!*"

Polaire's eyes widened. "How did you know about… No, now's not the time. We'll talk about it later. Mykaela's heartsglass still lives somewhere in this city. Given her current health, straying too far will kill her. I'm just propping her up till we can figure out something new." Polaire smiled nastily. "Once I'm through with that sack of dung that calls himself the Duke of Holsrath… No offense, Kalen."

"None taken. I'm inclined to think the same way."

"Zoya, Kalen, Khalad. You're to assist Mykaela and Polaire." Althy was always the quickest of us to adapt. "Don't let either of them out of your sight."

"Don't treat me like one of your sick patients, Althy," Polaire growled.

"You *are* a sick patient. Tea, Fox, Likh—stick close to Inessa and me. If something happens to our rose of Kion, the empress will have all our heads."

"Stop treating me like I'm not here," Princess Inessa complained.

Zoya took over Kismet's reins, and Khalad climbed up behind Polaire. The latter muttered another protest but had no strength to follow through.

"I'm not going with you," Kalen broke in.

I felt cold all over. "This is not the time for jokes, Kalen."

"I am not leaving Prince Kance. I promised to protect him." The Deathseeker's fists clenched, anger and guilt spilling out of his heartsglass. "I may not have been successful at that, but I'm not going to abandon him either."

"He isn't in danger," Khalad said quietly. "They have to keep his body physically healthy if they are to use his heartsglass."

But Kalen shook his head, stubborn to the end. "That doesn't matter. I swore an oath not to leave his side."

"You can't!" I cried. Strong as he was, he was no match for a whole army, and he knew it. Visions of Kalen fighting off soldiers as they surrounded and overwhelmed him until he was lost amid a sea of flashing swords, horrified me. "That's suicide!"

"You don't know me, Tea."

"I don't need to to know you're going to die!" My voice broke. "Kalen, please..."

He paused. "I'm sorry, Tea. More than you'll know." He turned his horse around, and my panic rose.

I felt apprehension on Fox's end, but he made no move to stop me when I drew *Compulsion* and directed it toward the Deathseeker.

"You. Will. Not. For once in your life, *do as I say!*"

Kalen stopped. He nudged his horse back to follow without another word, though his jaw had hardened. I could feel his outrage filtering through my shock.

I stared down at my hands, which were shaking. I didn't want to do that, least of all to him. But what else could I do?

I was breathing hard, and there were spots in my vision.

We had barely left the castle and already I felt like I could topple over any second. Wordlessly, Fox grabbed my hand and helped me onto Chief.

"Did she just...?" I heard Likh murmur, confused.

"Not now!" Zoya insisted. "Let's move!"

The walls crawled with men firing arrows that the *azi* avoided with ease. Already we were attracting attention; soldiers crept toward us with swords and bows at the ready. Zoya flung out an arm, and weapons flew from their hands. Another gesture sent them stumbling back. Likh and Altaecia flanked her, but Kalen remained where he was.

Tea. It was Fox, gently bringing me back to the present. *Now is not the time.*

I forced myself to speak. "I'm going to do something unusual. Fox, tell them not to panic."

"I will help you," Zoya said warily, "if you tell me what we shouldn't be panicking over first."

But I had closed my eyes, all my strength directed at the beast above us, eager to let the daeva in and chase away my guilt. The *azi* dipped down, close enough to send many of the men and women scrambling for cover or sprawling away.

There were a few asha and Deathseekers manning parts of the gates, but I knew none of them would risk fire or lightning at this range. Zoya was already weaving the air with her fingers, prepared to attack the daeva. Fox grabbed her arm. "Don't hurt it!"

"Grab my arm like that again, and you'll lose yours," the asha said ominously. "And why shouldn't I?"

"Because Tea's in its head right now," Althy said quietly. "Isn't she?"

I couldn't answer; the strain of keeping the daeva under control when it was so close to the city was too tasking.

Ram the gates? Fox suggested.

My mind recoiled at the potential casualties from his suggestion. *Absolutely not! The* azi *could kill everyone on those walls.*

I didn't mean with the azi, *idiot.*

I felt arms encircle me; my brother lifted me off Chief and transferred me to Likh's mount. "I'll need to borrow that!" he yelled at an approaching soldier, swiftly slamming his fist into the man's face to knock him out and promptly retrieving the latter's shield. Then he goaded Chief into a dead run toward the gates.

"Fox!" Princess Inessa shrieked behind me, and then both man and horse hit the barrier. There was the frightening sound of bone snapping and wood splintering.

Rise up! I screamed, and the *azi* flew so quickly that it became a speck in the sky within seconds. *What were you thinking?!* I screamed at my brother.

Were you expecting them to open the gates for us?

The rest of the group stared at the large, gaping hole Fox and Chief had left in their wake. "Ride hard!" Althy yelled.

A few asha struggled to block our way. Zoya whipped out a series of *Shield* runes that repelled arrows and sword thrusts. Althy was rougher; *Fire* and *Mountain* burst from the ground at times, surrounding attackers in either a ring of flames or stony obstacles. Likh maintained a *Shield* of his own, hovering it over the now-sleeping Mykaela and the barely conscious Polaire. I had stopped compelling him long before we reached the gates, but Kalen no longer showed signs of wanting to remain with us; his own runes of *Rot* and *Shake* sent fissures opening and walls crumbling behind us, preventing more soldiers from following.

Once our last horse was past the gates, I took hold of the *azi*'s mind again. The daeva landed, blocking the army's way and crowing belligerently. We kept riding, not stopping until we had reached the first copse of trees several miles from the city. From a small hill, we watched the daeva rise again, ringing the city but no longer attacking.

Fox and Chief waited calmly for us. Large splinters jutted out from my horse's legs, but that was the extent of his injuries.

Oh, but Fox... He was riddled with arrows, many protruding from his back. A painful-looking wooden stake was shoved through his chest, another through his neck. He had used the shield to bear the brunt of the damage, but the shoulder he had braced it against was nearly stripped of flesh, his bones sticking out.

And his face. I could barely recognize him underneath all the blood, and though I was reassured by the calmness of his mind, it was hard to reconcile that knowledge with what I saw standing before me.

Likh threw up. Princess Inessa slid off her horse and sank to the ground.

"Fox?" Even the normally sardonic Zoya was shaken. Khalad was a mixture of terror and curiosity.

Kalen slowly climbed down from his stallion, staring at my brother. "Are you all right?" he asked.

"Never been better." Fox's voice was brisk. "Chief can run for weeks if he has to, but the others can't do the same. We'll need to change horses frequently or at least find a cart to lessen the load, and that might pose a problem."

"Your arm is about to fall off, Fox," Althy said gently. "I think horses are the last thing on everyone's minds right now."

My brother glanced down at the arm hanging on to his shoulder by a few strips of flesh. He grabbed at the offending appendage and, with a quick twist, ripped it away from the rest of him. "Tea will patch me up later. Let's keep riding, people."

"I think I am going to be ill," Zoya said as Princess Inessa fainted.

THE PRIVATE CHAMBER LORD KALEN provided for me belonged to one of Emperor Shifang's many concubines. She, along with many of her other consort-sisters, had long since fled the capital, leaving only traces of her scent behind: lavender and jasmine, oiled perfume, and incense. But I was no longer accustomed to soft beds and thick pillows and thus spent a listless night with the fires from the approaching legions as my only source of light. The sight of those soldiers terrified me, but I did not fear for the inhabitants of Daanoris nor the fascinating, terrible asha who had seized power here. Instead, I feared the time the asha would summon her daeva, for I knew not even the most powerful armies of all the kingdoms would be enough. I feared for the advancing soldiers, who did not know they were approaching to die.

When I rose the next morning, the Heartforger remained in the throne room, and I wondered if he had moved from his spot after I had retired. The asha was sitting at the window near the throne again; she had changed her hua to suit the Daanorian style, with several layers of wispy cloth over rich purple silk and a waist wrap that began underneath her breasts and ended halfway down her hips. She watched the emperor dozing at a corner nearby. His hands and feet were still bound, but I suspected he would be in no shape to resist even without his restraints.

"You're up early," she observed.

"I couldn't sleep." My voice sounded rough to my own ears. *My gaze dropped to the pile of papers in her lap.*

"I have been writing. I sleep little nowadays, and my mind requires distraction." She gestured at herself. *"I do not think they will appreciate me wearing a* hua—*after all, I have long since been stripped of my title as an asha. I shall enjoy their discomfiture."*

"Where is Lord Kalen?"

"Still in our bedchamber." I blushed at her candidness, but she paid no attention. *"Use the next hour to prepare yourself."*

"For what?"

"They will want to make contact first, of course. They must have a lot of questions about me." Her smile was mischievous. *"Would you like another story while we wait? I imagine it'll take at least an hour for them to draw lots and decide on the unfortunate messenger, and Khalad is too engrossed in his work at the moment to hear us, much less be of use in conversation."*

"To be a perfectionist is not the same as being deaf," Khalad said without looking up, and the bone witch laughed.

13

WHEN I OPENED MY EYES, I became aware of three things: the gleaming waters of Lake Strypnyk before me, the savory smell of food, and Chief nudging affectionately at me with his head. I had drawn *Bloodletting* on him before I'd fallen asleep, and the Gorvekan stallion bore no traces of injury from the night before.

I reached out and felt the familiar touch of the *azi* on my mind. It was still at Kneave, discouraging any attempts at pursuit. I probed further but couldn't detect Aenah's presence beyond a faint hint that she was still in Odalia.

"Are you back with us, Tea?" Khalad carefully placed a few strips of bacon and a loaf of bread onto a large leaf. Likh was crouched over the fire, cooking the rest. Polaire and Mykaela were both fast asleep, made as comfortable as possible on the ground with thick blankets. Their heartsglass still rippled green, but it comforted me to know that, although exhausted, neither was in any pain.

I moved back to my spot and accepted Khalad's meal gratefully. "I'm surprised we even have food."

"Altaecia's doing. I think she brought the whole pantry."

"Well, that's shocking." I shifted, winced. "Where are the others?"

"Kalen's scouting ahead, and Zoya and Althy are bathing. I think the princess is with them."

"Has she shown you Prince Kance's heartsglass yet?"

"No. Althy said to wait till you woke up."

"Do you know where my brother is?"

It was the boy's turn to wince. "I don't know. I think he's distancing himself from us because it's disconcerting to look at him."

"Let's fix that." I stood, and the world tilted. Likh grabbed me just in time. "Vertigo," I panted. "A daeva's mind isn't the most relaxing place to be."

"I didn't know that was possible," Likh said, wide eyed. "Linking with a daeva, I mean."

"I don't think it's something most people want to try. Better than—"

Better than compelling someone you admire against their will, the rest of my mind supplied.

I stopped. Likh waited for me to finish, but I didn't. Instead, I stood, balance somewhat restored, and headed toward the lake.

"Wait up!" I heard him call, the crackling of leaves following me, but I trudged on, lost in my own misery and angry at myself for feeling so miserable. After all, I owed Kalen nothing. He wasn't a friend—he said as much. I'd saved his life. Surely that was a forgivable offense? There was no reason for my despondency.

I spotted someone bathing along the edges of the river. I was still sluggish, and as my mind told me this person was not riddled with wounds, not missing an arm, and therefore not my brother, Kalen reached for the clothes he'd left along the embankment.

I froze. So did he. I'd seen Kalen shirtless on the practice field, but I was too busy avoiding blows and his well-placed sarcasm to pay much notice. Now without any wooden swords in the way, I watched water drip down his muscled chest and felt ridiculous at how grateful I was that he had kept on his breeches. For a moment, I'd almost forgotten what I'd done to him. I tore away my gaze and raised my eyes to meet his cold brown ones.

There was no witty banter, no sardonic rebuttals. Kalen ignored my red face and walked in the opposite direction, taking the circuitous route back to camp without bothering to dry off.

"Is Kalen OK?" Likh asked from behind me, puzzled.

I had expected his reaction, but it did nothing to quell my guilt. "Not yet." He didn't even want to be a friend. But it hurt anyway, more than I wanted it to.

We found Fox staring out into the water. He'd taken off his shirt, having little of it left, and his whole body was riddled with deep wounds and pus. The splinters and arrows lodged in his body were gone, thankfully, but he had casually tucked his torn arm underneath the other like it wasn't of any import. I remembered the last time we were here at the lake—fighting the *azi*, trying to seize control of it from Aenah. Fox had been injured then too, and he had saved my life.

What I didn't expect was the Kion princess. She stood several feet from my brother, staring out into the lake like he was.

"Are you feeling better?" Fox asked me quietly, his gaze still fixed on the water's surface.

"Much better. I need to fix you."

"It can wait." His voice was harsh. "You're still worn out."

I saw the princess grip her collar with one hand and tug at it, refusing to look his way. "You are *literally* holding what's left of your arm in one hand," she snapped. "I'm surprised maggots aren't crawling over you."

"I've been dead for nearly four years. If maggots haven't found me appetizing all that time, I doubt they'd start now."

"I have to agree with the princess," I said rather crabbily, not in the mood to mediate. "I can rest later. You, on the other hand, can't afford to go anywhere looking like this."

Fox didn't look happy but remained still while I cut my finger and let the *Bloodletting* strands wash over him. It was a disconcerting sight, seeing the bones knit together and the flesh reform itself. Those wounds closed to become scars, thinning out and disappearing. His arm reattached itself to his elbow, sinews twisting and muscles distorting.

Likh was white but held on to his breakfast this time. Princess Inessa abandoned her pretense at ignoring him and watched. Her eyes traveled down his body before returning to the three large scars on his chest, the only part of him my magic couldn't cure.

Fox flexed his arm. "Almost as good as new," he reported.

"'Almost'?"

My brother finally smiled, and it was like the sun breaking out from behind a dark cloud. "Just a little spongy around the edges."

I took pity on Likh, who was making small choking sounds. "I don't think we should linger at Strypnyk for too long. When we can leave, Likh?"

The boy bobbed his head, relieved. "I'll ask Althy."

I turned back to Fox, but some of the levity had disappeared. The princess continued to stare at him until he spoke. "Am I done repulsing you, Princess?"

Inwardly, I groaned. "Your Highness, it might be best if you started preparing as well."

The princess nodded but looked back at Fox again. "If I'd found you repulsive," she said quietly, "I would have left the day I learned you were a familiar. Will you accompany me, Lady Tea?"

"As you wish, Your Highness." I felt a brief start of surprise from Fox's end, immediately stamped down.

The walk back to the campsite was quiet. A few feet shy of entering camp, she stopped.

"Do you think the prince is all right?" I finally asked, unable to bear the silence.

She took a deep breath. "I think so. No, I believe so. They wouldn't dare lay a hand on him."

"I'm going to kill them." It felt good to let the anger out. It was a better emotion to dwell on than the guilt.

She flashed me a small smile. "From what I've heard, and

from what I've seen with my own eyes, I'm sure you're more than capable of that." A pause. "I'd like to watch."

I laughed, surprising myself. "I'll try my best to arrange front-row seats, Your Highness."

"Are you close friends with my fiancé?"

Fiancé. That was enough to slide the smile off my face. "Yes. We are."

"It must sound strange then, talking about my fiancé when… I suppose you know about Fox and me," the princess said softly. "Of course you do. You must think badly of me."

"I don't," I said, confused. "I thought the opposite… I mean, he didn't tell you that he was my…"

"Familiar? I discovered that two weeks after meeting your brother. He didn't know I knew."

"And you're still…?"

She laughed softly. "After my grandfather's death, my grandmother took a consort-familiar. Dark asha have resurrected old lovers in the past. Kion are more open to these relationships than Odalia or other kingdoms. The only real problem with a familiar would be…the bringing about of heirs." She blushed.

"I understand," I said hastily, not wanting any more details.

"I didn't know about my engagement until a few days ago. I was furious when Mother told me. Kion empresses usually chose their own consorts. I swear on my life, Lady Tea, I never expected for my mother to determine my engagement when I met your brother and especially not after sleeping with him."

I was glad for the trees around us. I put my weight against

one, to recover my balance, which I'd lost again. Princess Inessa continued, oblivious.

"I will try my best to distance myself from now on, to spare him any more unpleasantness." Her mouth twisted. "He has made it abundantly clear that he wants nothing more to do with me."

"That's not true, Your Highness."

"It doesn't matter. I'm engaged to Kance. That's all there is to it."

Altaecia and Zoya sat by the campfire, looking grimmer than usual. Likh was with them, still green about the gills. Polaire and Mykaela were still fast asleep.

"I wondered where you'd gone off to," Althy said, looking up at us. "We need to talk, Tea."

"I know I promised not to overexert myself. But Fox couldn't go around looking like…"

My voice trailed off when Altaecia placed Aenah's book on a large stone beside her. "I think you owe us an explanation," she said quietly.

·· ⇃⅟⇂ ··

Althy folded her arms across her chest. "Whatever made you think you could handle spells so powerful—and from a Faceless, no less? I'm equally disappointed in you, Fox."

"My first loyalty is to my master," my brother said serenely, absolving himself of all blame.

"I would have told you, but I didn't want Polaire to know that—" I bit my lip, casting a look at the sleeping asha.

"I see. Was this about Polaire all along?" Althy gave me a searching glance. "Don't lie, Tea. I taught you to read heartsglass, and I know when you're evading. You know she's only looking out for your best interests."

"She didn't trust me enough to tell me about the betrothal, and she's constantly belittling me. I know there's a way to heal Mykaela using this book, but Polaire's more concerned about kissing up to the asha elders!"

That was going too far. Althy didn't slap me, but I wouldn't have blamed her if she had. As it was, her words came like a blow.

"Not at the expense of your life, she wouldn't. You claim to do this for Mykaela, but did you ever think about what *she* wanted? Would she want you to follow the same path she had, working herself almost to death for people who want nothing to do with her, losing her life with every flicker of spell and drawing of rune? Did you not stop to think how Polaire feels, watching her best friend die a little each day for years? Did you not stop to realize how horrified they would be, knowing that you would do the exact same thing?"

I looked down, embarrassed and guilty. "But Mykaela's dying. It's worth that risk."

"Mykaela doesn't think so and neither does Polaire. And neither do I, for that matter. Tea." Althy's voice broke. "People have killed renegade Dark asha for far less than this."

"Are you going to kill me?" I was angry and tired and sick of people telling me how I had to be strong enough to protect other people from these monsters, but not strong enough to defend *myself* because my life was worth less than their fear. "Do it then. You were there when Mykaela killed Illara, right?"

She sighed. "If you were anyone else, I might have. But there is an *azi* someone has once more resurrected that is running amok, and you are the only person who can control it. Illara was a different case. She was blighted from darkrot, Tea. It corrupted her, made her become something much like a daeva, and she had to be put down. No matter how foolish your choices were, none of this warrants killing—though the asha association might think otherwise."

"Are you going to tell them?"

"I would have, no matter my affection for you. We are honor bound to do so." Althy turned to Zoya, who was being unusually quiet. "And what do you think?"

"Well," the pretty asha said calmly, "judging from Polaire's current state, while she may not be keen on allowing Tea to sacrifice her life for Mykaela's sake, it's obvious that she's willing to sacrifice *hers* to do the same. Isn't this all a matter of perspective then? Don't you agree, Likh?"

The boy started. "Ah. I don't know. What Althy said makes sense…but so did what you said."

Althy shook her head. "You are right about one thing, Tea. Polaire would have never allowed you to use the book."

"But Polaire knew one of Aenah's spells," I insisted. The rune around Mykaela and Polaire glowed fainter but remained constant.

Zoya peered closer at the couple. "It's not any rune I've ever studied before, that is true."

"Polaire owes us answers as well," Althy conceded. "This rune's not life threatening at least. It's unusual to find this kind of rune in a Faceless's book, given the trust this requires."

"Don't be hard on either of them, Althy," Princess Inessa interrupted. "I know you better than most. And if Tea hadn't learned to control the *azi*, we would still be stuck in Kneave, right? If Lady Polaire hadn't learned this spell, it would have doomed Lady Mykaela. Incidentally, Lady Tea, can you reestablish a rapport with the *azi*?"

"Yes."

"Can't you force it to stay?"

"I can, but it needs its rest too."

"It sounds odd to hear you refer to that monster like it was a pet." The princess paused, reflecting. "You're going to let Tea keep the book, aren't you? Cat's out of the bag, so all you can do is limit the catnip."

"Not quite," Althy said firmly. "I will keep the book close to me for now, and there will be repercussions later. That shall be up to the association, though I shall ask for leniency."

I'd hoped she'd see things closer to Zoya's perspective. But I had committed many of the runes to heart, so the book's loss was not too great. "I understand."

"Now that that's settled"—Princess Inessa clapped her hands together, delighted—"I'd like to take a look at the book myself."

"It's not something Your Highness should be reading," Kalen said, breaking his silence in favor of admonishment.

"Why not? It's not like I'll be able to use the spells. And the more you say I can't, the more I want to."

A stray thought entered my mind. *The last time you wanted to see something you weren't supposed to, we wound up wearing each other out.*

I looked at Fox, now a bright red. The telltale embarrassment filtering through our link told me it was an inadvertent slip.

"But first, the prince's heartsglass. We need Khalad to take a look." Princess Inessa reached into her robes. Khalad scooted forward.

"Well?" Zoya demanded after several minutes.

"He's well," Khalad reported. "As well as he can be anyway. He has the same sleeping sickness as the other nobles Master visited."

"Is there a way to cure him?"

"Master was working on a possible spell for it, but he never left me any instructions for replication."

"Why were you and the prince wearing your own heartsglass?" Zoya asked. "Aren't you supposed to be wearing each other's?"

"Kance suggested that we wear our own until we're more comfortable with our engagement." A small smile played on her lips. "But neither of us reneged on the exchange, so I was able to sneak into his chambers with Althy and filch his heartsglass when the fighting started."

"When you create a memory, you take in several hundred impressions at once," Khalad said. "Smells and sights and touch make up only a small part of it. Whoever caused Kance's illness left a faint trace there…a desire to return to Daanoris."

"Daanoris?" Althy asked. "I doubt that Holsrath has ever been there, and there were no representatives from Daanoris at the betrothal. Emperor Shifang has been trying to woo Inessa for years, and we thought it wouldn't be appropriate to offer him an invitation."

The princess winced. Something flared up in Fox before it was swiftly shuttered away.

Khalad sighed and handed the heartsglass back to Princess Inessa. "That's all I can find. If Master were here, he might have found more."

"You said he was in Daanoris, right?" I asked.

"Looks like all clues lead there." Althy rubbed her chin. "Unfortunately. Daanoris was a closed nation until recently and not very keen on outsiders. Let's decide our next step at Ankyo."

"That might be more difficult than it looks," Kalen said. "We might have prevented them from sending an army after us, but that doesn't mean soldiers in every outpost from Kneave to Ankyo won't be on the alert. Pigeons fly faster than we can travel."

Zoya groaned. "I am not looking forward to fighting our way to Kion."

I spoke up timidly. "I have a suggestion."

"What is it?"

"I know a means of travel faster than any pigeon can fly."

"You can't be serious!" Zoya burst out. "You're not saying we fly on that *azi*, are you?"

Althy arched an eyebrow. "It will take at least a week to get to the Kion border," she said slowly. "But an army from Kneave can use the ports to arrive at Ankyo earlier than that. How long would it take your *azi*, Tea?"

"You can't be serious, Althy!"

"It's the best option we have, Zoya. Can you guarantee our safety, Tea?"

"I think so."

Zoya shivered. "It's cold-blooded, the way you can traipse in and out of that mind like it's an evening stroll through the Willows."

"Then to the *azi* we go." Althy allowed herself a faint grin. "I must confess I am curious. Kalen, the township of Lizzet is a fifteen minutes' ride from here. Bring the horses there, save Chief and Kismet. The rest will be of little use to us at this point." Althy skewered me with a look. "We will talk about this again, Tea."

I nodded, glad she hadn't decided on a worse punishment. Still, it was hard to meet her gaze with the disappointment there.

"I just hope Mykkie and Polaire are going to be all right." Likh sighed, gazing back at where the two still slept.

"I'll need a horse," Kalen said.

"You can use Chief," I offered quietly. "He can bring you back here in under half an—"

"I'm taking Kismet," he informed me, swinging up onto the stallion and riding off before I could respond. I swallowed and looked down, doing my best not to cry. We weren't friends, but surely—*surely*—my compelling him was a forgivable offense?

"Can you turn it on and off like a tap?" Princess Inessa asked me as we hurried to pack.

"Turn what on and off?"

"All the familiars sharing space in your head. Do you have to focus on them, or do their thoughts come unbidden?"

"Proximity helps," I admitted. "Animals don't have those mental barriers in place, but their thoughts aren't strong enough to intrude on my own. It's trickier with people because there's a give and take required. If they don't choose to meet me halfway, I don't sense anything beyond a general idea of where they are." Granted, the only experience I'd had with a human familiar was Fox, and it was hard enough to pry any thoughts from him unless his guard was down. My hold on Aenah was a lot more tenuous, almost nonexistent at times given the mental barriers she has in place.

"But he has a silver heartsglass…"

"Only because I do. He can't channel magic himself, but he has the same restrictions we have. Asha can't take back our heartsglass after giving it away, for example. It's the same for familiars."

The color drained from Princess Inessa's face, and before I could ask why, she was already stammering excuses as she turned to flee, red-faced.

Whenever we were unruly, my mother had a habit of grabbing us by one ear and twisting to keep us compliant. I put that to good use now when Fox drew close.

"If you'll excuse us," I said to an astonished Likh and a rather amused Zoya before dragging him off so I could scream at him in private. My brother might no longer feel pain, but he reacted on instinct, his protests ceasing only after I let go.

"How serious is your relationship with Princess Inessa exactly?"

Fox rubbed his ear. "I'm not sure that's any of your business."

"It is now. She said she hadn't expected the empress to choose a husband for her especially after—in her words—having slept with you." I'd been chewed out for the better part of the morning by Althy, and I wanted to do the same to someone else. "As you can imagine, her apology came as a complete surprise."

Fox's face was perfectly devoid of expression. "That's *really* none of your damn business, Tea."

"I don't want any more details. After my talk with the princess, I *definitely* don't want to know—but you need to tell me if your relationship is important enough to ruin diplomatic ties."

"I don't know!" His mask slipped. "I didn't even realize who she was until after I saw her watching practice for the *darashi oyun* with her ladies-in-waiting!"

"Did she know you were an asha's familiar?"

Fox coughed.

"Fox!"

"Not telling her was my fault, granted—"

"Every girl deserves to know whether or not they're in a relationship with a familiar from the very start, Fox! What were you thinking?"

"I wasn't apparently." My brother's voice was loud with the things he didn't say.

"Did you meet her again after you both found out? Or after you ended things?"

Darkness, the rustling of hay—slim hands against my pants, tugging—Inessa's voice, breathless against my ear. "I hate you," she gasped, meaning every word—

"Oh no, no no no nonononononono!" I clapped my hands over my ears like that could stamp out those thoughts. I summoned the *Veiling* rune and focused on my shield, wanting to scrub out the insides of my head with sharp thistles.

The thoughts retreated. Blood rushed to my brother's face. "Yes to both. I'm not proud of it."

I sighed. "You really liked her, didn't you? More than Gisabelle?"

"That was uncalled for, Tea."

"I wasn't prying into your head. You're just not compartmentalizing well enough today to hide your mind from me." I sat beside him. "What now?"

"Pretend nothing ever happened. Look, you need to talk to her—and soon. I don't want to stand there to make sure you do, but this can't go on. Can't you at least bury the hatchet with her? Having her angry is to no one's advantage."

"It's not that simple."

"At least try."

A wry smile crossed his face. "You don't have to worry about it."

"Kalen's back," Althy called out.

I stood to leave, but his voice stopped me. "Hey."

"Yeah?"

Fox kept his gaze on the ground. "I know I should have told you earlier. But when you found out…were you OK with it? About me and…?"

I grinned, feeling a little better, and rapped him lightly on the head. "Of course I was. Obviously, I had some reservations. But she's a nice person, and I know she made you happy. I'm *not* pleased that you aren't happy now, but…well, that's all I really want—for you to be happy. You know that, right?"

He smiled briefly. "Yeah. Thanks, Tea."

We returned, and I focused on the *azi*. It continued its cautious patrol around the city but perked when my mind touched its own.

Come.

With a jubilant cry, it turned and sped off. I could feel trees and hills blurring underneath my talons as we raced to the lake we called home.

The ground around us rocked as the daeva landed before me. Zoya swore and jumped back, and runes glittered in the air as both Kalen and Althy reacted on instinct.

But the *azi* cooed. It attempted to lick at my face, but I put a stop to that immediately. As far as anyone knew, I'd started controlling the *azi* today and not in the previous year, and its affection might draw suspicion.

"I don't know about this." Zoya's voice was strained.

I led Chief up its massive frame to the spot I knew was most comfortable. "You're not afraid, are you?"

Zoya glared at me, then made a show of stomping up the beast, tottering a little. "Definitely not!"

Likh looked like he would much rather stay put, but when Khalad clambered eagerly up the *azi's* back, he followed gingerly. Althy hefted first Mykaela and then Polaire on top of the dragon, settling them securely on the base of its three necks like she'd done this many times before.

Princess Inessa was next, not bothering to hide her fright. I watched Fox hesitate, then hold out a hand to help her up.

I turned to Kalen, who was glaring at me. "I'm sorry," I began.

"No, you're not," he snapped and climbed up before I could say anything else.

Can't you at least bury the hatchet with him? Having him angry is to no one's advantage.

Shut up, I growled, and then the *azi* was back in the air with a happy cry, hurtling through the air toward Ankyo over the sound of Zoya and Princess Inessa's screams.

*T*HE ARMY RAISED A WHITE *flag at dawn to signal for a tempo-*
rary truce—an unusual course of action for an army that
surrounded a fallen city and had yet to attack.

There was no crowd when the small contingent marched down
the empty streets. Kion had sent in too many soldiers, far too many for
a compromise. But the bone witch let them pass through the palace
gates unmolested; perhaps the daeva still camped outside, watching
the newcomers with eager eyes, were enough of a deterrent.

The Dark asha was prepared; the throne room had been removed
of the injured, who had been moved to a smaller hall. Khalad and the
Daanorian princess had gone with them. Lord Kalen had disappeared
with the emperor, and I didn't want to know where the Deathseeker
was hiding him.

A fresh bouquet of flowers had been brought in from the royal
gardens. It was a strange idiosyncrasy of hers; even during her exile
by the Sea of Skulls, she had kept garlands in her cave. "Monkshood,"
she told me, smiling. "And a rare flower called a belvedere. Are they
not beautiful?"

The Empress Alyx of Kion swept through the door of the throne
room, flanked by her personal guards, in as grand an entrance as
could be mustered given the situation. With her was a shriveled
old woman, short and bowed over but wearing the most unwieldy

hua *I had ever seen; it traveled for several meters behind her and a couple more on either side, her form nearly swallowed by the bulky fabric. Striped-yellow carnations were painted on it, an odd choice for an older woman. Her white hair, pulled in a tight bun above her head, was almost hidden by the collection of zivars piled atop it, each ornament more ostentatious than the last, but all eclipsed by a jewel crafted to resemble an azalea flower at its very center. Despite the woman's slightly ridiculous appearance, I thought the bone witch flinched, though she recovered quickly.*

Another asha joined them, dressed in a somber hua *of tinted blue and gray and wearing a pinched face. Despite the simplicity of her dress, her heartsglass case was the most extravagant of them all. Hammered gold vines and inlaid leaves circled her neck and folded behind her silver heart. She would not stop staring at the bone witch's black heartsglass, hatred blazing from her eyes.*

The last asha was a woman in a hua *of brilliant blue, wave patterns dotting its hems. Her long golden hair billowed out behind her, and her gaze was trained on the bone witch's face. The bone witch had frequently described Lady Mykaela as beautiful, and I could see that she did not exaggerate. But there were lines across the older woman's face, which was marred from a lifetime of tragedies.*

"It's been a while, Tea of the Embers." The empress had a reputation for flamboyance and playfulness; none of that was in evidence now. "We thought you dead. Imagine our surprise when word reached us of you raising daeva along Tresea's and Daanoris's coasts."

The bone witch had the gall to grin. "If it makes you happy, many times these last few months, I thought I should have been dead too."

"*Fool!*" *The old woman in the elaborate* hua *flounced forward.* "*I did not spend my hard-earned money on you only to bring down our reputation! Oh! If I could go back in time and stop you from ever darkening the Valerian's door!*"

"*I'm surprised you volunteered for this, Mistress Parmina. Though I am honored that the empress herself came to see me.*" *She paused.* "*And how are you, Lady Mykaela? Are the others at camp?*"

"*Our friends are all waiting for us in Kion; I came alone for this campaign. You're looking well, Tea.*"

A specter of a smile appeared on the girl's face. "*And you haven't changed at all, Mykkie.*"

"*As always, Tea, you are a magnificent liar. Where is the emperor?*"

"*At peace.*"

"*Tea—*"

"*I did not kill him, Mykkie. You have my word on that—if my word is still worth anything to you.*"

"*Do not speak like you still talk among friends, bone witch,*" *the woman with the vines-and-leaves heartsglass thundered.* "*You broke our agreement, Tea of the Embers. We had an understanding, and you sought to steal from our very noses—*"

"*I stole nothing, Hestia.*"

"*You gave us your heartsglass. In exchange, we promised to spare Fox's life!*"

"*'Sparing' his life is an overstatement. My brother would fare well even without your attempts.*"

"*You broke our treaty!*"

"*Is that what you call a treaty? To resort to blackmail as I lay on the ground, weak and helpless with death, in the sands? Black hearts-glass will always return to you regardless of anyone's control, whether you wish it to or not. Someone told me that once upon a time."*

"Shut up, Hestia." Lady Mykaela cupped the bone witch's face with her hands. "Oh, my sweet child," she said softly. "We searched for you for months. Fox was grief stricken, his only consolation was knowing you were alive. By the time reports reached us of a strange creature sighted along the Sea of Skulls, it was too late. Why are you persisting in this insanity? You will destroy Kion!"

"Not Kion, no. But there are injustices entrenched in Kion that deserve death."

"I will not allow such talk from a traitor!" The fire burning in the palm of Mistress Hestia's hand was frighteningly real. But when she raised her arm to unleash the flames, the bone witch's hand moved. The elder asha paused in midthrow, eyes wide.

"Traitor?" the girl asked softly. "You are the last person to speak of treason. I should let you burn for all you've done."

"Let her go, Tea!" Lady Mykaela raised her hands, gesturing firmly. The bone witch's lifted in response, and Mistress Hestia was pushed aside by some unseen force, still trembling with both anger and fear.

The battle the two asha waged was invisible to our eyes. Occasionally, one would flinch from some veiled blow, but neither wavered. Another elder asha, smarting over her mistress's humiliation, sent a quick streak of flames slicing toward the Dark asha's direction—only for another of her colleagues to stumble into its path. Her hua *caught fire.*

"*Water!*" *Mistress Hestia shouted, and within seconds, cloud-bursts appeared; the woman was shaken and singed but alive. She remained frozen to the spot, her eyes panicked.*

Lady Mykaela lowered her arms. "Tea," she said. "Please."

The fires died out completely, and the elder asha sank to the floor, gasping for breath. The bone witch turned away from the monkshood flowers and rearranged the belvedere. "I reject your offer and give you my own: leave Daanoris. Stand in my way and suffer."

"You know we cannot do that, Tea," the empress said.

"Then we have nothing to discuss."

The wizened old lady with the overabundance of zivar paused, eyes resting thoughtfully on the flowers the asha tended. "We receive your message perfectly. Our time with this foolish child has been wasted."

The empress bowed—bowed!—and left with Mistress Parmina.

"Well, Hestia?" The bone witch's voice was soft—so very soft. "Are you prepared to face me?"

The elder asha hesitated but hurried out after her colleagues.

"It's not too late, Tea," Lady Mykaela pleaded.

"I have no choice. You still do not believe me."

"Then swear to me that you didn't kill her, Tea. That she didn't die by your own hand."

But the Dark asha was silent.

The older woman lowered her head and left.

Now alone, the bone witch stared down at her hands. "I cannot," she whispered. "The gods help me, I cannot."

14

It's easy to dismiss the asha-ka association as nothing more than old women in overly elaborate *hua*, sipping tea and passing gossip. But as one who speaks for asha all over the world, their word is law in the Willows. I have seen grown women falter under their watchful, accusatory gazes. Now those eyes were trained on me.

"To keep the spells of the Faceless merits harsh punishments, especially for a practitioner of the Dark. What do you say in your defense?"

"Certain mitigating circumstances forced me to—"

"I see no mitigating circumstances," said their leader, Mistress Hestia of House Imperial. "Such spells have been banned for good reason."

"But the book speaks of a way to save Lady Mykaela's life."

"Saving one woman alone is not worth the dangers."

The elder's voice was harsh. "It would be foolish to imperil the kingdoms to sustain a life already on the verge of flickering out. It would be idiocy to go against Odalian's decree. We already risk much by accepting your claims of sanctuary and do so only at Princess Inessa's insistence. We will not trespass into Odalian affairs. I expected more from Mykaela, though Polaire had always been an eavesdropping little busybody."

They knew. A contingent of asha had ridden to meet us outside Kion before we had announced our arrival, though my *azi* fled quickly and escaped notice. Fox traded an Odalian prison for an Ankyon one, whisked away even before we had reached the Willows, and Princess Inessa was sent back to the empress's palace over her protests. I had no chance to see how the others fared, for I was soon brought to the association hall to stand before the tribune.

The asha-ka association wished to remain in Odalia's good graces. But they knew I was too powerful a tool to be sent back, even to cement an alliance.

"Rumors fly on swift wings," one of the elders said. "They say you and Mykaela poisoned the crown prince. That this is a Kion plot, carried out by the princess at her mother's command, has spread. What say you in your defense?"

"What is the true ending to Blade that Soars and Dancing Wind's story?"

They stared at me, statues dressed in expensive dresses and elaborate coiffures. "I beg your pardon?" one of them asked.

"Is that too difficult a question?" I had escaped from the wolves only to find myself in the lion's den. Propriety was the last thing on my mind. "It must be, for instead of doing everything you can in your power to save Prince Kance, you are here, building fairy castles against a threat that does not exist to pacify an actual threat from Odalia. Here is another question then: Where have you hidden Lady Mykaela's heartsglass?"

That earned more than a few gasps. Mistress Hestia looked ready to strike me down where I stood. "While we sift and root out facts from accusations, you are to remain at the palace dungeons until we—"

Someone coughed, and heads turned toward the sound.

I had never met the reclusive Empress Alyx of Kion in person, but she commanded full attention wherever she went. She wore gowns so sheer that it would be more respectful to look away than to look at her, and gemstones of every size ringed her neck and arms. Her smile was impish, making her look younger than her forty years. Like the asha, she too wore intricate zivars in her hair for show and for protection.

With her was Mistress Parmina, looking severe in her black-and-golden *hua*, and Councilor Ludvig of Istera.

"Did I arrive in time?" Cheerful sounds like Empress Alyx's voice were rare within the great hall. "I thought of cobbling together an army of guards to make our arrival more impressive, but I decided haste would be better than pomp. These few should suffice." She indicated the row of soldiers on either side of her.

"This is a private meeting, Your Majesty!" Mistress Clayve sputtered.

"This hall was built from the royal coffers. That gives me

some say as to what goes on inside it." Empress Alyx laid a friendly hand on my shoulder. "My daughter has been telling me wonderful stories about this young lady, and I *just* had to see her for myself."

"We are in the middle of an official interrogation!"

"Not without my presence." Mistress Parmina had never been on good terms with the Mistress of House Imperial, and her thin voice had syrupy overtones. "By law, the association must inform me of tribunes where any of my charges stand accused. I received no missives."

"There are questions that must be addressed!"

"Even I know the answers, Elder," Councilor Ludvig scoffed. "Was the prince poisoned? Absolutely. Did this girl poison him? Absolutely not. The Duke of Holsrath wishes to distract us from the real issues, including his long-desired ascension to the throne at the expense of his nephew. Is Lady Mykaela guilty? No, for the same reasons. Shall you punish them? No, despite your threats and tantrums. If they are innocent of poisoning the prince, then why should they be held?"

"She has in her possession a book—"

"Oh, posh." Empress Alyx laughed. "Books are only dangerous to those who keep their flock uneducated, Elder. I shall be taking charge of this girl now."

A subdued and angry silence followed as the empress led us out of the hall, the guards close behind.

"Ah!" the empress sighed. "Talking to those old women is like having your teeth pulled by a herd of tortoises. I hope you don't mind, Lady Tea, but I instructed the guards to free your brother.

It's about time the association stopped using my dungeons for their personal whims." The trek to the palace was eliciting stares, but the guards surrounded the empress, matching her stride.

"Empress Alyx...words can't even begin to express—"

"Then don't. My daughter is as much embroiled in this mess as you are and just as innocent." She paused. "You should be blaming me, not thanking me. I agreed to the betrothal over Inessa's objections. She still hasn't forgiven me for that either."

"But why would you arrange for an engagement, Your Majesty?"

"Tea!" Mistress Parmina snapped. "You do not talk to the empress that way!"

"That's all right, Parmina. She asks a valid question." The pretty woman grinned. "When Telemaine first proposed the idea, I wondered. Odalian nobles rarely married outside their own kingdom, excluding the occasional treaty with Arhen-Kosho. But I suppose politics there are not as stable as one might think, and Kance is a good man and would make an able son-in-law. Besides, I was curious to see how Inessa would react."

"Less talking, more walking, Your Majesty," Councilor Ludvig interrupted. "There are eyes around us." He patted me on the shoulder. "Although I am glad to see you safe, Tea. It seems you've had quite an escape."

"I am glad to be here, milord."

The guards saluted smartly as we entered the palace, and the empress led me past the magnificent throne room and into a smaller hallway, toward the royal chambers. Princess Inessa was already there, staring moodily out the window. So was Fox, at the opposite corner of the room. Kalen stood between them, an apple in one hand from a banquet spread out on the table before him: fresh flatbread with hummus, feta cheese drizzled in honey, lamb stew and carrots, and rows of fruit and sliced vegetables dipped in yogurt. Kalen refused to look at me, anger still simmering in his heartsglass. Khalad perched nervously on the arm of a long couch, nibbling on a piece of carrot.

"Did they give you any trouble?"

Fox asked the question, but it was the empress who answered. "They were about to exile your sister into perpetuity if I hadn't threatened them. I'm sure they're obstinate enough to try again."

"Where are Mykaela and Polaire?" I asked.

"Resting comfortably. Altaecia is watching over them." She turned to her daughter. "Well?"

Looking irritated, the princess reached into her dress and pulled out both Prince Kance's and her own heartsglass.

Empress Alyx grabbed at Kance's without warning. There was a brilliant flash, and the older woman reeled back.

Princess Inessa rose to her feet, mouth agape. "Mother! You know you can't take his heartsglass without permission!"

"I had to try." The empress frowned. "It's too dangerous for you to have it right now."

"I can handle it."

"Don't be ridiculous," Fox said harshly. "There are people who can better protect his heartsglass."

"Try to take it then," the princess said stubbornly. "You

know how heartsglass work. Kance gave it to *me*. I'll guard his heart with my life if necessary."

Their stares clashed. Fox was the first to look away.

"I hope neither of you were too uncomfortable," the empress said cheerfully to the other boys.

"It's no problem at all, Your Majesty," Khalad said meekly.

The woman smiled. "I remember how you used to play with Inessa, Kance, and Kalen when you were children, Khalad. I'd always hoped that you would stop by the palace when you and your master visit, though you never do."

"My master doesn't like the nobility, I'm afraid."

"I'm not surprised. He's had to deal with the worst of our lot in his trade, and that would wear down anyone. He holds Odalian nobles in greater contempt though. I'm surprised he took you in."

"I stopped being a noble the day I agreed to be his apprentice, Your Majesty," Khalad answered.

"Why did you bring us here?" Kalen spoke up. "It feels like we've been freed from the control of one kingdom only to be taken over by another."

"Kalen!" Khalad exclaimed, shocked by his rudeness.

The empress only laughed. "If you're clever enough to realize that, Kalen, then you're clever enough to understand why. We have a problem. My daughter's betrothed has taken ill under suspicious circumstances. My daughter also has his heartsglass, which does not portray her in a good light, and this is all exacerbated further by her fleeing Odalia with a handful of other suspects. What, then, are we to do?"

"I can leave Kion," I offered quietly. "Tell them I compelled her to leave with me. If you think it will help protect Prince Kance—if anything happened to him because of me..."

"You care for him?"

The empress, I feared, was a keenly perceptive woman. I forced myself to look in her eyes. "I care for him as one of his most loyal subjects," I said steadily, surprised by how the words came easily. "I will not see him harmed. I've done enough damage."

Empress Alyx cocked her head to one side. "Damage? It is the duke who has caused this turmoil, not you, child. You are not to blame."

"But..." Except I had. I had compromised Prince Kance. And I'd compelled Kalen, forced him to leave...

And broke his trust.

I stood still, realization breaking through. Kalen might not have wanted to be my friend, but he had trusted me in spite of it. He would not have trained me if he hadn't. He would not have talked to me about his father and of his childhood or shared his fears. And it was the thought of losing that trust that had frightened me. I could have borne his criticisms and his hostility but not this. Knowing that I had made me want to cry.

Empress Alyx continued on, following her own train of thought as I stood there, blinking rapidly and trying not to look in Kalen's direction. "Your exile won't stop the duke. The best option, I think, would be to clear all your names. And for that, we'll have to cure the prince. Perhaps the Faceless's book will be of some use." She grinned at our astonished expressions. "Althy has kept me abreast of developments. And of course, regarding matters of the heart, a heartforger is required. Your master is missing, Khalad, which makes you the next best choice."

Khalad startled. "He's missing?"

"We do our best to keep tabs on the both of you, even when you wander off to other kingdoms. You and your master are rarer than Dark asha. My spies lost sight of the Heartforger after he entered Santiang."

"Then he might know something about Prince Kance's illness, which is similar to the Daanorian princess's," Councilor Ludvig said, finally speaking up, having been silent through most of the discussion. "Locating him is our priority. Fortunately, the Daanorian emperor is notoriously fond of asha, even despite his occasional animosity. A contingent of asha on a diplomatic mission might be viewed with greater favor."

"Why can't we sneak into Daanoris instead of announcing ourselves to the emperor and his officials?" Kalen interrupted. I still couldn't look at him.

"None of us look Daanorian. It's only been some years since Daanoris opened its borders to the rest of the kingdoms, and we would stick out."

"We can wear disguises."

"Not all the time and not if the princess is with you."

"I am going," Inessa said stubbornly.

"Do you think that's the best option, milord?" I asked Councilor Ludvig.

"We have little choice. Tresea and my own Istera are too

far away, Drycht cares little for the world outside its borders, and Arhen-Kosho has historically sided with Odalia. The Yadosha city-states might intervene but only if the cause threatens their own territories. War must be averted. Diplomacy should incur the least amount of casualties."

The empress clapped her hands. "Tea, Fox, and Kalen, you are to accompany Khalad to Daanoris and reestablish contact with the old Heartforger. Tea, bring four or five other asha along. The emperor is enamored of dragons and, as a result, of *azi*. Perhaps we can introduce you as its keeper."

"The elders won't like that."

"The elders don't know. Althy and I took great pains to keep your new bond with the *azi* a secret. Hiding a book is easier to defend than hiding an *azi*, which I'm sure you would have told us sooner or later."

"I don't think I would have," I admitted quietly, choosing honesty for once rather than more subterfuge.

Empress Alyx patted my arm. "I'm not accusing you of anything. You're in a position no one else has been in, and that requires making a lot of hard choices."

"I'm going with them," the princess said sharply.

"No." I didn't think Fox wanted to voice that thought aloud, but it was too late.

Princess Inessa spun to face him.

"And why not?"

"You're useless," he told her bluntly. "You can't fight, you can't defend yourself, and you can't protect Prince Kance's heartsglass."

"Thank you for reminding me how thoroughly irrelevant I am to your objectives," the princess snapped, "but Emperor Shifang has been trying to court me for the better part of three years. Daanoris is a suspicious nation. My presence ensures he will welcome us."

"He's right, Inessa." Her mother shook her head. "It's too dangerous."

"I'm engaged to Kance, aren't I?" The princess lifted her chin. "I promised to protect his heartsglass with my life if I have to. You might have forced me into the arrangement, but I do not go back on my word. Or do you break promises once they becomes inconvenient for you?"

The empress glared at her. "We shall talk about this later, Inessa."

"And what if we can't find him?" Kalen asked.

"There is one other Heartforger in the room."

Khalad paled. "But I'm not skilled enough."

The empress wagged a finger at him. "Old Narel has never been one to heap praise on a subordinate. But he would have released you from his apprenticeship long ago if he didn't think you a worthy successor. He's rejected half a dozen candidates before taking you in and twice more since then."

Khalad looked shocked.

"We must be prepared for all eventualities, Khalad, whether you feel ready or not. A time may come when you shall need to prove your master right." Empress Alyx turned to me. "I will have your *hua* and possessions transferred here within the day.

My servants shall take you to your rooms to recuperate in the meantime. We'll talk more about Daanoris later."

"Is there anything you can do for Prince Kance?"

She shook her head. "Not at the moment. But I will do my best."

"And of Polaire and Mykaela?"

"The same amnesty I give you." Empress Alyx smiled sadly at me. "Althy is doing her best to support Mykaela. I understand that your mentor cannot leave Odalia at the cost of her life, but Polaire's sacrifice buys us time. You must thank her when she wakes."

"Thank her?"

"The attempt on Grand Duke Besserly's life—some of the Faceless's followers who'd escaped vowed revenge, so Polaire claimed credit to shield you. They've all since been captured or killed by the Yadoshans."

I swallowed hard. "Thank you for telling me this, Your Majesty."

"Councilor Ludvig," Khalad said, "I'd like to ask you more about your friend's sleeping illness…"

Kalen was the first one out of the room, and I hurried after him, blocked his path. "Kalen! I didn't have a chance to—"

"Then don't."

"Kalen, please. I want to apologize. I know I had no right to compel you, but I had no choice—"

"No choice? *No choice?* You compelled me against my will, but now you're telling me *you* had no choice? And now you ally yourself with the *azi*? The daeva that had killed many of my friends?"

"I—I—"

I had no good answer to that. Kalen strode away, and I closed my eyes, desperately willing away tears.

There was a small cough from behind me before Althy spoke up. "Polaire is awake, Tea, and asking for you."

I took a deep breath, trying not to show how much his anger affected me, surprised by the strength of my upset. "All right."

·· ゝl∠ ··

One would have thought it was Polaire who had lost her heartsglass, that it was Polaire withering away all these years. The asha's cheekbones were jagged peaks stretched across a barren landscape of skin; her eyes like faded twin moons. Mykaela slept on the bed beside hers, an unnatural glow about her serene face, and her heartsglass pulsed softly in tandem with the brunette's.

"About time they brought you here." Mykaela's voice was the only thing familiar about her; it was subdued and weaker but still vibrant. I wanted to throw my arms around her and beg for forgiveness, but I was afraid of her frailty.

"I am sorry," I sobbed, the tears running freely. "I should never have doubted you. I didn't—"

Polaire shook a gaunt finger at my face. "How pathetic," she said, coughing, "and how embarrassing. Little things have never tired me before. You have a poor understanding of your priorities, but I was young once and very much like you. Mykaela and I are fine, despite how we look. Our unwanted distance from Odalia has given us a heavier load to bear, but we will survive this." Her eyes drooped. "The empress told me you are going to Daanoris to find the Heartforger."

"I'll find him." I squeezed her hand. "I promise I will."

"I know, Tea. That I never doubted." Polaire sighed, her eyes falling shut. "I have been sharing my heartsglass with Mykaela for months now. Another month or so will make no difference. *Heartshare*. A *Compulsion* that us regular asha can use."

"For *months*? Polaire, how did you know of the rune?"

"Her study," Polaire mumbled. "Hestia."

"*Mistress Hestia?*"

But Polaire was already asleep, her breathing steady.

·· ⌇ ··

The oracle's temple looked the same as when I had last left it: the same winding halls and confusing corridors, the same fiery pit burning at the center of its only room. The oracle herself was unchanged. Despite the heavy incense, she wore a thick veil to obscure her face. Asha are expected to meet her only thrice during their lifetime: before they are accepted into an asha-ka, when they become an apprentice, and again when they become a full asha. I have visited her twice more after that. She had predicted my bond with the *azi* and Aenah's imprisonment. Now I return a third time, seeking more.

Without waiting, I threw one of my zivars into the fire, watched the shiny opal gleam for a moment before disappearing into the flames.

"Did you know this would happen?" I demanded. "Did you know the prince would take sick?"

"As it was written," the oracle whispered, a chorus of voices accompanying the sound.

"Will he get better? Will Mykaela and Polaire get better?"

"With death shall come enlightenment. It is not Kance who you shall weep over, broken and bleeding. You shall weep once for regret and another for family, one more for mercy and two for love. You must tread on a path of dead, asha. Only then will you find your shadowglass."

"What deaths?" I cried, but it was useless. The oracle turned away and said nothing more.

Standing outside the temple much later, I made a fateful decision. I scried and reached out—but not to Fox. I followed the spiral of thoughts leading toward the asha-ka and into House Imperial. The mind I entered was a rigid maze, full of right angles and narrow lines. I felt suffocated, undercurrents of thought pushing me in directions I did not want to go. At least with the *azi*, in its swamp-like mind, I could choose my own paths.

I swam against the tide, struggling, until I found the memory I feared I would find: carefully locked away in a hidden drawer of the mistress's study was a familiar book of bound leather, the embossed upside-down crown stamped on its cover. But Mistress Hestia's mind reared up, alarmed, and the image disappeared.

*D*O NOT LET EMPRESS ALYX'S *submission deceive you. She is wiser than many of the other elder asha."* The bone witch continued to linger by the flowers, inspecting each bud. *"Did you notice Mistress Parmina's* hua?*"*

"I wasn't sure she could fit through the door, milady."

"The larger and more flamboyant the hua, *the more she liked it. She wasn't fond of flowers, and yellow carnations are typically worn among the younger asha. It suggests youth not usually attributed to someone of Parmina's age."*

"Perhaps she didn't think about the implications."

"No. Parmina had always been vain about her appearance, always quick to follow the conventions of dress. She is craftier than the elders who rule the association at least."

"It will take some time before they can muster any attack," Lord Kalen said, watching the women and their guards ride out of the city from the window. *"In the meantime, you need practice. How long has it been since you've used your sword?"*

The asha had not backed down when up against an empress, an elder asha, and her former mistress. But under Lord Kalen's raised eyebrow, she wilted. *"Several weeks maybe."*

"Tea."

She raised her hands. "I mourned you for months, and the only thing you single out is that my sword skills are rusty?"

"Are they? Did you seriously think I was going to change because I died?"

She glared at him, and he glared back. She surrendered. "I suppose not."

Without warning, Lord Kalen pulled her close to him and kissed her hard.

She whimpered softly.

"Get your sword."

It was a dance of blades. Her fierceness met his skill, matching him stroke for stroke. The bone witch worked hard for every parry and blow, but the Deathseeker's shoulders were relaxed, deftly avoiding the brunt of her attacks but taking his time to counter.

Finally, the asha's blade snapped against his shin. They stopped; the girl was breathing hard, and the boy not at all.

"You let me win!" she finally growled, but the frown never quite reached her burning eyes, bright from more than just the fight.

"I always let you win." He sidestepped her fury, caught her mouth in his again. She resisted at first, still in protest, but gave up soon enough, leaning into his taller frame. Red-faced, I turned to watch Khalad at work instead. The Heartforger's eyes were on the clay before him, but he was grinning. "Get a room, you two."

"A good idea." The Deathseeker lifted the asha in his arms and carried her across the hall, her halfhearted, half-laughing protests carrying through the corridors, the first genuine sounds of mirth since we had arrived.

15

I HAD NO DELUSIONS THAT KALEN would resume his sword practice sessions with me after everything that happened, so I took the initiative. The revelations my scrying uncovered had kept me awake the night before, and I was haunted by their implications. If Aenah spoke the truth about Hestia, then was she right about others? Did the elder asha hide Mykaela's heartsglass and not Vanor?

I chased those thoughts until morning and found, despite my lack of sleep, I had excess energy that needed spending.

I knew Kalen trained at dawn. The look on his face when he found me waiting at the courtyard, my practice sword at the ready, would have been funny in any other circumstance.

"Get out," he said curtly, though it was he who turned to leave. I was ready for his rejection, shrugging off the twinge of hurt.

"You promised Prince Kance you would protect me."

He stopped. I pushed on.

"You might not like me right now, but I'm prepared to make it up to you any way I can. I want to save him too. And if that means learning to defend myself better, then I'll be damned if you let your opinion of me break your oath to the prince."

For several moments, he stood as still as the wind. I closed my eyes, prepared for him to rebuff me again. Images of the *azi* passed through my mind; it was sailing leisurely along the Sea of Skulls, by Tresea's coast. I watched the sparkling waters underneath us, wishing I could sink down into it.

A rustling noise made me open my eyes again. Kalen had stripped off his coat, his chest bare. I remembered how he looked at Lake Strypnyk, near naked and soaking wet (*magnificent*, a hidden voice inside me trilled), and I frantically ripped away my gaze, looking up to meet his brown eyes instead.

"What are you waiting for?" he rasped.

An hour later, I regretted my offer. Fox had wandered in—first to watch and then to keep score. Seventeen for Kalen. A measly four for me.

I hopped back and charged again. He parried my attack and swung overhead, but I was ready this time and blocked. He was tougher and more relentless than before, and I realized then how much he'd been holding back in our previous spars.

"Stop," Fox finally said after Kalen scored another hit. I dropped to my knees, puffing, annoyed that he'd barely even broken a sweat.

"Better form than usual," the Deathseeker said,

surprisingly. Then, because he could never stop at a compliment when he could also add an insult, he continued, "But not all that much better."

I bit back a retort. I was used to Kalen's snide criticisms, but I wasn't used to the cold way he said them, like he meant it this time. The *azi* let out a baleful sigh, sensing my thoughts.

My brother approached us, weapon in hand. "Too tired to go another round?" he asked, grinning.

"Not after this small fry." Kalen abandoned the practice sword for his own steel blade.

Watching Kalen and Fox fight was like watching two of Vahista's best asha perform the *Lament of the Goddess*, the most difficult dance in the academy's repertoire. I moved back and caught sight of Princess Inessa standing nearby, away from their line of sight.

Fox moved first. Steel sang as blade met blade. Both men moved far quicker than I ever could, switching tactics and counterattacks in mere seconds.

Fox charged forward, and Kalen shifted to one side, sword sliding inches past my brother's ear. Without hesitating, he turned and swept his blade up, but Fox ducked underneath the blow and swung again, only to be met by another parry. Princess Inessa took a step forward, hand over her mouth.

"Don't," I said quietly. "They're having fun."

She nodded, her eyes straying back toward the fight. "How are Mykaela and Polaire?"

"Still unconscious." Althy had told me that sleeping was

their body's natural response to healing, that neither was in any immediate danger.

"Fox never told you about me, did he?" she asked softly. "I presumed many things about your bond that were not, in fact, accurate."

"It isn't any of my business, Your Highness."

"Call me Inessa." We watched the two in silence for several minutes, neither of them gaining the advantage for too long. "I've known Kalen since I was very young," she said finally. "He's Odalia's best fighter, better than any in Kion. Your brother is extremely competent."

"He told me he wasn't very good back when he was alive." The princess winced at my words. "But he had to match with the best in the kingdoms to be my protector. I sensed some tension between you and Kalen," she said. "Are you all right?"

"Not really." I should've be watching my brother, should've be cheering him on, but I had eyes for only Kalen.

"Should I talk to him?"

"No!" Inessa blinked, and I hastily lowered my voice. "No. I have to work out things with him on my own."

"Do you like him?"

I looked at her but couldn't think of anything to say. Me, like Kalen? Of course not, I liked…

"I don't know," I said. "I want him to like me, but…"

Inessa smiled reassuringly, patted my hand. "Sorry. You don't need to say anything. I understand. I was confused for the longest time too, trying to figure out what I wanted—who I wanted." Her gaze drifted back to the sparring. "Fighting styles weren't likely to come up in conversation when I was with him."

"So you were often with…how…?"

She grinned. "As often as I could. They say Kion princesses enjoy more freedom, but that's not true. Oh, we have the run of the palace, but it is a different story beyond castle walls. I snuck out one night, determined to see more of the city I was to one day rule yet knew little of.

"I was curious about the dancing houses that are so popular among the people. An atelier had once made me a dancer's *hua*. It was the most fun I've ever had. My dancing tutors were asha, so I reckoned I could perform with the best. It was easy to slip on a veil and pretend I was just one of the many girls there."

Her voice softened. "Fox arrived in the middle of my performance. Unlike his friends, he was embarrassed to be there, but he couldn't take his eyes off me. He said my dance reminded him of a dance he'd seen his sister perform." Summer over Istera, I remembered. "I found it adorable, the self-conscious, almost guilty way he stammered, like he'd stumbled onto secrets he wasn't supposed to know."

I tried to imagine my brother as self-conscious and stuttering and couldn't.

"I snuck out a week later and saw him again. His friends told me he visited the dancing house every day, hoping to see me." The princess blushed, faltering. "He never told you about me?"

"Being my familiar doesn't mean he tells me everything." Both Fox and Kalen showed no signs of letting up, and a curious crowd had gathered to watch them spar. Among the onlookers, I saw some of Kalen's friends, fellow Deathseekers I had met before: Ostry, Mavren, and Alsron, Farragut and Levi. I continued, "I knew there was someone he was very much taken with. It didn't feel right to pry."

"I intend to honor my engagement. My mother might have agreed to it in my name, but it is my duty to follow through." She laughed. "We're good at keeping up the pretense of free will. Few people know what few choices we truly have."

She turned to look at me. "I wanted you to hear my side of the story. Not that it matters now."

"It does." It was my turn to pat her hand. "And I admit, I would have wanted to learn about this sooner. But Fox *cares* about you." I stressed the word, watching her surprise. "Still does. It doesn't sound like you're ready to let go of your relationship, and I know he isn't either." I could meddle as well as my sister Daisy if I wanted to.

Something akin to hope appeared in her eyes and spread across her heartsglass. "Do you—"

A shout from the field made us turn. Fox had made a slight mistake—a forward jab an inch more than he should have. Kalen altered the stroke of his swing, and the blade glanced off Fox's shoulder.

I gasped, and Inessa's hand gripped at her collar, nearly yanking it off. Her heartsglass burned a bright blue.

Fox moved back, grinning ruefully. "Point to you."

The audience broke into applause, Ostry and the others

leading the cheers. "Fine job, you two!" The burly Yadoshan called to them. "Never thought I'd see the day someone could give Kalen a run for his money!"

"A run for *my* money too," Levi grumbled. "I bet Alsron the familiar would win."

"Watch out, Kalen," Mavren laughed. "Sir Fox shall outstrip you soon enough!"

Kalen wrinkled his nose, used to his friends' jesting, but he was smiling.

Inessa grabbed one of the wooden swords propped against the wall and made a beeline for them.

My brother moved quickly in battle, but he seemed paralyzed as the princess approached. The crowd went quiet.

"You told me I was useless because I couldn't protect myself or my fiancé." Inessa planted herself before him, one hand on her hip. Her heartsglass wobbled between unsteady blue and deep maroon, but she lifted the sword and pointed it at him. "Teach me then. Teach me how to use a sword."

"Kalen would make a better instructor."

"Kalen is busy seeing to Tea." I turned red at her remark. "You are the only fighter here who can match his skill." Inessa lifted her face, defiant, and threw the sword at his feet. Her other hand came up and tugged at her collar again. "Or are you not good enough for a princess?"

There was a long silence. Finally, Fox spoke. "Pick up the sword."

Inessa paused, her turn to be wary.

"Pick it up, Princess. When facing an opponent in battle, the last thing you should do is throw your only weapon at his feet. Bravado only gets you killed." Fox sheathed his own blade and picked up the wooden sword. "Put your dominant foot forward, grip the sword like this, and don't lock your elbows. I said do it!"

The words cut through the air like a whip, and though Inessa looked both alarmed and murderous by this sudden change in attitude, she hurriedly complied.

Being a bastard to her isn't going to help, I told Fox.

That's not my problem.

Sometimes I want to throttle you.

Get in line. It's a long one. "Now stab me."

"What?" the princess asked.

"First rule of swordsmanship. You take the pointy end of that weapon you're holding and try to stab me with it."

"Shouldn't we put a stop to this?" Mavren whispered to Alsron.

"You try. I'm not going to put myself within sword range of either."

"Do they know each other?" Ostry asked me. "I didn't realize."

"It's a long story."

The princess's technique needed work, but her strength was surprising. Her blade rammed hard into his side. She stopped, panicked. "Why aren't you defending yourself?"

"Because you don't want to harm anyone, and that will kill you. Until we wean you of that fear, you're useless in a fight. There is no room for hesitation in battle, Inessa." He paused. "And if you want to vent any frustrations you might have at the moment, I'm the only person in Ankyo who can take it."

I could see Inessa was tempted by the offer—for all of two seconds. She raised her sword and threw it. The sword whizzed past Fox and clattered against the wall behind him. To his credit, my brother didn't blink.

"I wish I could," Inessa informed him quietly, breathing hard. "I'd like to. But even if I wanted to hit you, the only trouble that would cause is to Tea. I won't hesitate if it comes to a fight. But I don't want to always be a victim. Teach me to be useful. Please."

A reluctant smile found its way to Fox's face. "You have a good throwing arm."

"But very poor aim," she informed him, and he started to laugh.

Kalen waited long enough to ensure neither Fox or Inessa were going to kill each other, then quietly withdrew. I caught up to him by the entrance to the palace.

"Are you going to ignore me from now on when we're not sparring?"

He ignored me. I grabbed him by the elbow.

"Can't you at least let me apologize?"

"Why? So you can do it again at the next opportunity?" His voice was cold.

"They'd torture you if you stayed behind! They'd execute you, duke's son or not!"

"That's my decision to make!"

"No, it's not!" A few people stared, but I was too caught up in my own emotions to care. "You know you could do nothing for Prince Kance if you remained behind, and he would've never forgiven us if you got yourself killed for the most idiotic of reasons!"

"You do not speak for Kance!"

"Yes, I do! His last request was for you to protect me, and I am making damn sure you carry that out! Kance wants you alive, Kalen, and so do I! I want you to be with me for as long as we can be together. I don't want you to die, you ass! I had a choice between letting you kill yourself and keeping you alive but having you hate me for the rest of your life, and I chose the latter!"

The Deathseeker paused.

Emboldened, I pushed on. "And even with that, I still want you to like me. If not as a friend, then as allies working to make sure Prince Kance is safe. So yes, I'm selfish. I've always been selfish. That won't change anytime soon. And you may not like me, but you're *my* bodyguard now. And if the only way I can stop you from throwing away your life is to compel you and everyone in Ankyo, I will if I have to!"

The hall was silent by the time I was done. I was not making any new friends with my words, but I was too focused on Kalen to care. I wove *Heartshare* briskly, and his eyes widened.

"This is the rune Polaire cast over Mykaela." My voice was quieter, reassured that no one else could see. "It's used mostly for healing, but it also grants one person control over another willing spellbinder. The only way I can think for you to forgive me is to put myself in the same position I put you in." I guided the rune toward him; it hovered over his heartsglass. After a moment, he accepted, the rune flaring around him before disappearing.

"I'm not going to dispel it," I continued, "which means you can choose to take control anytime you like. Go ahead. I'll submit to whatever you want."

The Deathseeker stared at me, and his silver heartsglass shifted to a bright, brilliant red. Why was my offer making him madder?

"This is the least sincere apology I've ever heard. Did you think I was going to take you up on your offer? To do what? Clean the barracks for me?"

My cheeks burned. "I'm trying my best! I don't know any other way!"

"Do you know what I really want, Tea?" He stepped closer. "Do you want another look inside my head?" He forced my chin up so I couldn't look away.

This was different. *He* was different. He was using me as an outlet but for an anger that was, oddly enough, no longer directed at me. "If you knew what I was thinking, would you still be so willing?"

We were still, him and me, staring at each other, my breathing embarrassingly loud. *What does he mean?*

"I don't need the rune. If you promise to stay out of my head," he continued, in a lower voice, "then I will obey Kance and protect you with my life. That's all the apology I want."

His animosity had retreated. There was a strange gravity to his words.

"I promise, with all my heart," I said softly. "I'll never do that to you again."

He placed a hand on top of my head—easy to do given his height but annoying to be on the receiving end of given my temperament. He drew closer again—*too close*—and my heart sped up.

"Apology accepted. For now. Inept as it was."

He walked away. This time, I didn't chase after him. He didn't reject the rune but neither did he take me up on my offer.

The spell continued to hover between us, along with all my other unspoken questions. But though I tried to lift my fingers to dispel the rune, I couldn't find the courage to carry out the act.

•• ⟩⊮ ••

The room allotted for me at the palace was three times as large as my old room at the Valerian—staying at my asha-ka would not have been prudent. As I walked in, I was stunned to see it filled with beautiful *hua* of every fabric and color. My dresser overflowed with countless zivars where all kinds of gemstones shone. From within the hidden depths of my mind, the *azi* stirred, curious at the glint of jewels. Zoya was in the room, a dreamy smile on her face.

"What's going on?" I sputtered.

"As part of the delegation into Daanoris, the empress said we must look the part—which, by Kion standards, is to be as ostentatious as possible. We shall all be the poster girls of *hua* excessiveness before this is over."

"There you are!" A loud, booming voice was the only warning I received before I was swept into a bear hug by Rahim. Chesh popped up from somewhere behind him, grinning, and with her was Likh, who had shed the customary black clothes he had been given and now wore something more familiar to me: a *hua* of amber and blue, with beautiful koi swimming down the folds. Councilor Ludvig accompanied them, smiling.

I squealed happily and turned, trying to wrap my arms around Rahim's massive shoulders. This was proving difficult because he refused to relinquish his bear hug. I settled for clinging to one giant forearm instead. I extended my other hand to Chesh, who wasted no time hurrying in for a hug of her own. "I missed you guys." It hadn't been that long since the last time I'd been in Kion, but after our escape, it felt like years had passed.

"We were so worried!" Chesh stroke my hair. "We heard about what happened to the prince. I'm glad you're here!"

"The empress, she says it is dangerous for you to walk in the Willows still," Rahim proclaimed, still holding me in his death grip.

"Fah!" I said. "What do elders know? They go around, grimacing in their dull *hua* and their shades of blech. Shall they decide who I can and cannot take in as clients? Even if Empress Alyx did not insist, I shall dress you well and spit in their faces! *Pshah*, like so! And so here I rush, armed with my best designs. You represent the ateliers of Kion and must have only the best to show! I can't possibly afford all these!" I protested.

"The empress is footing the bill," Chesh pointed out. "She

insisted we provide you with the highest quality silks that Rahim possesses, as well as the best of the zivars in my inventory. That goes for you too, Likh."

"Me?"

"I understand that the elders have not yet made a decision regarding your petition, but the empress insists you be outfitted as an asha regardless."

Likh's eyes filled with tears. "Thank you, Lady Chesh."

"Don't lose heart so easily, Likh my dear." Chesh hugged her former assistant. "Let's get to work! Lady Tea, I have several accessories I want you to look at. Empress Alyx wanted me to fashion the strongest protection spells for you."

"A rightful decision of the empress," Mistress Parmina snorted, stomping into the room with Shadi and Althy close behind. "And at such exorbitant rates, even for you, my dear Rahim! What of our wayward Dark asha?" Mistress Parmina gestured at me. "Mykaela missing in Odalia, and Polaire along with her. My Dark asha, wanted fugitives in Telemaine's kingdom! The elders in particular are not happy about you and the empress defying their wishes! Imagine how much revenue that will cost our asha-ka, hmm? A wardrobe full of *hua* and zivars will not be enough if we are known as criminals!"

For the right price, Mistress Parmina would stick a knife into every one of those elders herself, but two years living under her asha-ka had taught me the importance of silence. I waited for Shadi to speak up. She did not disappoint.

"I've just received our account reports from Ula this

morning, Mother. All our asha in Kion have been booked solid for the next six months."

Mistress Parmina's head spun so fast, it was like an old barn owl swiveling its head. "How so?"

"The nobles are intrigued, Mother. To be a fugitive in Odalia is not the same as being a fugitive in Kion. Even given Tea's unavailability, it is enough for them to be associated with the asha-ka she belongs to."

"And also, my dear Parminchka," Rahim broke in, releasing me so I could finally draw breath, "you forget about the untapped potential that is the eager Daanorian public. Their emperor is enamored of both our princess and of asha. Perhaps in the near future, there will then be visitors from Daanoris, asking for beautiful asha of the Valerian they have heard so much about?"

Mistress Parmina visibly thawed. "Well. I suppose the asha-ka must continue to grow. And as the Empress Alyx has vouchsafed all expenses, I see no reason why you should not do as she asks."

Rahim winked at me.

I drew Althy to one side. "I think the elder asha might have something to do with the troubles in Odalia," I told her quietly.

She stared. "And how did you come to that conclusion?"

"Polaire didn't learn of the *Heartshare* rune from the book. She told me she'd found it in Mistress Hestia's study."

"She's not in the best frame of mind. How can you be so sure?"

Telling her I'd snooped in Mistress Hestia's mind would only land me in more trouble. "I trust Polaire."

"But why would they do that?"

"I don't know yet. I was hoping you could help me with that."

Althy looked troubled. "The elder asha and I don't always see eye to eye, Tea, but to accuse them of what is practically treason… you might not like them, but they are loyal to Kion."

"Please, Althy."

The older woman sighed. "If you believe there is something suspicious there, then I will take a look. But we must keep it quiet. We are already in enough hot water without more accusations."

"A moment of your time, Lady Tea?" Councilor Ludvig asked me as Althy left.

"I have been struggling with my conscience for a while now," he continued as Rahim pounced on Zoya and Likh in turn. "Alyx is aware of this latest development, and I feel it is important to let you know."

"What is it, milord? Did something happen to Mykaela or Polaire?" I asked with concern.

"No, there is no change in either. I am close friends with the father of Baron Cyran, the youth who succumbed to the sleeping illness some years ago. The lad woke up yesterday."

"What?!"

"Say nothing of this to anyone, save your brother and Khalad—and perhaps your small circle of asha friends who will be going with you to Daanoris. Istera is keeping his miraculous recovery a secret from the rest of the kingdoms, and I trust you will do the same. The Heartforger came to us with a cure last month."

My hands shook, hope bubbling inside me. "Then that means...Prince Kance—"

The old man shook his head. "I do not know yet. It was the forger who requested secrecy, and I suspect he is at Daanoris, attempting to do the same to Princess Yansheo. He left us no clue how to replicate his cure. He is the key to Prince Kance's life, Tea. This is promising, but locating him is imperative."

Likh and I emerged a short time later with an armful of *hua*. Zoya remained behind; I saw her take Shadi's hands in hers as we were leaving. Likh clung to his share, terrified that someone might snatch them away from him at any minute.

"You better get used to this," I told him, my head still spinning from Councilor Ludvig's revelation. The forger could cure Prince Kance. *The forger could cure Prince Kance!* "Rahim's been looking at you like a cat looks at tuna. He's been looking for a new model for his latest summer collection."

"I hope I don't cause trouble for him," Likh said, worrying. "Or Chesh."

"They're the most popular artisans in their trades, and their opinions aren't easily dismissed. You're an asha whatever the association decides, Likh. Don't you forget that."

"And if they decide against me," the boy said dreamily, rubbing his cheek against the exceptionally soft satin, "then at least I'll have all this to remember it by."

*T*HE HEARTFORGER PAID LITTLE ATTENTION *to the approaching army outside, more concerned with the strange lightning-shaped beads he was forging. His calm unnerved me.*

"There will be no more lives lost among the Daanorians, Yansheo," the asha promised the princess. "Not while I breathe."

"But how? At least two kingdoms stand against us."

"Trust me. Khalad?"

"A day or two more is all I need."

"What is he doing?" I asked. "What are these urvan? *Who do these souls belong to, and what do you intend to do with them?"*

The Heartforger and the bone witch glanced at each other. "I told you how the old Heartforger had an antidote to the sleeping sickness," the girl said slowly. "This is part of the remedy."

"But no one is afflicted with the sleeping sickness here."

The bone witch smiled. "Khalad and I have since found other uses for the antidote. I have learned that when heartforgers are involved, nothing is impossible."

Lord Khalad shrugged. "No more so than Dark asha. Silver heartsglass cannot be raised from the dead, Tea—yet my cousin stands here with us. I have worked easier miracles."

"For what use?" I insisted.

"To you, deprived of heartsglass, seeking Blade that Soars's

path," *she quoted.* "Take that which came from Five Great Heroes long past and distill it into a heart of silver to shine anew. *Khalad remembers every heartsglass he touches and can create copies of their urvan if needed. I wear Hollow Knife's darksglass, but I shall need lightsglass. I intend to have both before long, to create shadowglass.*"

"*You intend to become immortal?*" *I was crushed, betrayed. What good was her hatred for the Faceless when she walked the same path?*

The bone witch looked back out the window.

"*I intend to die,*" *she said.*

16

OUR GROUP WAS TO BE few in number: Fox, Kalen, Councilor Ludvig, and me. I had told Fox about Baron Cyran's recovery and the forger's visit, and he agreed it would be prudent not to say more to anyone else. But after thought and my last encounter with Kalen still on my mind, I had told the Deathseeker as well and asked if he would accompany us.

Then Likh came, unusually insistent and blushing. At the last minute, Inessa announced she and Althy would also be joining us.

"I want Khalad to take another look at Kance's heartsglass," she explained. "He might have something in his workshop that can provide more clues."

The Willows was different from the rest of the city. Magic was a mandatory experience among the asha-ka, and one expected to find beautiful women there in expensive garments, with runes as easy to discern as the wind. Most people in downtown Ankyo, from the richest nobles to the lowest trader, steeped their bodies in magic. I could smell it in their hair, in their clothes, in the jewelries they wore.

Shops sold clothes with runic spells stitched into the fabric at a quality below authorized atelier shops, but the garments were affordable to most. There were different strains of inferior runeberry drinks, zivars promising all sorts of dubious abilities, and quack love potions. Numerous stalls lined the streets, specializing in spells of varying successes. What they lacked in authenticity, they more than made up for in demand.

"Kion," I heard Kalen mutter behind me, the wryness in his tone unmistakable. "The city of plenty."

We traveled through the widest, busiest streets first, where people wore heartsglass cases in elaborate metalwork. But the spells grew fewer and the garments simpler as the streets narrowed until we reached the poorest districts, where mud-smeared children played in front of decrepit gray houses. Men and women in drab clothing and hard faces hung linens from clotheslines or loitered in groups and stared as we passed. The air smelled of rotten eggs and discarded trash, unflavored by spells.

"For a city that looks as rich as Kion, I never imagined it would have such poor in these numbers," Inessa murmured, looking stricken. She gripped her cloak, and I saw numerous cuts and bruises covering her hands and arms. Fox was as hard a taskmaster as Kalen.

"Cities are the same the world over," Councilor Ludvig said.

"The greater the stench of the city's poor, the more extravagant the lives of the city's rich."

"We try our best," Inessa said. "We created food programs. We try to find them decent places to live. But sometimes people slip through the cracks."

"These are mighty big cracks," Fox said. Princess Inessa looked away.

Our journey ended in a narrow lane too small to be called a street at a shack between two crumbling houses abandoned by even the most desperate. The path was filled with people, wretched and sickly.

The princess took a step back. Kalen forged on ahead, but a chorus of angry cries greeted him when he stepped past the line. I grabbed his arm, tugging him back.

"We were here first!" an old woman shouted shrilly.

"We've been waiting to see the boy!" another man shouted. "My child is sick. We will not wait another day more!"

"What is all this?" Likh gasped.

"They have come for the Heartforger," Althy said. Few here could afford heartsglass cases, so many kept them in small bottles worn around their necks, and most glowed an unhealthy green. "They cannot afford a doctor."

"And Lord Khalad and his master treat them?"

"As frequently as their time allows. The Heartforger is often away, so these duties have fallen to Khalad. Why did you think he left the palace?"

Kalen scowled. "We'll be lucky to see him today."

"Their ailments are common enough," I observed, watching a heartsglass near me flicker the bright emerald color of bronchitis. "Fox, where is the nearest shop selling pots and pans?"

"There is one not too far from here," Kalen said before my brother could speak. "I've been there before."

"Purchase half a dozen of the largest pots they have. There are a few more essentials I need that might be harder to find. Silver needles and thread, a mortar and pestle, some small vials to put medicine in." I reached into my bag and drew out several poultices.

"You knew why Khalad left the palace, didn't you? He and the Old Forger always open their doors to the sick around this time of the month."

"Khalad prides himself on being both a healer and a forger. I wasn't expecting this many patients though."

Kalen smiled, his eyes softening. "Write them down. There's an apothecary nearby."

"Can you find clean water?"

"There is a fresh stream that runs through the eastern district. It's near the Deathseekers' barracks, and they see to its maintenance."

"Thank you. Fox, clear some space and find wood for kindling. Likh, make a fire where he shows you."

"What do you intend to do, Lady Tea?" the younger boy asked.

"Khalad has too many people to see. Perhaps I can whittle down the number." I looked at Althy, who was looking wordlessly back at me. "Althy? Is something wrong?"

"Merely looking at one of my better achievements," the older asha said gravely. "Move over and make some room for me."

Kalen returned promptly and departed again with a longer list of items. I filled two of the largest pots with water, setting them atop the fires Likh and Fox tended. Once the water boiled, Althy placed the instruments into the second pot and ladled some of the liquid into a smaller bowl. I plunged both my hands into the bowl, gritting my teeth at the scalding heat. Some of the people watched us warily but did not protest.

"Princess Inessa, would you mind grinding these herbs?"

"I've never ground anything before," the girl said dubiously.

"Place them inside this bowl, Your Highness," Fox said quietly, "and pound them with the mortar until they are as fine as you can make them. I'll show you how."

The princess hesitated, looked back at the crowd, then nodded.

Councilor Ludvig rolled up his sleeves. "I worked as a healer's apprentice in my younger days," he said. "This brings back memories."

I approached the old woman who had called out and the young girl with her. "She has food poisoning," I said, watching her heartsglass pulse yellow.

"Are you an apothecary, milady?"

"A bone witch," I said honestly. "Her fever will grow worse before you can expect treatment. Let me help."

"I do not have much money to spare…"

"I ask for nothing."

The woman cast an agonized glance at the long line of people before her and nodded.

I led them to the space Fox had cleared, took up the ground herbs Princess Inessa made, and placed them inside a metal bowl. I ladled hot water into it, then poured it all through a sieve. A little of its contents I poured into a vial and handed it to the old woman. "She must drink everything," I instructed. "Boil two spoonfuls from this pack in a glass of water, and have her drink it every two hours for the next eight. She should be fine by morning."

"Bless you, miss!" the old woman said, nearly crying, clasping the small vial to her chest. The young girl no longer looked as ill, pink creeping back into her heartsglass.

There were people who decided against leaving the line, but there were many others, tired of waiting, who approached Althy and me for help. Together, we prescribed treatments for horserash, persistent coughs, small chills, and migraines. Althy set splints and stitched open wounds, and I wrapped sores and cuts in clean bandages. Kalen was constantly coming and going, leaving us new vials, herbs, and gauze. Likh and Fox manned the growing number of fires where pots boiled and smoked, the former stoking them with well-placed runes and the latter maintaining their heat. Both stopped to assist us when we needed bones set. Princess Inessa had grown proficient with the mortar and pestle, grinding at the wooden bowl with gusto.

I worked on a dislocated shoulder, Councilor Ludvig holding the man in place and Inessa waiting with clean bandages, her face turning pale with every crack and pop.

"Red limebeet?" someone asked.

"Yes," I said, looking up. The crowd had thinned noticeably, and the half dozen people remaining stepped to one side to allow Khalad closer. Dark shadows lined his eyes, and he looked wan.

"Have you been treating patients all morning?" I demanded.

"And all of last night. I wondered why the number I have seen to seemed less than the number I'd observed outside."

Likh rose with a clean towel and gently wiped Khalad's face. Blushing hard, he sat back down as the forger smiled his thanks.

"We would have offered assistance had you told us," Althy admonished him.

"I didn't think about that," Khalad said meekly. "I've always done things on my own."

"Well, get used to us." With a sharp jerk, I snapped the man's shoulder back in place, the patient's cries muffled by the clean rag I had forced on him. Inessa swayed. Fox placed a hand on her shoulder to steady her, and she leaned into him.

"Keep all weight off for at least a week," I told the man. "Drink this to ease the pain."

Inessa had let go of Fox but did not move away. Kalen was watching me, no longer angry as he'd been the day before but still oddly cryptic.

"Did you bring the heartsglass?" Khalad asked Princess Inessa.

"Well, I... Yes." The girl started to take it out.

"Not here." Khalad glanced around. "My home isn't much, but I'd prefer we do this inside."

"Do your hands hurt?" Fox asked quietly as the others followed Khalad.

"The herbs make it sting," Inessa confessed ruefully. "My cuts haven't fully healed yet."

Fox took some leftover poultice and rubbed it on her palms. Inessa's heartsglass glowed. Memories flickered through my brother's bond, of conversations and laughter, of him rubbing her fingers when she complained about the cold and lifting them to kiss.

Fox froze. Inessa froze. Without thinking, my brother had been lifting her bruised hands toward his mouth.

Shaking, Inessa quickly let go. I hurried inside, not wanting to show them how much I'd seen.

•• ⧽∣∕⧼ ••

To call it a house was an overstatement; Khalad's home had only one room that could barely accommodate us all. Glass cabinets filled with bottles lined the walls. Some vials had labels, like *Loss* and *Grieving* and *Childbirth*, which presented more questions than answers. There was a curious sign plastered against the lone window—

GUILT—1 sigloi
MELANCHOLY—2 sigloi
LONGING—4 sigloi

A table, two small chairs, and two narrow cots were the extent of the decor. A few loose stones served as paperweights, some carefully balanced over the others. *Both forgers share similar habits*, I thought, remembering Khalad's pyramid of pebbles at the inn in Odalia.

"But you're both Heartforgers!" Princess Inessa burst out, shying away from the meager furniture like it was corrosive to the touch.

"He offers his services for free, Your Highness," Althy pointed out. "He derives no income from treating ailments since he does not charge for them."

"There must be over two hundred bottles in here," I marveled.

"My mother should be treating you better than this, Khalad!" Inessa was still in disbelief. "I will not sit back and allow an Odalian prince to live in such squalor."

"We refused her offer. Three times. We charged exorbitant heartsglass prices for the rich snobs Master didn't like, as part of the Heartforgers' oath, but he gave most of it to charity. He said he'd rather live like one of Her Majesty's poorest citizens so she'd occasionally remember to treat them better."

"But that doesn't apply to you!"

"It does. I took the vow too, remember? If he'd been here, my master wouldn't have welcomed you in, Your Highness. He would've turned you out on your rears and then laughed about the irony over tea."

"And you've been keeping house for him while he's away?"

"We mostly treat the sick here, like today. I'm only an apprentice, but the demand's so high, he lets me do my own projects." A shadow crossed Khalad's face. He played with the pile of paperweights. "We were knee deep in orders, and it really wasn't a good time for him to leave. But he insisted it was important."

"It was," Councilor Ludvig murmured. "The sleeping sickness—the forger said it was caused by a strange rune. One he'd never seen before."

"None of the runes in the Faceless's book speak of sleeping sicknesses," Althy said.

"Perhaps he left a clue to the cure somewhere around here?" Princess Inessa took out one of the largest vials from the cabinet, a purple container with "Sad Sleep" written across its surface.

"Your Highness, please don't touch any of the—"

Inessa pulled the cork free. I was immediately assaulted by visions of—

—*a young woman, weeping by the grave of her betrothed, laying flowers upon the*—

Khalad snatched the bottle out of Inessa's hands and hastily stoppered it. "Careful, Inessa! It took months to find this!"

"What was that?" Likh asked, swaying on his feet. "I thought I was…kneeling on a grave…"

"Inessa," Althy admonished. "This is Khalad's home. It is discourteous of you to take things without his permission. This is not the palace where you can do as you see fit without repercussions."

The First Daughter's shoulders slumped. "I apologize, Khalad. I just feel…helpless. Is there nothing we can do for Kance?"

"I'd like another look at his heartsglass." Khalad squinted at it. "See here? There's an empty space between his heartbeats. It's small and very easy to miss, but I'm not mistaken."

"I don't see anything," Likh confessed.

"I do," I said. "He's right, but I wouldn't have noticed if he hadn't pointed it out."

"I told Lady Tea and Sir Fox how the victims of this sickness are descendants of each of the Five Great Heroes. Something was taken from them—Master called it an *urvan*, the soul."

"A soul?" Kalen sounded skeptical.

"It's the essence of who you are, so to speak. It's your memories that define and shape your soul, mold it into the person you are. Drawing Heartsrune nourishes your soul further. People have longer lifespans with heartsglass, are less prone to diseases."

"I don't know much about repairing and making heartsglass," Princess Inessa confessed, "but why would anyone want to steal a soul?"

"According to the Faceless's book, it's an important ingredient for making lightsglass, which in turn can create shadowglass. And with their victims asleep and unresisting, heartsglass won't fade. Without knowing where the Five Heroes' graves lie, taking their descendants' *urvan* is the next best choice."

The white-haired boy gestured at the bottles behind him. "Why do you think the master and I spent years collecting them? They are to us what cloth and silk are to ateliers, what herbs and spices are to apothecaries. Souls remain, even when our heartsglass have been taken. But take away the soul and I can do nothing. What good is a heartsglass if memories can't form around a soul to make them real?"

"Excuse me? Master Khalad?" A young boy peeked in,

flustered by the crowd inside. "I saw your sign and was wondering… Broke me mum's good vase by accident, and she's all put out. I was hoping I could get her something nice, but if you're busy…"

"That's all right, Jobie. Let's get your ma a new vase." The forger gestured at us to keep our silence. The young boy sat down, and Khalad produced an empty vial. "Don't be so nervous, Jobie," the white-haired boy said soothingly. "You've done this enough times before."

"I know, but it gets me worried every time. Can't you take my worry with my guilt too?"

"Close your eyes. You'll feel more relaxed that way."

The forger traced two of his fingers across his forehead before withdrawing. A small strand of something thicker than smoke and heavier than fog curled around them. He tipped it into an empty vial, and I caught the faintest whiff: Jobie looking stricken, hovering over a shattered vase on the floor. But Khalad pushed the cork in, and the image was gone.

"It's done, Jobie."

The boy slid off the chair, grinning. "I feel much better!"

"Do you remember anything?" the forger asked. "Do you remember the vase?"

"The vase? What vase?" Jobie frowned, trying to remember. "Buying me mum a vase, wasn't I?" he asked, after a moment.

"That's right, Jobie. Here's the money for it."

"Don't know what Mum needs with two vases. She's got a perfectly good one at home." Shaking his head, the boy left.

"I had no idea you could do that," Likh breathed.

"It's easier than it looks." Khalad took out a heartsglass from a cupboard. Its colors were faded, not quite as clear as they should be.

"I don't have enough of my own memories to create heartsglass for everyone who needs them. The master and I can't pay much, but the people here are grateful for every bit we can give. Guilt's a popular ingredient. Everyone's always looking to unburden their guilt. It's the other emotions people have trouble parting with. Happiness, always. Even sadness. Most people don't want to part with their sadness, surprisingly enough. You'd think it was the opposite. Guilt is cheaper, but I try to give a fair price."

"Old memories for new," I echoed quietly, thinking about the ones I had given to Khalad over the last couple of years. How many of them had he used for new heartsglass? I had never thought to ask before, but seeing his workshop made me wonder. Would his patients remember traces of the memories I'd supplied? Of dancing around my father's forge, of curling up by his feet as he told me stories? Of me as a child, sitting on Fox's shoulders as he raced through the streets, my brothers and sisters giving chase? And what about my time at the Willows? When they fell in love, would that love bear a trace of my crush on the prince? My friendships with Mykaela and Polaire and everyone else? Would their nightmares come with raised skeletons or three-headed dragons?

"This is for an old man who lives a few streets down who is suffering from dementia," Khalad continued. "I'm building him a new heartsglass. Can't do much with his mind—old age will do that. But I've placed some happy memories here: of being loved by a wife and by children. There're some sad ones to balance everything out and then guilt that goes well enough as conscience. Each heartsglass is different. You can't fit people with the same heartsglass every time."

"But they're not his memories," Fox said. "Won't he remember a different wife, different children?"

"That's the beauty of forging. You don't always need the memory itself, just the emotions that go along with it. Memory's always been tricky—you think you remember a brown dog with a white spot on its nose, but years later, when your mind isn't as sharp, you could easily believe it was a white dog with a brown spot. He'll be confused for a day or two, but his own memories will reassert themselves and take their shape. Those old memories I'd bought will be gone, of course. It's why I keep the newest memories for a while, to make sure those who sold them won't have a change of heart and want them back, though most of them have trouble remembering what they'd sold."

"Did it help?" I found myself asking. "My memories?"

"Absolutely," Khalad promised, almost reverently. "You helped a lot of people, Tea, and they know. I made sure of it."

"You're doing good work," Likh was wide eyed with admiration.

"I'm still an apprentice," the forger said, smiling. "But I've managed complicated hearts on my own. People think Master's an old codger, but he's really kind."

"I'm going to do you both better," Princess Inessa said. "Kalen, please return to the palace. Tell the commander I require the sturdiest wagon he can find, enough horses to pull it, and two dozen of his best soldiers."

"What are you planning?" the Deathseeker asked her.

The First Daughter set her jaw. "Odalia will be after you, Khalad, and your small house will make a poor defense. You don't know your master's cure, but our enemies don't know that. You will be safer in the palace, so I am bringing all your tools with you."

"Master won't like that."

"Your master isn't here, Khalad. That's part of the problem."

T HE ARMY MADE ITS MOVE *at dawn, approaching the unguarded gates. Despite being heavily outnumbered, the Daanorian soldiers in the palace began their preparations to repulse the enemy, their bravery shining brighter than armor.*

Lord Kalen drew their leaders aside, speaking to them in their language. The men looked uncertainly at him and then at each other.

"They will not be fighting today," the Dark asha said from behind me. "My daeva will be more than adequate for the task."

"But they draw too close to the palace." I did not believe that the incoming army would spare the Daanorian civilians the way the bone witch had, and the daeva were too large to be careful should the city be overrun.

The smile she shot in my direction was almost cruel. "You forget that I too have an army."

Her hands drifted lazily, sketching runes I could not see. The wind died for a few brief moments, and a strange hush fell over the palace, extending out toward the city and past the gates.

An earthquake rocked Santiang, the force pitching me to the floor.

The Heartforger calmly snatched a falling vial in midair, setting it on the floor before returning to his forging. I grabbed at the windowsill and chanced a look outside. The daeva remained where they were below, still waiting placidly.

Beyond the gates, I could see the army struggling to regain footing. And then another wave hit us, and the ground around the soldiers broke apart. I saw skeletal hands reaching up to clasp the now-frightened infantry by their legs. I saw horses rear up, throwing off their riders as the undead clawed out from the soil in easily twice their number.

And then the screaming began.

I dashed from the window and fell to my knees, vomiting.

"They're eating them," the Dark asha said matter-of-factly, "though I don't suppose the undead have much appetite."

"My lady!"

"I warned them. I told you of our language of flowers, Bard. Yellow carnations mean rejection, and striped ones tell me that the elder asha refuse to compromise. Parmina's azalea-shaped zivar said she is concerned for me, but nonetheless, she is power- less to order the army's retreat. I responded with monkshood to warn her of traitors in their midst and then belvedere—merciless war—should they proceed. They did not listen. They made their choices, and I made mine. If I cannot sway them with kindness, then they shall die."

She took a step forward, doubled over. Her shoulders shook from pain, and Lord Khalad abandoned his work to reach her side, worry etched on his face.

"It would appear," she gasped out, "that darksglass is starting to take a toll on me earlier than I would have wanted."

"You expected this?" The Heartforger demanded.

"There is a price for this much power, Khalad." She straightened

again, a sudden burst of strength. "There is no need for concern. I will finish this one way or another."

"Kalen—"

"Kalen knows. That is why he is fighting out there instead of me."

I staggered to my feet and glimpsed the soldiers defending themselves, cutting off limbs and heads. Their actions did little to stem the tide of undead.

The Dark asha watched the chaos her creations caused with a smile on her face. "Something similar happened in Kion many months ago."

"I—I remember the reports. An attack on Ankyo, they said, by the Odalian army." I could not look away from the horror unfolding before me.

"An eye for an eye, Bard. I do not forget."

17

FOX LOOKED ON WITH AMUSEMENT as I sat on the lid of my overflowing trunk, endeavoring to close it despite all evidence to the contrary. Sensing my irritation, the *azi* tossed and turned within the depths of my thoughts, strangely uneasy.

"There," I grunted, finally latching the lid and allowing the servants to carry it out. "Perhaps Princess Inessa might decide to forgo the trunk and ship my whole closet to Daanoris instead. I must be bringing more than she is."

"She's bringing twice what you have."

"How do you know that?"

"She and the empress haven't stopped fighting about whether or not she should accompany us. I could hear them from the other end of the palace as clearly as I could hear everyone in between."

Likh peered into the room. "Althy says we're to leave at

first light, with either a small legion of soldiers or, er, a dozen depending."

"Depending on what?" I asked.

"On whether the princess or the empress wins the argument. Although it seems moot at this point. I am told a pigeon from Daanoris has just arrived. The emperor refused the delegation unless the princess comes with us."

I groaned. "Perhaps my *azi* can swoop down and bully the emperor into helping us find the forger."

"Tea!"

"I'm serious. If I had a choice, I'd stay here. I don't want to leave Mykaela and Polaire."

"I know. At least they'll be well rested when they wake."

I laughed. "Likh, you really do look on the bright side of every situation, don't you?"

"I try. We need all the positivity we can." Likh shifted. "Tea, are you close friends with Khalad? Do you know much about him?"

"As good a friendship as a bone witch and a Heartforger are capable of having. Why do you ask?"

Likh stared at a wall. "I didn't know there was another option for male spellbinders beyond joining the Deathseekers."

"Khalad is an exception. The Kion forger is the only remaining master of his trade, but he's also extremely selective when it comes to apprentices."

"And you give Khalad memories for his ingredients?"

"Yes. Asha replenish their own memories. Regular people can't."

"So I can give memories too?" Likh's face was earnest and easy to read.

"Well, yes. Why are you—?"

Several things happened instantaneously. The *azi* reared up in alarm. Its wings spread, and all three heads hissed angrily, then the beast shot out of the lake it had been nesting in.

At the same time, there were shouts along the corridor, the sounds of running feet and frightened yelling. From the direction of the Kion city gates, I could see dark, heavy smoke rising into the air.

I felt the sudden flicker of a *Compulsion* rune, saw the surprise on a servant's face before her expression turned blank. Wordlessly, she picked up a poker she had been using to tend the fireplace and raised it at Fox's unprotected back.

A barrage of wind swept into the room, the *Hurricane* rune gleaming in Likh's hands as the maid slammed into the door, knocking her out.

A sudden scream ripped through the air, and Fox was out the door in a flash.

"What's going on?" Likh cried, alarmed, but I was already chasing after my brother into the royal chambers. Empress Alyx was on the floor, stunned. Princess Inessa stood before her with a sword in hand, eyes wide as the unfamiliar guard approached her, his own blade raised.

Fox took one look at the faint bruise marring the princess's cheek and a growl rose from his throat. One broad stroke was all it took to send the soldier on his back, but I leaped forward before he could deliver the killing blow.

"No, Fox! He's being compelled!" I forced my way into the fallen man's mind, the *azi* giving me the strength I needed to fight through the barriers in my path, and commanded him to *sleep*. The man obeyed.

"Are you hurt?" Fox's eyes were still blazing. I could taste his fear.

"We're fine, just shaken up. What's going on?" the princess asked.

"The city is under attack."

"Someone's compelling people!" I shouted. "We need to—"

I broke off and stumbled, my mind on fire. White-hot heat scorched my vision. All I could see was *the strength of our wings as it kept us aloft in the wind, our three heads snapping at invisible attackers as we continued our inexorable trek to Kion. Danger*, the shadows breathed. *Danger, Master.*

I could feel warmth and a pair of arms as someone carried me down the hallway, shouting, before setting me somewhere soft. A babble of voices washed over me, concerned and questioning. I heard brief snatches of conversation, swimming in and out of focus—

"—what's wrong with Tea?"

"—collapsed. Not a coincidence—"

"—no demands that we surrender. Going too far, even for him—"

"—tried to attack Princess Inessa and the empress! Barricade the door!"

"—aren't you allies? Would he go so far as to—"

"—betrayed—"

"—battering the gates. It will fall before long—"

"—battering the *doors*. They've gotten into the palace—"

"—must leave." The empress's voice broke through the fog. "This must be the duke's doing."

"What makes you think this is the duke's doing?" Zoya asked. "We would have sensed if he were capable of magic."

"It's too much of a coincidence for there to be an attack so soon after your arrival. My scouts are reporting Odalian colors in the field. If this is not the duke's doing, then someone is doing this with his approval. He's after Khalad and Tea, we know that. Kance's heartsglass too, I warrant."

"No asha can pry his heart from me," Inessa argued. "I'm going with them, Mother."

"Surely Althy can think of some way—"

"I cannot," Althy cut in, and something cool was pressed against my forehead. I heard hammering at the door, interspersed with sounds of fighting. "There are limits to what spellbinding can do, and matters of the heart stand high on that list. The princess is right. Where Prince Kance's heartsglass goes, she must go along with it."

"The *azi*," I croaked, staring up at the ceiling.

"Tea?" Rahim's voice drew close. "What is happening? Even my assistants I had to fight off—"

"The *azi*'s coming," I gasped, my voice thick as sandpaper. I was seeing double, the throne room overlapping with my vision of the city of Kion on the horizon. "It's going to—"

And then I felt it, the reason for the daeva's anger. Underneath its wings, I saw the army, twice the size I knew Odalia's army to be, spread out for miles around us.

And over half the army was visibly rotting. Strips of armor rusted on their bodies, and their faces were of those long since dead, decaying and desiccated. Those closest to the city gates threw themselves at the walls, heedless of broken bones and torn flesh.

"They're dead!" I cried out. "All of them dead! It isn't an army of soldiers at the city walls, Your Majesty. It's an army of dead."

"Impossible!" the empress said. "No one could summon that many—"

"Yes, they can," Althy said with a grim smile. "The *Puppet* rune, wasn't it? To do this successfully requires immense power."

"Seeking stones." Through the *azi*'s eyes, I saw soft globes of light wafting from among the corpses. "They brought seeking stones with them!"

"What's a seeking stone?" Princess Inessa asked shakily.

"It amplifies an asha's power," Althy told her. "Whoever controls the corpses is channeling through them. Tea, how many do you see?"

I concentrated. "Seven."

Althy grimaced. "A normal spellbinder would already be suffering from darkrot. No one can command seven stones at once and retain their sanity. Your Majesty, we must be prepared for the worst."

"I am not leaving Kion and my people to these hordes of undead, Altaecia!"

I squeezed my eyes shut. To concentrate on two perspectives was draining, so I struggled to focus on the one where I could do some good. The *azi* purred when it felt me graze against its consciousness, opening its mind to allow me entrance. We headed straight for the undead horde amassing outside. They battered the city gates without mercy, and all three of the *azi*'s mouths opened.

The undead soldiers made no sound as they burned, consumed almost immediately by the blazing fireballs that slammed into them from overhead. We cawed in triumph and dove toward the city entrance. I saw the Ankyon soldiers manning the towers, fear etched upon their faces as death approached, the bravest of them shooting arrows at us in desperation.

I ignored their attacks and turned at the last minute, lashing out with our claws and ripping away most of the undead still hammering at the gates. I circled around and unleashed three more streams of deadly fire. The undead died again, lost in the inferno.

We next directed our ire at the pulses of magic amid the throng, at the seeking stones. I guided the *azi* through the air, using its winged body in place of my hand as it wove the *Strangle* rune in my stead. The rune shone large in the sky, and through the daeva's eyes, I could see the telltale flickers of the seeking stones dotting the army below us. At my command, the daeva landed before one of the soldiers that carried a seeking stone, and the *azi*'s middle head snapped out to grab the glowing orb in its jaws before rising up again. I flew the daeva straight into the center of my rune, and the seeking stone exploded into oblivion. Again and again, we singled out the dead warriors, and soon, a greater part of the undead stopped, unmoving, until we put them out of their misery with more flames.

Dimly, I felt someone grab hold of my human body, attempting to shake its shoulders, and sensed someone pushing them away. "No!" Fox's voice said, cold and clear in the confusion. "Let her be. She's saving us."

I swooped down and sprayed the men with fire until bonfires dotted the fields. We circled the city hungrily, awaiting more signs of movement, but nothing else stirred. The undead army lay smoldering. I sent my mind out, probing, but I was certain none of the seeking stones survived the onslaught.

A babble of voices erupted again, excited and joyful. I was more cautious, arrested by a sense of wrongness.

They are coming, the *azi*'s mind boomed, already reaching out to the horizon.

"It's not over," Fox said, voice brittle and bleak. "They are coming."

It was not the dead that came in droves this time but the army of the living, in gleaming armor with polished swords, marching toward the city of Kion. From their flank streamed the flag of Odalia, flashing bright gold and red. Zoya might not be sure if the duke led this attack, but the presence of Odalian soldiers made a compelling argument for it.

"We need to leave now," Kalen said, putting my own thoughts into words. "They will keep attacking Kion as long as we remain in the city. There is no more time, Your Majesty."

"And what of Inessa?" Empress Alyx demanded.

"She will not be safe here. That is out of our hands. If the Faceless can infiltrate the palace, then she and Kance's heartsglass will be safest by the Dark asha and the Heartforger's side, wherever that may be."

Mother and daughter looked at each other without speaking. Finally, the older woman reached out and hugged her daughter. "I should have let you make your own decisions," she said roughly, unshed tears salting her voice. "Protect your betrothed's heart, Inessa, and may the gods watch over you."

Zoya spoke up, "I'd like to know how we are leaving the city, surrounded as we are."

Wordlessly, Fox pointed toward the sky.

"*Again?!*"

"You can either stay or join us, Zoya. I won't force you on the *azi* if you're not comfortable with it," I replied.

"You say, 'comfortable.' I say, 'it's a freaking flying three-headed dragon, you sod.'"

"I don't think we have much choice, Zoya," Shadi said gently.

The asha looked at her, squared her shoulders. "I did give my word, didn't I? But you have every right to refuse, Shad."

"I go where you go, Zoya. We promised each other." The doe-eyed asha took Zoya's hands in hers, and the normally abrasive girl blushed.

"I'm going," Khalad said quietly.

"So am I," Likh said immediately.

"I cannot." Heads turned toward Althy. "Someone needs to stay and ensure the city remains protected after you are gone.

Zahid and most of the Deathseekers are away from Kion, and among the other asha, I am the most qualified to take command. We cannot leave Ankyo open for the taking, Your Majesty. And I, for one, cannot leave Mykaela and Polaire alone."

"But what about my daughter?"

"You will not find worthier people than them, Alyx. They have fought worse demons than I have and saved this city more times than you are aware of." Althy smiled at us. "I trust them. Zoya, you know Daanorian, so I expect you to take charge."

Zoya sighed. "I'm surrounded by heroes."

I opened my eyes. "We need to get out of Kion. Tell them to open the gates for us and to keep as many men away from it as possible."

"That will be difficult," Althy murmured. "To leave the city defenses unmanned might provoke the soldiers to step up their attack."

"They won't," I promised. "But whatever you do, don't distract me. I want to keep my hold as tight as possible."

Althy nodded. "May the Blade's path guide your way, Tea. Protect the princess. I will do everything in my power to hold down the fort here."

I clasped her hands. "Althy. Remember what I told you about the elder asha."

"Tea…"

"Don't let them near Polaire or Mykaela. Promise me."

The asha looked troubled but nodded. "I swear it."

"We will help them, Tea," Rahim promised. "I am Tresean.

It is in my blood to fight. And Chesh and all the rest—we will help protect the city with the empress and Altaecia until you come back. So you must come back!"

I tried to smile, but the daeva's thoughts slammed back into mine. My stomach plummeted as it dove straight toward the center of the army, and I forced it back toward the sky without inflicting any casualties, though a trail of arrows followed in our wake. I goaded all three mouths into opening again, and the resulting fire raked across the regiments in front, a blazing line in the ground that prevented them from pushing forward.

I could feel Fox lifting me again, felt him run. I heard sounds of battle and the surge of magic as we fought our way out of the palace. And then I heard Chief close by, nickering, and Fox murmuring softly to the stallion.

I could see Deathseekers and asha engaging the soldiers. Capitalizing on the *azi*'s work, they summoned more *Fire* runes until a wall of flames faced the army. The Deathseeker Ostry was calling out orders, and at his command, sharp stalagmites burst from the ground, a natural defense against attackers.

I heard Inessa cry out from somewhere behind us, sensed Fox hesitating.

"Protect the princess, Fox," Kalen's voice drew closer. "I'll stay with Tea." I felt him take my brother's place, pressing me against his chest as he took command of Chief. I leaned into his warmth.

I shifted tactics. The daeva made for the entrance of the city, landing with such force that the whole of Kion shuddered.

The Deathseekers had retreated, Ostry and Alsron yelling at

their companions not to provoke the *azi*. We deliberately turned our backs on them, bayed thirstily at the Odalians to do their worst.

A fireball came out of nowhere straight toward us. My first instinct was to dodge it, but the human part of our mind was screaming, reminding me that the people behind me would be the first to suffer from that choice.

Daeva were immune to most forms of attack but not to pain, and the *azi* hissed as the fire licked at its skin. *There are spellbinders in the Odalian army, Fox*, I hissed, and he started. *Send word to Althy to investigate the asha and Deathseekers in Ankyo. There may be more traitors hiding there.*

In the distance, something flared.

A seeking stone! Another flare lit up among the soldiers and then another.

The men, once so hesitant to fight, went rigid, unnaturally silent. And then, as one, they shuffled forward.

Fox, tell the others to stay back!

The army picked up speed. I swept my mind out into the crowd, reaching for the stones—and encountered a barrier. The men kept running, swords falling uselessly from their hands. This was a suicide mission, a show of force. If the *azi* didn't kill them, they would dash their brains out against the city walls.

I searched for the seeking stones a second time and encountered a *Compulsion* so great, my mind snapped back from the force. If I had not been inside the daeva's mind, if the *azi* had not pushed away that corrupting magic, I could have easily been turned.

"Deathseekers, to me!" I heard Ostry yell. I felt another

surge of magic as *Shield* runes popped up behind us, braced for impact.

The *azi* struggled, eager to defend itself, but I forced my full will on the beast, shouting at it to *keep still, do not move, do not hurt them.*

The *Rot* rune appeared under the soldiers' feet a second before the ground disintegrated. The opposing army slid down the steep embankment as a large sinkhole opened beneath them, deep enough to make climbing out difficult.

"It's Althy!" Zoya was awestruck. "She's literally sweeping them off their feet!"

From within that strange barrier, I finally found cracks I could slip through amid the confusion and located the stones.

"Kalen!" Fox yelled. The Deathseeker and I had outpaced the others, mostly because of Chief. "Right field, by the flag bearer!"

Kalen scanned the army quickly and wove the air around us. Bursts of wind and fire spiraled out, directed toward the location Fox had shouted, and snatched the seeking stones with accuracy, leaving flames in their wake. Fox called out more locations, using my sight for his own, and Kalen stole them away, gathering them all in the air above us. I briefly shook myself free from the *azi*'s mind to weave the *Strangle* rune around them. The sound of the seeking stones shattering gave me immense satisfaction.

I could feel rage and consternation, and then the unseen mind was gone. The soldiers stumbled and fell to their knees, shaking their heads groggily. Many had collapsed, unconscious, but their lives were intact.

I could feel Fox and the others arriving at the city gates, Princess Inessa screaming at the Deathseekers to let them through. I opened the doors of my own mind to the *azi*, felt it snake its way in, closing around me like a fitted glove. Through the *azi*'s eyes, I saw Likh and Princess Inessa shrinking back and Zoya bravely standing her ground in front of Shadi despite the fear in her eyes. Alsron and Mavren tensed, but Ostry remained where he was, his mouth open as our three heads bowed to him. "Tea?" Those two syllables left his mouth in a near squeak.

I laughed; the *azi* rumbled. In this form, they looked strange, almost grotesque—as if it were them and not us who were the unnatural beasts.

Play, I told the *azi*, searching its memories and latching on to a vision of another city of stonework and marble, its ivory domes unmistakable. The *azi* cawed, and its wide wings lowered.

I felt the group scrambling up our back and a "Y'all really gonna climb up *that*?" from Mavren. We explored the fallen soldiers for any remnants of that powerful mind and found none. Deathseekers and asha were hard to surprise; after their initial amazement, they went to work, grabbing our trunks and tossing them up to my companions.

"Wouldn't want you ladies naked in Daanoris!" Levi guffawed, always the quickest to find levity in any situation.

"Come back in one piece, you reckless loonies," Ostry yelled at us.

We rose, Zoya leaving more invectives in our wake as we flew at breakneck speed. The city of Kion was soon gone, replaced by an endless landscape of trees and mountains.

The wind gave little opportunity for conversation, and it was all the others could do to cling to us as we flew. The land soon disappeared, and the crisp blue waters of the Swiftsea took its place.

It felt like eons had passed before I saw approaching land, the Haitsa mountains at a distance, though it must have only been an hour. The *azi* called out a warning as it descended, and we soon found ourselves standing in the kingdom of Daanoris, dirt and heat rising around us with the pearl roofs and spiral towers of its capital city, Santiang, only half a day's ride away.

A NEW SOUND REACHED OUR EARS—*AN explosion. At this, the bone witch abandoned her story to rush toward the window. She stared eagerly out at the carnage below. Large fireballs rose and fell, consuming the Dark asha's undead by the dozens. Still more fire rained down on Santiang, and I froze in fear, imagining the asha's efforts to protect the Daanorian citizens coming to naught should the city burst into flames.*

Before anyone could stop him, the Deathseeker leaped out the window. The Dark asha's cry was drowned out by the cawing of the azi, who swooped in and caught him easily. Kalen swung up on its back as it made for the army. The bone witch inhaled noisily, let her breath out slowly. "That idiot," she muttered.

"I wonder where he learned that trick?" the Heartforger drawled.

"Shut up, Khalad."

The azi flew into the path of the fireballs heading our way. A current ran through my body, sparks singing through the air as Lord Kalen's magic took hold. Almost immediately, ice crept up around the incoming flames, freezing and turning them into rocks that shattered midair, their pieces falling uselessly back to earth. Every attempt by the enemy asha was quickly repelled, and the Deathseeker was quick to turn the battleground to his advantage; new hurricanes savaged the area, and what legions of the army had retained their formations despite the undead assault were soon dispersed by the whirling tempest.

But the army's asha had not been idle; I could see the earth breaking up underneath some of the cadavers, saw many of them falling into the pits. The girl smiled, and I could feel the crackling of energy around her. The zivar pinned to my shirt grew hot to the touch. "Mykkie must have learned that from Altaecia," I heard her murmur to herself. "But she forgets the one glaring difference between humans and corpses." She lifted her arms, fingers moving deftly.

More cries and shouts of alarm came as the corpses reconstituted themselves and clawed their way back to the surface. Limbs reattached and heads returned to their bodies as the Dark asha's magic took hold again, willing ashes and bone back to life. Now I saw the wisdom of bringing these undead from every grave she could find in Daanoris and burying them before the city. Already the army was demoralized and broken, and the daeva still waited beyond, refreshed and eager to participate.

The army retreated, carrying their dead and injured with them. I watched them disappear over the hill, while the corpses stood like rotting mannequins.

The azi returned with the triumphant Deathseeker. The bone witch rushed to him, giving him little time to respond as she took his face and kissed him hard.

"You are to never do that again," she panted when they finally broke apart. "For a moment, I had forgotten that you were...that you were..."

There was a boyish grin on Lord Kalen's usually serious face. "Call it payback from last time."

"Shut up," the girl said and kissed him again.

18

HOW COULD YOU NOT TELL us that your pet could get from Kion to Daanoris *in one day?*" Zoya was not having a very good morning. We were camped outside Santiang, Daanoris's capital, to finish our preparations. The *azi* had long since left; none of us wanted another panic, much less in a potentially hostile city. I could still feel it nearby, making itself at home in a nearby forest.

"It never came up in conversation before. And I've never been to Daanoris." I felt ridiculous changing into an elaborate *hua* in the middle of nowhere, but there were delegates to consider. The presence of the *azi* had not gone unnoticed, and a small contingent of ambassadors, diplomats, and three times as many soldiers had arrived barely an hour after the *azi*'s departure. Though they were most respectful, with Zoya and Shadi fluent in Daanorian to prevent any misunderstandings, they were also very insistent that we meet the emperor immediately.

The look Zoya shot my way was scathing. "Well, there better not be any more surprises. We're treading on unknown territory, and your daeva isn't helping matters any. Can you keep a leash on your *azi* at this distance?"

"Distance doesn't really mean anything to us."

"Good. Let Shadi and me do all the talking. Back me up even when it sounds like I don't know what in Mithra's ass I'm talking about." Zoya smoothed her dress. We were all decked out in our best *hua*, Inessa included, while Kalen, Khalad, and Fox dressed in gray woolen robes. It was odd to see Kalen in clothing that wasn't black, and it was clear that the Deathseeker didn't like it.

Zoya was uncharacteristically meticulous, fussing over each of us. "You're going to have to take the lead at some points, Your Majesty," she told the princess. "You're going to be speaking for all of Kion, and it's necessary to be assertive. Keep Prince Kance's heartsglass hidden at all times. Have you ever been here before?"

"Once, on a ceremonial visit. Mother did most of the talking."

"Channel as much of your mother as you're able to. I'll be whispering in your ear every now and then, like I'm your closest adviser. The emperor's own counsel does this frequently, so it won't seem out of place." Zoya sighed. "They've waited long enough. Let's get this over with."

A crowd had gathered by the time we entered the city. As we were led down the streets, the people knelt, touching their foreheads to the ground.

"The emperor has his subjects well trained," Kalen murmured softly and received a sharp jab in the side from Zoya.

There were certain similarities between Kion and Santiang. The roads here were narrower, but the sharp roofs and curved arches so popular in Ankyo had first taken root here. Kion was constructed with aesthetics in mind, but Santiang was built with utilitarian intent. The walls were made of a mix of wood and concrete. Though roughly hewn and unpainted, all looked capable of lasting for decades. We passed sturdy houses and well-maintained pavements, all in varying shades of gray.

Most of the people wore short robes and sandals, and I saw nothing in their dress to distinguish among different professions and trades. The only magic I could sense were in the *hua* and zivars we wore—no one we passed wore anything bespelled. Nobody wore heartsglass. It would take considerably more effort to use magic on someone without one, a clear disadvantage for asha.

"Something doesn't feel right," Likh said nervously.

Zoya wove a rune in the air. It sputtered against her fingers. "Still works," she said, "but it's not as strong as it should be."

"If runic magic isn't used here, then how did the sleeping Daanorian princess acquire a heartsglass of her own?" Fox asked Khalad.

The forger shrugged. "Master thinks it was a foreigner. I don't think it was an asha though—that would have caused a stir—and Princess Yansheo wouldn't have understood its significance. Most Daanorians think heartsglass are nothing more than pretty trinkets."

"Makes what happened to her even more heartless," Fox said. "Literally."

The Daanorian palace was the only spot of color in the city. Pearl-white and luminescent, it was ringed by golden towers and sloped roofs, which shone like ivory. As we approached, I saw the reason why—the exterior was covered in marble slates, polished until they reflected the sunlight. I shuddered to think how hot it would be in the height of summer.

"They have an extensive irrigation system that pipes cold and hot water into the rooms within and can be adjusted according to preference," Shadi murmured. "It keeps the palace temperate, no matter the weather."

Something felt wrong the instant we stepped inside. Zoya stiffened, her fingers moving. "Wards," she whispered.

"Someone warded the whole palace?" I could see the barriers writhing above us, tied in complicated knots. I sketched out *Compulsion*, but nothing happened. I pressed my hand against the protection stone I wore around my neck but found no response to it either. I tried *Scrying*, to similar effect. These wards were stronger than those in Aenah's jail if not even the False runes worked.

"We should have expected this," Shadi said softly. "Magic is banned in Daanoris. Whoever was responsible was also very thorough. And extremely competent."

"Master never mentioned these protections though," Khalad said. "This was added recently."

Likh stared intently at the ceiling, at the magic beyond our grasp. "They may be more complicated than the wards around Aenah, but they don't look all that different from the spells we wove into zivar at Chesh's," he murmured. "Will this put us at a disadvantage?"

"Not completely." I reached out with my mind, felt my brother's response, his comfortable nearness. Moving farther out, I detected faint thoughts from the *azi*. Our connection was not as strong as I was expecting, but it was assuaging to know our link had not been severed.

The *azi* was drifting lazily somewhere in the middle of the Swiftsea. I tried to nudge it with my mind, tried to get it to turn around—and found that I couldn't.

"My bond with Tea is intact," Fox confirmed.

"And the daeva?" Zoya asked.

"Not quite. I can sense it, but it doesn't respond to my commands."

"Isn't that bad?" Likh asked. "Who's controlling it while you're here?"

"It's not going to attack."

"How sure can you be? It's a daeva!"

"I've been inside its head. It doesn't like cities. Unless... someone else controls it."

Zoya groaned.

Even the floors and walls were made of marble. I could hear the soft rushing of water from somewhere nearby as we were led down large hallways. Servants and courtiers stopped to kneel as we passed, their foreheads pressed to the floor as the people outside had done.

At the end of a very long corridor stood two heavy doors.

A band of trumpets sounded, and the doors opened almost instantly.

The throne room was even more ostentatious than the one at Kion. It was a dazzling display of white, from the embossed columns to the large, open windows shaded by soft curtains. Golden banners hung from the ceiling, and my heartsglass wavered when I saw they bore the silhouette of a three-headed yellow dragon, the emperor's personal crest.

In the wake of such rich displays, Emperor Shifang stood out like an afterthought. He sat on a gilded throne that looked more expensive than all our *hua* combined. I was curious; common folk were not allowed to look on the emperor's face, and at the last *darashi oyun* he attended nearly two years ago, his head had always been veiled.

But the emperor wore no concealment now. He was tall with long black hair; curiously intense dark eyes; and, while on the slim side, was easily one of the handsomest men I'd ever seen, rivaling even Prince Kance. His robes were heavily embroidered and wrapped in gold foil, and jewels adorned his wrists and fingers. Three dragons were carefully embroidered in his robes, entwined so closely that they gave off the appearance of being only one creature.

The emperor of Daanoris rose to his feet, and the people in the room genuflected. I stood uncertainly, unsure if I was expected to follow suit, but Zoya stood straight and proud, and we followed her lead.

The emperor made a speech in Daanorian in a surprisingly

firm tone, his eyes never leaving Princess Inessa's face. Zoya stepped forward and delivered her own speech, her confident voice echoing in the room. We were introduced, and the emperor looked surprised to find that I was the Dark asha.

"How can one so small and harmless looking command such power?" Shadi translated. Clearly, the emperor and I were starting off on the wrong foot.

Khalad was announced as a healer, Fox and Kalen, bodyguards to Inessa and me, respectively. The princess's movements were likely to be restricted, so Fox and I decided our bond would help us keep in contact without arousing suspicion.

The emperor asked Zoya a question, and she responded, gesturing at me to step forward.

"What are you telling him?" Princess Inessa muttered without visibly moving her lips.

"He talked at length about your beauty and waxed poetic about your eyes, Princess," Zoya said quietly. "I won't bother you with the details. But he wants to know more about the *azi*, considering they patterned their royal crest after it. Speak clearly, Tea, with as little information as you can divulge. The emperor won't understand us, but some of his advisers will. This is for their benefit."

We'd already discussed what I would say, but speaking before an audience always made me nervous, and another headache was forming. "I am the keeper of the dragon," I announced. "We have come from Kion to pay our respects to the emperor of illustrious Daanoris, for whom we hold high esteem. We wish to foster a closer alliance with His Majesty and are pleased to be given the opportunity to do so. We regret that we cannot bring the dragon into the city, for it fears enclosed spaces and always yearns for open sky. But we have summoned it here, as a sign that we wish good fortune upon your kingdom."

Emperor Shifang smiled. He turned toward his audience and made an announcement in strident tones. A hushed whisper spread among his courtiers and nobles. Zoya remained calm and composed, and the faint blue tinge blooming in her heartsglass was my only warning. She launched into another monologue, addressing the emperor directly, but the royal cut her off with a curt wave of his hand. A dismissal.

"What's going on, Zoya?" Inessa asked again.

The asha's face was set. "The emperor has gotten it into his head that you are here to offer yourself in marriage, Your Highness. He said this was the agreement your mother sent him as part of your visit to Daanoris."

"That's impossible!" To her credit, Princess Inessa's face was outwardly serene and smiling, though the words issuing out the side of her mouth were anything but. "I'm already engaged! Surely he knows that!"

"Nobility from other kingdoms are beneath them, Your Highness. They believe that any contracts they make supersede those of other nations. Either your mother agreed to this betrothal or some miscommunication occurred between the envoys."

"No, this stinks of my mother's schemes. I was wondering

why she was so adamant that I not come with you. He will not be happy if I refuse, will he?"

"We don't have much choice," Kalen said tersely. "As long as these wards remain, we can do little. We need to find the source of the magic."

Emperor Shifang might not have understood us, but I supposed our body language spoke volumes. His eyes turned flinty, and the next words issuing out of his mouth had a threatening air about them.

Immediately, there was a clanking noise as the guards in the throne room lifted their spears, their tips leveled at us.

"So much for diplomacy," Shadi murmured. "How goes the daeva summoning, Tea?"

"Oblivious to my commands."

"So I assume asking the daeva to rain down fire is out of the question?"

"No." Princess Inessa shook her head. "I'd like to scale back on the calamities. We've had enough misadventures. We must find the Heartforger, and that will be difficult with the whole country in chaos. The emperor might be fond of your *azi*, but I suspect his people want nothing to do with it." She stepped forward. "Emperor Shifang," she began, her voice strong with none of the anger and frustration she'd expressed only seconds ago. "The First Daughter of Kion agrees to your offer. We hope that this engagement will mark the start of a new and better alliance between Ankyo and Daanoris and that prosperity shall smile down on both our kingdoms with this union."

She turned toward Zoya, who was staring at her. "Make sure you translate that properly, Zoya."

"Are you certain about this, Your Highness?"

"As you said, there are undoubtedly a few advisers here who understood me, so there's no going back. It will give us the freedom to find the Heartforger and several days' respite while I think of a way to turn him down without insulting another kingdom."

The guards' spears retreated. The emperor smiled broadly, the epitome of congeniality once more, and stepped down from his throne to take Princess Inessa's hands in his own. Another court official, an elderly man with a long beard and a tall hat, scuttled forward and made several more announcements. To this, a younger man began to protest. They argued for a few minutes before the emperor interrupted them both with an irritated wave. The two men bowed and shuffled away, scowling at one another.

Khalad frowned. "That younger man," he said. "He looks familiar. I believe he knows the master."

"That's unusual," Kalen said. "The younger man wishes to postpone the ceremony to a later date, while the other wants to carry out the king's orders without delay."

"You speak Daanorian?" I asked.

"I understand the language better than I speak it. The old man's name is Tansoong and the other, Baoyi. We might have some trouble with the latter. He believes we're swindlers out to fleece the king, and he's ready to send us to the hangman's block if he has his way."

There was a certain smugness to the older official's voice as he announced that the next two weeks would be spent celebrating the engagement, with us as their guests of honor.

Emperor Shifang looked over at us appreciatively and added something else in a suggestive tone I would have understood regardless of language.

"The Daanorians have a longstanding tradition of concubineship," Zoya said dryly, "and it is not unusual for noble visitors to present the emperor with a few as a show of their appreciation."

"He wants Princess Inessa to give him a concubine?" Likh asked incredulously. "But he just announced their engagement!"

"It's the custom," Shadi confirmed. "The number of wives and concubines is directly proportional to one's power and influence—or so it is believed. That he is granting Princess Inessa the status of first wife is one of the highest honors in Daanoris, considering she is foreign born. The position is usually restricted to local nobility."

"I'm flattered," Inessa said, sounding anything but. "Truly."

The emperor spoke again. Zoya cleared her throat. "He's already made the decision apparently. His words translated verbatim are, 'I am particularly enchanted by the lovely concubine in the beautiful red dress.'"

"Me?" Likh squeaked. "I'm not sure I meet the requirements he's looking for."

"Do you want to turn him down?" Princess Inessa turned back to the emperor. "Tell him we accept the conditions if he will agree to one of our own."

Likh blanched. Khalad patted him awkwardly on the shoulder.

The emperor looked puzzled but nodded.

"One of my subjects is missing. He was last heard from in Santiang, and I would like to ask the emperor's leave to search the city for him on the morrow."

"What is his name?"

Inessa looked to Zoya, who nodded slightly. "His name is Narel."

Baoyi looked astonished, his mouth falling open. Tansoong burst into a flurry of protests, but the younger man intervened again. They argued for several seconds before the elder withdrew, not looking happy.

"That's a surprise," Zoya said. "The other man insists that we be given every assistance to look for him."

"He's Master's friend," Khalad said. "I'm sure of it now."

The official continued to speak. Zoya listened closely, and understanding dawned on her face.

"The emperor agrees but not tomorrow—only after the immediate danger is over."

"What immediate danger?"

"I am beginning to realize why the Daanorians and their emperor are so quick to push forward with this betrothal, Your Highness."

"Oh, great. What is it this time? Should I be offering him more concubines? Will Kalen suffice instead?"

"This is serious, Princess. Daeva almost never make an appearance in Daanoris, but he says there have been sightings of a gigantic frog-like creature with webbed talons and yellow eyes."

"The *savul*," Fox said bleakly, his hands balling into fists.

"They do not have the means of defeating it," Zoya explained. "They are very eager to see the Dark asha in action as soon as they can figure out where it is."

I SPENT ANOTHER RESTLESS NIGHT; THE army no longer posed an immediate threat, but I knew they would not give up so easily. Not with the power the Dark asha displayed, the lengths she had proven she would go.

She had risen earlier than I had again that morning, though it was clear she had less sleep than me. She sat on the throne, one leg slung over the armrest, displaying the long scar on her thigh. She had been writing again; the thick bundle of papers before her was testament to that. Lord Kalen and the Heartforger were nowhere to be found, and I surmised that the latter, at least, had finally gotten some much-needed rest.

To my surprise, she handed me some of the sheaves of paper.

"If yesterday was any indication, I will have many busy days ahead of me," she said. "The rest of my story lies within these pages. Perhaps you can find a song there."

"What else are you writing?"

"A letter—for my brother to read." She laughed. "You look shocked."

"I assumed that you were not on cordial terms."

"That's never mattered before." She looked down at her papers. There is a strange scar marking her right palm, silvery from age. "If I do not survive this," she said with less mirth this time, "then neither will he. But in the event that I succeed in my quest, he will live regardless of how I die. And I owe him an explanation. Mykaela too."

"But how?"

"Some secrets I intend to keep a little longer. Do your best not to get caught in the crossfire, Bard. We are only just beginning, and I cannot foresee the future beyond my own, however much I plan."

"They are quiet today," Lord Kalen noted, entering the room. "But I suspect they are growing desperate."

"Let them come. I defy any of them to get past my daeva." The bone witch stopped. Her eyes widened. "But it looks like someone already has." She rose to her feet. "Stop."

I looked around but saw no one.

She sighed. "And here we have another complication. Come to me, Princess."

I still did not understand until a cloaked girl marched stiffly into the room. Lord Kalen's sword made a hard ringing sound as it slid out of its scabbard. Already he was halfway between us and the stranger.

"How did you sneak in here, Inessa?" The bone witch's voice held grudging respect. The Deathseeker stopped in his tracks, astonished, as Lady Tea dispersed the magic surrounding the newcomer.

"Don't you remember? For a very short time, I actually ruled this kingdom. You should know; you were there." It was a soft voice, light and lilting. The princess tugged her hood down, and I found myself staring into a beautiful face with bright-blue eyes framed by reddish-brown curls. Her heartsglass gleamed cherry red.

"This is not the warm welcome I had hoped to receive," said the First Daughter of Kion.

19

"OUR DUNGEONS?" TANSOONG ASKED, STARING. "But why?"

"We are the princess's guard," Shadi told him. "We must be kept abreast of any dangerous felons in the city, and that includes those in your dungeon."

Khalad had stayed behind to examine the sleeping Daanorian princess. Princess Inessa and Likh were elsewhere for some court function. Kalen was off to measure the scope and extent of the wards in the palace, hoping to find the means to unravel them, leaving only Zoya, Shadi, Fox, and me.

Tansoong, the elder statesman, was solicitous but also very inquisitive, constantly peppering Zoya with questions. He seemed particularly interested in Dark asha, and more than once, I felt his curious eyes on me when he thought I wasn't looking. The younger court official, Baoyi, was the complete opposite, not bothering to hide his dislike. Clearly, he was here only because his emperor had ordered him to be and maintained a sullen silence with us. He had a nervous-looking servant with him who appeared to be a secretary of sorts.

It was unfortunate that I couldn't cast *Scrying* on either official; I wondered what kind of minds they had. Likh had asked them about the wards around the palace and received blank stares from both. Inessa had questioned the emperor and gotten the same reaction. Either the barriers were placed without their knowing or they were magnificent actors.

"We only have two prisoners at the moment," Tansoong explained, "both servants caught stealing from the kitchens. They shall be transferred to the larger jails in the city, so her betrothed will have little reason to worry."

Zoya studied the prisoners while I peeked into the other empty cells. With a sigh, I glanced down at the floor, where some bored prisoner or guard had piled a few stones in one corner. Dirt was strewn across the floor, and many of the cells had no locks. The prison cells were rarely maintained, Tansoong explained, because few people would dare to commit crimes so near to the emperor. It was wishful thinking to have hoped that the old Heartforger was here.

It was only after we left that Baoyi finally spoke. "Why do you ask to examine our princess?" he demanded.

"We have a noted healer with us," Shadi explained. "He offered his services."

"What do I know of this man's qualifications? What assurances do I have that you will not poison her?"

"It is the emperor's orders, milord."

His secretary cleared his throat and murmured something in a soft, placating tone. Baoyi scowled, then barked an order to some of the soldiers.

"He wants the guards increased at Princess Yansheo's room," Shadi murmured. "He is protective of the girl."

The girl herself, Jade of the House of Weixu, lay sleeping on a golden bier, surrounded by flowers. A glass case separated her from the rest of the world, like she was a character from an old fairy tale. Zoya told me the glass was removed every three hours for the attending servants to bathe her hair and anoint her body with the choicest perfumes, which Zoya learned had been on Baoyi's orders. To spread rumors that the princess was dead was a jailable offense.

"They found her by the gardens outside the ballroom," Khalad said quietly. Whatever wards were in place, his forging skills remained unaffected. "Her heartsglass is missing, but someone had drawn her Heartsrune. I can still feel the spell lingering around her."

"None of the Daanorians are owning up to that," Fox said. "Curious."

Tansoong excused himself, glancing at me as he did. Baoyi stood over the princess and folded his arms, still glaring.

"He doesn't believe that a young girl like you is capable of putting down a *savul* when their army has failed," Shadi whispered. "It is the kingdoms of Tresea and Istera that hold the nearest daeva burial mounds, so Daanorians know little about the beasts. They always considered asha an ornamental profession, more to do with entertaining guests than slaying daeva."

"It is a belief they should consider amending," Zoya said shortly. "Daeva have not been sighted in this kingdom for more than five hundred years, but a creature's habits are never constant. Times are changing and so must they. Once they pinpoint the current whereabouts of the *savul*, Tea, you should prove them wrong. Show them asha are more than concubines for princes."

"'Princes'? Did a prince say something to you, Zoya?"

"Not to me," the asha growled.

Shadi squeezed Zoya's hand. "Don't be jealous. I declined their offers."

"Still makes me want to kick each and every one of their satin-clothed behinds."

"You know I'm for you alone, Zoya. I thought I made that very clear last night."

"*Shadi!*"

"I'm going to see how Khalad's faring," I said glibly, stepping away from the red-faced Zoya and her grinning lover. Fox followed me.

The glass case was removed at the forger's request, but Baoyi and the stern, harsh-looking soldiers surrounding the bier remained. Oblivious to their scrutiny, Khalad continued his examination, his gray eyes large behind his spectacles. "Did you find anything else?"

Khalad sighed and rubbed at his eyes. "She was dancing at

a ball held in honor of her fourteenth birthday when the sickness took her."

"This is nothing we haven't heard of before," Kalen said, coming up behind us.

"I'd like to show you something." Khalad's hand hovered above the sleeping girl's chest. I saw the swirl and eddy of colors and then a faint image from the princess's point of view: a man bowing down to kiss her hand, the cut of his clothes more Odalian than Daanorian. There was no mistaking his face. The vision lasted only for a few seconds before sputtering out of view.

"Holsrath," I gasped.

"My vision is limited," Khalad said. "I can pull out a stray memory or so but not for long. This was the last thing she saw before losing consciousness, that much I can ascertain."

Kalen frowned. "Considering my father was supposed to be in a jail cell during this time, it's something of a surprise."

"But how did he get out without anyone knowing?" Fox demanded. "Short of King Telemaine himself setting him free, that's impossible."

"Still not as many questions as I would like answered," I confessed.

"We need to discuss this in private," Khalad said with a sidelong glance at Baoyi. "Let's get Shadi and Zoya and return to my room. We may be the emperor's guests, but that's not a guarantee his hospitality will hold."

"Where are you going?" Baoyi wanted to know. "How will you cure the princess?"

"It will take time, milord," Khalad told him gently. "We will do everything in our power to help her. Is there anything else you can tell us about her sickness?"

The court official nodded, the scowl momentarily slipping from his face. "There is very little to say beyond what is already known. She was found sleeping in the gardens with no evidence of foul play."

"Did you see anyone running away?"

Baoyi thought. "There was one person—a young upstart by the name of Shaoyun. He was one of Princess Yansheo's admirers, but she had shown little interest. A few people reported seeing him leave the gardens around the time she took sick."

Khalad cleared his throat. "Lord Baoyi. You might not remember me, but I am Narel's assistant. He introduced me to you once."

Baoyi peered curiously at Khalad; then his expression changed, softening. "My apologies. Khalad, wasn't it? I remember, we met at Kion once. I had no idea... Is Narel in trouble?"

"I don't know. He has a habit of leaving when it suits him," Khalad lied glibly. "He hasn't returned from Santiang, and I was worried."

"I am sorry we are meeting again under these circumstances." Baoyi thawed considerably. "The situation has been complicated further by your...princess's...arrival. I shall send out search parties of my own in the city."

"I hope you don't mind if we still conduct our own search?"

"Of course not. I wish us both all the success." His clerk hurried forward, looking harried with a clipboard tucked under his arm. He murmured something in Baoyi's ear, and the other man nodded. "I must go. Let me know if I can be of more assistance."

"We will. Thanks."

Shadi lowered her voice as we left the room. "What are your thoughts on the emperor and this Baoyi, you two?"

"It's difficult to say for sure without a heartsglass," Khalad said. "But Baoyi does sound genuinely concerned about Master."

"It might be good to keep communications with him open," Zoya decided. "He might find information we may not have access to. The emperor's an admirer of asha, without a doubt, but it doesn't seem likely that it was he who engineered these palace wards. It must have been someone of great skill, and I don't see a Daanorian having that ability."

"Have you ever considered that the elder asha might have a hand in this?" I asked quietly.

Zoya's mouth fell open. "That's crazy, Tea. Whatever their mistakes, they would never sink so low as to betray Kion."

"They possess a False book much like I had."

Shadi frowned. "They might have confiscated it from someone else in the past. Do you have any other proof?"

"No," I was forced to admit. That Aenah had told me didn't mean much either. But...

The pretty asha patted me reassuringly on the shoulder. "Let's keep an open mind. I would say the duke is a far more viable suspect in this, with more evidence stacked against him."

"I take it magic isn't something they can easily get at in Daanoris?" Fox asked.

"Daanorian emperors of old have banned the practice of magic. Some nobles once dabbled in them or at least paid those skilled in the runes, with horrific results. The Daanorians imposed little restrictions on their magic, and twenty years of war soon decimated their population. It took Odalia, Kion, and the Yadosha city-states to put an end to the fighting, and every Daanorian ruler since then has pledged to never use runes. Even heartsglass was prohibited. That they have wards in place is suspicious in itself. Using magic to prevent other people from using magic sounds a little hypocritical to me."

"But Emperor Shifang himself is keen on magic?"

"Not quite. His interest lies in the *azi* for the most part, given its similarity to his royal crest." Shadi shrugged. "Hopefully, Emperor Shifang's fascination with Princess Inessa shall work in our favor. In the meantime, Fox, try not to get yourself stabbed. You're a little harder to explain."

"I'll try, milady."

Khalad shut the door behind us, briefly pressing his ear against the door. Then he prowled the room, carefully tapping at the walls.

"Why all the secrecy, Khalad?"

"We need to go into the city," the forger said quietly, pitching his voice lower. "I tried to earlier, but the guards stopped me under Tansoong's orders."

"The old man might not be as accommodating as we thought," Kalen growled. "Didn't they promise to allow us to search?"

"Sure—eventually, once the *savul* has been neutralized.

Sorry, Tea, but the sooner we can get to that daeva, the sooner we can search."

"I'd have done it already if I knew where it was," I said. "Or if I could control the *azi* to search for it. But how certain are you that the Heartforger is in the city?"

"Master keeps a small house in Santiang."

Zoya stared at him. "Why didn't you tell us?"

"It slipped my mind," Khalad admitted. "He treats patients as a regular physician would, without using any magic, so he's never gotten into trouble."

"Do you know where this house is?"

"No, but I can find it."

"Let's give ourselves a few days to assess the politics in the palace first," Zoya suggested. "I do not want to have to fight my way out of another kingdom so soon. We'll need to ferret out more information about this Shaoyun fellow. It's a long shot, but at least it's a lead. Besides, I was never one to do things halfway."

"No, you don't," Shadi said serenely, and Zoya blushed again.

·· ≥I∕ ··

It was difficult to find answers from the servants using only gestures and the most basic Daanorian I knew, but I finally found the gardens where Emperor Shifang was giving Princess Inessa the royal tour. It was an immense field, with each bush carefully clipped and tailored so none were out of place, and much of the shrubbery was shaped into different variations of dragons. The emperors of Daanoris, I thought, had a particular and peculiar fetish.

I felt Fox's irritation. My brother leaned against a tree, glowering. Princess Inessa's heartsglass told me she was bored, though she sent enthusiastic nods and wide smiles her fiancé's way. She maintained a death grip on her collar and frequently snuck glances back at Fox to reassure herself she was not alone with the emperor.

I could understand his impatience. Every day we lingered, the chance of Prince Kance dying increased. Not for the first time, I cursed the barriers. Without them, we might have found the old forger by now, broken Inessa's engagement under the threat of the *azi*, and left.

"Tell me more about Daanorian empresses," Inessa said sweetly. "Were they brave fighters? Did they take command of armies?"

"They were as able as men," came the proud response, translated through Tansoong. "Emperors are selective when it comes to wives. Should a ruler become incapacitated, they take over in his stead and command the same obedience. When Emperor Hansun fell dangerously ill, it was Empress Kalka who led the army to victory against Tresea, with only six hundred men against their thousand. And Queen Meili successfully conquered Arhen-Kosho when she married the sickly Emperor Jien, losing that kingdom only after her death. All young, blushing innocents before their marriage—as is required of them, naturally—yet with the courage of the gods in their blood. And with you by my side, my love, we shall lead Daanoris into further greatness." He took her hand and kissed the inside of her wrist. Chagrin surged out at me from Fox's end.

Where's Likh? I asked quietly.

I think Inessa took pity on him and sent him to his room was the terse response.

You know, if you're really bothered by this, you should speak up.

Who said it was bothering me?

You're not as good at hiding your emotions as you were before I first drew the Veiling, *Fox.*

He scowled at me. *That's none of your business.*

That's never stopped you before.

I don't like it, all right? It's one thing to be engaged to Prince Kance, and it's another to be betrothed to an emperor from another kingdom she knows nothing about! I saw the way he eyes her. She isn't a person to him—she's just another expensive ornament to display! I'd like to strangle that royal neck!

We've been in the Daanorian palace for barely a day, Fox. Let's not set the fastest world record for bad manners.

I'm not going to lose my temper in front of her. I'm just…I'm just…

You're what?

I don't know. Nothing. It was not like Fox to sound so helpless, and my heart went out to him.

I could have told Fox to forget her, that Inessa was capable of handling herself or, failing that, her choices were her own to bear. But living inside his head and being more susceptible to his emotions changes one's perspective.

Talk to her. She's as scared about this as you are. You can't be this dense.

He didn't try to deny it. *Not when the emperor is glued to her side all day, drooling like a little lapdog.*

Do I have to do everything myself? I didn't know if I was breaking Daanorian protocol by approaching the emperor, but I did it anyway. "Your Majesty?" My Daanorian was terrible, so I directed the words to Tansoong. "I'm sure you must have questions about the *azi*. Perhaps if you have time today…"

The emperor brightened at the mention of the *azi*. "But of course," Tansoong said with some reluctance. "Perhaps after his majesty has shown Princess Inessa around the rest of the gardens—"

"Oh, that won't be necessary," Princess Inessa broke in cheerfully. "I've taken up far too much of His Majesty's time today, and I'm quite tired. I think I shall retire to my rooms. I would appreciate it if he can keep Lady Tea company."

Tansoong relayed this to the emperor, who nodded. "If you say so, Princess. Some of the other concubines shall accompany you back to—"

"That won't be necessary either," Princess Inessa said, shying away from the suggestion. "I—I…"

"I'll escort her back," Fox interrupted.

Tansoong looked scandalized, and Princess Inessa hurriedly added, "He's my personal guard after all. I'm used to having him near."

A muscle ticked in Fox's jaw, but he said nothing else.

Emperor Shifang looked puzzled but nodded once her

request was translated. He took Inessa's hands in his and kissed them again. "Until we meet again, *qin'ai*," he said in the common tongue, with only the slightest accent.

"*Qin'ai*, my ass," Fox growled as he stomped after the Kion princess.

The emperor was inquisitive and not as oblivious or as simple as he first appeared. With Tansoong acting as translator, he asked me several questions about the *azi*, and I told him how instead of killing the daeva, I had found myself bonded to it, leaving Aenah's role out of the tale.

"I am glad you did not," he said. "Dragons have always been a symbol of prosperity in Daanoris. We have always considered the *azi* a noble beast. And you control it?"

"My influence is absolute, Your Majesty," I lied, not wanting any suggestions of weakness. "It is a good companion to me."

"I understand that Kion is quite different from the true kingdom. I have only been to Ankyo twice, and your customs are perplexing."

"I can understand why. In Kion, for example, the practice of concubinage has fallen out of use."

Emperor Shifang looked startled and laughed. "I thought asha were something of concubines themselves. Now I understand your surprise when I asked for Lady Likh. We did not mean to offend you."

"Does this mean His Majesty will no longer pursue…ah, Lady Likh?"

The man shook his head. "As I have decreed, so it must be

done. Lady Likh will be treated well. Royal concubines are highly respected here. Many would consider this an honor."

So much for extricating Likh. "We are accustomed to taking only one wife or husband in Kion."

The emperor shrugged. "I come from an unbroken line descended from gods and can take as many to wife as I wish. Some of my councilors do not like my choice of a Kion princess, but Inessa is different. Empress Alyx is wise to accede to my wish."

"This is my first time in Daanoris, and everything is new to me," I apologized, retreating from dangerous ground. "Our healer has finished his assessment of the princess, and he wants to know if anything unusual happened before her collapse."

The emperor frowned, worried. "I do not think so. My cousin was quite the typical Daanorian noblewoman—quiet and refined for her age, though keen on attending parties, as girls are wont to do."

I sensed his impatience and soon begged my leave. I caught up to Tansoong as he too left the king. "Our healer has questions about Princess Yansheo. Did anyone visit her in the days leading up to the party?"

"No, our women do not interact with foreigners beyond our social functions."

"What about Princess Yansheo's admirers?"

"Minor nobles, no one she should've treated seriously. Prince Mailen and Prince Feiwong come from good enough houses. And there was the young Shaoyun, an impulsive young man, prone to speaking before thinking. His family is of some minor importance in the outer provinces, and to set his sights on someone like the princess displays arrogance on his part. I have not seen him since she fell sick, and good riddance to that."

I hid my distaste. "Did you invite foreign visitors to her party?"

"Yes, mostly from Tresea. Of course, we extended an invitation to the Kion express and the Odalian king, but they were unable to attend. But I do recall Odalia sending a representative."

"A representative?"

"Yes. It came as a surprise, for we did not know he was coming until he was already at Miekong." The official's beard bristled. "But we learned he was a relative of the king's, and he was quite contrite. Perhaps his messengers had gotten lost, and his missive failed to reach us."

"Who was this relative?"

"The Duke of Holsrath, milady. Brother to the king himself. He was quite cordial to the young princess at her party, as I remember. We rarely have people from Odalia at important functions, and she was quite pleased that he had come all the way to make her acquaintance."

*T*HE HEAD COOK OF THE *Daanorian palace's kitchens, while understandably frightened, displayed that brand of courage common in those who take immense pride in their work and refused to leave his domain for something so trite as a hostile takeover. The Dark asha had chosen not to impinge on his territory, asking for very little in her choice of viands during our stay, but it was difficult to scale back on banquets when you had spent most of your life serving as an emperor's chef.*

Today was a different story. Word of Princess Inessa's visit was quick to spread, and at the bone witch's command, a table was wheeled into the throne room, sideboards groaning with many Daanorian delicacies: sweet and sour pork in a delicate plum sauce topped with coriander, diced chicken in simmered dried chili and fried peanuts, strips of roasted duck wrapped in celery and served in a sweet-potato-and-vinegar soybean sauce. Fried wonton and lamb dumplings rounded out the sides of the silver plates. This was a banquet fit for kings, and my mouth watered from the savory smells as each tray was uncovered.

Not even the princess remained unaffected for long. She eyed several of the dishes with longing and appeared to be summoning every measure of willpower not to reach for the nearest plate.

"These aren't just for display," the asha reminded her. "They're all quite edible."

"I'm not that hungry." A small growl issued from her stomach, amplified by the silence.

"If you've been traveling with the army, then you've had little to eat the last few weeks. The food is not poisoned if that's what you're concerned about." To prove it, the asha selected a small strip of chicken and bit into it. "Bard, you are more than welcome to join us."

I confess that my hunger was quick to overpower my good manners. I reached for a piece of lamb dumpling; it tasted like heaven.

"Bard?" The princess stared at me, then back at her. "He is here to tell your story because you have no intentions of surviving this, do you?"

"Why are you here, Inessa? Judging from the lack of guards in your wake, you told no one you were coming. Not even Fox."

"I'm good at sneaking in and out of palaces. And I've had ample time to explore the Daanorian palace, as you know. You stationed no guards."

"Your entrance did not escape my daeva's attention. It takes great courage to walk past them, knowing full well what they can do."

The princess gulped. "I was terrified. But I know you could not possibly be the monster they are making you out to be. Please, Tea. Stop this madness. Kalen would not have approved of you seeking revenge on his behalf."

The bone witch ladled out tea into three porcelain cups. "I am not doing this for revenge on Kalen's behalf, Inessa."

"Prove me wrong!"

"Kalen, the princess is asking for you."

The princess froze, mouth agape, when Lord Kalen and Khalad

stepped into the room. She rose to her feet and fought to maintain her composure, though her voice still trembled. "The elders told me that… It's not possible…"

"The elders told you many things that are not possible," the bone witch said.

20

H E SWORE THE DUKE WAS there?" Khalad asked as he examined Prince Kance's heartsglass. For the last couple of days, the forger had shut himself in his room, only leaving to examine Princess Yansheo. While we were treated like honored guests, we still could not leave the palace compound to explore the city. Both Kalen and Fox had been keen to defy the orders, but Inessa and Zoya convinced them otherwise, arguing it was too big of a risk to attempt at the moment. The hunt for the *savul* was still under way, but without our help, it was a slow process.

Princess Inessa frowned. Today she was dressed in riding breeches and a plain shirt, much to my surprise. "That's impossible, isn't it? How can the duke be in two places at once? Is there a rune for something like this, Tea?"

"I know of an *Illusion* rune that might be feasible."

"Whoever did it could draw Heartsrune." Khalad turned Prince Kance's heartsglass, as if the glint from it could unlock secrets from within. "I've seen Holsrath's heartsglass, and he has no inclination for it. What about the other Daanorian suitor?"

"Yuanshao? Nobody's seen him since the party. His family lives in the Mekong province, so it's going to take a while to reach out to them for questions about his whereabouts. From what Zoya's gathered, the boy is something of the family's black sheep. He hasn't been home in months."

"I've been talking to Baoyi, like Zoya suggested," Khalad said. "He has his men combing the city but has found little."

"But you're sure you can find your master?"

"I think so. I know a few things Baoyi doesn't that I'd rather not share. He seems trustworthy enough. He relies a lot on his clerk, who seems pretty competent and good at keeping his master's secrets. But I can't say the same for any soldiers." He looked worried. "Normally I would trust Master to look out for himself, but this feels different. I hope he's all right."

"Would you like to hold it?" Inessa asked suddenly, offering Prince Kance's heartsglass to me.

"What?"

"I don't need to learn to read heartsglass to see how worried you are for him. I don't know how much you can see, but…"

I nodded, my fingers hovering over the delicate case. Prince Kance's heartsglass felt warm even from there; I could see a steady pulsing nearly hidden within its depths, like a heartbeat.

"Draw *Heartsrune* over it, Tea," Khalad instructed.

"The wards are still here, Khalad."

The white-haired boy only grinned. "Just do it."

I obeyed and was stunned to see the rune shimmer into life. Wisps of it settled around Prince Kance's heartsglass like a cloak— and flared up again, images blooming at its center.

I spotted glimpses of memory: of Kance as a child, playing tag with Kalen and Khalad while Inessa toddled after them, begging to join; of him as a teenager, poring over heavy tomes and old parchments; of riding on horseback at his father's side as they explored the limits of their kingdom's territories.

I saw sadness and grief from his mother's passing, carefully bottled away. I saw compassion and understanding as he calmed a weeping Kalen when word reached them of Holsrath's imprisonment. I saw fear and worry as he watched Khalad's heart flame silver, marking his brother's path away from the throne and into the often-unappreciated life of a Heartforger. I saw resignation mixed with determination when he was made King Telemaine's heir—no longer the second son but next in line to rule Odalia. I saw the comfort and strength he derived from having Kalen as a protector, Khalad for his support, and Princess Inessa as a trusted friend and confidante. But I saw no romantic love for her there.

And then I saw our first meeting, watched as I blushed and stumbled over my words with Fox grinning by my side. I saw the Falling Leaf *cha-khana* and how he kept his head, kept me safe from the horde of skeletal rats I resurrected. I saw his admiration and respect as he watched me take down the *aeshma*, his pleasure and happiness when I presented him with that ill-fated pendant for his birthday.

But though I scoured his heartsglass, I could find no love for me either.

I bowed my head. I had never expected it, surely never demanded it, whatever my feelings for him. But the blow wasn't as bad as I had expected. A few months ago, this might have devastated me. Now I felt only a wistful sadness.

And, inexplicably, like a weight had been lifted off my shoulders. That revelation stunned me.

Do you want to talk about it? I could hear Fox ask.

There's nothing to talk about. I don't chase after people who don't feel the same way about me as I do about them—who I just realized I don't have the feelings for that I thought I had. Didn't you do the same thing with that Jezebel girl and her Maharven?

It's Gisabelle. *And why do you keep remembering that blasted man's name but not—*

I giggled aloud and stopped. Khalad and Inessa were goggling at me. "Sorry. I was…thinking of something else."

"You're not angry?" Inessa asked.

"Actually, I feel relieved. As odd as it sounds."

"I'm sorry."

"I'm not. I don't regret it." And then I did a double take. "You knew?"

The princess laughed. "Not this, no. If anything, it confirmed something else I had already suspected. How did you do that, Khalad?"

"Heartsrune is a forging rune more than it is a regular rune or a Dark one, though we can all draw from it. Wards block both offensive and defensive magic, but forging is neither."

"I didn't know this," I confessed, though that somehow made sense.

Khalad grinned. "We don't give away our secrets. Weren't you due at the courtyard for practice with Kalen?"

"I'm coming with you, Tea." The princess tucked Kance's heartsglass inside her shirt. "I'm supposed to be training with Fox."

"Thank you." It was easy to underestimate Khalad. He was quiet and unassuming, but there was a reason the old Heartforger had chosen him for his successor.

"Don't mention it. Zoya and Shadi should be along soon." His silver heartsglass gleamed. *This too shall pass*, it seemed to tell me.

"There's something I want to talk to you about while we walk," Princess Inessa said. "Something I'd like your opinion of. It's about my engagement to Shifang."

"What about it?" I asked.

She flashed me a grin. "I might know a way to wriggle myself out of it."

·· ⁣࿊⁣ ··

Kalen and Fox were already in the courtyard, and so were an alarming number of guards and courtiers who had come to watch. To my astonishment, Emperor Shifang was present, and so were Tansoong and Baoyi. Likh was also beside the Daanorian ruler, his tall, slim figure wrapped in the exquisite peach-and-silver *hua* Rahim had made for him, with a cluster of shorter women in flowing silks nearby; obviously, they were some of the royal concubines. The emperor made no bones about paying court to the male asha, having taken the latter's hand in his. Likh was looking around frantically, trying to find an excuse to step away without causing offense.

But all eyes soon turned to Princess Inessa. Aside from her casual shirt and breeches, her hair was pulled back and her face unadorned.

Tansoong was sputtering. "Princess, it is scandalous to wear such clothes in public!"

"This is what the women of my kingdom wear for sword practice, my lord," Princess Inessa said gravely. "It is our custom."

"But you have no need for a sword! You are the emperor's betrothed!"

"For as long as I have a kingdom, then I will always have need of a sword. And I am prepared to fight for it as well as any man here."

There were a few murmurs among the Daanorians. Emperor Shifang asked Tansoong a question, and the official stuttered out a response.

The emperor laughed and clapped his hands. Likh took the opportunity to move away to my side. "I was so sure he was going to find out about me," he breathed.

"Likh, you're more feminine than I am."

"Oh, I wasn't referring to that...although that had me

worried too. I was snooping around the palace when he found me
and asked me to accompany him here."

"What were you looking for?"

"I was looking at the palace wards. Kalen was right—it's
more complicated than regular spells, but I think there's a way to
untangle them."

"Are you definite about this, Likh?"

He grinned. "It's similar to zivar making, really. Think of
magic as a spool of yarn. You can make complex patterns with it,
but sometimes, some of Chesh's spells get a little too heavy for
the accessories we use. I'm usually the one tasked with unraveling the thread back into the spool, so to speak. It just takes
patience."

"You do know I don't understand half of what you're saying,
right?"

"I guess it's something those with purple heartsglass understand more than those with silver," the asha admitted. "Give me
more time to figure it out."

"His Majesty has had training with the sword as well," Baoyi
translated, looking like he'd taken a bite of lemon. "If the princess
wishes to defend Daanoris together with him, he would enjoy an
exhibition of her prowess." It was clear Baoyi wanted to express
more of his views about that, but his secretary tugged nervously at
his sleeve, shaking his head.

"Would you like to spar with me, Your Majesty?" The
princess sounded coy.

If anything, the emperor laughed even harder. Already, a

servant was hurrying forward with a small, ornate sword, the hilt meticulously covered in jewels despite its wooden blade.

Are you sure you want to let this happen? I hissed at Fox.

I know enough about etiquette not to scold the princess in front of another kingdom's emperor. Besides, she's good enough to beat him. Look at how he carries his sword. The gems on it are too polished to be anything but ceremonial. The emperor might think himself competent, but I know he isn't.

That's exactly what I was afraid of!

Tansoong was frantically shaking his head, issuing admonitions in Daanorian. The emperor paused and made a counteroffer.

"No fighting," the councilor said, this time to us. "Instead, the emperor and the princess shall display their skills for the public to judge."

That sounded like the better choice to me. Our hosts' hospitality would come to an abrupt end should Princess Inessa accidentally skewer the emperor with her blade.

Shifang started first. His series of maneuvers were nothing special, similar to the ones I was taught as a novice.

Princess Inessa responded with more intricate movements, her sword slicing through the air with precision. I was impressed. Fox was either an extremely good teacher or she was an exceptional student.

The emperor, however, was clearly not pleased. The routine he performed next was a little more complicated than his first, though still not up to par to the princess's initial display. The applause was louder when he finished but not entirely genuine.

Princess Inessa watched him carefully and proceeded to

sabotage herself when her turn came: dropped swords, flimsy moves, and clumsy spins. "I must concede to the emperor," she announced as she ended. "I cannot begin to match his skill, and it would be futile to continue this further."

The message was relayed back to the emperor, whose spirits were noticeably buoyed. I felt Fox scowl. Princess Inessa bowed prettily to the emperor and handed her wooden sword back to my brother, her hand now tightly clutched over her collar, as was her habit.

Lose the battle to win the war, I reminded Fox.

I know, but I can't stand that she's forfeiting to that insufferable ass.

One soldier glanced over at me and said something to his comrade. They laughed.

Kalen snarled something in Daanorian, cutting off their laughter. Then one of the men offered what sounded like a challenge. Kalen's face broke into a wolfish grin.

"We're going to do something different today, Tea. You're going to face off against those two arrogant idiots in mock combat."

"What?!"

"At the risk of sounding immodest, fighting me is a lot different than fighting two guards who can barely tell which direction to parry. I've seen them spar. Trust me, you'll do fine."

"But—"

"Anything I wanted." Kalen's voice was soft and studied. "You promised me, remember?"

It's a good way to measure your progress, Fox murmured.

"If it means anything to you," Kalen continued, "he said

you didn't look like you knew how to use a man's sword, except to act as its sheath."

"Really?" I stared hard at the men.

"Really."

"Well, there's a compelling reason to hit their faces with something sharp. Are you sure?"

"Trust me." Kalen's voice sounded odd, any emotion in his tone stifled. But there was quiet confidence in the way he looked at me, and that gave me courage.

"OK."

One of the men lagged behind as the other strode forward to face me first. I held my sword at an angle, waiting. He had several inches over me though was still not as tall as Kalen. But the Deathseeker had trained me to calculate my reach against people of varying heights. By the time he'd shifted his sword and lunged, I knew what to do.

My blow took him by surprise. The insult still had me seething, and I'd placed more strength into it than I normally would have, knowing it would hurt worse. The man's sword passed harmlessly over my head because I had already ducked and slammed the tip of my blade up into his chin. A regular sword might have decapitated him; this knocked him out immediately.

The crowd cheered, Likh and the concubines being the loudest.

"Don't get cocky!" Kalen yelled at me.

Not wanting to suffer the same fate as his friend, my second opponent was cautious, circling me and biding his time. I took the initiative this time, striking only to have it parried. Without pausing, I moved again and scored a glancing blow on his side. The man was fairly competent, but I'd been training with the best fighter in Odalia for months. To be competent was no longer enough to beat me.

I delivered quicker, more decisive hits on his legs and shins while he desperately tried to move his blade in time to counter mine. But I was faster. I might not have been as strong, but my mind was mapping the holes in his defense, finding the best moves to use. My training wasn't enough to fight Kalen on equal terms, but it made me much more than adequate when facing others. I just hadn't realized it before.

I spun, angling my sword as if to attack his midsection. He moved to block, and I switched targets in midblow. The man dropped to the floor, stunned and a little concussed.

The courtyard was silent. Inessa and Likh stared at me in awe, but Fox was beaming. Tansoong looked at me with amazement, and Baoyi was silent, though there was a small, reluctant smile on his face. Even the emperor was studying me carefully, like he was seeing me for the first time.

A loud sound broke the quiet.

"That's *my* Tea!"

Never had I ever seen Kalen laugh that long or that loud. He was nearly doubled over, one hand against the wall to hold himself up. But there was no derision in his heartsglass, none of the dry amusement usually on display.

There was only pride—fierce, unabashed pride.

"YOU HAVE AN ULTERIOR MOTIVE *for coming here, Princess,*" *the Dark asha said.* "*You aren't here to ask me to stop my work. You're here to plead for my brother's life.*"

Princess Inessa stiffened. "*I will not deny that. If you die—*"

"*Then so will he. Every action I do against the kingdoms and the elder asha will increase the likelihood of retaliation against him. He knew the risks. You knew the risks.*"

The noblewoman trembled. "*I don't care.*"

The Dark asha smiled and took the princess's hands in her own. "*You trusted me enough to walk past the daeva guarding the palace, knowing you would not be harmed. Trust me for a little bit longer.*"

"*Is there no way for me to change your mind?*"

"*If I succeed, then you will have everything you want. No more wars, no more daeva.*" *She turned back to the window.* "*No more magic,*" *she added softly.* "*How is he?*"

The princess hesitated. "*Worried about you.*"

I watched the asha's lips move, sounding each word carefully, afraid that they might take the shape of other emotions she did not want to voice aloud. "*Tell Fox I am sorry for everything. But there is no turning back now.*"

"*Apologize to him yourself, Tea!*" *The princess rose from her seat, trembling with anger.* "*He's been waiting for you for all these months!*"

He can no longer sense your thoughts through your bond, but he refuses to believe you've abandoned him! Even now, he waits!"

The bone witch folded her hands behind her back. "I did it with his best interests in mind."

"Then come with me to see him!"

"What would you have me say, Inessa?" The Dark asha's voice hinted of winter. "Would you have me return to Kion to be tried and executed for crimes I did not commit? For my brother to die with me? You told me of your grandmother's dalliance with a familiar. Did she regret it? Will you regret loving a dead body given a semblance of life? In time, you will resent him for not being human. Will you spend the rest of your life loving a corpse, Inessa?"

The princess was pale. "You have no right to speak to me that way."

"My brother lives because of me. I have every right."

"If you are innocent, then my mother will—"

"Do nothing. The Willows' influence is far too ingrained in Kion's psyche to grant me a fair trial."

"But you killed her, Tea. Fox saw you."

The bone witch's hands clenched. I heard the rumblings of the daeva outside, the aeshma's hiss.

"You killed so many people, Tea. They were your friends—"

"Enough!" The daeva's howling grew. Then came the sound of stones shattering; one of the beasts had struck a column, destroying it with a violent sweep of its tail.

And then Lord Kalen appeared, his hand on her shoulder. The Dark asha closed her eyes and took long, steady breaths. The daeva quieted but was still uneasy. "If I cannot convince you of my innocence,

Your Highness, then there is no hope for me, and we do nothing now but waste time. You have my word that I will do everything in my power to save Fox. I make no promises for everything else."

The bone witch's hands unfurled. Her nails had scored deep, painful-looking grooves into her skin, red blood dripping down the floor.

21

THE NUMBER OF SOLDIERS IS often directly proportional to the importance of the noble in tow; in Prince Kance's case, over half of the standing army had been dispatched to protect him while I slew the *aeshma*.

The emperor of Daanoris was not only the troops' undisputed leader but was also venerated by the people as a god-king, so nearly the whole army turned up for the hunt, to my horror. Daeva are not predictable creatures, and my worry during Kance's excursion was magnified tenfold here.

Emperor Shifang was just as adamant about seeing me in action, perhaps inspired by my impromptu match against his soldiers. Inessa was as insistent too.

Khalad, the most prudent noble of the bunch, elected to stay behind with Likh and Shadi. Both Tansoong and Baoyi accompanied the emperor. Zoya was practically purring, here in the open, away from the palace, where we could once more channel runes. As soon as the wards were gone, I had instinctively reached out to find the *azi*, and the relief when it responded to my thoughts was enormous.

I had taken the opportunity to scan the emperor and his officials with *Scrying* but could not find anything out of the ordinary. Shifang was oftentimes too concerned with himself for his thoughts to be relevant. Tansoong's mind thrived on petty details such that most issues of substance were beyond his capacity. Baoyi's thoughts were calm, his mind sorting through the paperwork still needing work in the palace, though that was overlaid by apprehension concerning the daeva we now hunted. Experience told me this did not exempt them from an alliance with any of the Faceless, but it seemed less likely somehow.

Fox was quiet; we were riding separately for once, with me on Chief and him on a gray Daanorian stallion beside the princess. I understood the emotions thrumming through his head: anger and annoyance that Inessa was along for the ride and the same frustrations I felt about the potential casualties. But riding at the forefront was grim eagerness. We were finally going to face the daeva that killed him. Revenge had been a long, exhausting road, and we were nearing the end.

I rode with Kalen. We had little chance to talk since reports came of the *savul* being spotted near Lake Kaal. In this vast expanse of fields and small hills, I could feel the *azi* more keenly in my mind. Free of care, it coasted along the edges of Daanoris far above the clouds, aimless and happy. I envied it.

"Kalen?"

"Hmm?" His eyes were trained ahead, where the lake gleamed back at us.

I toyed with the sword on my hip. "You always said my fighting wasn't up to par."

"That's true."

I glowered. "I would have appreciated a little more encouragement."

"There's no encouragement on the battlefield, Tea. Surviving means you've improved, but that doesn't guarantee living through the next fight."

We were the first to reach the lake. I dismounted quickly, as did he, and heard the others behind us following suit. I stared out into the waters. It looked no different to me than the lake back home, and I wondered if the *savul* too had made Lake Kaal its home the way *azi* had made Lake Strypnyk its residence.

"It's so peaceful here," Princess Inessa murmured.

"Be on your guard, Princess," Zoya told her. "We're in the daeva's territory, not the other way around. Fox, don't let her out of your sight."

"I'm not planning to."

The princess frowned. "I'm not going to run around and get myself lost, Zoya. I'm not a child."

"When you decided to tag along, you became exactly that," my brother told her.

The girl muttered something under her breath. They had

finally stopped avoiding each other outside of training, though being civil was still difficult.

The emperor looked around disdainfully and issued a question.

"What did he say?" I asked Zoya.

"The emperor may look regal, but I'm not sure if he takes his brains out to exercise often enough for my taste. He wants to know why the *savul* hasn't shown up yet. Do you sense anything amiss?"

I directed my thoughts toward the blue waters. I felt the *azi* graze against my mind. "No, there's nothing here."

"The *savul* may have moved on," Inessa suggested.

"It's a creature of camouflage," Zoya said. "It can mask its presence well enough that you would barely know it was there until it was on top of you."

"But if Tea couldn't sense anything…"

"No," Fox broke in quietly. "It's nearby."

"How do you know that?"

"Because *I* can sense it." Fox clutched at his chest. His face was strained, but I could not feel his pain.

"Fox?"

"My scars…hurt."

Inessa drew in her breath. "Was this the daeva that…?"

"I want most of your soldiers surrounding the king and Princess Inessa at all times," Kalen instructed Tansoong. "Do not approach the lake until we investigate. I want the rest to spread out and search. If you find it, do not engage the beast in battle. Do not attack and neither should you incite it to attack you. Avoid it at all costs and report to either Lady Tea or me immediately." He was already on his horse, leaving me to glare at his retreating back as they rode away.

Fox, stay with Inessa.

Tea, where are you going?

I ignored him and clambered up Chief to ride after the Deathseeker. He was deliberately ignoring the other groups of men, making for the thicker parts of the woods surrounding the lake all on his own.

I caught up to him a few minutes later. Trees hid the lake from view, and within the heavy cluster of trees, it was like no one else was around.

"Are you seriously thinking of facing the daeva on your own?" I demanded, sliding off my horse. Kalen was already standing, sketching out runes in the air. I watched as *Light* flickered dimly, drifting higher up into the trees and bathing our surroundings in a soft, muted glow. Another rune was directed toward the ground, and I felt it spread, stretching out into the distance.

"I can look after myself."

"What is that?"

"A *Tremor* rune. If there's anything large and heavy coming our way for a good thirty miles around us, I'll know."

"What if it's in the lake?"

"Same premise." He stared at me. "Why are you here?"

"At the fight…" I paused. I'd seen pride for me shining as clear as day in his heartsglass, but there was another, much more profound emotion there too, though I couldn't describe it.

He hesitated. "It's natural to feel satisfaction, knowing my training had paid off."

"Are you still angry at me?"

He didn't answer.

"My offer still stands. You can do anything you want to me."

Kalen's jaw dropped half a heartbeat before I realized why.

"No! I meant that if I promise to do anything you want—no, that's not right either! I forced you against your will, so now I'm giving you the right to order me to do anything, even if I don't like it. No, wait!" I clutched at my head. "The words aren't coming out the way I want them to!"

"I understand what you're saying, however ineptly you phrase it." He stalked toward me, and despite my earlier bravado, I found myself pressed up against the trunk of a large tree with Kalen looming over me. "Anything and everything I want?"

I couldn't tell if he was kidding or if he was riling me up, as was his norm. There was both an earnestness and a reluctance to his face I'd never seen before, contradicting emotions warring for primacy, like he was about to tell me something he was going to regret but that had to be said. I couldn't glance down to gauge his heartsglass; he was too close, giving me little room to move, little room to look anywhere but up at him.

He looked intimidating, almost menacing, despite his lack of anger. But I wasn't afraid. If anything, I was…expectant. I could feel his heartsglass flare—with the *Heartshare* rune I had offered him back in Kion, I realized. I had not dispelled the magic; while diminished by the castle wards, out here in the open, it shone brightly.

"Do you really want to know what I want to do to you, Tea? Would you still be so willing if you did?"

He had never said my name that way before. I could feel his warm breath against my lips. He smelled nice, like pine and musk.

The sides of his mouth curved up. The rune flickered.

"I want you fighting five soldiers next time," he said quietly.

"Wh-what?"

He was already drawing back, the smirk still on his face. "Two soldiers is child's play. You're going to improve by *my* standards and not by anyone else's. I don't know how long we're going to stay here or what Inessa has up her sleeve to wheedle herself out of the emperor's marriage contract, but if you can't fight five soldiers by the time we leave, then you're still incompetent. Your heartsglass is palpitating, by the way."

With a growl, I pushed hard against his chest, but he barely budged. "You bumbass!" I shouted at him, clapping a hand over my heartsglass. I thought...I was so sure that he was going to—"I hate you!"

He chuckled. "Now we're *almost* even."

"Almost?! You—"

"Shh."

"Don't you dare shush me, you—"

"No, keep quiet." Kalen dropped to the ground, pressing his hand against the soil. "Do you feel that?"

I shook my head.

"Something large is moving this way."

"How can you be sure?"

He stared at me.

"Forget I said anything. Where is it?"

He stilled. "It's in the lake."

"That's impossible! I would have sensed it when I was—"

And then it was my turn to drop, the pain unbearable. I had dizzying visions, all juxtaposed on top of one another: an image of Kalen in front of me; an image of the *azi* in the air, roaring and veering off course; an image of Fox on his knees like I was, clutching at the scars on his chest and howling in pain; and an image of swamp water and marsh and of scale-tipped claws.

"Fox!" I gasped out. "Take me back to Fox!"

Kalen needed no explanation. He was already on his horse with me in his arms before I'd finished my sentence, Chief cantering behind us.

Zoya and Inessa were administering to Fox. My brother was breathing hard, his heartsglass wavering between silver and green. It was the first time I had ever seen it change color. His shirt was stained red.

"What's wrong with him?" Baoyi asked in alarm, riding up to us. "Who attacked?"

"No one." Inessa had a death grip on Fox's hand and was on the verge of tears. "He just collapsed."

I tore Fox's shirt open. His wounds had opened up and were bleeding profusely.

I traced the *Bloodletting* rune in the air, to no effect. Desperate, I dove into his mind and staggered back from the overwhelming pain there.

"What's happened to him?" Zoya asked grimly.

"He has some connection to the *savul*." I turned back toward the lake, allowing the new, strange mind into my own. The *savul* might have been good at camouflage, but Fox's unexpected link to the daeva was my only chance at detecting it.

It was there; basic, primal thoughts I could sense but could neither touch nor influence and a vision of something dark and foreboding rising to the surface of the lake.

The *savul* broke through the surface, screaming. While it was the color of the blue waters it had jumped out of, it shifted to a spectrum of olive greens when it landed among the grass. It was corpulent as wide as a barn, its massive fishlike scales shining.

Lightning shot out of Kalen's hands, peppering the creature's hide. It hissed in anger, turning to face him.

"Get the princess and the emperor out of here!" Zoya yelled to the army, most of whom were staring at the *savul* in horror. Tansoong was the first to act, grabbing Emperor Shifang's hand and leading him away, shouting at the guards around them to follow, though he was quaking so hard, it was a wonder he managed to remain upright.

"No!" Inessa refused to relinquish her hold on Fox. "I'm not going!"

"Princess!" Zoya shouted. "Stop being a twit and go with the soldiers!"

But the girl shook her head doggedly, lifting my brother to his feet and staggering under his weight.

I put myself between her and the *savul*; I could touch its

mind, but try as I might, I could do nothing to commandeer its thoughts, which stood heavy and putrid against my own. I could feel Fox's pain through our bond, but I gritted my teeth and forced my way through it. My best chance at helping him was to attack the *savul* first.

Zoya had taken up defenses beside Kalen, fire shooting out from her fingertips as she spun runes as large as she was, sending torrents of flames upward. But despite all their efforts, the *savul* simply shook off the excesses and cawed mournfully at the sky. It leaped into the air, its six limbs extending like a twisted, grotesque toad's, and landed on one of the soldiers unfortunate enough to be in its way. There was a sickening crunch, and the creature's head lowered, prepared to enjoy its feast.

"It's not working!" Zoya hollered.

I turned toward the sky. I could feel the thrum of the wind underneath the *azi*'s spread wings as it closed the distance.

The *savul* turned to look, almost quizzically, at my brother on the ground and at the princess still clinging to him. It took a step toward us and then another.

"Zoya, take them away," I said through gritted teeth, trying to sort out all the different contrary perspectives running through my head as I wove more *Compulsion*. But the runes did nothing, and the *savul* continued its inexorable trek toward us, yellow eyes filled with malice.

One of the soldiers beside Inessa turned, his eyes suddenly blank. He lifted his sword, and both the princess and Zoya were too busy watching the daeva to realize the danger.

"Look out!" I screamed, tearing myself away from the *savul* and redirecting the *Compulsion* swiftly into the man's mind. I found the exact same barrier that had stymied me back in Kion when the Odalian soldiers had attacked the city.

Before the blow could fall, a hand reached up, gripping the blade of the sword. Blood flowed down his arm, but Fox was relentless, ripping the blade away. The soldier staggered back, and Fox punched him, hard enough that he was out in an instant.

Don't worry about me, Tea! Focus on the savul*!*

Zoya dragged both Princess Inessa and Fox away, leaving me to face the approaching daeva. "Some of the soldiers are being controlled!" I yelled behind me, and she understood. A few more soldiers, eyes glazed over and swords raised, were already ambling toward Inessa and Fox but were thrown back several feet by a surge of *Hurricane* and a quick weave of Zoya's fingers.

"Tea!" I could hear Kalen yelling, but I refused to budge, concentrating on the solitary speck in the sky flying above us, growing closer and closer until—

The *savul* lunged forward with its serpentlike tongue extended and jaws open to reveal several rows of brown teeth. And then Kalen was there, grabbing me and angling his body so his back was exposed to the *savul*, *Shield* runes popping up around us.

Master.

With a loud wail, the *azi* landed, one of its heads biting savagely into the *savul*'s neck before it could strike us, sending deep-ocher-colored blood spurting up from the wound. With a horrible cry, the beast fell back, righting itself before turning to face the new threat.

"Are you OK?" Kalen whispered against my hair.

I nodded, fighting off my dizziness. The confusing perspectives were now down to only two—my own and that of the three-headed dragon before us. "You idiot. Why did you...?" He couldn't have known that the *azi* was on its way. And yet he...

"Because you make me careless, Tea." He punched out more *Shield* runes that glowed in the air as more of the blank-eyed soldiers turned. "What's happening to them?"

"Same as in Kion. There are seeking stones here." I wove *Strangle* this time, still keeping my eyes on the *azi* and *savul*, who continued to watch each other. I've never seen daeva fight each other before, and I didn't know what to expect.

The runes took hold, and I found a glow inside one of the soldiers approaching Inessa and Fox. With all the strength I could summon, I poured everything I had into shattering that light. It broke, dissipating from view, but the soldier gasped. He stumbled forward, blood pouring out of his mouth, and collapsed.

I watched him fall, stunned, and tried to move forward. Kalen pulled me back. "Focus on your pet, Tea!"

"But..."

The *azi* hissed. Its three heads threaded through the air and its wings extended, drawing to its full height and span. Not to be outdone, the *savul* squatted and let out a hoarse croaking sound, blowing up its body like a bullfrog's. Its outline shimmered in the air, green scales becoming more and more translucent until, before our eyes, it faded from view.

"Camouflage!" I saw nothing, but the grass bent, web-shaped footprints stamping onto the ground, toward the *azi*. And then they stopped.

"It's jumping!" I barreled into the *azi*'s mind. We swiveled to face the *savul* just as it reappeared, its scaly body slamming into us. I felt its talons rake into our body, and we cried out, both in pain and with rage.

We opened all three of our mouths and breathed firestorm onto the *savul*. It shrieked, the heat from the flames intense enough to burn its limbs and a goodly portion of its body. Runes didn't work, I realized, but daeva could kill its own.

The air reeked of charred flesh and smoke, the stench burning our eyes. Our chest hurt, the wounds from where the *savul* had raked its talons pulsating with every heartbeat. I could still feel Fox's pain as he struggled to defend himself and Inessa from the soldiers going after them. Inessa had yanked out a sword from one of the fallen and was training it on the approaching mob, trembling. "Get out of here!" Fox rasped.

"I'm not leaving you!"

Zoya successfully kept most of the Daanorians at bay, but I knew she was tiring quickly. Of the elemental runes, *Wind* required the most strength, and she'd been slamming dozens of soldiers into the ground with it.

I was conscious enough of my own body to know that Kalen still held on to my limp form. I could feel the power of the runes he was hammering in the air, following Zoya's lead and pushing the soldiers away with more *Wind*. But he was tiring too.

"Tea, leave one of the stones untouched if you can! I've got an idea!" Zoya clapped her hands above her head, and a sinkhole opened underneath most of the men, sending them tumbling down.

"Copycat," Fox murmured.

"I'm saving your ass, you ass!" Zoya had been around Polaire more often than she should have.

Kill, I told the *azi*, not wanting to prolong the fight and Fox's pain, and we unleashed more torrents of fire in the *savul*'s direction. It avoided the onslaught, leaping high into the air again.

Its attack patterns told me the *savul* preferred close fighting, relying on its camouflage to get away unscathed. I kept ourselves still, one of our heads remaining immobile and presenting itself as an obvious target as the nearly invisible daeva descended toward us, its talons primed to strike. I shoved away my disgust and poured myself into the *azi*'s mind, anticipating the blow.

It never reached us. From behind the *savul*, both our other heads lashed out, jaws snapping at either side of the *savul*'s neck. A fountain of blood spurted into the sky.

The frog-like daeva squalled. It thrashed its nearly decapitated head frantically from side to side, but that did nothing to stop the torrent of russet-colored blood from flowing to the ground, staining and rotting everything it touched. The Daanorian soldiers stumbled back, clutching at their heads. The *Compulsion* surrounding them lifted briefly, and I could finally see the source: two of the men carried glowing orbs hidden within their clothes, and I wasted no time reaching for one with my mind and destroying it quickly.

"Over there!" I yelled at Zoya, pointing at the second man, and the asha moved with great speed. A small hurricane all but slammed the man to the ground, knocking him out.

I tried again. My *Compulsion* bored straight into the *savul*'s mind without any other interference. I could feel a part of it struggling still, furious that someone else had been given access to its brain.

And then, just as suddenly, I found myself punted out of its thoughts as the other presence occupying its head took back control.

Howling, the *savul* dissolved from view. I could hear it leaping, this time away from us, and just as quickly, its presence was gone.

The pain in my head diminished. Fox staggered to his feet, breathing easier, and dropped his sword as Princess Inessa hurled herself into his arms, heedless of his bloody state, and buried her face against his chest. Slowly, his arms closed around her waist.

From the corner of my eye, I saw Zoya rise from beside a fallen soldier. She caught my eye, smiled grimly, and carefully pocketed the seeking stone she had extracted from him.

Thank you. I was never sure to what extent the *azi* understood me, but it was enough. I stepped away from Kalen and allowed the *azi* to caress my face, nuzzling at my neck and shoulders as if searching for injuries. Finding none, all three heads cooed.

Master.

I watched the *azi* rise, tired but triumphant, to resume its exploration of the skies as it had been before we had interrupted its peace.

I turned to find Kalen looking back at me. He smiled, and I found myself smiling back, a warm glow settling over me. "We didn't kill it," I said, feeling foolish for stating the obvious.

"But you hurt the daeva badly. For now, that's good enough."

One of the men rose behind him. The Daanorian already had a knife drawn, too close for Kalen to turn in time, much less respond. One look at his mind told me this Daanorian was not being compelled, that he acted of his own volition.

I reacted on instinct. The *Compulsion* rune still hummed in the air, but the man was already swinging his dagger—

Die!

—and missed Kalen completely, the blade ramming into his own stomach.

Blood bubbled up from the soldier's mouth; wordlessly, he fell. Shocked, Kalen turned to see the Daanorian collapse on the ground, dead. But the man's eyes stared blankly back at me, wide open and accusatory.

*T*HE MAN HAD ARRIVED IN *the early morning, and like the princess,
no one barred his entry at the gates. He showed no fear before
the daeva that guarded the doors. His sword was useless in the face of
the horrors, but he held it as if that made no difference. His clothes
told me he was a military official of some importance. He was tall and
broad shouldered, and his long hair was tied back from his face. But
he had the Dark asha's eyes and coloring and the same stubborn set to
his mouth as hers did. He had visible cuts around his face and arms,
old wounds that showed no signs of healing.*

The monsters attempted intimidation; the nanghait *drew its
two faces close to the man's and hissed out its venom. A snarl rose from
the soldier's throat, and the beast flinched. The* savul *took a small hop
forward, but the man moved swiftly, flinging out his arm so the blade
he carried was a hair's breadth from its flattened snout.*

"Try me," he seethed, though the savul *did not. "You are lucky,
you blasted toad, that I no longer feel pain from your nearness, but I
will slice off your legs if you so much as blink those hideous eyes. Where
is Inessa? I swear by every god I know, Tea, if you have gone so far as to
harm her…!" He swung his sword in an arc to include both the* taurvi
and zarich *in his threats, both of whom were endeavoring to sneak up
behind him. "And leash your beasts!"*

Lord Kalen stepped through the doors of the palace, Princess

Inessa behind him. The man's gaze slid to her face. Reassured by what he saw there, he turned to the Deathseeker. "They said you were dead."

"What difference does that make? You are still against us."

"I have never been against Tea."

"Not from where I stand."

"She killed people, Kalen. She raised the undead to massacre soldiers!" His voice shook. "They ate men under my watch!"

"And your men would have massacred these Daanorians if she hadn't. What makes you any better?"

"You've changed since dying, Kalen. Are your feelings for my sister hindering your judgment?"

"Are your feelings for the princess hindering yours, Fox?"

They stared at each other, stubborn to the end, convinced it was the other that was wrong, like the disagreements all wars were made of.

Lord Fox moved so quickly that it took the sound of steel meeting steel for me to realize the fight had begun.

"Stop it!" Princess Inessa cried, but she was ignored. This was not the playful sparring sessions between friends that the bone witch had so fondly recalled. This was a brutal fight, waged by familiars who fought despite knowing neither one could be killed by the other.

A stroke of Lord Fox's blade was parried; a swing of the sword by Lord Kalen was countered. It was the Deathseeker who first drew blood. A flick of his wrist and a cut appeared over the other man's shoulder, though the latter showed no pain. Lord Kalen dealt a second blow to his side and then a third across his cheek, but Lord Fox rallied with two slices against the other man's shin and hand.

"Enough!" The air crackled from the force of the words. Both

combatants froze in midstrike. The bone witch stood by the entrance, hands fisted on either side of her. Princess Inessa stood with her, arms folded over her chest and looking just as furious.

"You've been practicing," Lord Kalen said. "You're much better than when we last fought."

"And still I struggle to keep up with you," Fox conceded wryly. "You're stronger than I remember. Inessa snuck out of camp to come here," he added in a quieter voice as they both turned to face their fuming paramours. "You were defending Tea. Why are we the ones in trouble?"

Without changing expression, the Deathseeker replied, "I don't know."

22

THE ENGAGEMENT CELEBRATION WOULD PUSH through regardless of the army's losses; Emperor Shifang insisted it would. "It is not the custom for the emperor to rescind his own orders," Tansoong informed us. "He is infallible."

"Half his army has fallen victim to someone else's *Compulsion*, and he worries about his *infallibility*?" Zoya was in a fighting mood. Her attempts to explain the spell had fallen on deaf ears. It took all our persuasion to keep the emperor from executing the soldiers for treason, finally getting him to understand the nature of *Compulsion*, if barely. The only good thing to come out of this was the emperor honoring his promise to let us into the city, to finally find the old forger. Not for the first time, I cursed my inability to act then, to seize the azi and turn on these Daanorians. But the old Heartforger was still somewhere in the city, and Inessa continued to insist on diplomacy despite everything.

"There is little to be learned about Kalen's would-be assassin," Shadi spoke up. "His name was Leehuang, and he was a loner. What is strange is that he joined the army voluntarily instead of waiting to be conscripted, like most."

"Did he have a family?" I asked quietly. "Children?"

Zoya and Shadi glanced at each other. "No family or friends," the latter said gently. "It's not your fault, Tea."

"I killed him. Of course it is."

"You told me he wasn't under any *Compulsion*," Zoya chimed in. "The chances that he was in league with one of the Faceless is likely. This isn't a man who was being forced to act against his will."

"What about the other man? The one I killed when I destroyed the seeking stone on him? Did he have family?"

"Tea..."

"Did he have family?"

"A wife and a son."

I bowed my head. We had gathered in Khalad's room, with Princess Inessa and Likh conspicuously absent. As the guest of honor, the Kion princess was preparing for her engagement party that night, convincing the court concubines that she needed only Likh to help her dress. Shadi and Kalen had combed through the palace, hunting for any more seeking stones in the vicinity, and came up with nothing.

Some of the dead soldier's blood had gotten under my fingernails. I rubbed my hands frantically against the sleeve of my *hua*, but try as I might, I could not rid myself of it.

"Are you OK?" Fox asked me quietly.

"I'm fine."

Do you want to talk about it?

No.

I think we should talk about it.

There is nothing to talk about.

Tea.

There isn't!

"What about the Shaoyun boy?" Shadi asked. "The missing suitor. Any word of him?"

Zoya shook her head. "They've questioned his family. They haven't heard from him in more than a year, but they also say that's not unusual. He travels frequently and spends most of his time in the cities."

"That makes our jobs harder. I hope the old forger's OK. Baoyi hasn't found any reason to think he's injured or worse, but it's hard to be sure when we can't find him ourselves."

"Inessa's finally convinced the emperor to let us visit the city tomorrow, at least. Now that we know there are Faceless agents inside Daanoris, let's err on the side of caution. Likh says he might know how to remove the wards."

Everyone turned to Likh, who had just entered the room.

"It's only a theory," he mumbled, blushing.

"Any theory's worth discussing at this point," Khalad said, encouraging him.

"Well," Likh began shyly, "the main problem is that there's not a separate ward in each room. It's one large ward woven throughout the castle, so I can't undo one part of it. But without access to any runes, I don't see how I can—"

"And that's why I'm brilliant," Zoya said with a grin, fishing out the seeking stone she'd taken during the *savul* fight. "The *Unraveling* rune doesn't need as much effort to channel. We can probably muster enough magic with this to destroy the wards, as long as we focus on the one spot that will undo the whole spell."

"I can start this instant," Likh babbled, jumping to his feet. "It might take a few days to figure out the weakest point, so the sooner I begin, the better."

"Don't dismantle anything until we find the forger," Zoya cautioned. "They might stage some new devilry if they knew what we're doing. Khalad, go with Likh."

"Why?" Khalad asked.

"*Why?*" Likh echoed.

"The forger's good at untangling complicated spells," Zoya told them brightly. "He'd be a big help. Get on with it already."

"Zoya," Shadi remonstrated. The asha shot her an innocent look.

"Usij isn't at the Haitsa mountains then," Kalen said suddenly after a beet-red Likh led a slightly confused Khalad out. "Everything points to him being in Santiang."

I killed my first man when I was fifteen, Fox continued doggedly. *I threw up for an hour afterward. I know how you feel, but you can't let it take over you.*

Leave me alone.

Tea, I'm only trying to help—

"Well, you're not!"

Startled faces look back at me. "Tea?" Zoya asked.

Flushing, I scrambled to my feet. "I have to get ready for the party," I mumbled, avoiding my brother's gaze. "I'm going ahead." I hurried out before anyone could stop me.

The long walk back to my room felt like it took forever, and my legs gave out the instant I reached my bed. I threw myself onto the covers and spent half an hour weeping furiously.

I'd never killed anyone before. Perhaps it was foolish of me to think I never would. Even worse, I knew I would do it all over again. I felt revulsion; I felt sick.

But I felt no remorse, not even for the poor soldier with the wife and son. With the assassin, all I could remember in those moments leading up to the kill was anger, fear that he would kill Kalen—and a curious sense of satisfaction.

Am I a bad person?

I hadn't expected Fox to answer, given how I'd left him, but his words came quickly, wrapping around me like a warm cloak.

You worry too much about being a good person to be a bad one.

I killed someone.

So did I. Many times. Does that make me a bad person?

Of course not.

I can't say that it gets easier, Tea. We may hold the sword, but it's circumstance that deals the killing blow. He sighed. *I don't know how to make this easier for you, love. That's always been the problem—it never gets easier. But taking a life is not supposed to be easy, and you are a good person. I never had any doubts about that.*

Thank you. I smiled into the darkness, the weight off my shoulders for the moment. Still, I looked down at my heartsglass, half expecting to see the beginnings of black there, as Aenah promised it would. But all I saw was silver.

•• ⌇ ••

Kion royal parties and balls were extravagant affairs, but the Daanorians put those memories to shame. I do not know how much was spent to finance this ball, but I was certain it surpassed the annual budgets of other smaller fiefs. Fireworks dotted the sky with explosions of color and light, and the resulting smell of gunpowder was an odd contrast to the scents of incense, roses, and perfume hanging heavily in the air.

Ice sculptures taller than I was depicted scenes from Daanoris's past: the successful war against Tresea; the first emperor of Daanoris, Golgolath, leading his soldiers into battle; his marriage to the beautiful Faimei. Some of the sculptures were not as historically accurate. One ice scene had the Great Hero Anahita the Mighty riding the skies on the *azi*, and the Daanoris's subsequent battles against Istera had not been as triumphant as these scenes made them out to be.

Five long tables were piled high with food, most of them delicacies I was not familiar with: roasted crackling pork belly, dumplings surrounded by soft, silken curds made of soy milk, spicy noodles in red and green pepper sauces, and braised white chicken in ginger-oyster dressing. I parked myself in front of the banquet table and helped myself. Morose as I was, I did love food.

Not for the first time that night, I wished Fox were there to make amends with, though no doubt he thought I needed more time to myself. The language barrier made it difficult to initiate conversation with the Daanoris, but a few of the noblemen persevered. Word had spread about the fight with the *savul*. Since the *azi* was venerated by the people of the kingdom, I soon attracted, much to my horror, a throng of male admirers clamoring for a dance.

Asha are trained to be more than fighters; we are entertainers, conversationalists, listening companions. Not wanting to cause a scene, I accepted the men's invitations, trying to inject as much cheer as I could with the little Daanorian that I knew.

Already I'd seen Shadi and Zoya, each with their own bevy of admirers. Much to my amusement, it was Likh who attracted the most number of men, and the terrified expression on his face only spurred them on.

Khalad approached the group surrounding the male asha, oblivious to the dark stares thrown his way. The boy's face lit up when he saw the forger approach and wilted somewhat when the latter began to talk. A few seconds later, and Likh was excusing himself from his admirers, glancing wistfully at the dance floor and then ruefully back at Khalad as they left together. For someone whose job was to examine heartsglass, I thought, Khalad was woefully inept when it came to reading Likh's.

"Pet *azi*?" my dance partner asked, my seventh for the night.

THE HEART FORGER 339

Every suitor I'd danced with had asked a variation of the same question, and it was becoming harder not to force my smile.

I had racked my brain for the Daanorian equivalent of "equal" earlier on but had given up. "Yes," I lied, for the seventh time that night. "Pet *azi*."

There was the sound of drums, and all heads turned to look at Emperor Shifang at the doorway with Princess Inessa on his arm. The Kion noblewoman was stunning, decked in gold and silver from head to toe, handmade embroidery trimmed the edges of her dress. There was a hush over the onlookers as their ruler led his betrothed to the ornate thrones and then the sound of knees falling to the ground as everyone prostrated toward him and their future empress.

Once seated, Emperor Shifang called out a command, and the dancing resumed. All too quickly, I was whisked away again by another Daanorian waiting his turn.

"Beautiful," my partner breathed. "Stay in Daanoris longer?" He rattled off a string of words I didn't know, going on and on until finally ending with a question and looking back at me hopefully. "Pardon me?" I managed, not entirely sure what I was answering or if a guesswork yes would bring me more trouble than a no.

"Mind if I cut in?" a voice to my right interrupted. My suitor wasn't as fluent in the common tongue, however, and Kalen had to repeat it, this time in Daanorian, adding in a few other words I couldn't understand. The boy visibly gulped, cast a fearful glance at the tall Deathseeker, and stepped aside.

"Likh and Khalad are off to map the rest of the palace wards,"

Kalen advised me. "Zoya thinks Likh can use the seeking stone to overcome the wards' restrictions and channel enough magic to untangle the threads all on his own."

"How long will it take them?"

"Most of the night, according to Likh. Zoya told me to come here and tell you in case anything else happens."

He started to step away, but I grabbed his arms and guided him across the floor, taking note of several women eyeing the Deathseeker. Odalian nobles were oblivious by nature, I decided. "And here I thought you just wanted to dance with me."

"I can't dance." But he didn't pull away, and we moved slowly to the music while the people around us spun.

"I thought you could do anything."

"Do you want me to learn?"

I looked up. He was staring at me again in that strange, exhilarating way he had in the woods by Lake Kaal.

I faltered and mumbled at his boots. "Not if you don't want to."

We danced for a few minutes without saying anything. A Daanorian woman worked up the nerve to approach us but backed away when I glared at her.

"Angry about something?"

"You do know there are women itching to kill me right now, right?"

His grip tightened. "Did someone compel the people in the palace? The wards are still in place."

I sighed. "That's not what I meant. Never mind." His breath tickled my ear, sending goose bumps along my skin.

"Want to talk about the *hanjian* instead?"

"*Hanjian?*"

"Traitor. The emperor decreed that the man who tried to kill me be labeled as such. It's the lowest form of insult among the Daanorian army apparently. If you don't want to talk about him, how about the other soldier who died then?"

"You sound exactly like Fox."

"We're very similar in a lot of ways."

"I don't think you've ever forced a guy to kill himself," I said bitterly.

"There isn't much difference between forcing him to and running him through yourself. You were looking out for me."

"I'm no longer certain you're worth the effort." I wanted to rile him up, but that only made him laugh.

A familiar song began. Shadi and Zoya were dancing *The Fox and the Hare*, popular among the kingdoms and a common repertoire in asha performances. Even the crowd, unused to our style of dance, fell silent as they watched the couple sway to the music, flowing to the rhythm with little effort, gliding from one intricate movement to the next.

"Don't make it a habit of shutting people out," Kalen said quietly as everyone else watched. "Your brother cares for you. You shouldn't make him worry."

"I know. I'll find him later and apologize."

"The first time I killed someone, I was thirteen. She was a Tresean soldier."

I gasped. "She?"

"There're a lot of women soldiers in Tresea. They fight as well as any man I've ever met. This one was a deserter, part of a roving band of thieves and pirates who'd managed to sail into Odalian waters, robbing and setting fire to our merchant ships. I didn't know until much later that she hadn't taken part in the raids we'd been tracking. The ship she'd previously been on had floundered, and they'd picked her up only the day before. She felt honor bound to fight with them, I suppose, but I still cried myself to sleep for two nights running."

"Cry? You?" Kalen had always seemed made of stone. Emotions of any extreme seemed out of place on him.

"I wasn't always a bastard."

That made me giggle. "That's hard to remember."

"You're holding up much better than I did."

I sobered. "I don't feel guilty. I feel bad that I had to kill both of them, but I also feel bad about not feeling worse about it, as I know I should. What does that make me?"

"That means you have more of a fighter's temperament than I do."

I snorted. "Nobody's more of a fighter than you. You're the bravest, strongest, most amazing man I've ever…"

I stopped. So did he.

"I mean, you're all right," I finished feebly, wanting desperately to kick myself.

"Tea."

I froze. Kalen was looking down at me with a vulnerability I never thought possible with him.

"I think I'm going to take you up on that offer again."

He drew nearer, and I wondered, in some part of my brain that was still functioning, how I must have looked to him. Did I look shocked? Nervous?

Eager?

"Don't move," he whispered. No two words had ever been so hard to obey.

His mouth hovered a few inches from mine, and I overcame the desire to close the distance. But he stopped, and I wondered if I'd misinterpreted his intentions again. But his eyes were fierce and hungry and desiring and a million other emotions all at once, and I could not look away.

He kissed me. In full view of the nobles, in full view of the emperor and anyone who wanted to see, his mouth hot against mine. He tasted like everything I wanted, and he kissed like I could reach into his heart and take everything I desired from it. I was inexperienced at this—too young in Knightscross and too busy in Ankyo, the little time in between spent daydreaming about an infatuation that paled when compared with the reality that was Kalen. But I kissed him back like I wished I could do better, like I *could* do better if it was always with him.

The Fox and the Hare ended. Shadi and Zoya curtsied, their fingers linking together as their captivated audience broke into applause.

Kalen stepped back. His face was expressionless, but he was breathing harder than he had during our sparring sessions, as if realizing he'd gone too far, too fast, with nothing to show but the truth of a kiss still hanging in the air between us. His heartsglass gleamed a combination of brilliant silver and warm apple red.

"I promised Zoya I'd make a few more rounds tonight. I'll see you tomorrow, Tea."

I watched him walk away, Shadi and the emperor's curious eyes on me the only barriers stopping me from pursuing him. It was not quite a faux pas, the kiss…but Mistress Parmina would have frowned on it all the same. I took a deep breath, trying in vain to quell the happy, nervous butterflies sprouting in my stomach, and turned back toward the throne.

And stopped. Inessa's seat was empty.

I followed Fox's thoughts and found her with him, away from the crowd. They swayed noiselessly on the veranda, dancing without the need for music. Inessa's head was against my brother's chest, her eyes closed and a small smile on her face. Fox looked down at her, his own expression unreadable.

I wanted to leave, but instead I parked myself between them and the rest of the guests, ready to sound the alarm if anyone headed their way.

"Your Majesty," Fox said quietly, formally, "we can't stay here for much longer."

"I don't want to leave."

"Your Majesty."

"Are we on formal terms again, Sir Fox?" Inessa let go. Her hand gripped at the neckline of her dress.

"It's your engagement." Fox's tone was wooden. "Stop tugging at your collar. You'll ruin your dress."

"You've done that enough times before." Inessa pulled harder in response.

Fox's hand folded over hers.

"Princess Inessa!" I heard Tansoong trill from somewhere nearby, and her arm jerked up.

Something small and sparkling flew through the air, landing in a metallic clink as it hit the floor.

The princess staggered back. "I'm going," she mumbled.

"Inessa, what—"

"Keep it!" The words rushed out with a heartbroken sound, and Inessa fled.

Fox knelt. With shaking hands, he picked up the small pin Inessa had left behind—a silhouette of a fox dotted with tiny crystals.

PRINCESS INESSA AND LORD FOX were silent when she finished. Lord Kalen had stepped out to oversee the rest of the Daanorian soldiers and Khalad had resumed his toil at his forge, bent studiously over his task.

"Princess Inessa has been good to you, Fox," the Dark asha murmured to ease the tension. "You look like a soldier for once. A royal uniform now instead of the threadbare shirts and breeches you're so fond of."

"I didn't realize you'd seen us at the party," the princess whispered, her cheeks coloring.

"It was none of my business."

"But your leaving was my business, and you knew it." The Dark asha's brother's face gave away no emotion. "You raised monsters and invaded a kingdom, and now you fight against Inessa's own people. Still my business, all of it."

Her head dropped, avoiding his gaze. "I had no choice."

"No choice?" His voice was flat, but his words were cutting. "You had a choice, but you left and gave me none. You blocked your thoughts from mine, and still I sat and waited for months because I was a fool and thought I knew you better. Do not stand here and tell me you had no choice when it was you who gave me nothing to choose between."

"*Because you didn't believe me!*" She fought back, her words coming out in quivers and hitches.

"*The elders said—*"

"*The elders said!*" the asha shouted. "*The elders said! Exactly that! They are lying cowards, and yet you heeded their words over mine!*"

"*I saw you, Tea.*" His cold facade shifted, and my heart twisted at how broken the man now sounded. "*I saw you kill her.*"

She trembled. "*I didn't. I couldn't.*"

"*And you don't believe me either. You don't trust me, Tea. Because even as I stand here, you still have the* Veiling *rune in place between us.*"

"*Inessa and I shouldn't be here,*" Khalad said softly.

"*No. The time for secrets is over.*" The bone witch's hands curled, held at the ready, fearful of the next fight. She closed her eyes briefly, relaxed. Some magic I could not see thrummed between them, dissipated. Lord Fox started in surprise.

"*It is gone.*" A queer sob, all the more strange and sad because it came from her. "*I don't know. I don't remember. All I remember is the screaming, and even then I don't recall if it was mine or hers. Some nights I wake up and scream still because I can see the blood on my hands. It never goes away, even with all the soap and the scrubbing. Hers is the only death you can lay at my door. If I killed her, then I will pay for that soon enough. But I killed no one else, no matter what they tell you. I swear on Kalen's grave, Fox. I told you nothing because you hated me then, didn't trust me—and because if you knew, they would cast you out as well. Do not deny that—I understand.*

"*For the longest time, I hated myself. You can hate someone and still wait for them, but I didn't want you to wait. I left because it meant I would live, that you would live. But even that is not enough. I cannot give you half a life, Fox. Neither you nor Inessa deserve that. So I took the daeva and made my plans without you because I knew you would stop me. I swear on Kalen's grave. I swear."*

The man watched her with eyes so like her own. It was as if he could delve into her soul with one look and discern her lies from her truths. "And what are those plans?" he asked quietly.

"I do not want a fight with either Odalia or Kion. My war is with the elders and with Drycht. I will remain in Daanoris a few days more, and I will leave the city unscathed. As a sign of good faith, I will do nothing against the other asha. When I am done with King Aadil, they will no longer matter. Command your armies to return home, Inessa. They give the dead nothing but stomachaches."

"Come back with us, Tea," the man insisted. "We can talk to Empress Alyx. Mykaela will understand."

"Empress Alyx and Lady Mykaela do not make up the whole of Kion, Fox. Not anymore. They will put me on trial for my crimes, and I will be publicly executed for the world to see. I have gone too far, Fox. There will be no other judgment, no matter what Mykaela or Zoya or anyone else claims." Beside him, Inessa froze, her fear thick enough to touch. "And when I die, so will you."

"If you declare war against Drycht and die in battle, then so will I. What difference will it make?"

"Because my odds there are better." The bone witch rose, a knife in her hand. She cut her finger, drops of blood welling up. "Should I find what I seek in their mountains, then you will survive this, Fox.

Or did you forget that there was once a spell in Aenah's book you forbade me to use?"

She leaned forward, placing her injured finger against her stunned brother's cheek. I watched as the small wounds on his face and arms healed, disappearing as his flesh knitted back together. "And I will use it, Fox. You will live. Regardless of how I die."

23

Y OU WANT ME TO COMPEL them to sleep?"

"It's the fastest way."

After that initial stab of disappointment at Kalen's nonchalance, like nothing significant had happened between us, I swore not to let it show. "People without heartsglass are harder to control."

"There're only two of them."

"You know, for someone with decided views about compulsion, you're pretty open when it comes to compelling someone else."

"So I'm no different to you than some palace guards?" Kalen asked.

I looked at him, but he was already directing his next question at Khalad. "You sure you can find him?"

The boy adjusted his spectacles. "I'm positive. If the forger is anywhere in the city, I will locate him."

Shadi spoke up. "Zoya and I are going to stay behind and snoop for a bit."

"Isn't that dangerous?" Likh asked, concerned.

"I doubt we'd look suspicious," the doe-eyed asha said with a smile, "but I can defend myself if I have to. And I'll have Zoya with me."

"Where's the princess?" Fox asked.

Zoya cleared her throat. "Since the *savul* expedition, she's been under heavier guard. I don't think it's a good idea for her to come with us, especially since Emperor Shifang has been taking up much of her time."

Jealousy slithered through his mind like a serpent. "Fox, stay at the palace," I ordered. "I don't think anyone should be leaving the princess alone with people we don't trust, her fiancé most of all. She told him you were her guard. What guard leaves the palace without his charge?"

Fox looked torn. *And besides*, I added, *you both have issues that need resolving.*

"I'm not going to let you go without me watching your back."

"I'll protect her," Kalen volunteered quietly.

Both men looked at each other. Some unspoken understanding passed between them, and Fox nodded reluctantly. "Not one hair on her head," he warned.

"I am perfectly capable of taking care of myself," I complained.

"If you say so," Kalen replied.

Walking into the city was an unexpected, blessed relief. There were still wards there, preventing me from establishing contact with the *azi*, and when Kalen tried out a few of his own runes, they were still less than half the strength they should've been, as Zoya had found out the day we first arrived in Santiang. Still, it was better than nothing, and I drew *Compulsion* for a few seconds, just to savor the feeling.

Compelling someone without a heartsglass was like walking underwater with the current against you, and the lesser potency of the runes here made it even harder. I hesitated—the half rune I'd traced lingered in the air, struggling to retain its shape.

"Tea?" Likh whispered when it became apparent that the guards accompanying us were still walking of their own volition. I hesitated again.

"What's wrong?" Kalen asked quietly.

"I don't—" My eyes moved from the guards back to him. "I don't…maybe I shouldn't—"

The Deathseeker's face cleared, understanding. "You don't have to if you don't want to. We'll do it some other way."

"No." I forced myself to finish the rune, and the guards froze, their eyes blank.

"Are you sure?" His voice was low. "You're right. Not after— it's not fair to ask you to do this."

"It boils down to necessity, I guess." At my silent command, the men began to move. Just to be sure we were unwatched, I explored the surroundings carefully with my mind and found no spies. "And *you're* right. You're different from those guards."

Kalen looked at me, moved to speak, then thought better of it.

I goaded the soldiers into a nearby inn, made them pay for rooms, and soon they were fast asleep on their beds. Before we returned, I would coax them into waking, with none of them the wiser.

Santiang was a city both strange and familiar. I could see the same influences in their architecture that defined the homes and temples of Ankyo, from their arched slopes to their slanting roofs. But while Ankyons had a preference for bungalows and residences no more than two or three landings high, Santiang houses were tower spires that reached as high into the sky as they dared, with different families occupying every floor. The roads were narrower than Odalia's, save for the one leading from the palace out to the city gates.

Khalad walked like he knew the way, pausing every now and then to get his bearings. "I can sense Master's workshop," he explained. "The memories and half-finished heartsglass there burn as bright as a beacon."

The people of Santiang were noisier than their Kion counterparts. Tiny stalls crowded every conceivable corner, selling dried fish and pickled vegetables next to fishing rods and rat repellent. The people spoke with loud, raucous voices whether they were arguing, bargaining, or telling jokes.

Children played on the street with paper balls and spinning tops, running to one side and giggling when heavy wagons came creaking past. Teashop owners and tavern proprietors—in many instances one and the same—wheeled out tables and chairs along sections of road to accommodate more customers. Everyone we

RIN CHUPECO

passed wore plain robes of muted colors, and it was difficult to distinguish the successful merchant with a flourishing business from the average bricklayer.

Khalad led us through busy intersections where long lines of carts and horses were at a standstill, through roads so full of people and merchandise it was a wonder we could pass, and finally to smaller alleys that stank of beer and vomit, as the crowds thinned out and the voices faded, until we were standing before a small shack, not unlike the Heartforger's hut in Kion.

Abandoned lots lined either side of it, and an open canal overflowing with rotten fish and garbage appeared to be the reason why.

"We traveled half a continent only to reach the same place again," Likh said, staring.

I reached for Fox without thinking, then remembered he wasn't with us. I sought him out with my mind instead and saw him at the courtyard with the princess. There was a marked improvement to Princess Inessa's swordsmanship, and I wondered how many other sessions they had finished.

We found the forger's hut, I whispered.

Another *hut?*

That was Likh's reaction too.

Sounds promising. Be careful. Out of the corner of Fox's eye, I spotted the emperor striding toward them, his face livid.

You better get out of my head, Tea. This isn't going to be pretty.

But—

You've got more important things to do. Scram.

"Tea?" Likh waved a hand in front of my face. "Are you with us? Tea?"

"Um...I think the emperor isn't happy about Fox and Inessa spending so much time together."

"Why?"

"That's a conversation for later." Kalen took a step toward the shanty. Despite the city wards, I could feel waves upon waves of powerful energy, almost as strong as a seeking stone's pull, emanating from the small, innocent-looking hovel. "Wait." Khalad blocked his path. "Something's wrong. Master's not this careless. This is too much concentrated magic. It's...overwhelming."

"Stay back, Khalad." Kalen approached the shack slowly, runes already half-formed. He pushed open the rotting wooden door with one foot. "Doesn't look like anyone's been here in a while."

The hair on the back of my neck prickled. "Guys?"

"The Heartforger isn't here, that's for sure," Likh said, peeking in.

"Guys?" I had little knowledge of how sewage systems worked, but surely canals didn't froth and bubble like that. Surely still water didn't swirl that way...

"I'll go first," Khalad said. "He might have left something behind."

"Let's not be hasty," Kalen said. "Your master isn't in the habit of laying traps for unwanted visitors by any chance?"

"No, he's not—"

"Guys!" I drew out my sword. The canal behind us went *goop*, and something rose from that putrid pool. The stink alone was nearly enough to make me faint, but what staggered out was the stuff of nightmares. It was an emaciated figure, a cross between flesh and skeleton. Tattered strips were all that was left of its clothing, and stringy black hair puffed out around its empty skull. It was small, easily a child or a young woman, but there was nothing human about its face.

More monstrosities crawled out of the canal, decomposing corpses of either human or animal remains or a revolting hybrid of both. The dogs no longer howled, but their teeth were sharp and yellow in their cadaverous mouths. They sprang forward faster than their human counterparts.

I drew *Compulsion* and was once more confronted by a barrier that was becoming familiar to me. "Someone's controlling them!"

One of the skeletal hounds leaped for me. I stepped aside and cleaved its head off as it passed, slamming the hilt of my sword against its legs. "Break as many bones as you can!" I ordered. "They'll keep moving if you don't!"

Kalen whipped out an arm, sending a group shattering against a nearby wall. Khalad froze as more dogs approached, but Likh planted himself between the forger and the corpses, weaving his own runes. Lightning lanced through a nearby skeleton, blasting it into pieces.

"No lightning, Likh!" Kalen lifted a few of the cadavers with *Wind* and clenched his fist. The undead were immediately crushed into powder.

"Sorry," Likh squeaked, shifting to *Ice* and *Water*, freezing bones and limbs. Despite their strength, it was clear that Likh and Kalen were having a harder time creating runes because of the unseen wards in place, and they were tiring quicker.

"Cover me, Kalen!" I *scried* and cast my mind around me, trying to find the mind responsible. Fox's presence spread over my consciousness, calm and comforting as he wordlessly added his will to mine.

I punched through the haze of *Compulsion* around the monsters and found my target—and recoiled instinctively in disgust. The thoughts I found were human enough: they belonged to a man in a small, dark room, wizened and bald and dressed in expensive robes. But his thoughts reeked of such depravity and greed and insanity that my reflex was to push him away, desperate for cleaner thoughts to breathe in.

He sensed my intrusion and attacked. I saw rivers of blood, of people torn to bits by wild animals as he basked in their blood, of him ripping through flesh with his own bare hands. I fought not to retch; I would rather wade into the sewage canal than into the depths of that grotesque mind.

But Fox had stronger willpower, and he took over, pushing past the horrifying images and burrowing deeper into the man's mind. While the man gloated over my horror, he had left me an opening to sever his link with the corpses.

The backlash was terrifying. I could not feel the pain that lanced through the man when his bond was broken, but I could sense its intensity. Screaming, the man reeled back, and our connection was gone.

Likh and Kalen stood, bewildered, while discarded bone and decaying carcasses surrounded them. Kalen was quick to catch me as I staggered.

"There was a man," I gasped out. Kalen's arms felt good around me, and my shivering abated. "His mind was...repulsive. I think it's the same person controlling the *savul.*"

"Is he still here?"

"No. I don't think so. Fox hurt him."

"The poor people," Likh mourned, crouching down beside one of the remains. Bones and bits of hair were all that was left of it, along with scraps of bright-red clothing. "Khalad, are you OK?"

The forger was breathing hard, but not from fright. His eyes were a bright gray behind his glasses, and he was staring at Likh like he was seeing the other boy for the first time.

"That was amazing!" Khalad clasped his hands around the boy's. "I've never seen anyone spin runes like that before. It's like a performance at the *darashi oyun!*"

"What did he look like, Tea?" Kalen asked as Likh quickly went from worried to mortified.

"Bald but with a beard past his waist. It took Fox and me to get past his defenses—I certainly couldn't do it on my own."

"Sounds like Usij."

"So he really isn't at the Haitsa mountains?" Khalad asked.

"Never underestimate a Faceless. Usij's the oldest of the three—and the most degenerate."

"But why plant a trap here?" Khalad dropped Likh's hands.

"Wait!" Likh cried, but the forger had already entered the shack. With an uncharacteristic curse, Likh tore in after him.

Are they all gone? Fox asked.

Yeah. Thank you, I owe you one.

Glad to be of use while I'm stuck in the palace.

Has the emperor killed you yet?

She was amazing, Tea. Fox's tone was admiring, and blips of memories popped into my head: Inessa with her hands on her hips, confronting the Daanorian emperor with *I shall train with my personal guard whenever I wish* and *I am your fiancée and not your chattel!* and also *You cannot select me for my independence only to turn around and complain that I am being too independent!* The emperor was not a skilled debater, unused to anyone disagreeing with him to his face; Shifang could only shake his head and stomp petulantly away.

Good for her. I was worried.

So was I when I saw what crawled out of those sewers. Why is Kalen—

Tell me the rest later. I pushed his thoughts out. I was in a good place, and I was not going to give him time to ruin it. "Thank you," I mumbled into Kalen's chest, not quite ready to move away.

"That was a pretty good swing. Guess you're not as bad at sword fighting as I thought."

I rolled my eyes. "Yeah, I'm so terrible at this. Two soldiers at a time is my limit."

"They said you were too small to be a bone witch, too delicate looking to be a fighter. That Odalians and Kions weren't of the same caliber as their Daanorian women." His grip on me tightened. "I wanted to confront them. I wanted to tell them they were idiots who didn't understand they were watching the strongest girl I'd ever known, a girl who had faced off against demons and creatures beyond their imagining and won. That they didn't deserve to be in the same room with her, much less in the same fight.

"But you winning was better than anything I could have said, better than anything they would have believed. I laughed because there was nothing else I could say that was better than what you had just proven."

I listened to Kalen in stunned silence, thrilled by his words and the rasp of his voice. The voice in my head that had started as a dull murmur since leaving Odalia was shouting now, that damn little upstart no longer refusing to be ignored. *You like him,* it taunted, *you're in love with him, have been since Strypnyk. It's why you couldn't leave him behind, you fool.* My own thoughts rose louder, terrified and elated but still partly, desperately in denial, going *Oh no, oh no,* oh no.

"Tea! Kalen!" Likh yelled from inside the small hut. "You've got to see this!"

"Let's go," Kalen said quietly, and I shoved all those confused jumbled thoughts out of my head, falling back on the meditation techniques I was taught to try to tame the raging of my heartsglass. *Later.* The mantra throbbed in my head. *Later. Deal with it later.*

The room was similar to the one in Kion, with the same disorganized mess of bottles, papers, and potions. It had the same shelves, the same kind of stones piled over each other as paper-weights. Khalad was already crouched along one wall, fishing out several sheaves of letters and notes from a small brick-shaped hole while Kalen glared at a nearby cabinet.

"I found it!" Khalad said triumphantly, waving the papers in the air. "He wrote me a note!"

"How did you know it was there?" Likh asked.

"I know all of the Heartforger's hiding places."

"What does it say?"

"I haven't opened it yet—there's a lot of his more recent work here, including how to completely rewire heartsglass to actually *improve* people's personalities—"

"Khalad!" Kalen barked. "*What does the letter say?*"

The forger hurriedly unfolded the paper. "'To my foolish apprentice: If you are reading this, then you have disobeyed my orders to remain in Kion and attend to business there. You are a complete and utter disgrace to our profession, and sometimes, I wish I'd never taken you on as my apprentice.'"

Likh blinked. "That's rather harsh."

"Don't worry about it. That's just the way he talks when he's irritated." Khalad paused. "At least, I hope he doesn't mean it. He's always had a poor way with words—"

"Khalad!" Kalen roared.

"'—but I suppose that's beside the point now,'" he continued reading. "'We have far greater problems on our hands, my boy. I have had my suspicions for close to a year now, and it irks me to know how often I am right, though I would wish otherwise.

As you know, I have been investigating the sleeping sicknesses, convinced that this was no natural disorder. Princess Yansheo's case was particularly curious, as the sickness requires the presence of a heartsglass when she should have had none. I had also received an unsigned message from Daanoris, warning me of magic being carried out in the palace, so I endeavored to see for myself. It was also a chance to investigate reports of the Duke of Holsrath having visited Daanoris.'"

"So he suspected it too," Likh murmured.

"'It was astonishing to discover that Holsrath had been at the Daanorian ball in the princess's honor on the very same night I visited him in his cell, for he had been sickly as of late. Either the duke has a doppelgänger or he possesses skills not even I am aware of, which is highly unlikely given my abilities.'

"Modest too," Kalen murmured.

"'The danger is closer than I could have ever imagined. Usij has infiltrated Daanoris, Khalad. The iron fortress in Haitsa was a bluff, a means to convince the emperor that his enemy remains isolated in the mountains. The Faceless has entered Emperor Shifang's palace just as Aenah has infiltrated the Odalian court.'

"'My antidote replicates the *urvan* of the sleeping nobles—to restore their missing "souls," so to speak. With his father's permission, I tested it on Baron Cyran, with promising results. The young man is awake and without any ill effects, and the whole of Istera still has no inkling of their kinsman's recovery, as King Rendorvik and Councilor Ludvig have been sworn to secrecy. Despite all my efforts, however, I believe the Faceless has learned of my cure.'

"'There are agents after me, and I believe they are under the command of a man named Tansoong. I cannot remain here for much longer. I hope to return to the Daanorian palace and perform the same cure on Princess Yansheo. If you find this—or worse, if you find this letter after receiving word of my death in Daanoris—you must look for my friend, a man who has the least reason to cause Princess Yansheo harm. Find Baoyi. Tell him old Narel sends his regards and show him this letter. I have told him nothing about the princess's sleeping sickness or of its magical symptoms to spare him from further worry, but he and I have known each other for a long time, and he will give you sanctuary.'"

S HE SAYS YOU ARE A *bard*," Princess Inessa said softly.

"I wish to one day tell the world her story, Your Highness." We stood by the entrance of the palace. The bone witch had not accompanied her brother nor the princess, much to the latter's disappointment. Lord Fox said nothing, remaining solemn and quiet. Lord Kalen was already arranging horses for them.

"I would very much like to hear her story. I know so little of her—much less than I thought I did. She saved my life many times. I would do everything in my power to save hers if I could." She looked up at the daeva standing before her; they gazed curiously back but made no approach. "But she is right. Her people will kill her, even without a trial. The Tea I knew would never have thought to invade a kingdom with the very daeva she had sworn to put down." It sounded like a question.

"I am their chronicler, not their confidante."

"She plays a lone hand. She no longer trusts us. I don't even know if she trusts Fox anymore." She looked back at the palace. "But Fox trusts her now. I know, even without his saying so. Kalen is with her, and so is Khalad. If there is a voice of reason among us, it is Khalad, despite all he's been through himself. He has every reason to hate Tea, but he does not. I can always trust Khalad." Her voice broke, and her tears fell. "I have to. Otherwise, nothing makes sense anymore. It was good to see him. It was good to see Kalen."

"Let's go, Inessa," Lord Fox said, already astride his horse.

The princess turned. "We gave in so easily. We could still convince her to come back with us."

"When she reestablished our bond, I knew we could not convince her. There are blighted folk in Daanoris, Inessa. We must return to see if any are hiding among our own army before it's too late." Ignoring her gasp, he looked at me. "I don't know what Tea plans. There is still much she refuses to share. I do not know if we can withdraw our forces or convince the empress, but I will not lose my sister again, no matter what she says." For an instant, the grim lines around his mouth faded, and Lord Fox's eyes lightened to a gray mist instead of starless midnight.

He nodded at the Deathseeker. "It's good to see you again, Kalen. Protect her for me."

"I always have."

"Write her a good story, Bard. They say the best tales spare no mercy and spare no lies." He paused. "But spare her anyway," he added quietly and nudged his horse onto the road that would lead them out of Santiang.

A kind man, *I thought as I watched the two ride away.* Too kind. But of all I have seen of war, kindness makes the best of commanders and the finest of soldiers.

·· ᰔ ··

The bone witch knelt at the center of the throne room, studying her hands as we entered. Gently, the Deathseeker took her wrists, turning them over so he could see the damage her nails had wrought.

"Did I kill her?" The Dark asha asked him, despair in her voice. "Fox said I did, and he would never lie. Her blood on my hands, and my brother as a witness. What if I took in too much darkrot and killed her in my rage? How could I do that? What if I am as guilty as they say?"

The man said nothing.

"I killed a king, Kalen. And then I killed two more of our own. I did not want to kill her, but I did it anyway, and they cannot say it wasn't deliberate. And the other…my own…"

She whimpered, hand grasping at her chest, breathing hard. "I can feel the Dark in my soul. I thought I could stand it, but now I am afraid of what I can do. Of what I might do. I have killed Faceless and innocents alike, and whether they were one or the other, I am afraid it will no longer matter to my conscience. I tried. I wanted to show them how my daeva can choose not to kill, that I can choose not to kill. Inessa was right—I'm no longer the Tea they know. But did they ever know who I was to begin with? Did you? Did I?"

Lord Kalen bent down and kissed her forehead.

"Promise me, Kalen. If I succumb to the darkrot before I finish, you must kill me. Quickly and without hesitation." She found his hands. "I am sorry for bringing you back only to suffer this. I thought I was stronger. I thought that being with you would make me stronger."

The Deathseeker kissed her cheek, her nose, her lips. "I promise. And whatever happens, know I will be with you. Until the very end."

24

T O SAY THAT BAOYI WAS as suspicious of us as we were of him was an understatement, though his suspicions extended to those in Shifang's royal court, particularly toward Tansoong. There were guards stationed not only outside his room but also inside it, and the man himself was dressed for battle, with a short sword in one hand and the other twitching toward a broadsword mounted on the wall of his room. Though he and Khalad seemed to have come to a mutual understanding, Baoyi remained incredulous of our motivations until Khalad handed him the old forger's letter.

"This is his handwriting," he said, studying it carefully before opening a drawer and taking out another piece of paper. "This is the letter Narel sent me a few months ago, noting his intentions of visiting Yansheo. But he never arrived, and I assumed he had changed his mind. When you told me that you were searching for him, I had no idea he was in trouble." Baoyi sounded almost accusatory.

"How do you know the old forger exactly?" Zoya asked him.

"He is an old friend of my father's since childhood, before an asha discovered his skills in magic. The emperor tolerates him only because he returns to heal our sick. But I have known him since I was a little boy."

"Narel is Daanorian?" I knew the forger was not Odalian or Kion but little else. "Narel isn't a Daanorian name, and he doesn't look Daanorian."

Baoyi laughed. "He looked Daanorian enough when he was younger, though I believe he has Kion ancestors on his mother's side. Old age makes it harder to ascertain one's nationality, I've found. And he felt it necessary to adopt a different moniker for his new life. He was no longer a citizen of Daanoris but rather a citizen of the people. But Narel and my father remained close." He waved at his guards and issued a few clipped orders; the room was empty of soldiers within seconds. His clerk glanced at us and asked Baoyi something in Daanorian. When he replied in the affirmative, the nervous man gathered his papers and dashed out, looking relieved.

"You are not charlatans?" Baoyi asked. "This is not an intricate plot to bewitch my emperor, and the woman you call Princess Inessa is truly who you say she is? And Narel is truly in danger?"

"And you're not a complete jerk who makes it a point to insult and demean foreign visitors when they visit your city?" I demanded. Likh gulped. Khalad fidgeted with a few of the small gemstones that decorated Baoyi's mantelpiece, but Kalen grinned.

"Ah—Lord Khalad, please be careful with those. They are precious jade stones dating back to the Harshien Dynasty. But I was very much a jerk, wasn't I?" Baoyi sounded almost embarrassed. "I thought you were clever crooks who wanted to make a fool of my liege. I even wondered if the *savul* was a cunning illusion concocted by your spellbinding skills. We heard that the Kion princess had been engaged to King Telemaine's son and thought it impossible that Odalia would break their engagement so easily. It did not seem likely the princess would come and offer herself to Shifang."

"Princess Inessa has always been an impulsive girl, milord," Fox growled.

"I haven't seen Narel in over a year. But I shall order the guards to conduct a search in the city."

"We have reason to believe that Usij has spies in Emperor Shifang's court, milord," Shadi cautioned him. "I would advise you to select only the men you trust for such an expedition."

"Usij?" The man scowled. "We have been hammering at the Haitsa iron fortress for close to a decade now, and he has shown no signs of abandoning the place. Do you mean to tell me that he has been here in Santiang all this time?"

"He is not one to be taken lightly, milord."

"I do not know what he plans. Princess Inessa's wedding to the emperor takes place on the morrow. Would he do anything to disrupt it?"

"There are many reasons to oppose that wedding, milord," Fox said quietly.

"How goes the search for Shaoyun?" Shadi wanted to know.

Baoyi sighed. "There is no trace of him. I do not know if he is in league with Usij, but given everything that has happened, I would no longer be surprised if he is. Perhaps his interest in Princess Yansheo was all a deception to gain access to her. He shouldn't have been difficult to find—the boy dresses like a scarlet peacock and would easily stand out in a crowd. I will ask my soldiers to search for any gray jewels that may turn up, just in case." He turned to me and held out his hand. "This is how you make peace in Kion, isn't it?"

"What is?" I asked.

"To shake your hand and bury the hatchet, so to speak. My intentions were pure when I thought you were here to bespell the emperor, but that does not excuse my behavior. Can we be friends?"

"Of course." Grinning, I took his hand. "I too would like to apologize. My mentor would beat me over the head and send me to scrub outhouses for life if she knew how I had conducted myself."

"If there is any way you can heal Yansheo, then I am in your service and in your debt." Baoyi's face softened. "I have known Yansheo since she was a child. She is a charming, sweet girl. I would do anything to see her laughing again."

"We'll do our best." Likh promised.

"Do you speak for Khalad now, Likh?" Shadi asked impishly, and Likh turned red.

Zoya was a brimful of orders when we returned to Khalad's quarters. "Kalen, we need to patrol the palace for any behavior out of the ordinary. Tea, stay with Khalad. Keep in contact with Fox at all times. After the attack in the city, let's not take any more risks."

"I'm always in contact with Fox, Zoya. It's not like I have a choice."

But the asha wasn't listening. "Likh, how goes the unraveling?"

The boy asha nodded, looking exhausted. "I've figured out where to undo the knots. One big tug and I think it'll all crumble." He shuddered.

"Was it your first time seeing raised corpses?" Shadi asked him sympathetically.

"I felt bad for them." His lip trembled. "Did anyone even miss them, I wonder? That one boy...he could have been my age. There was nothing to identify him beyond the red cloth and black hair, but surely he had family and friends looking for him? The ones that looked like young girls, with their scraps of dresses and small faces...surely they all had family?"

"You're a good person, Likh," Khalad said, and the boy averted his gaze.

"We're forever in your debt, Likh. Get a good night's rest. The same goes for you, Shadi," Zoya instructed.

But the girl folded her arms across her chest. "I am just as capable of patrolling the castle with you, Zoya. I have no inclination for either Dark magic or forging magic, and I would be quite useless here."

"We have a long day ahead. You need sleep too."

"And so do you. Most of my duties in Kion may have revolved around entertaining guests and visitors at *cha-khana*, but I am not some frail flower that must be hidden away at the first gust of wind. It was sweet of you to treat me like a princess back in Kion, where there was little danger and we could indulge. This is different."

"Shadi, you know I would…" Zoya trailed off, realizing that they now had a rapt audience listening to their conversation with undisguised interest. "*Shadi*."

"Are we still hiding us from them?" Shadi challenged her. "Are we still a secret? If there is something you need to tell me, Zoya, then raise your voice and let them hear."

Zoya cleared her throat—several times. Then she leaned over and kissed Shadi, full on the mouth. "Shadi, my love, you know I would never forgive myself if anything were to happen to you. Surely you can understand my reluctance."

"Haven't I proven myself? Haven't I shown that I am more than capable?"

Zoya gave up. "Shadi, would you like to patrol the palace with me?"

The other asha smiled happily, linking arms with her lover. "It would be my pleasure."

"You know," Khalad said mildly as the two left, "I'd always thought it was Zoya who made the first move. I might have been mistaken."

Kalen stood. "I have to see to rounds myself. With the wedding tomorrow, people are on edge."

He nodded at the others before taking his leave, glancing back at me as he did. I opened my mouth but couldn't find the words—didn't even know what I wanted to say. Not in front of everyone else.

"I should take a look at Fox." I was feeling antsy, and I wanted to do something more than sit around pretending to sleep.

"Zoya wants you to rest," Likh reminded me.

"I'm not going to leave the room—not yet anyway." I tapped the side of my head. "If something needs my attention, shake me."

"I'm not going to—" I heard Khalad say, aghast, but I was already off.

Emperor Shifang would not be happy to see Fox and Princess Inessa in the same room again, but the princess had never been one to take no for an answer. She was by the window, staring out, while Fox had his back toward the door, watching her watch the city.

"Move away from the window, Princess. You'd make for an easy target."

"Is that all I am to you, Fox?" Inessa asked, turning her head. "A target? Someone to protect?"

"Move away from the window."

Inessa obeyed, crossing the room so she stood before my brother, starting stonily up at him. "You've stopped talking to me after the fight with the *savul*," she said angrily. "You've never felt pain before, but seeing you that way…and then you stopped talking to me."

"That's a lie."

"After that fight, you went back to talking to me like you were my subordinate. Not like how it used to be before."

"Brides shouldn't talk in this manner," Fox said quietly, an odd note to his voice. I tried to withdraw, but his emotions pulled me back again.

She unfurled her hands. "You're doing it. Right now."

"Enlighten me, Princess. Tell me what am I to expect of someone who, not satisfied with finding herself engaged to a noble from one kingdom, goes ahead and affiances herself to another?"

"Because I'm useless!" The sound bounced off the walls. It was not the answer Fox was expecting. He looked astonished.

"I'm useless," Princess Inessa repeated in a softer voice. "You can train me to fight, but you will never train me in time to be as competent at the sword as Kalen or Tea or anyone else. I will always require the most saving, the most protection. Do you know how horrible that makes me feel, that I can do nothing?

"All I have to offer is my crown, my perceived value as a princess, a potential bride. I may not have had as much say in my engagement to Kance, Fox, but I certainly do with my obligation to Shifang. I know this betrothal is the only reason we are allowed to remain here in Santiang to find the forger, and I will ensure that this betrothal allows us to remain here long enough to heal Kance's heartsglass and help the poor Daanorian princess. And if I have to wed the emperor on the morrow for us to do that, then I will."

"But I don't want you to!" Fox moved. Now it was the princess against the wall, Fox trapping her there with his arms.

Something glinted at his collar; Inessa's eyes gravitated toward it. It was her fox pin that he now wore.

"A thousand times I wanted to shout it to the world," my brother said through gritted teeth, "but a thousand times I kept my peace. Because it wasn't my place and because I knew my jealousy talked louder than my respect for your royal customs. But your wedding is tomorrow, and I have stayed silent long enough. Don't do this, Inessa. I'm begging you."

"Why tell me this now?" Inessa whispered.

Fox's hand shook. "Because in my arrogance, I never thought you would wed anyone else so willingly. Not Kance and definitely not Shifang. I thought I could wait long enough for you to realize my feelings, when I should have spoken out."

Trembling, Inessa placed her hand against Fox's heartsglass. "I remember the first time I asked you about this," she said quietly.

A muscle ticked in Fox's jaw, but he said nothing.

"I thought the silver meant you were a Deathseeker-in-training. You laughed and said that being a Deathseeker would have made your life a lot less complicated." Her fingers traveled past his heartsglass, up his chest and neck, to touch the silver fox pin. "Do you remember what you told me then?"

Fox's mouth worked. "I asked you to trust me."

Inessa smiled. "And then, four months later, when I told you I loved you. Do you remember what you said?"

Fox was silent, his head bowed.

"You told me you couldn't accept my love, that if you couldn't tell me the reasons for your silver heartsglass—"

"—then I can't promise you what I know you deserve."

She wept, and her tears tore at him.

"Inessa."

She looked up, her beautiful eyes still bright with tears. They widened when she saw what he was holding out to her.

"I can promise you nothing but what I already have."

Inessa stroked his lower jaw. "You offered me your heartsglass instead."

"You were right to reject me." Fox's voice was hoarse. "I couldn't promise you anything. I still can't—not as a familiar. When I learned you were the First Daughter of Kion, I knew you were out of my reach. Familiar-consorts weren't unheard of in Kion—but Kion empresses and princesses also needed heirs. I was too much of a coward to tell you what I was, knowing it would end what we had."

"No. I rejected you because I was stupid and because I was terrified. I was raised to believe in those ridiculous storybook romances, where love was meaningless unless it comes without fear, without selfishness. I thought you weren't willing to fight for me, that you were going to give me a heartsglass that would fade in time, to pacify me for the moment."

"Silver heartsglass don't fade, Inessa."

"I know that *now*." She looked back at him fiercely. "Tea told me, back at Lake Strypnyk. I saw you walking with her in the Willows once, you know. I was angry and jealous until they told me she was your sister. I was still angry, but it wasn't because I was repulsed that you were a familiar. I was angry because you never trusted me enough to tell me."

Fox lowered his head. "I was afraid of what your answer would be."

Inessa closed her eyes. "I know that now too. I...can't guarantee what my mother might think about this, Fox. But at least let us try." She kissed his neck. "It's your turn to trust me," she whispered. "When tomorrow comes, promise that you'll trust me, Fox."

His fingers tightened on her hair. "I promise."

The kiss was chaste for only a second, before Fox gathered her in his arms and deepened it, Inessa returning the kiss with the same fervor.

Gross. Please don't make me watch this. Already I was embarrassed, trying to pull my thoughts back again, but this time, Fox helped me snap free.

I think it's about time you left, Tea.

I fled his mind, knowing I also had a matter to resolve.

•• ⃰ ••

I found him in the gardens, the night air cool against my cheeks. We paused to savor the crisp breeze, neither of us speaking for the longest time. Kalen's heartsglass swung, and I saw the reason for his hesitation in its silvery depths. But I didn't want to prolong the silence. I was desperate to clear the air about Odalia, about Lake Kaal, about the dance.

"Kalen. About the compulsion..."

"I'm not holding that against you anymore, Tea."

"But I have to explain myself!" I blurted before I could change my mind. "I was frightened."

"Frightened?"

"Because I was selfish." He looked surprised. I pushed on. "I wasn't frightened about leaving Prince Kance in Odalia. But I was when you said you were staying."

"I don't understand." Yet I saw glimmers of hope in his heartsglass belying the words, and I plucked up the last of my courage.

"You know how I feel—what I *thought* I felt—for the prince. But staying with him never crossed my mind. I could argue that I knew he would be cared for, that he wouldn't be harmed. But that's not completely true. I should have been as worried as you were."

"You knew you had no choice—"

"But I gave in so easily, without putting up a fight. When *you* said you were staying…" I swallowed, my eyes straying to the floor. Tonight was a night for confessions. Perhaps my brother's resolve was influencing me through our bond, giving me more backbone to do the same.

"The thought of you in Odalia, alone, scared me so much that I did what I'd sworn I'd never do. I shouldn't have forced you to come. It was cowardly of me, even if I thought I had the best intentions."

"Cowardice has never been one of your vices, Tea. You killed a man for me. I wouldn't have asked that of anyone."

I had to smile, still not meeting his gaze. "What I did to you felt worse. That doesn't say much about me."

"Did you know what I thought the day you made me the offer to share heartsglass? When you said you'd do anything I wanted?"

"Are you going to throw that in my face again?"

"I couldn't accept your offer. The last thing I wanted was to force you to kiss me."

My stare flew to his, disbelieving.

"I've been in love with you," he said quietly, "since we fought the *azi* by the lake."

It sounded like an accusation as much as it was a confession, but for a man like Kalen, maybe they were one and the same. His words worked the way runes did, kicking up a whirlwind of emotions around me: trepidation, shock, happiness.

He loves me. But he looked so unguarded and open, like he was preparing himself for a rejection he knew was coming, and I wanted to weep and laugh all at once. I wished he could see himself the way I saw him: strength and familiarity and warmth in a dark cloak, brown eyes as steady and as comforting as the dawn. *He loves* me. "You never said anything."

"Your life was problematic enough without involving me in it." He sounded gruff. "And I thought your affections were engaged elsewhere."

"They're not. Not like this."

"Tea." His voice was so soft and low, I almost couldn't make out his words. "Are you still in love with Kance?"

"Why?" I had to hear him say it so there wouldn't be any more *now we're almost even*'s and *you bumbass*'s between us.

"Because if you are in love with him and if he stops being an idiot about it, then I can protect you both without any regrets."

"And if I'm not?"

"Are you, Tea?"

I wet my dry lips. "No."

There was no time for anything else but Kalen's mouth descending on mine, his hands cupping my face, his lips and tongue going straight to my head like wine. I matched him kiss for dizzying kiss, giving back every thought and word and heart, happier than I had ever known. I felt the flicker of *Heartshare* still around us, a rune I'd offered and forgotten, not wanting to dissolve even this meager connection.

It didn't matter who saw; there was only me and Kalen underneath the moonlight and the wind spinning around us.

"I can't court you the way Kance would have," he said much later, still adorably unsure despite all we'd shared between us. "I have no head for poetry and no patience for rituals. I can't worship you with words or song; I never know the right ones to sing."

"I don't need worship."

"Yes, you do. With my hands." His arms tightened around me. "With my mouth." His lips pressed against the side of my jaw, kissed me again before I could protest that he was wrong because he'd always had the right words. Then he slid down to his knees.

"Kalen," I panted, as he pushed the hem of my dress to one side, high enough to reveal my leg. "Kalen, what are you—"

He pressed his mouth against the scar on my thigh, that ugly, jagged line of raised flesh that deserved no affection, least of all from him. The *azi* was my weapon, but it had also killed fellow Deathseekers and injured his friends.

"Kalen." The words came out as a sob. "Please."

"With my heart," he murmured against my bare skin. "You better be damn sure, Tea. The last thing I want to be is a consolation prize. But if you want this, then to hell with Kance and everyone else because then you're *mine*." His eyes darkened. "And I'm yours."

"I have never been so sure of anything in my life." It was my turn to take the initiative, grabbing him by his shirt and tugging him up to me. It felt so wonderful and *strange* to know you are your own person but begin to understand how you could also belong wholeheartedly to someone else. "Show me how to worship *you*."

Tea!

I groaned. "Oh no."

Kalen stilled immediately, questioning.

"No, not you." I latched on to him again. *I think I'm owed some privacy, Fox. You have the worst—*

There's an Odalian army at the gates of Santiang!

What?

There are ships on the horizon—at least fifty that I can see. War has come to Daanoris, and we're right smack in the middle of it all over again!

I'M DONE," THE *HEARTFORGER SAID wearily, leaning back. The five slivers of forged* urvan *lay on the table, glittering. "Here are the replicated souls of the Five Great Heroes."*

The Dark asha ran her hands through the urvan *and then the heartsglass before enveloping the startled Heartforger in a hug. "You saved me, Khalad," she whispered. "In the coming days and weeks, no matter what other people shall say about me, remember only this: you saved me, and you saved us all."*

The Heartforger smiled sadly and hugged her tighter. "Is there really no other way, Tea?"

"There is none." She looked back at her lover, and the air changed. She no longer smiled, and her mouth grew pinched, like she was about to do something neither of them wanted. "Kalen, bring him in. Make sure the princess is not here to see—it will not be a pleasant memory to remember His Majesty by."

25

IT WAS AN HOUR BEFORE the wedding. The tension and worry I knew the day would bring, coupled by Kalen's kiss the night before, had made rest almost impossible. I was wide awake, adrenaline coursing through my body. Kalen and Fox kept a close watch on the approaching army; there was nothing else to do but wait and fort up in preparation of a siege.

A history of constant warfare had instilled discipline in the Daanorians—or perhaps they were used to following orders. The emperor called all officials to the throne room, us included, to give a long, sonorous speech that Shadi was quick to translate.

"Are you kidding me?" Fox was disbelieving. "He intends to push through with the wedding?!"

"He believes the Odalian army is here in protest of his engagement to Inessa," Shadi said. "And by making their wedding official, there will no longer be grounds for Kance's betrothal taking precedence. Let's not dissuade him of that belief just yet."

"This is insane," my brother growled.

"Insanity or not, we are trapped," Zoya muttered darkly. "An army outside and traitors within. Stuck between a rock and a hard place." She frowned. "Still…I am certain we are overlooking something important." She raised a hand. "Let me think. I'll figure it out. I always do."

Beside her, Shadi sighed.

·· ⇃⊢ ··

"Baoyi can accuse Tansoong in public of his crimes," Kalen said, "but we don't have any evidence that can hold up to their judgment. There's still Baoyi's testimony, but his and Tansoong's families have been rivals for generations. It would be easy to dismiss this as another play for power on Baoyi's part."

We were on top of the battlements, where we could see the docked ships and the Odalian army amassing. Kalen estimated that it would take another couple of hours for them to arrive at the gates, so Emperor Shifang had announced that the wedding would take place in half the time. I had to admire the emperor's arrogance; he was so used to being the center of which all Daanoris revolved that he assumed Odalia would follow suit.

"I hate this," I groaned. "We've got the Odalian army chasing after us *again*, we can't muster any proof against Tansoong, and we still haven't found the forger!"

Kalen placed an arm around my shoulders, pulling me close. "Just another day in the life of an asha."

"And of a Deathseeker." I snuggled closer to him. "I love you."

"Tea, you don't need to say that just because I—"

I smacked him lightly on the side. "Shut up and let me finish."

He laughed. "Go on."

"I didn't realize it until the day we left Odalia, when I compelled you. I didn't know why your anger bothered me so much. I was terrified you would never forgive me, and it took me a lot longer to ferret out the real reason why."

"I *was* angry," he admitted. "But I was also angry at myself. I knew I had a duty to stay and protect Kance, even though I'd done a horrible mess of it at that point, but I also didn't want to let you out of my sight."

I remembered something else and started to laugh.

"What's so funny?"

"You. When Daisy made a pass at you back in Odalia and I intervened. I had no idea why you were acting so strangely."

"I was stunned."

"I thought I was doing you a good turn. But when you kissed me on the cheek...maybe I was a little jealous you weren't being as rude to her as you usually are to me."

"I didn't want to be the only one out of sorts." He kissed me now. "We're supposed to be on watch," he said brusquely but didn't move away. "Are you sure Inessa intends to go through with this wedding?"

"I think she has something up her sleeve. Zoya too. She went down to the city again this morning."

"Zoya with a plan makes me nervous. What is she up to?"

"I don't know. She asked me if I'd told anyone beyond our group about any specifics of the sleeping sickness. I'm pretty sure no one did."

"Odd. She asked me the same question." He looked back at the army. "They know we have the *azi* on our side, that the army has no chance. Why come all the way here?"

I had no answer to that either.

•• ∖∕∠ ••

It was a solemn affair, and no one but the emperor looked happy. Baoyi and Tansoong stood on either side of the aisle and traded dirty looks when they thought he wasn't looking. Zoya and even Shadi seemed unnaturally nervous. Likh was staring at the ceiling, his mouth moving soundlessly as beads of sweat appeared on his forehead. Kalen glanced occasionally at me and then out the window. Fox's placid exterior bespoke an inner turmoil: disbelief that the marriage was taking place, worry about the growing army outside, and anger that he was doing nothing to stop either.

We can call this off, you know, I told him.

I promised her, came the grim response. *I told her I'd trust her, and I will.*

Daanorian wedding ceremonies were not a lengthy affair. All that was needed to cement the marriage was for the emperor to take his intended bride by the hand and declare to all those watching that she was officially his wife. And as Inessa walked serenely down the aisle, courtiers strewing roses in the path before her, she never once wavered. As she passed us, I saw her eyes stray toward Fox, and her heartsglass bloomed a rosy-red glow before she deliberately turned away.

We watched as Emperor Shifang took her hand, turned toward us, and in a remarkably brief speech, no doubt ushered along by the situation outside, officially proclaimed her his wife. On cue, the court fell to their knees, and at Zoya's quick gesture, we followed suit. Fox was seething with grief and rage entwined.

Cries rose up from outside. The army had reached the gates. Battle was about to begin.

Emperor Shifang gave a curt order. "Send word that the Princess of Kion is now the Empress of Daanoris," Shadi translated for us. "Prepare the troops. As soon as I give the word, we shall attack."

Zoya stepped forward, speaking in Daanorian. "A moment, Your Majesty."

A few courtiers gasped, and the emperor scowled. He turned to ignore her, but Inessa shook her hand free from her husband's and stepped back.

"What is the meaning of this insolence?" Tansoong demanded.

"We have reason to believe that there is a traitor in our midst and that it is one of your own advisers, Emperor Shifang. This traitor bespelled your army and summoned the *savul*."

"And who might that be?" demanded the emperor.

Zoya raised her hand. It swept past Tansoong and pointed unerringly at Baoyi. "Him."

I was astonished. From Kalen's and Fox's expression, I wasn't the only one.

"Lady Zoya?" Baoyi looked as stunned as I was. "I beg your pardon?"

"You poisoned Princess Yansheo under the guise of an Odalian duke. For your help, Usij promised you lordship over Santiang and most of Daanoris. It was you who secreted those seeking stones within the emperor's army in the hopes it would distract our Dark asha long enough for her to be killed by the *savul*. You have betrayed Emperor Shifang and you have allied yourself with the Faceless."

The man lifted his hands. "Emperor Shifang," he beseeched. "I have served you faithfully for years. I am innocent of these accusations. Surely you do not believe these lies?"

"Let us not get ahead of ourselves, Baoyi." I didn't like Tansoong, but he was a master politician, quick to take advantage when the tide turned in his favor. The advisor said, "I have been keeping a close eye on you for many months, and I have many reasons to suspect that what they say could be true."

"Is he in on the plan?" I heard Shadi whisper to Zoya.

"Of course not. He's talking out of his ass, but at least the emperor's paying attention."

"They're going to hear you," Khalad mumbled.

"It's not like most of them understand me. And at this point, it's too late to be offended."

"My suspicions began when you arrived from Tresea last year with several pieces of what you claimed were jade stones," Tansoong continued.

"I have always been a collector, Tansoong."

"Collector my foot. I know what jade looks like, and those certainly weren't precious gems. After Yansheo fell sick, I pored through many magical tomes from Kion, trying to find an antidote even if it went beyond our own laws. In my desperation to see the princess well again, I came upon many magical treatises written by asha. What you call jade looked like what the asha call 'seeking stones.'"

"You're getting blind in your old age, Tansoong," Baoyi accused.

"Oh, I know my vision isn't what it used to be," the old man drawled, enjoying his time in the spotlight. "You spirited them out of the palace as quickly as you received them, but I had my spy steal one of your 'jades' to confirm my suspicions. After that, I had my men deliver it, along with an anonymous letter, to your old friend, Narel, at the shack he frequents in the city. He and I had never seen eye to eye, but I knew he wouldn't let your friendship get in the way if you were up to something suspicious."

The realization that Tansoong was telling the truth and Baoyi was our enemy all along triggered something in my brain. I remembered Baoyi's quarters, the jade stones Khalad had arranged on the mantelpiece. The Heartforger had piled three of them on top of the other, a careful display of balance. I had seen that somewhere else in the palace...

Baoyi shifted uneasily. "That means nothing."

"No, but it explains many other things." Zoya spoke up again. "The men in your army who sought to attack you, Your Majesty, were influenced by these same seeking stones."

"Then there is all the more reason to suspect you and your group, not me," Baoyi protested. "I have no skills for magic, and of all of us here, you would be the most likely—"

"You talked about conducting a search for the princess's heartsglass yesterday. How do you know what heartsglass looks like?"

"I have read texts of them, that they are red in color and shine like rubies. It is common enough knowledge."

"What isn't common knowledge was that this particular sleeping sickness turns their hearts gray. None of us told you about this particular detail, yet you told me you had ordered your soldiers to bring back any gray jewels they might find. How do you explain that?"

Sweat beaded on Baoyi's forehead. "Narel told me."

"The Heartforger explicitly stated in his letter that he told you nothing to spare you from worry. Once I realized that, I focused my attentions on you. The jade you like to display on your mantelpiece are very similar in shape and size to seeking stones. How easy would it be to smuggle them under the guise of unpolished gems? The forger also mentioned a recent visit, yet you denied he ever came. Either he was talking to an impersonator—highly doubtful, since it would be too risky to have two of you in the palace at once—or you lied because you didn't want to be the last man to see him." Zoya was in fighting form, her eyes glittering.

"A coincidence!"

"You talked about Shaoyun, Baoyi. *A scarlet peacock*, in your own words. The lovely Lady Likh mentioned finding a corpse in the city—a corpse with bits of red cloth still clinging to its body. Red is an unusual color for a typical Daanorian, who prefer their grays and browns. Shadi and I took the initiative to bring back his remains. I spent quite a long time piecing together the bits of cloth he wore, which contained a crest. We compared it with his family's herald. Shall we have the Dark asha raise him to confirm to see what stories he could tell?"

"You—you—" Baoyi took a step toward her, his face livid.

"Now, Likh!" Zoya commanded.

Instantly, I felt the wards around us disappear, as Likh forced the spell to dissipate. Baoyi's clerk dropped to his knees, a pained howl dribbling from his mouth as a sudden rush of magic filled me, too fast and too soon that I swore that my whole body was thrumming from the power alone, a desperate need to compel everyone I saw nearly overwhelming.

But my training returned, my mind clinging to my meditation runes almost on instinct, to focus on the matter at hand, at my role in this drama playing out. Already I was completing the spell before I'd realized what I was doing, and the *Piercing* rune spiraled into the air toward the strongest source of magic in the room—not Baoyi but his *clerk*. The spell bound him like rope. I squeezed, and a ripple *went through* the man, like he was merely a reflection in the water.

I felt a force attempt to clamp down on my mind, trying to

prevent me from going further. But I was ready. The protection stone felt hot around my neck, and the *azi* rose up and roared at him, barreling into his mind with all its might.

With a frantic yell, Baoyi's assistant dropped his guard, and I surged forward. The illusion around him shattered, and the remnants of his disguise peeled away. I found myself looking at a shriveled old man, far older than even Tansoong, bald but with a full beard.

"Usij!" Emperor Shifang roared.

The man ignored him and turned to me, a slow smile spreading across his wrinkled face. "I am impressed, bone witch. I have heard of your exploits, including Aenah's capture. Neither she nor I had ever been able to tame the *azi* completely. Your willpower is formidable."

"You dare bring this foul magician into the palace, Baoyi?" the emperor thundered.

"I am no longer Baoyi of Daanoris, fool. Just as you have forsaken your kingdom for magical creatures and Kion strumpets, so have I forsaken mine to serve the Great Prince as his favored disciple."

"How could you?" Khalad raged. "You were my master's friend!"

Baoyi was unmoved. "Neither you nor your master know how the world truly works. Daanoris has stepped out of its self-imposed exile only to discover that we lag behind other kingdoms. Only through magic and these monsters at our bidding can we finally stand as gods before all. *I bear my own silver heartsglass,*

Your Majesty. Master Usij found me, drew it for me, showed me the way. I could have risen to such heights had it not been for your foolish ban on runes."

"You killed Shaoyun," Zoya said grimly.

"As you said, your friends have already met him." The Faceless's smile turned my stomach. "And after all the effort we took to implicate him."

"You filthy, loathsome man."

"Now, now, this is not the time to trade compliments. I have conceded this battle. Let me go."

"Preposterous!" Emperor Shifang all but screamed at him. "The hangman's noose shall be your fate! Why should I release you?"

Still inside the traitor's head, I sensed the sudden shift, familiar and strange, creep into his mind. I had a vision of scales and yellow eyes.

A wild cry rose up from outside the city, the scream penetrating and loud.

"My *savul* is at the city gates," Druj said, "and the city shall run red with blood before the day is out."

Then he struck. I was waiting for it; the *azi* took most of the blow, its shield strong enough to deflect what could have easily incapacitated me, and I could still feel my ears ring from the force. I staggered backward. Usij whirled to attack again—not at me but at the emperor.

Shifang froze, eyes strangely blank. He snatched a sword from one of his guards and turned to Inessa.

But Fox was ready. The emperor's blade passed through my

brother's shoulder, and a deft twist of Fox's wrist disarmed the Daanorian. Another hard blow knocked him out.

There was the sound of shattering glass.

Kalen, Zoya, and several of the soldiers rushed forward. A small net strung across the city below had taken the brunt of both Usij's and Baoyi's fall, and I saw several passersby—no, Usij's followers!—helping them to their feet.

"Barricade the city gates!" Tansoong roared. "Don't let them get away!"

"We have more to worry about now," Fox said grimly, ripping the sword free from his body. Through the broken glass, I saw the *savul* heading toward Santiang, and its shrieks rattled the panes.

"Stop that!" Inessa said irritably as more soldiers drew their swords on Fox. "You've seen him stabbed. It's not going to work. Lower your weapons or I will stab you all with *mine*." She further demonstrated by fishing out a small knife she had hidden within the folds of her dress, pointing it at the nearest guard and then repeating the words in Daanorian.

"Your vocabulary needs work, Your Majesty," Shadi cautioned helpfully as the trembling soldiers obeyed. "You told the men you were going to stab them with your hamster."

"Then do the translating for me, Shadi. Tell them that while the emperor is incapacitated, I'm assuming command, as is my responsibility. Just like the Empress Kalka and the Empress Meili before me, I claim rulership of Daanoris in my husband's stead while he recuperates. Order the army's retreat, Tansoong. This war shall not be won by drawing human blood."

I was already moving toward the door, brushing past the frightened guards, who made no move to confront me. *The dungeons, Fox*, I whispered, frantic. *The dungeons!*

The jade stones on Baoyi's mantelpiece. And Khalad absently building a tower of pebbles in the Kingshead Inn—and then again at the forger's hut in Kion.

Got the habit from Master, he had said.

The prison was just as dark and as dank as I remembered, for all appearances empty. I stopped at the farthest cell and stared into it. I could see nothing within.

I looked down at the broken debris that littered the dungeon floor. The pile of stones I had seen at my last visit was still there.

Kalen and Khalad had caught up to us. "What's happening?" the Deathseeker asked.

"The forger is here."

"I don't see anyone."

"I know." I closed my eyes and took a deep breath, wove *Heartsrune*.

There were three people in the room. But when I focused on the number of heartsglass that I could detect from sense alone, I could feel four.

This was Khalad's first time in the dungeons; his face was pale.

"He's here," he croaked. "Master's here."

To pierce through the veil of the Illusion rune, it is important to believe that what is in front of you is not what you truly see...

"What is in front of me," I echoed, "is not what I truly see."

It was easy enough to puncture Usij's mirages when you're certain what you are looking for. But all I had to go by here was a hunch and a pile of stones at my feet.

But there was someone in this cell, someone that a rune convinced my mind was empty. There was someone here because I could hear his heartsglass pulse and rise and fall, as real as my own. There was someone here. There was someone here!

I drew the *Piercing* rune, unshakable in my newfound belief, and put everything I had into that small cell. It was uphill work and slower than I imagined, like weaving thick taffy. I also felt resistance—not from another's thoughts but from the nature of the spell itself—and forced the image of the forger that I remembered through it.

There was a sound, at least to my mind, of glass breaking.

And from what had once been empty air, the old Heartforger lay, huddled by the straw bed, unconscious.

*T*HE DEATHSEEKER RETURNED WITH THE *struggling emperor and deposited him in the middle of the room. The Dark asha stepped toward him, her fingers busy.*

"The time for deceit is over, Your Majesty," the asha told him. "You have been hiding under this form for many months, and the people suffered under your tyranny. You have killed the worthy Tansoong and recruited many of your own into positions of power in the palace. You have wallowed in luxury and allowed your people to live in filth. You survived our last battle but at a cost. Even now, my wards wrap around you, and you are no longer strong enough to break free. I let you keep your illusion only because every Daanorian soldier in this city would want your head if they knew, and the last thing I wanted was a mutiny before the forger was done. But now you have outlived your usefulness."

"Lady Tea," I implored her, hoping to find some mercy left inside her, "Emperor Shifang's death will do more harm to your cause."

"But Emperor Shifang is no longer with us, Bard. I knew it when I scried my way into Daanoris from the Sea of Skulls and confirmed it when I saw the hanjian, *Baoyi, directing the soldiers against us." Magic burned. The emperor threw his head back and screamed. He thrashed desperately on the floor, twitching, as his features twisted and writhed—and melted, like wax dripping over some great bonfire.*

I watched, horror stricken, as a new face emerged from that ruined expression, a mask peeled away to reveal the face of an old bald man with a long beard, gasping in pain on the floor.

"Meet the scourge of Daanoris," the bone witch said. "The Faceless, Usij."

26

NEITHER THE DAANORIAN NOR THE Odalian army was a match for the rampaging *savul*. It tore through their front flanks like they were made of paper. Inessa called out orders to retreat as Shadi and Kalen stood guard over the unconscious emperor. I scanned the rest of the guards for any signs of *Compulsion* and found none, but as I directed my thoughts farther out, delving into the city, I felt the wards outside diminishing my reach. If Usij had been planning for such a contingency, he was alarmingly good at it. The barriers were still not enough to deprive me completely of my magic but enough to keep me from intervening in the battle with my full strength as long as I remained in Santiang.

Even more telling, the *savul* made no move to attack the marching Odalian army. The implications were clear—and the idea that the Duke of Holsrath or someone else was possibly in league with Usij made me sick.

"Why didn't you tell me about Baoyi?" I hissed at Zoya.

"I found confirmation just before the ceremony began. I had enough time to tell Shadi and Inessa. We wanted to expose him as soon as possible, but Inessa wanted to wait until after the ceremony." She flinched. "I would have looked foolish if I'd called out Tansoong."

"You were planning on assuming command all along," Shadi said to Inessa. "That speech was a little too practiced to be spontaneous."

The princess grinned. "I've been reading up on Daanorian history. Whenever the emperor was incapacitated, his empress could use as much power as she wanted and expect the same obedience as was due the emperor."

"Were you expecting to knock out the emperor yourself?"

"I asked Althy to bring me some herbal preparations before we'd left Kion. One of them was a sleeping remedy I'd slipped in his wine earlier for the toast. I wanted to be prepared for any eventuality, but Fox punching him was an unexpected bonus."

Shadi looked impressed.

"I am not looking forward to telling your mother we have *another* unwanted international incident on her hands, Inessa," Zoya scolded.

"Then maybe she shouldn't have dangled me in front of Emperor Shifang all these years. Or offered the betrothal to him in the first place."

"The Daanorians have retreated back into the city, Your Majesty," Tansoong reported, hurrying forward. "We have barricaded the gates, but I fear that will not last long."

"Have the men stand at the ready, and keep an eye out for any other spies within. Report to either Lord Kalen or Lady Tea immediately should any soldier begin acting strangely. There may be a few more under the effects of the seeking stones."

"Nothing says loyalty better than the newfound devotion of a man whose rival you helped depose," Zoya noted sarcastically as the man scuttled away.

"Do you think Aenah is behind this somehow?" Likh asked. "She's the only Faceless we know of in Odalia."

"It's hard to tell at this point. Zoya, I want you and Shadi protecting Inessa and the old forger."

"He's not going to die, is he?" Likh asked worriedly.

He and Khalad were tending to the still-unconscious Heartforger, the relief I saw in Khalad's heartsglass the only bright spot this morning. A bed had been carried in, water and clean cloth brought forward, and Khalad had dug into his medicine pouch, administering treatments. "He suffers from a lack of water, but he's still as strong as they come."

"You must really love him, don't you?"

He hesitated, smiled. "I suppose I do. He has his odd moments, but he's been like a second father to me."

"I wouldn't go that far, boy."

Khalad pounced on the old forger, who was already struggling to rise. "No unnecessary movements, Master!"

"Every one of my movements *is* necessary, boy," the old man scowled, resisting. "And what's necessary is that I get up from this contraption!"

"It's called a *bed*. If we'd ever saved enough money for one, you'd know. And what's necessary is to keep you well rested and healthy, you old codger. If you keep struggling, know that I am a lot stronger than you and will use force if I have to."

"You wouldn't dare!"

"Try me!"

Master and apprentice glared at each other. The former finally relented, sinking back against the pillows with a grunt. "I should be gone more often. You've got some of your hotheaded-ness back, boy."

Khalad sagged. "You scared us, Master."

"I scared myself too. I was certain it was the end of the road for me." The forger nodded in my direction. "That was very perceptive of you, girl. Thank you."

"I'm glad you're all right, sir."

"I'm not all right. I can't be all right when that bastard's still running free! I must be getting soft in my old age, giving him the benefit of the doubt simply because I knew his father. Is the princess still asleep? Unharmed?"

"She is," Likh confirmed.

The old forger stared at him. "You're a pretty girl, but I don't know who in the seven hells you are. What's happening?"

"Daanoris is being attacked by Odalia, and Usij is out there using the *savul* to create widespread panic," Zoya growled. "Nothing out of the ordinary."

"Master, you should rest…"

"Rest, my foot. We've got enemies surroundings us at all

sides, and the bastard who locked me up is at the forefront. Where is he? I need to punch him. I'm glad his father's no longer alive to see his son fall into such depravity. Always been a weak boy, wanting things he didn't want to earn. The princess is all right, you say? Take me to her."

"We should," Khalad said. "It's the safest room in the palace at this point."

"And where are you going?" Fox demanded as I headed for the door.

"I'm not going to stay here while a daeva is making short work of the people outside, Fox. Stay here with Inessa."

"Don't do anything stupid, Tea!"

"When have I ever?" I was out of the room before he could reply, but I could hear the pounding of feet behind me as Kalen gave chase. I raced up the staircase, making for the highest tower in the palace—the same battlements Kalen and I stood on as we watched the Odalian army approach a few hours before.

"What do you think you're doing?" Kalen yelled, catching up to me as I reached the top. I could see the *savul* approaching, the soldiers in disarray. At the same time, I could feel the *azi* drawing closer to where I stood.

I faced him. "I can't fight the *savul* from this far away, Kalen."

"You can't handle both the *azi* and the *savul* at once!"

The thought of Mykaela back in Kion, still fighting for her life alongside Polaire, only filled me with more resolve. "Does it look like we have a choice?"

And then I leaped off the edge of the tower.

Looking back, I knew it was a foolish thing to do. But after being deprived of the Dark for so long, it was difficult to shunt away the heady power filling me. At that instant, I felt almost omnipotent, ready to take on the world and everyone in it.

I had a few moments of clarity, saw Kalen's shocked face and open mouth staring down at me, rapidly falling from view as my descent continued. And then the *azi* was there, swooping me up so quickly and effortlessly onto its back, just like during those midnight rides we shared before the rest of the world knew of our connection.

Are you crazy?! Fox all but screamed into my head.

This was quicker than riding through the city. I felt sorry, but the giddiness from being full of the Dark had not disappeared. I could only let out a strangled giggle, still drunk on the power, even as the *azi* changed direction, the battlefield before us its new destination.

It did not take long to arrive, and by then, I had taken back control of my faculties, forcing the sweetness of the magic away, not without regret. I needed my wits about me; there were two wars on this battlefront, and my enemies could easily unite against me.

In another corner of my mind, I could feel Fox moving, barking orders. I had fleeting images of Daanorian servants and courtiers with wooden faces and blank eyes shuffling toward them, my brother fighting them off.

"Perhaps we shouldn't have been so hasty with unraveling those wards," I heard Shadi say, and through my brother's eyes,

I watched her slam a heavy vase against the side of a man's head, watching him crumple.

"Curse that old geezer," Zoya growled. She was keeping the bulk of the enemy at bay, weaving *Wind* through the corridors so a small tornado sent people flying left and right before any of them could get too close. "Fox, where is your wayward sister now?"

"Off to fight the *savul* on her own," Fox growled, his frustration bleeding through. "Kalen's on his way."

The *savul* was still injured from our previous fight. I saw the ugly scars along its neck where we had been dealt our fiercest blow, its blackened limbs moving with difficulty. For all its ferocity, the *savul* was clearly in excruciating pain. A brush against its mind told me that it's participation today had not been a willing decision; the faintest edges of Usij's mind touched mine, and I drew back immediately. I felt the Faceless push harder, but the *azi* responded in my place, snapping at the intruder until he retreated.

You've trained your pet well, bone witch.

Would you like some advice for yours? The *azi* was docile because I had shown it nothing but respect. Usij had mistreated his daeva, and despite all the harm and chaos the *savul* had caused, I could not help my sympathy. How long had he been enslaving the creature?

Longer than you have been a bone witch, child. The simpering old crone tasked with killing it was easy enough to dispose of. The chaos it caused rampaging through Odalia's territory!

I allowed myself a grim smile. I knew he was somewhere nearby, for we needed proximity to our beasts to garner the greatest control; perhaps the old man had already hidden himself among the Odalian soldiers. *Thank you, Usij.*

Oh?

If it were not for your savul, *my brother would not have been killed and I could have lived the rest of my life oblivious to my true abilities. You are the reason I am standing here, and I am the reason you will die today.*

He snarled into my head, and then his mind was gone. The *savul* let loose a horrible cry and jumped; the *azi* responded with a barrage of flames, but not even the extreme heat was enough. The reptilian daeva slammed hard into us, and quick thinking and reflexes saved me from being skewered by its powerful claws, which dug into the *azi*'s hide. My daeva reared up, howling in pain, and I held on to its neck, knowing one lost grip could mean falling to my death.

Tea!

Protect the princess! I screamed back. There was nothing Fox could do at this point to help me, and the quick *Veiling* rune I wove kept the bulk of his thoughts away from mine, kept him from being distracted. It was more difficult this time. I had no one to look after my physical body and so could not completely immerse myself in my daeva. At my command, however, the *azi* raised its spiked tail, still scrabbling with the *savul.* It was the toad-like beast's turn to shriek, as the spike plowed through its midsection, puncturing the skin. It stumbled back.

The army hesitated. Seeing the fallen daeva, they pushed forward cautiously. I wove *Dominion* over as many of them as

I was able but fell short. Only a dozen or so responded—I was too exhausted to extend my reach, and there were thousands of them still.

I saw Kalen approaching with his horse, staring up at us in horror. I stuck my head out over the *azi*'s side.

"Get out of here!" I yelled.

"I could tell you the exact same thing!" Kalen turned to face the Odalian soldiers. It was a magnificent, petrifying sight: my black-clad warrior, facing off against an army—the very fate I had hoped for him to avoid when I compelled him in Odalia. My fears were mitigated only because I could sense no other spellbinders there beyond Baoyi and Usij. "What makes you think I'm going to let you do this alone?"

As the men surged forward, Kalen spread his arms, tracing dual runes in the air at once. A fog rose, the mist so thick and cloying that it was difficult to see a hand in front of your own face. Cries of dismay rose among the ranks as soldiers stumbled into each other.

Kalen wasn't done. Borrowing a page from Althy's book, he slammed his hands to the ground, punching another series of runes into the soil, and a large sinkhole opened up underneath the mass of swirling fog. More yells came from the soldiers as they tumbled down the unexpected ravine.

"Showoff."

He said nothing, flashing me a smug grin.

With the soldiers off our backs, I focused on the *savul* again. I slipped cautiously back into its mind and felt Usij's rancid presence as he screamed and railed at his creature to rise. The *savul* could only moan piteously. The *azi* had withdrawn its spike, leaving a large bloody hole at the center of the daeva's body; I could feel the life stealing out from it. Usij's mind withdrew, leaving it to suffer a slow and painful death.

Breathing hard, I commanded the *azi* to lower its head so I could slide down to the ground. Usij had abandoned his former pet, and I felt no resistance as I probed lightly into its mind. Its thoughts slid over me, warm and accepting of its approaching demise with a relief I could not help but feel pity for.

"*Stay*," I told it gently, and it shuddered.

Pain lanced through my mind. I screamed; behind me, the *azi* reared up, all three heads howling at the sky. I felt something wrench them from my mind, and then their presence was gone.

Kalen's arms caught me before I could collapse, but I could barely hear his voice. The loss of my *azi* had left a sudden gaping emptiness in my chest, like Usij had wrenched my heart out along with my control.

I heard a wheezing chuckle from nearby. As my vision cleared, I saw the old man standing before the fallen *savul*, smiling. "You might have bested the Odalian army, my dear," he said laughing, "but empathy remains your weakness." He turned to regard the *savul* with disdain. The creature was lying on its side, no longer moving. "A waste of flesh and power. The weakest of the lot as far as I'm concerned. But now, the *azi*…"

The *azi* took one step toward him and then another. It bowed its heads at his feet, and rage coursed through me. "Oh, the *azi*! That is a different beast entirely. The only daeva to have never been conquered by a human army or slain by a human hand. Aenah's a fool, but that bitch knew how to tame daeva. If not for your efforts, Tea, I might never have found so powerful a prize." He laid a hand on one of its heads, and the *azi* did not flinch. "It is time to replace your old master with one of better conviction," he told the daeva. "*Kill her.*"

With a low hiss, the *azi* rose, its three heads trained in my direction. Trails of flame simmered from its snouts. Kalen raised his hand, palm outward, and *Shield* runes shimmered.

Despite the protection, the heat was intense. Fire licked at us, stopping several inches from us as it hit the barrier. The *azi* rumbled and let loose another torrent, and Kalen, his face grim and perspiring, shouldered the burden.

"Not today, Deathseeker."

Kalen stiffened, his eyes wide with surprise. He let go of me, and I tumbled to the ground, still dazed. The *azi* had backed away, but Kalen remained upright, his eyes staring into the distance. The runes around us faded. I moved to stand, but Kalen's foot pressed against my back, pinning me down.

"I think this would make for a better end and for better irony," Usij drawled. "A bone witch slain by her own protector's hand. Is that not a more fitting epitaph?"

Wordlessly, Kalen turned to me. He drew out his sword.

"Kalen…" I tried to enter his mind, desperate to find an opening, but Usij had been using compulsion for far too many years on far too many victims.

Kalen raised the blade over my neck. I changed the direction of my thoughts, pushing myself into the mind of the next best thing, knowing full well that I would not wrest control before the blow came.

"*Kill her, Deathseeker.*"

The blade fell, and I closed my eyes.

It struck the ground beside me, inches from my head. Usij snarled.

"*Kill her!*"

Kalen did not move. The sword trembled in his hands. I felt weak; there was a tug at my heartsglass, leeching strength from me.

"*Kill her! Kill her!*" Usij howled.

Kalen raised his sword, lowered it again. And then I saw the *Heartshare* rune, bright and glittering by his heartsglass, and I understood. He was resisting.

So did Usij, who laughed. "Foolish, besotted little man. Here is a better idea. *Kill yourself in front of your beloved bone witch. Slice your own throat and let her bathe in your blood. Do it!*"

The sword rose, but Kalen's hesitation gave me time.

Usij let out a strange, strangled gasp and fell to his knees. The blade dropped from Kalen's hands.

The Faceless looked down, eyes bulging, at the large claw now sticking out of his chest and at another talon protruding from his stomach, organs and entrails slithering to the floor.

"Impossible," he wheezed as rivulets of blood flowed down his mouth, a waterfall of red that soaked his chin and neck. And then he fell on his face and stopped moving.

"Tea," Kalen whispered. He was beside me, his rough hands cupping my face, his lips against my brow, my cheek, my lips. "Tea."

"Beating him was tantamount to fighting at least five men, don't you think?" I whispered against his mouth, exhausted beyond belief. Kalen's chest heaved with relief, with laughter.

I focused on the *savul* again, and it withdrew its claw. At the same time, the *azi*, independent of any control, wrenched its tail spike away from the old man's body with a sickening, crunching sound.

With difficulty, Kalen helped me up, his stare cautious as his eyes rested on the three-headed dragon before us.

"It won't hurt us."

"You're not compelling it, Tea. It can attack at any moment."

"It won't hurt us," I repeated. "When Usij was distracted, it killed him without my urging." The *azi* bowed all three snouts, resting its long necks on the ground in an act of submission.

"But that's impossible."

"What's one more impossibility today?" The yellow eyes that watched me approach were trusting, and the rumbling noise that started from the back of its throat was almost kittenish. "You shook free of his control all on your own, didn't you?" I asked in wonder, laying my hand on the *azi*'s head, as I had done so many times before. It purred again, and I felt its mind open to mine, inviting as, for the first time, a daeva bowed before a human master of its own free will.

*T*HE RAMIFICATIONS WERE BOUNDLESS. EMPEROR *Shifang* was an imposter. *The man who had been leading Daanoris all these months was its greatest enemy. Now I understood the bone witch's hatred; now I understood her murder of the* hanjian.

The pain of having his spell so violently dispersed took its toll on the Faceless. His eyes rolled to the back of his head as he shook, and foam bubbled from his mouth. His hands and feet were still bound, but these were no longer deterrents; he was clearly in no shape to break free.

"You survived, you old fool," the Dark asha said, almost appreciative. "Old as the mountains, your hands full of guts and viscera, and still you survived. But severely weakened. Maintaining this Illusion *rune must have taken everything you had.*"

"You…stupid…bitch…" *he snarled between choking gasps.*

"To you seeking Blade that Soars's path," *the girl quoted,* "take that which came from Five Great Heroes long past and distill into a heart of silver to shine anew. *I have need of your heartsglass, Usij. Black heartsglass was silver once, and lightsglass has purifying effects. And the rub? I do not require your permission. Khalad, do it.*"

The Heartforger was quick; he grabbed at the Faceless's heartsglass, which rippled violently. With one hand, he forced the first of the five *urvan into its center, the lightning-shaped glass disappearing into its depths.*

Usij howled and tried one last time to break free, but Lord Kalen held the Faceless's arms and Lord Khalad forced the second and then the third urvan in. Usij's face swiveled to stare into mine, and I froze. It was like the face of a desperate animal, willing to do anything to free itself. The zivar I wore shone, but nothing else happened.

Kill them.

Feeling bemused, I rose to my feet. There was a small table by the side of the door, with the remains of our last meal. I took one of the larger knives there, examining it closely to gauge its sharpness. Quickly! The thought ran through my head.

I ran toward Lord Khalad's unprotected back, knife raised and ready—and stopped as a new presence bored into my mind. The zivar burned again, so hot that I could feel it scalding into my skin, could imagine the sizzling of flesh there. I screamed aloud. The knife clattered to the floor.

"Desperation brings out strength," the bone witch said. "Warded as you are, weakened as we made you—and yet able to reach out and control the bard still. You are a dangerous man, Usij. The land shall be glad to be rid of you."

The Heartforger forced the last of the urvan into the black heartsglass and the room filled with unexpected light. The Faceless's heart was no longer black like the Dark asha's but instead a magnificent array of silvers. The girl ripped the heartsglass free from Usij and held it aloft in her hand.

"Leave," she ordered, and a terrible languidness came over me. My feet moved independently of the rest of me, shuffling toward the room next door, even as a part of me struggled and screamed at the aeshma that now lumbered forward with horrifying eagerness.

"*Tea!*" *the Heartforger pleaded. "Don't do this. Kill him if you must, but let it be quick.*"

The bone witch trembled. With what remaining access she had to my mind, I could sense her thirst for the darkrot, her yearning to be cruel.

"*Tea,*" *Lord Kalen said, adding his supplication to his cousin's. "Please.*"

After a moment, the aeshma *sniffed, retreating. I was already out the door and into the corridor, and what else happened in that throne room afterward, I knew not. My mind was peaceful and deprived of thought, and for that I was glad.*

27

EMPEROR SHIFANG HAD NOT QUITE fully recovered from his ordeal. His eyes were bloodshot and glazed over as he looked out into his city and saw the remains of the carnage that stretched out before him, from the bodies of the Daanorian soldiers that had not survived the battle to the two hulking daeva out in the field.

He was no longer the perfectly manicured and well-dressed emperor who had greeted us with spears and threats when we first entered his throne room. But for all his faults, his formidable arrogance and assurance of his gods-given right to rule remained very much in evidence, even as he defied Tansoong's orders to set out and see the daeva for himself, despite all reasonable arguments against his doing so.

The *savul* was still alive, still breathing despite its mortal injuries as the litter carrying the emperor arrived. With them was everyone else: Zoya and Shadi, Likh and Khalad, and the elder Heartforger. The old man was stooped and exhausted, though the fire was back in his eyes. Khalad supported him, with Likh on the other side. Zoya and Shadi looked just as tired. Princess Inessa walked beside Fox instead of behind the emperor, as should have been customary of all noble Daanorian wives. The silver fox pin she wore on her collar glinted in the morning light. Fox said little, though the pain from his proximity to the *savul* had not faded.

We had borne away the dead and the dying. The Odalian army had not recovered from the sinkhole Kalen had opened beneath them, and from their stunned expressions and their incredulity, I surmised that most of them had fallen victim to compulsion, though which Faceless was responsible still remained a mystery. The Odalian army was, in fact, not quite the Odalian army after all.

"Hired stooges," Kalen muttered angrily. "I wondered why I saw no familiar faces among them, why their uniforms were out of order. Bandits and thieves, for the most part. Their leaders were paid handsomely to wave the Odalian flag and march in beat, but no one can tell me their purchaser. We are still hunting for Baoyi and the others."

"A quick scry into their minds tells me nothing, though I would say Usij is the likely culprit. Holsrath would have sent the army itself." I still had one last task to accomplish. The Faceless's body had still been warm to the touch when it had been carted away to be thrown into a nearby ditch for the crows to feast on.

I had drawn out my knife but paused. The logical part of me knew that the *savul* should die. And yet…

"Do you want me to do it?" Kalen asked quietly.

I shook my head and turned to Fox, still watching me with that same unshakable gaze. "Here's your revenge," I told him.

He shook his head. "You avenged me the instant Usij died. This is just another one of his victims." His eyes searched mine. *You don't want to kill it. But you must, Tea.*

Had this been Kion, I might have found another way. But this was Daanorian territory, and the kingdom bayed for blood.

After a moment, I took Kalen's sword and presented it wordlessly to Shifang. He understood well enough. It was not every day that an emperor could claim a daeva kill, even on a technicality. But he dismissed my paltry weapon and summoned an underling to bring him the sword he so favored, littered with ornate jewels but with no sharpness to speak of. The *savul* would not die quickly from its blow.

The emperor raised his hand, his sword glittering in the light, while I quietly wove my *Raising*. "*Die*," I whispered softly as Shifang struck, and the *savul* complied before his blade landed. A faint cheer rose among the soldiers.

"Take this carcass and dispose of it," the emperor ordered. Tansoong scuttled forward, issuing more commands of his own, and the soldiers converged around the fallen beast, uncertain where to start.

The deed done, the smile faded from the emperor's face, and he turned toward his wife. Inessa remained standing apart from him, as regal as any queen could be, and I could see the Empress Alyx in her stern face.

"You have brought many things to my kingdom," the emperor added soberly. "The good and the terrible."

Inessa inclined her head. "Perhaps our marriage has been looked on with disfavor from the gods."

"Perhaps that is so." But yearning lingered in the man's voice. "Perhaps…perhaps it is still possible—"

Inessa shook her head. "You knew long before today that we are not compatible."

The emperor's gaze strayed toward Fox, contempt and anger now evident. "I can make things difficult for the people of Kion," he said, falling back on threats when honeyed words would no longer work.

I was done with all the intrigue, and the Dark swirled in my blood, enough to desire to offend. "And I can make things difficult for His Majesty." I glided forward, and the emperor shrunk back, his fear palpable. I hid my smile. Was I no longer the small harmless thing he described at our first meeting? "I am the keeper of the dragon. Harm one hair on your queen's head, harm any of us here…and we will wreak havoc upon your land until your own citizens shall beat their chest and rue the day you assumed your throne."

Perhaps that went too far, as I was not in the mood to be cordial. But it had the desired effect; Shifang did not need a heartsglass for me to smell his fright, as sharp and as sweet as the breeze around us.

"What the Dark asha means," Zoya countered, as soft as syrup where I was as rough as granite, "is that the Faceless's plans to sow discord will succeed if we are divided against them. We must stand united, Your Majesty, but we must do so by means other than marriage."

The emperor bowed his head, scowling, but nodded. "That is true. My people…have not looked on this betrothal with favor. But Inessa and I are already wedded."

"We are not, Your Majesty," Inessa interrupted. "A binding stipulation of an emperor's bride is that she must come to her husband's bed pure and untouched. I…cannot fulfill such a requirement."

To have Inessa declare this before her husband, much less in front of an audience, was positively scandalous. The emperor drew away from her in horror, her audience gasped, and I hid a grin.

I moderated my tone. "There will be no shame in you declaring the marriage to the First Daughter of Kion annulled. Kion will do nothing in retaliation, and you keep your honor in the eyes of your people. For all intents and purposes, it is us who have been rejected and turned away. But you, in your magnanimity, have offered us a chance to enter into better trade agreements with Kion as a means to bolster our friendship in spite of the failed union."

The emperor was a proud man, but he was no fool. I saw him taking to the idea the longer he thought. "It is the only way," he said slowly. "As much as I…appreciate the Princess Inessa, I am not willing to put my affection for her before Daanoris. The magic you wield…it is too much for my kingdom, for any kingdom, to contain. See what terrors you have wrought upon my people because of it. My ancestors have done well to ban the practice."

He looked up at the *azi* silhouetted against the sky, ever watchful for new signs of trouble.

"See what terrors you will bring upon Kion," he added.

·· ⋛⋚ ··

"You and Inessa planned this," Fox said as my knife sliced into the dead *savul*'s flesh. At my request, the Daanorians abandoned the attempt to carry the daeva away, and all had retreated to a safe distance, fearful. Zoya and Shadi were in deep conversation with Tansoong. Now that his most hated rival had been dishonored before all, the old man was predisposed to be friendly. Kalen stood a few meters away with his lip curled, watching me, and the heat in his gaze sent a warm glow through me.

"Have you been reading my mind again?"

"No, but when Inessa declared her reasons for annulling the marriage, you barely batted an eye. You were surprised she announced it so publicly but not why she did so to begin with."

"I'm not a child, Fox. I know very well what your relationship with Inessa meant."

Fox reddened. "You've talked to Inessa about this before. About annulling her marriage."

I nodded. "It was her idea. She had read up on Daanorian history and knew emperors had strict requirements when it came to choosing their brides. The emperor had already broken one of the cardinal rules by taking a foreign woman to wife. She knew he would be even less willing if she'd broken yet another, especially one that would hurt the emperor's pride the most."

"And if he persisted anyway?"

"I would have called on the *azi* to threaten the city." I sensed his shock. "Never to harm or kill the people, Fox."

"Accidents can happen. Given the *azi*'s size, it would have been inevitable that someone would get hurt."

"I know, but we needed a last resort. Inessa seemed confident that her plan would work though. That's why she declared it before his whole court, to force him to save face. Her reputation's a bit sullied if you measure it by their standards, but it worked."

"You're changing, Tea."

"People change, Fox."

"The Dark is changing you. And I don't know if it's for the better."

"We've come out of this unscathed, with the best possible outcome. Surely it cannot have been for the worse." I dug my hand into the corpse and brought out the *savul*'s bezoar. The daeva crumbled into dust, and shouts rose from the Daanorians. Their dread was nearly tangible; I savored it before coming to myself and forcing that pleasure away.

Fox shook his head before walking away. I watched as Inessa saw, gave chase.

"He's right, Tea," Kalen said. "The magic is changing you."

I looked down at my own heartsglass. "You think so?"

"Mykaela always said that drawing in too much of the Dark leads to darkrot, but there are many dangerous stages in between. The Dark makes you more reckless. More inclined to take risks where none should have been taken."

"I did what I could to survive this, Kalen."

"I know. I think I understand that the most out of anyone else here."

"Fox is mad at me."

"Everyone is, a little bit. That was a chancy thing to do, Tea."

"Did you expect me to have acted differently?"

"No," he admitted bluntly. "But you still need someone to tell you when you're doing something stupid."

"I know. I'm sorry. I...don't think. The Dark came too much, too fast, and I felt like I was the most powerful being in the world. Mykkie always said that was my problem. I like magic a little too much." The princess had caught up to Fox. "And I want you to tell me when I am being impulsive. I don't know if I'll listen though. But I'll need you for that task because Fox's starting to outgrow me."

"When you're constantly in each other's heads, I imagine that can't be easy."

"I want him to have a life of his own away from mine," I said. "That's why I wanted to fight the *savul*, to bury his vengeance. That's why I wanted to be an asha. Sometimes I think he forgets that."

"Sometimes I think you forget it too," Kalen reminded me. "He didn't need the *savul*'s death to find his own peace."

I bowed my head. "Point taken." The Kion princess reached out to grab Fox's hand. "You think they're going to be OK?"

"Inessa has always been a fighter. And if Fox was able to handle coming back from the dead, I'm sure he's perfectly capable of handling whatever it is he needs to be for Inessa."

"You make it sound like the second's harder than the first."

"With Inessa, I wouldn't be surprised."

I looked away, suddenly self-conscious. The adrenaline was wearing off, my desire to wallow in the Dark diminishing somewhat in his presence. "And...us?"

Kalen bent down to kiss me in full view of everyone, ignoring the delighted gasps from Likh and the *Well, finally!* from Zoya. "We can be whatever we want us to be too."

·· ≥⁄⁄≤ ··

We had overstayed our welcome in Santiang. Though he had agreed to our conditions, Emperor Shifang was a sore loser. With Inessa, he was even more abrupt, so fully encased in his armor of hurt that his arrogance was even more unbearable. Shifang had formally declared the annulment before his courtiers and officials, and Zoya's foresight ensured that the emperor had no time to present his bride to the citizens. Rumors that the wedding had been interrupted before it could be concluded were encouraged to spread.

"How was it to be the empress of Daanoris for a couple of hours?" Shadi asked Inessa lightly.

"Like a weight around my neck," the princess admitted sourly. "Once we return to Kion, I would like to spend a few hours yelling at my mother."

We had one other task to attend to. "Without Princess Yansheo's heartsglass, we find ourselves facing the same predicament as Mykaela," Shadi admitted.

"There's one way to make sure." Zoya looked at Tansoong. "Have you kept Shaoyun's remains like I asked?"

The official nodded. "He will have a state funeral, given the circumstances."

"I'm afraid he has one more duty to the kingdom. Bring his body here."

Tansoong looked apprehensive. The emperor, no longer bothering to hide his curiosity, barked at him to hurry.

There was not much to retrieve of the unfortunate boy. His meager bones and the scarlet cloth instrumental in identifying him were brought before us, carefully wrapped in a small blanket.

I summoned *Raising*, and a small stampede broke out as officials and courtiers scrambled out of each other's way, as far from the corpse as they could get. Emperor Shifang stood his ground, though he looked ready to join his subjects at any moment. The only Daanorian unmoved was Shaoyun himself. He studied his hands with a strange detachedness common in the newly risen and concentrated on me.

"You will not be inconvenienced long," I told him, with Shadi translating between us, and the dead boy inclined his head in affirmation. "Was Baoyi responsible for Princess Yansheo's collapse?"

"It was a foreigner," came the grim reply. "An Odalian. He drew a strange red light from the princess's chest, and she fell. But then he too shimmered and changed, and I saw it had been Baoyi's servant all along."

"Where is the pendant now?"

Slowly, the boy shook his head.

"The princess is ill. We need it to restore her health."

He shook his head again, but the movement was strangely hesitant.

"Shaoyun." This time it was Shifang who spoke. Even in death, the emperor held some sway over his subjects. The boy froze in recognition, limbs creaking as he began to kneel, almost from instinct.

"There is no need for that," the emperor ordered. "This woman speaks the truth. If you care for Princess Yansheo, then where is the pendant?"

The boy's lips moved. "I snatched it from him before he could work more foul magic. I ran, and they pursued me. The—the pendant filled me up."

"What does that mean?" I asked Shadi, sure something was lost in the translation.

But the asha was just as puzzled. "I don't understand it either."

"The pendant filled me up," Shaoyun repeated, "and the servant was furious. He...took control of my thoughts, but try as I might, I could not tell him what I had done with it. That was the last thing I remember before the pain. And then nothing."

"That doesn't make sense though," Zoya muttered. "Where did the heartsglass go?"

Khalad was pale, stepping forward. "I am a Heartforger," he told the corpse. "I don't know if the title means anything to you, but I can heal the princess. You loved her, didn't you?"

The corpse closed its eyes and sighed its regret.

"You protected her from one who wished her harm. And now he is dead, and she is safe—but you still possess what is needed to restore her to life. Will you help me?"

The slightest of nods was his answer. Khalad lifted his hand—and plunged it through Shaoyun's chest. Slowly, he drew it back out—and in his hands was a luminous sphere made of brilliant red light that glittered back at us. "Thank you, Shaoyun," he said sadly. "Rest easy, knowing that the princess is safe."

A ghost of a smile appeared on the young Daanorian's lips. I dissolved the spell, and the undead boy was once again rendered into nothing more than ashes and bones.

"How did you know?" Kalen asked his cousin.

"I didn't. But few people remember that we use heartscase exactly for this purpose—to keep heartsglass at a fixed point. When you love someone enough, it's almost instinctive to keep their heartsglass as close to your own heart as possible." He looked down at the remains and sighed. "I haven't been in this trade long, but I'm slowly realizing that when it comes to matters of the heart, nearly anything is possible."

·· ＼١∠ ··

The old forger and Khalad stood on either side of the sleeping princess's bed, the former holding out a vial where a thin sliver of thread lay nestled within. The last few weeks had taken their toll on the old man, the strength gone from his heartsglass. He could no longer attend to his duties when we return, and the expression on Khalad's face told me he knew that. "It should have taken us three days to make," the old man said. "But Khalad here found a way to shorten the process to six hours. Would never have thought of it either. If you didn't keep sedating yourself into insensibility, taking out your own memories to fashion heartsglass for every poor soul who asks, imagine all the things you could have done by now."

That didn't sound like a compliment, but Khalad beamed like it was. "I'm glad you approve, Master."

The man laid a hand on his shoulder. "Your father's a mess of a man and more a fool for rejecting you for prejudices you have no control over," he said gruffly. "But you're as close to a son as I've ever had, however badly I word it at times, and I don't think I'd have been any prouder, even if I had one of my own."

Khalad swallowed hard. "That means a lot to me," he said, his voice thick with emotion.

The old man clapped him on the back. "Let's get to it anyhow. Girl's been sleeping long enough." He held up the small container. "We never forget any of the heartsglass we've touched," he said. "I can replicate each of the sleeping noble's *urvan* at this point, and I'll show Khalad every one too, just to be sure."

"But that also makes you a target all over again," Princess

Inessa told him, troubled. "The Faceless won't need their heartsglass anymore—all they'll need to replicate shadowglass is one or the both of you."

The old forger smiled. "That's a problem for another day. Khalad?"

Reverently, Khalad placed the shimmering heartsglass on the sleeping girl's chest, and it shone a bright ball of red and pink hues.

The Heartforger carefully unstoppered the lid, and the new light burned brightly in the room; it was like looking into the sun. I shielded my eyes from the glare, endeavoring to peek through my fingers. Both forgers appeared unaffected. As I watched, Khalad lifted the small yarn-like thread out of its container and extended his hand toward the sleeping princess.

As if seized with a life of its own, the thread drifted slowly toward the girl, landing on the center of her heartsglass—and passed through it like it was slipping through water. The surface of her heart rippled.

Princess Yansheo opened her eyes and noisily sucked in a great big gulp of air. It was done.

*T*HE BODY WAS DRAPED IN *heavy black cloth when I returned, and the blood had been cleaned; I knew enough not to ask questions. Princess Yansheo came with me, white and trembling. I had told her all I remembered, but she took the discovery better than I had. "Shifang was always arrogant and selfish," she said, "but he was never wicked. Your story explained many things he had done these last few months. I was fortunate enough not to be harmed, but others were not so lucky."*

I did not have the heart to tell her that Usij kept her unharmed because he intended to harvest her urvan *once more should the forger fail to help him. To tell her, I decided, was unnecessary cruelty.*

The bone witch never looked down at the corpse and continued to watch from her window. "Tell the soldiers to draw back the gates," she said quietly. She still held the Faceless's heartsglass; though Usij was dead, his heart lived on. It was no longer the sooty black it had been in life but a sparkling silver.

"Ironic," the bone witch said with a smile, "that we would recreate Blade that Soars's lightsglass from the most repulsive man I ever had the displeasure of meeting." She looked down at her own heartsglass and sighed. "And that I would recreate Hollow Knife's in mine. Open the gates."

"What are you doing?" I asked.

"We are leaving Daanoris. We have what we came for." She

turned to Princess Yansheo. "Whatever your people might think of this in the coming years," she told her, "know that I leave your kingdom without a madman on the throne."

"But who will lead us? Usij killed my true emperor."

"The Heartforgers proved that you are descended from Great Heroes, more fit to rule Daanoris than Shifang ever was. You called for change, Yansheo. I see no more qualified person to lead this kingdom."

The princess took a deep breath. "I have my own councilors, people I trust. I—I owe that much to my Shaoyun. I will make him proud of me. I will work hard to be a good ruler. I will be one, a true one, the next time we meet."

There was a faint hesitation on the bone witch's part before she nodded.

"I will go with you," the Heartforger said.

"It's too dangerous, Khalad. Stay in Santiang for the meantime."

"Danger has never stopped me before. I go with you."

The bone witch paused. "I cannot promise your safety. You are still needed by the people. You can do well here."

"That will not stop me from doing what I believe is right, and the quicker we can prevent war, the fewer lives will be lost." He trembled. "I've already lost too much. You know that."

"What do you intend to do?" I asked.

Lady Tea placed the silver heartsglass around her neck, next to her black one. "We are going to face the army, Bard, and see how badly they want me dead."

"And this is not even the craziest thing we have done today," the Heartforger sighed from behind us.

28

THE CELEBRATION BACK AT ANKYO was a muted and silent affair. Tensions remained high and the city was on alert, with Deathseekers and soldiers patrolling the borders separating Kion from Odalia. That the First Daughter had fled with a handful of asha and a Deathseeker had been a carefully guarded secret, and it was a surprise to most when we came riding back to the city gates with no *azi* in sight.

Empress Alyx was nearly apoplectic in her relief, clasping Princess Inessa tightly and refusing to let go until her daughter gently pried herself free. Althy was in attendance too, no worse for wear than when I had last seen her and smiling broadly. "Polaire and Mykaela are much better" were the words she greeted us with, even as I dashed into her arms. "They're eager to see you."

She was right. Polaire was still weak and exhausted looking, but of the two, Mykaela had fared better, color returning to her thin cheeks. It was difficult to recount everything that had happened since we had left Ankyo for the doubtful safety of Santiang, and not even Polaire's fragility could shield me from her criticism, all of which I bore in a much better spirit than I had back in Odalia. Now that most of the lingering effects of the Dark had faded from my consciousness, I had more time to reflect and more time to consider my rash decisions.

"You married the emperor?" Empress Alyx asked her daughter, horrified, to which the latter could only manage a sheepish shrug.

The older woman turned to Zoya with blazing eyes. The asha put her hands up in protest. "Annulled as soon as we could. We might have also threatened the emperor with more daeva if he refused and then also offered him trade and a better alliance in the same breath."

"I am glad that I was not awake long enough to take part in this," Polaire muttered. "Inessa's, Zoya's, and Tea's ideas of diplomacy seem to stop just short of declaring war."

Mykaela, perhaps still too weak to scold, laughed instead. "It worked out for the best, Polaire. We might not approve of their methods, but we cannot fault their success."

"Was the annulment more than a political ploy?" The empress's eyes fell on Inessa's hand, which had found its way to Fox's.

My brother moved to step away, but Inessa only tightened her grip, staring back at her mother with a wary fierceness. "And what of it?"

"You might have found your way out of one engagement, but there is one more with Odalia that comes to mind."

"Odalia attacked us, Mother. In light of such events, I don't think it's unreasonable to break off that engagement."

"And is that the only reason, Inessa?"

Her daughter took a deep breath. "No, Mother."

The empress's eyes shifted to Fox. "You do realize that he is a Dark asha's familiar."

"Really? I thought he was a raven prince from Tresea."

Empress Alyx allowed herself a small smile. "We'll talk about this later."

"No, we're talking about this now." Inessa straightened. "If you find anything wrong with my relationship with Fox, then say it to my face. I have been hiding my feelings for years when I should have been honest about him from the start, and for that, I am sorry. But I am tired of hiding."

The empress regarded her daughter for several long moments. "I find nothing wrong with the nice Pahlavi boy. But I was worried for his sake. You are not the world's most amiable noble, Daughter." Inessa's mouth fell open as her mother continued. "I was cautious, of course, as any mother would be, but if I had had any pressing issues with him, I would have voiced my concerns two years ago."

"You knew?" the princess sputtered.

The empress grinned; it was identical to the one Inessa wore so often. "Of course. Did you think it would have escaped my notice, given the frequency you snuck out of the palace? If I had disapproved, I would have nipped it in the bud early on. Remember: your own father was a general from Arhen-Kosho, and I was no stranger to eluding my chaperones in order to arrive at a promised rendezvous. Gods, I miss that man. As straitlaced as they come, except when it came to me. He sent dozens of marriage proposals after our first meeting, so prim and proper and quite *ironic*, given our circumstance. I accepted only after he could admit our relationship was more meaningful than simply saving my honor and his."

She sobered slightly. "There is, of course, the question of offspring and whether or not a familiar can give me grandchildren… Should I discuss that with you in front of everyone else?"

"No, Mother." Inessa's face was scarlet.

Empress Alyx laughed.

"How are you two faring?" Khalad was on his knees beside Polaire and Mykaela, examining their heartsglass.

"All bed rest and no excuses," Althy said from behind him. "Over the sounds of Polaire's lamentations and expletives, I might add."

"I feel better now, Althy!" the brunette said, scowling. Althy shot her a glare right back; Polaire acquiesced eventually, sinking back onto the pillows, huffing.

"That's amazing," Zoya said. "You've managed to get Polaire to sit and stay."

"I found it entertaining." It felt good to hear Mykaela giggle again, clear and bereft of pain. "She's been on my back for months, and now it's payback. But where is the *azi*?"

"Usij broke our bond during the fight. I don't know how he did it."

"And you're no longer linked to the *azi*?"

Before Daanoris, I would have kept this a secret. I'm learning from my own foolishness at least. "No. I reached out to it again."

She sighed. "Tea."

"I forged no new bonds with it. But I learned that I no longer needed to compel the *azi* for it to obey me. Familiarity might have something to do with it. It's free to come and go as it pleases, but it's choosing to stay near."

"I'm not happy about this, but I understand. Can you control it again if you have to? I don't think we can trust it acting independently, however noble its intentions."

"I think so."

"Good. Its help could still be invaluable, and we have few choices for allies." She turned to the old forger. "It's good to see you again. We thought we lost you at Daanoris."

"Truth be told, I was very nearly lost. You have a very clever protégé here."

"We have high hopes for her," my sister-asha agreed.

"Although she still acts without thinking half the time," Polaire said, still frowning. "Althy has been telling me about the Faceless's book. How you could not deign to tell us earlier? I don't—"

"I know, and I'm sorry." I wasn't sure if this was the right place to ask, but curiosity was getting the better of me. "You knew of the book too—the *Heartshare* rune."

Polaire hesitated, then sighed. "I suppose I owe you an explanation. I've flouted the rules a few times myself."

"A few times?" Althy quipped. "At least a hundred times is my best guess, and that is a conservative estimation."

"I recall many nights in my youth misspent because of all the trouble you talked Althy and me into," Mykaela chimed in.

Polaire rolled her eyes. "Fine, I am the scoundrel of this bunch. But I stumbled upon the rune quite by accident when I was your age, Tea."

"Did you find it in a book?" Kalen asked.

Polaire shook her head. "I came upon it at Mistress Clayve's study actually. She was the former head of House Imperial before Hestia took over, more than ten years ago. We had our dance exams, and I thought I had made a bad mess of it. So when an opportunity arose and I found her study unguarded, I snuck in to see my results, possibly to change any unsatisfactory scores and criticisms. I found several papers on the rune on her desk. It gave comprehensive details of its usage and effects. I had never been a good student, even at my best, yet it burned itself into my brain—I could not forget it if I had wanted to. I suspected that it was forbidden, and perhaps that was its appeal. I never thought to use it until recently, when Mykaela grew worse and I was desperate."

I felt cold. "But why would the elder asha have a Faceless's rune?"

"I was foolish enough to ask Mistress Clayve then," Polaire snorted. "She nearly went into hysterics at the question. She refused to answer and dumped chores on me in retaliation. I snuck into her study again afterward, but the papers were gone.

They were nowhere to be found, no matter how hard I searched." She gazed steadily at me. "Do you think there is a connection?"

"There has to be. This cannot be a coincidence." *Hidden runes wielded by Dark spellbinders, lost over time—deliberately—by the asha, to prevent Dark witches like us from rising too high.* I felt sick to my stomach, remembering Aenah's words.

Althy shook her head. "But why would they hide such runes from us? I have made my own inquiries into the matter like you asked, Tea. I could find nothing incriminating."

Mykaela frowned. "Althy says that they have been very vocal about us since you left Daanoris. The empress refused to allow them to see us, but they were very persistent."

The plump asha sighed. "It is still not a sign of guilt, but it is obvious there are details they are hiding from us. Not surprising, really."

Zoya frowned. "The association has been a thorn in our side since Likh. There must be a reason for their meddling. Did Aenah give you any reasons, Tea?"

"No, unfortunately. Just that they wanted to control what Dark asha can do to some extent."

"Perhaps it is prudence?" Althy suggested. "The book is proof enough that some runes shouldn't be drawn."

"I think it's more than that though. Aenah hinted that there was some big secret they didn't want us to know."

Empress Alyx paced back and forth. "There is still the matter of Prince Kance's illness and the Duke of Holsrath on the throne in Telemaine's stead. We cannot afford to divide Kion when there is still Odalia to deal with. We can deal with the elders afterward."

"Kance takes priority," Kalen said tersely. "Khalad, how quickly can you re-create an *urvan* for the prince?"

"I should have everything done by tonight."

"Which brings us to another problem," Zoya said. "How exactly do you propose to sneak back into Odalia when practically every armed person there is after us, knowing full well that someone has woven compulsion over many of the soldiers and possibly over the king himself?"

"Wasn't that Usij's doing?" Likh asked.

Zoya replied, "I'm not sure yet. If someone else is controlling the men there, whether or not it's Holsrath's doing or if the duke was under Usij's thrall, it pays to come prepared for any eventualities."

"I'm impressed, Zoya," Polaire said. "You actually thought this through."

"We flew thousands of miles on the back of a dragon to reach a kingdom where an emperor had forcibly kept us hostage in a warded palace. I want the odds to be better for us next time."

While Zoya, Polaire, and the empress worked out the details, I drifted toward the small veranda, and Fox followed, his expression somber. "Do you still feel the *azi*?" he asked me.

"In a fashion. I'm sorry. I know I messed up, Fox. I wasn't thinking straight, and I worried you more than I should have." I took a deep breath. "But you kept secrets from me too, you know."

"Ours were not the same, Tea. Yours had greater repercussions—"

"Really? You still think that after being involved with a princess who has had two royal engagements to powerful kingdoms? A princess who is breaking both because of you?"

He winced. "You have a point."

We stared at the night sky for a few minutes before he spoke again. "Where do we go from here?"

I closed my eyes. "I don't know. Do we still make it up as we go along?"

"Isn't that what we've been doing?" He paused again. "Inessa wants to make our relationship public. The empress seems to like me at least, but the elder asha won't feel the same way."

"They're going to look at this as a political move on my part—a way to exert more influence over the empress and her daughter," I said.

"I know. And that's why I'm breaking from our longstanding tradition of keeping secrets from each other and telling you first. If you think this makes life difficult for you at the Willows, then I'll—"

"You'll what? Turn her down? The last two years have shown me how easy it was for you to reject her." I grinned at him. "I understand, and thanks. But you aren't dead, Fox, so stop treating yourself like you are or like my life has more importance than yours. I don't care what anyone else says. You have a heartsglass. You're in love. You're much more alive than other people I know. You know what it is to die, and that's why every second of life has a sweetness that only you understand. You deserve a chance at living, and Inessa does too."

He smiled wryly. "When did you get to be so wise?"

"I've had time to think about a lot of things. And it offsets some of my dumber moments." I gave him a playful push. "Talk to her. Stop keeping your heart from her. She loves you enough to accept your flaws, and you do the same to her. Go on and prove the empress wrong and give me lots of cute nieces and nephews."

He really colored this time. "I don't even know if familiars are…ah, capable of—"

"Talk to the forger or to Khalad. They're working miracles, so I don't think one more challenge is going to stump them. Look at what they were able to do with Mykaela's—"

I stopped, staring up at the sky in shock.

Mykaela's heartsglass. Mykaela's heartsglass. It all came back to where Vanor had hidden it, lost all these years. To save her, Polaire had given part of her heartsglass to Mykaela, the way Dancing Wind had given hers to Blade that Soars in the legend. Khalad and Shaoyun's corpse, the forger's intuition, his breakthrough, Khalad telling me once that Vanor loved Mykaela, though Vanor had refused to reveal her heartsglass's location.

"Tea?"

"I need to talk to Khalad and the forger. I might know where Mykkie's heartsglass is." My hands tightened against the hem of my dress, knowing that my proposal would not be popular. "But to do that, we'll have to return to Odalia as soon as possible."

•• ⁄|⟨ ••

Councilor Ludvig had not been idle, and his official retirement from Isteran politics in no way put a damper on his love for spying and intrigue.

"Odalia has done little since their abortive attempt at invading Kion," he reported, spreading a fan of reports on the empress's table. "Frankly, I'm surprised. It's not in the duke's temperament to give up so easily, especially after such heavy losses. I have read reports of them fortifying parts of the city by increasing their soldiers on watch, which is not unexpected. I see no siege preparations despite the rise of military activity, but they do not appear to have plans to mount another attack. The Odalians are fearful and unsure. The king has not shown himself for some time, and neither has the duke. As far as my spies are aware, Prince Kance remains stable, though there is no change in his condition."

The old man frowned. "Personally, I think Holsrath plays a waiting game, to see what we would do. News of Daanoris would have reached him by now. Surely you can wait before attacking?"

"Lady Mykaela and Lady Polaire are better, but they will only grow weaker in time again," Empress Alyx pointed out. "If there is a remote chance that we can recover her heartsglass, then we should do so before they take another turn for the worse."

"A pretty theory on paper, Your Majesty," said Zoya, ever the pragmatist. "But sneaking two asha, who are not exactly at the peak of health, into hostile territory makes for difficult logistics."

"Polaire and Mykaela are rallying at the moment, Zoya, but Mykaela will die, and Polaire, in her stubborn refusal to relinquish Mykaela at the cost of her own life, will soon follow." Althy sighed. "Your Faceless book deals very much with the process of using the *Heartshare* rune, Tea, but it says very little about repercussions. Which is not surprising, as Faceless think little of the consequences of their own actions. But it is very clear on one point—*Heartshare* is a temporary fix. In time, they both will die, and we cannot measure the when of it."

"Then what do you propose?"

Althy grinned, grim and purposeful. "Perhaps we should ask Polaire and Mykaela themselves. It is their lives at stake."

"Let's do it," Polaire said immediately.

"Polaire!" Mykaela protested.

"I love you, Mykkie, but I am not going to be tethered to you any longer, knowing you can weaken again at any moment. I can still fight, and I defy any asha to say otherwise. The sooner we find your heartsglass, the better chances we have of winning this war."

"I didn't have the chance to apologize to you," I told Polaire. "I made assumptions that I shouldn't have, and it was wrong of me not to trust you. I'm so sorry. If I could take back all the words I said…"

The brunette smiled and wrapped me up in a hug. "You are so much like me, Tea. Perhaps that is why I chose not to tell you, knowing full well you would act the way I would. I love you even at your most troublesome, you silly girl. You are stronger than I give you credit, so it's time I should start." She smiled coyly. "Kalen seems to have come to the same conclusion."

Nothing got past Polaire.

*W*E WERE FOUR AND THEY *numbered in the hundreds of thousands. But the fighting ceased; they retreated. They knew: our seven daeva outnumbered them all. It was the golden-haired asha who rode out to greet us, gesturing at the others to stay back. I saw some of the elder asha ignore the command, though they stopped several feet behind her when the bone witch approached. Unlike Lady Mykaela, the older asha sweated profusely under the hot sun, and the silk of their* hua *stuck to their skin in the least appealing ways. There were other asha and Deathseekers among the army—I saw glimpses of* hua *in muted colors and men dressed in heavy black. My zivar glowed almost as bright as their heartsglass.*

"Tea!" *Lord Fox broke through the ranks and stopped beside Lady Mykaela, frustration and anguish etched across his face.*

The Dark asha smiled at him. "I told you they wouldn't listen." *She gestured back at the city.* "All seven daeva at my command. But do you see the palace burning? Do you see chaos, anarchy? I spared the people as much as I could. I came here to kill a cruel man, no matter what falsehoods those old fools told you."

"Wretched little girl!" *one of the elders sputtered, her face red.*

"And the corpses?" *Lady Mykaela asked.*

"Stragglers I collected from graves on my journey here. If my undead did not attack, you would have done worse to Santiang. Do *not ask me to choose between the lives of an army you raise against me and the lives of citizens who did not ask to take up arms."*

"They are only Daanorians," the elder snapped and almost immediately hunched over, choking and pawing at her throat.

"And you're an ugly old woman hiding her mediocrity in expensive clothes. One Daanorian is worth more than a thousand of you."

"Tea!" Lady Mykaela exclaimed.

The old woman took in a shuddering gasp of air. The bone witch turned to her former mentor, her voice matter-of-fact. "Where is Empress Alyx?"

"Returning to Kion," It was Lord Fox who responded. "I'd convinced her that you mean no harm to Daanoris, and she seeks to boost Ankyo's defenses."

"Daanoris is intact, and I have reached an understanding with the Empress Yansheo."

"Empress Yansheo?" Lady Mykaela asked. "What has become of Emperor Shifang?"

"Emperor Shifang died many months ago. We have since disposed of the impostor." Lord Kalen stepped forward, a large sack in his hand. He tossed it to the ground before them. "You might recognize his head."

Wary, Lord Fox stooped down to retrieve the sack, ripped it open. He sucked in a noisy breath. "Usij," he said bleakly. My knees buckled.

"We have no intentions of fighting any of you. Do not stand in our way," Lady Tea pronounced.

"We are wasting time," another elder snapped, the same one who had accompanied the empress to the palace. "You will return

these daeva to their graves, and you will return with us to Kion, where you will be summarily tried for your crimes."

"My crimes, Mistress Hestia?" The bone witch mocked her. "My crimes? You were there the night they died, Elder. You have no intentions of returning me alive to Kion. Even now, your scheming mind plots ways to kill me."

"You killed your own flesh and blood!" the elder hissed. "That alone merits the executioner's axe!"

"And I will pay for that sin soon enough. But not today. I know you will not allow me to stand trial, Elder. Would you really allow me to provide a full accounting of what happened that final night?"

"You—you—" Mistress Hestia stopped, her eyes bulging. A peculiar change was coming over the woman along with some of her fellow elders. A queer gurgling sound began at the base of her throat, lower than her thin voice could manage.

Lady Mykaela stepped back in alarm, and so did the bone witch, looking as startled as the rest. Mistress Hestia clutched at her throat, stumbled, and fell to the ground. Her tongue lolled out as she jerked and spasmed, turning bloated and black.

"What did you do, Tea?" Lady Mykaela gasped.

"I haven't done anything!"

The elder moaned one last time—and insect-like wings sprouted from her back.

29

"GETTING INTO KNEAVE," ZOYA GROWLED, spitting out a mouthful of hay, "sounds infinitely better on paper than it is from inside a wagon."

Unlike the Odalian army that had showed up at Ankyo, there was no Kion army attacking the gates, but there were Kion asha and Deathseekers gathered around the city, led by Alsron and Shadi, staying out of view until they were called upon. Besides, the *azi* was an army all on its own.

Under my guidance, it attacked the outposts first. The watchtowers crumbled, and I forced myself not to think about the casualties, of how many unsuspecting soldiers had been there when the attack commenced. I could not think about it; the stakes were higher now.

The *azi* still waged bloody war above us, and the whole palace shuddered whenever it flew too close, striking the top of the battlements with its tail, destroying centuries-old architecture in one heavy swipe. I had no fear that any attacks Odalia might mount in retaliation would injure the *azi*, so for the moment, I was content to let it move independently, leaving a cautious note in its head to increase its distance to the city, to prevent any more citizens from being harmed. The daeva had the easier task; all it needed to do was distract the soldiers from us.

Our entrance into the city was a lot less conspicuous than my *azi*'s, and Zoya wouldn't shut up about it. "Whose brilliant idea was it to use a hay wagon of all things?" she sputtered as she crawled out from underneath the bales. Kalen was the first out the wagon, helping me to my feet. We were dressed like Deathseekers: black breeches and long-sleeved shirts further camouflaged us in the approaching evening. "Why didn't we use a fruit wagon or one of those covered wagons Yadoshans seem to be so fond of—"

"We could have a wagon made from goose pillows, Zoya, and you'd still be complaining." Polaire had recovered rapidly almost as soon as we had entered Kneave, nearly returning to her old self again. The color had returned to Mykaela's cheeks, and she no longer needed Polaire's help to move about, climbing down from the wagon with her old agility after Altaecia.

"Wasn't it *your* idea, Zoya?" Khalad asked pointedly, squirming out of the wagon after her. Fox, his face hidden underneath a dark cloak and hood, was the carriage driver, leading the horses. The *Illusion* rune I had woven around us had been most effective, and we had managed to enter the city unmolested.

"Perhaps I am slowly losing my mind like the rest of you. Among us, I'm practically the only one not on the duke's wanted fugitives list."

"We all have a part to play in this enterprise, Zoya," Polaire said sweetly. "And as you said, you have the least important part to play. You can stay in the city until we return if you'd like."

"And miss out on all the fun? Not on your life." Zoya brushed what straw she could off herself, making a face.

"A little less talk," Kalen said. "The entrance to the crypts shouldn't be guarded. Few soldiers keep watch there."

"Tea knows," Fox said with a sidelong glance at me, and I snorted.

The royal catacombs were as I had remembered them—gloomy and stale smelling, with the same statues and marbled columns. Kings of ages past loomed over us as we walked down the narrow stairway. Kalen brought up the front and Fox guarded our rear.

I could see the familiar shape of King Vanor's tomb looming before us and watched as Kalen took the initiative. *Fire* combined with *Mud*, and the stone and dried bricks crumbled from the vault where the king's body lay, the sound muffled by the ongoing chaos above us. Zoya and Polaire added their strength to Kalen's, and heavy currents of *Wind* drew the coffin out into the open.

"Your turn, Tea," Polaire told me.

As before, it was easy enough to compel the dead king to rise—much more difficult to compel him to speak. King Vanor showed the same stubbornness from when we had left off at his last raising. No sound issued from his lips, though his eyes remained trained on Mykaela as if the rest of us did not exist. It was clear that his presence pained my sister-asha. Pain and grief were evident on her face, and the anger inside me burned again.

"I can't do anything if he's not willing," Khalad reminded us.

"Where is Lady Mykaela's heartsglass?" I demanded of the corpse. As before, he made no reply.

Polaire frowned. "Perhaps we are asking the wrong question, Tea."

"What other question is there but that?" Zoya wanted to know. "We must be quick about it. I don't like exposing Mykaela to this royal degenerate any longer than is necessary."

"No," Mykaela said quietly. "I have been silent enough at previous raisings, despite my own doubts and fears. Many of my fellow asha tried to be kind. They thought my presence would motivate him to speak but also worried what toll his nearness might take on me. Not anymore. Do not treat me like glass—I am stronger than that. What must be asked are questions I was too afraid to have answered, questions that none of you dared ask out of respect for me." She looked back at her former lover. "Vanor. Did you love me?"

The silence ticked by. Five seconds. Ten seconds. Twenty.

"*Yes.*"

I jumped, for I had not expected a reply. Death had made King Vanor's voice harsh, but a strange contrite note laced it, modulating his anger but also imbuing his voice with unspoken emotion.

"Did you love me when you died?"

"*Yes.*"

"That's a bald-faced lie and you know it, Vanor," Polaire began heatedly. "You don't hide the heartsglass of the person you love for more than a decade and then refuse to disclose its location long after your death."

King Vanor said nothing, his eyes still on Mykaela. It was as if Polaire had never spoken.

"What do you think, Khalad?" Zoya whispered.

"I'm not sure. The lack of a heartsglass makes him harder to read."

"Other than stating the obvious, I mean."

"The dead can't lie, which means he isn't lying. But that doesn't mean he can't hide the truth," I said.

"I'm a prime example of that, I guess," Fox murmured.

"Maybe we're going about this the wrong way. We say that he hid her heartsglass because he didn't love her. But what if he hid her heartsglass *because* he loved her?" I suggested.

"That doesn't make much sense either," Zoya said.

"But it does," Althy broke in, frowning. "What if he was hiding her heartsglass to protect her? What was he doing in the days leading up to his death?"

I struggled to remember my history lessons. "King Vanor was visiting the emperor of Daanoris when he was attacked. That was Emperor Undol—Emperor Shifang's father. Daanoris was lifting the closed-border policies of its kingdom, and Odalia was trying to negotiate more lucrative trade agreements. It was at first suspected that Daanoris was responsible for King Valor's murder, but the investigations King Telemaine ordered could find no proof. Daanoris had everything to lose and nothing to gain by assassinating King Telemaine's brother. The last thing they would want at that point was to gain notoriety by killing the first king to offer a trade alliance with them."

"There were some theories that circulated, of mercenaries from Tresea killing King Vanor to shift the blame on Daanoris," Althy said, remembering. "But there was no proof to support that either."

"Well, why not ask the guy directly while he's here?" Zoya demanded.

"We did. He's never responded to that either."

"Don't any of you understand? *Why?* Why answer Mykaela when she asks if he still loves her but not answer anything else? Fox, what are you doing?"

My brother ignored Zoya, stepping toward the dead king. "King Vanor, who first suggested the idea of a trade agreement with Daanoris?"

"It was I," came the expressionless reply.

"Were you and Emperor Undol on cordial terms?"

"Yes."

"What did you have for breakfast that morning?"

"Bread and cheese."

"What is the point of all these questions, Fox?" Polaire asked him. "I don't see what bearing they have on the questions we wish to ask him."

"Exactly. Don't you see? He seems quite capable of answering questions as long as they have nothing to do with his death or as long as you don't ask him where Mykaela's heartsglass is. Don't you see anything wrong with that? The dead don't lie. I speak from experience in that regard. But if he does love Mykaela, then why wouldn't he help us?"

"Because he doesn't trust us?" Zoya suggested. "But Mykaela's here too."

"Or," I said with newfound understanding, "it's because someone was controlling his heartsglass and compelling him against his will before he died."

"Someone was compelling him?" Khalad asked, aghast.

"I have some experience in that area too. When Aenah compelled me in the past, I couldn't tell any of you what she was doing, even though I wanted to, and I was made to believe that I was acting of my own volition. Couldn't the same thing have happened to King Vanor?"

Khalad was already nodding his head. "It's possible. In fact, it's more than possible. If he loved Mykaela, his heartsglass would have remained with her. But if someone had cast a spell on him and compelled him otherwise…"

"Then that would explain why I couldn't retain my hold on his heartsglass," Mykaela finished, her eyes widening. "But how could someone keep control even after his death?"

"King Vanor," Khalad began, "do you know where Mykaela's heartsglass is?"

Silence.

"That was one of the questions he never answers," Zoya reminded him.

"King Vanor, is there a reason why you cannot tell us more about Mykaela's heartsglass?"

"Yes."

That he even answered startled us all, and the forger pushed on doggedly. "Is it to protect her?"

Silence.

"Are there certain questions that you cannot answer because you've been bespelled by someone before you died?"

No answer.

"Let me rephrase that. Are there certain questions you cannot answer but would like to if given the chance?"

"Yes."

"Do you know who killed you?"

"Yes."

"Can you tell us who?"

Silence.

"I still don't understand," Polaire said. "Why is he answering some questions but not others?"

"Because whoever bespelled him couldn't anticipate all the possible questions we could ask or the loopholes we could use. They never thought we would know that he'd been compelled, remember? None of us had considered the possibility before. As long as we do not ask him directly about the location of Mykaela's heartsglass or who killed him, he can answer."

"I repeat Mykkie's question. How is it possible for someone

to control him even after death?" Althy demanded. "I was one of the asha who examined the king when he died. We found no traces of spells on his person."

"The control could be through a rune we do not know, a spell we have not been taught—anything is possible at this point. Remember, there were missing pages from the Faceless's book."

"Vanor," Mykaela said softly. "Did anyone from Daanoris bear any resentment toward you?"

"No."

"From Tresea?"

"No."

"From Odalia?"

More silence.

"If that isn't an answer, then I don't know what is," Zoya looked smug. "He won't respond to certain questions, but if we limit his answers down to a yes or no and eliminate possible answers as we go along, then I think we've found our loophole."

"I hate complicated," Kalen grunted.

"King Vanor, was the Duke of Holsrath responsible for your death?"

Silence again.

"OK, not the right question. Vanor, did the Duke of Holsrath begrudge your relationship with Mykaela?"

"No."

"Did King Telemaine?"

"Zoya!" Kalen protested.

"Process of elimination, remember? We can eventually get

to the…" Zoya's voice trailed off. "He didn't say no. King Vanor, did King Telemaine resent your relationship with Mykaela?"

The king said nothing, and a chill crept up my spine. Surely that didn't mean…

Zoya swallowed. "Did King Telemaine wish to become king by assassinating you?"

Silence.

"Did King Telemaine wish he were the firstborn son instead of you?"

For the first time, Vanor tore his gaze away from Mykaela to focus on Zoya. "Yes."

"Was King Telemaine willing to do *anything* to become the King of Odalia?"

Silence.

Khalad gasped. Mykaela clapped a hand over her mouth.

"I can't believe that," Kalen said hoarsely.

I spoke up, voice trembling. "Do the elders have Mykaela's heartsglass?"

"No."

"Is the Faceless, Aenah, working with the elders?"

"No."

"Is Aenah in league with the king?" I asked.

King Vanor's gaze shifted to the shadows. That was the only warning I had, but it was not enough. White-hot electricity lanced through me, the pain barely fading before I found myself on my back. From the groans and startled cries around me, I knew I was not the only one.

"That was sheer genius. I must congratulate you all on your creativity."

Still unable to move, I opened my eyes—and stared straight into King Telemaine's smiling face.

"How could you, Telemaine?" Polaire hissed from nearby.

The king shrugged. "Vanor was a fool. Throwing his heart away for a Dark asha—he was the laughingstock of Odalia, and he was too besotted to realize it. Your *azi* can rage all it wants outside these city walls, Lady Tea, but it means nothing here, where I am in control."

"Impossible," Althy said through gritted teeth. "You have no inclination for runic magic."

"No, he doesn't," a voice behind him agreed.

I lunged upward, desperately clawing at the walls in a bid to right myself, to will myself the required energy to leap at the newcomer and attack her mind—to no avail. The pain in my head increased, and I slumped back down. The figure stepped forward.

"But I do," said Aenah.

I REMEMBERED THE HANJIAN AND HIS *painful transformation, his protruding tongue and blackened face before the bone witch killed him, before he could become one of those hideous creatures. I remembered the poor Daanorian soldiers. In these elders, I saw the same horrifying changes. Their features distorted and twisted until their faces were no longer familiar, and more limbs and appendages burst from their bodies until they were parodies of humanity.*

Twelve of the elders had undergone differing anomalies, though all resulted in the same kind of horrors: a bison-like creature with an armadillo's armor; a snake that stood several yards high with a long forked tongue, six hoofs, and a spiked horn that grew at the end of its tail; another with the jaws of a crocodile and the wings of a dragon; a praying mantis ten feet tall, with eight legs that ended in hooked talons.

Mistress Hestia was gone, and the ripped remains of her hua *were the only evidence she had once been a woman. In her place was a nightmare: a terrifying beast with a beak and the facade of a rooster but with lion's arms and a sentient tail of snake heads. Her wings fluttered, growing several feet on either side of her body, and three-pronged horns adorned her head in a terrifying mockery of a crown. Like the others, her silver heartsglass was fused to her chest, shining faintly.*

"Impossible!" Lady Mykaela cried out. "They've been blighted!"

The horned rooster crowed, laid its beady eyes on the bone witch, and opened its mouth. Something that looked like blue fire erupted from its beak, lancing straight toward her.

Fox leaped for the Dark asha, as did the Deathseeker. Magic sparked around Lord Kalen, and Lord Fox pulled Lady Tea to the ground, shielding her body with his own. But it was the savul that moved quickest, throwing itself in front of its mistress, shrieking as the intense fire burned through its skin. It sank to its knees.

Red-hot flames blazed atop Lord Kalen's hand, arching toward the hideous asha-beast. Almost at the same time, Lady Mykaela lifted her arms and lightning rained down from the sky. But the creature simply ducked its head, and both attacks glanced harmlessly off its hide.

"They are invulnerable to magic, just as daeva are!" I gasped.

"Send the rest of the soldiers back!" Fox all but snarled to his men, lifting himself up. "Protect the empress and the princess at all costs, but do not engage in this fight! Asha and Deathseekers, to me!"

"Fox," the bone witch said softly. "Thank you."

"Habits are hard to break," he said shortly, helping Lady Tea back to her feet.

"See to Inessa's safety first. Whatever you say, we both know I am no longer your priority. As it should be."

"Tea—"

"Go to her, Fox. If I die, then I will not deny you any minute you can spend with her." The rest of her daeva raced forward, teeth and claws bared, and when the first blows came, the world shook.

The daeva had been waiting long to fight. The nanghait drew first blood, savage fangs ripping into one of the snakelike asha-beasts, and the latter roared out its hurt, proof they could still be harmed.

The aeshma rolled itself into a large ball of metallic spikes and plunged through the monsters, tearing skin and bones as it went. The asha-beast that was once the Elder Hestia snapped at the taurvi, its beak sharp and poisonous, and the taurvi collapsed, whining. The savul and the akvan rushed to its aid.

Both Lord Kalen and Lady Mykaela had abandoned all attempts to fight the asha-beasts and began their retreat, though the Deathseeker stayed close to the bone witch. "Leave, Mykkie!" the Dark asha shouted at her mentor. "This is not a fight you can win!"

"I will not leave you, Tea!" The older woman raised both her hands and the asha-beasts paused, reeling as if dazed, struggling to shake off her control.

"Fox, take the bard and get out of here!"

The familiar obeyed, grabbing me and lifting me up on his horse with little effort. I looked behind me and saw the winged serpent shake free from the enchantment Lady Mykaela had cast. Already it was leaping toward the woman, its mouth horribly agape. Tea screamed once, and then I saw nothing else as the azi bathed my vision with more fire, obscuring my view as Lord Fox's horse broke into a dead run away from this battle of titans.

30

THEY KNEW. THOSE WERE THE words running through my head over and over, even as Aenah stepped past us toward King Vanor. They knew we were coming to the crypts, and they had planned for it. There were wards around the royal tombs, which were dormant until Aenah had activated them. Now her compulsion was strong enough to batter our defenses.

Frantic, I sought out the *azi* still on a rampage around the city. For a moment, its thoughts touched mine—only to be wrenched away as Aenah severed our connection.

"No, little lady. We wouldn't want that."

I had lost my hold on King Vanor, but he remained upright, no doubt now under Aenah's influence. His eyes stared unseeingly at the wall before him, paying the Faceless and his brother no attention.

"Father?" Khalad quavered.

"Surprised?" Aenah asked, smiling. She bent down and

slipped the protection stone off my neck. "You should thank Lady Mykaela. It was she who told Telemaine that you were skulking about the catacombs, hoping he would station a guard there. As you can see, Telemaine took Mykaela's advice to heart. And doing so has gone better than expected, my Tea. Usij was an eyesore. I had hoped to imbue you with runes and point you in his direction so I would have one less rival for shadowglass, whichever of you won. You have performed your task admirably."

"A liar, as always," I hissed.

"I spoke no lie. My offer to join our cause was genuine. You have always been a true child of the Dark, Tea. I knew it the instant our minds first touched."

"There's no time for conversation, my love," the king said. "Prepare what you need."

I watched Aenah as she moved around the tomb, ignoring Vanor. The runes she traced in the air were unknown to me. She smiled as she caught my eye. "Did you really think I would show you every rune I know, Tea? A shame really. We could have worked well together."

"You were imprisoned!" I had felt her distress at her warded cell, and it had been unfeigned.

"It was necessary to *be* imprisoned, to keep me uncomfortable and pliant to your coercion whenever you visited Odalia. Telemaine more than made up for it whenever you left the city."

"Did you silence Vanor with one such spell?"

She laughed. "There are spells that can seal his mouth, even without compelling him. You should know, Tea. It was one of the runes I used on you while you were a novice."

"How could you, Telemaine?" Polaire raged. "How could you be in league with that Faceless witch?"

"Why shouldn't I, Polaire?" Gone was the hearty attitude, the pretense of concern and compassion. The king's eyes glittered against the firelight, cold and calculating. "It was I who had Vanor killed, Polaire. I have been with Aenah for many years, long before you were an asha."

"Vanor was your brother!" Polaire protested.

"Forget it, Polaire," Kalen groused. "The king had no qualms about using my father as his scapegoat. But I now understand why he revolted against you."

"Ah, yes. Lance had always been smarter than Vanor but not by much. I'm glad I kept him alive all these years. Vanor was weak willed and spineless, more concerned at playing house with a bone witch, while other kingdoms slowly outstripped Odalia in power and influence. You may not think it, Polaire, but I am as much a patriot as you think you are. Our kingdom suffered at the hands of Vanor. Our army was in disrepair, and what did he do? Pin all our hopes and riches on some poor little village because it had an inferior runeberry patch. Daanoris encroaches on Arhen-Kosho's coastal territories, and he offers them a trade agreement! By the time he was done, Odalia would've been nothing more than a vassal kingdom, robbed of its status and power and at the mercy of Daanoris, Kion, or the Yadosha city-states. Vanor's death was a blessing, Polaire. I merely sped up what nature was too slow to accomplish."

Zoya wriggled slightly, attracting my eye before casting her gaze upward at the wards around us. Her fingers twitched.

"You're not telling us everything," I said. "Wresting the kingdom away from your brother was only one reason you killed King Vanor. You might not have shown me every rune you know, Aenah, but you should not have provided me with the blueprint to create heartsglass, even if you thought immortality would appeal to me. You didn't only need a silver heartsglass. You needed the most powerful one you could find for the best potency. But Vanor learned of your schemes and disrupted your plans by hiding Mykaela's heartsglass. You know where it is, but none of your runes can give you access."

"You have always been very perceptive, Tea."

"You might have sealed his tongue, but you cannot seal his intentions," I declared.

"And that is why I keep your Heartforger alive. Did you know they are capable of taking heartsglass without permission?"

I snapped my head toward Khalad in amazement. He flinched.

"Yes, it is part of the Heartforger's oath—to refuse those who are not willing. That is why so few people meet the qualifications for forging. This is their true trade secret, for fear others may take advantage of them. But seeing his friends tortured might give Khalad better motivation. Perhaps you would like to offer your own heartsglass in Mykaela's stead?" Aenah clapped her hands in delight. "We shall make it a contest. The first to give up their silver heartsglass shall be put out of their misery quickly, and the others will be left to torment."

"But Prince Kance!" I tried to lift myself off the ground, but it felt like a heavy rock sat on my chest. "Prince Kance is innocent! His own son!"

"Ah, Kance," Aenah sighed. "We had no choice with Kance. He was one of only two from Anahita's lineage to satisfy our requirements for shadowglass, and we could not spare the young Heartforger should old Narel die."

"Did you really think I would put Kance in any danger?" Telemaine asked scornfully. "Aenah took his soul and kept it safely hidden, knowing that Usij might strike him next. She merely planted a suggestion of Daanoris about his heartsglass in the hopes you would rise to the bait."

The Faceless woman giggled. "And Princess Yansheo has made a miraculous recovery. If Khalad works with us, then perhaps Kance too shall recover. Kance would be understandably grief stricken to discover that many of his friends have been put to death for treason while he was asleep...such as his uncle, the Duke of Holsrath."

A sound of both rage and agony fractured from Kalen's mouth.

"He was not in the best of health, and the added compulsion broke him. Fortunately, his role in this matter had already been completed."

A sudden spurt of laughter broke the silence. To my shock, it came from Khalad, his body shaking where he lay. "I wondered why you'd ignored me all these years, Father, only to start inquiring about me in these last few months. You needed me to forge this heartsglass. Does that still make me the royal disappointment?"

"Nonsense, Khalad," Telemaine snapped.

"Nonsense?" With a grunt, Khalad flipped onto his stomach. "You said I was a worthless heir, incapable of giving you grandchildren because of my 'unnatural proclivities.' You banned me from functions and put Kance in the spotlight long before my heart turned silver. And when it did, you turned me over to the Heartforger and said I was no longer your son. Is that what you call 'nonsense' nowadays, *Father*?" His lip curled. "I thought you'd changed the last couple of months, and, fool as I was, it gave me hope. But I watched Kance support Likh's appeal to become an asha, and you didn't. How could you when you'd rejected your own son for those same *unnatural proclivities*?"

Khalad was resisting the spell, struggling to his feet. "You couldn't even *pretend*. Couldn't announce to the people why you refused to champion Likh's bid when you couldn't look at me without disgust. So instead, you took the opportunity to make it all about Kance and his engagement. That was why my brother was in such a state afterward—he'd realized your aim. I could see it all over your heartsglass: *how dare this* catamite *upstart demand this from my obedient,* normal *son—*"

Telemaine hit Khalad across the face, and he went down. "I would beat your proclivities out of you if I could," the king said, seething.

Khalad choked on blood but laughed. "But you can't, can you? You could bend Kance to your whims, but you could never do the same to me."

"In the interests of scientific curiosity," Althy said calmly, "what exactly *are* you intending to do here?"

"Make shadowglass, of course." Aenah smiled. "Our forger here has done the impossible, replicating what we need." She smiled at King Telemaine. "We will be immortal, he and I, and Odalia shall prosper under our rule."

Fox's gaze met mine. Kalen was close beside me, and I wriggled as best as I could until my feet brushed against his shin.

"Wait," I spoke up. "Leave them alone and I'll give my heartsglass freely."

"Tea!" Zoya shouted behind me.

"How nauseatingly noble. *Come here, Tea.*"

Unwillingly, my body rose. Aenah laid a hand on my heartsglass.

"Such a waste, Tea. If events had gone differently, you could have been standing beside me."

"I would rather stand with daeva."

"Falling on misplaced courage now? You no longer control the *azi*, Tea. Daeva have no true master."

The ground around us heaved, caught in the throes of a sudden earthquake. It knocked both Aenah and King Telemaine off their feet, and Aenah's control wavered.

Fox and Khalad leaped forward, the latter plunging his hand straight into King Vanor's chest. The roof above tore open. The *azi* gazed down at us, purring, and its strength sang through me.

"Impossible!" Aenah shrieked. "You do not control it! Why is it defending—"

I linked my will to Zoya's, funneling as much of the magic as I could through her. The asha grunted, and I felt the wards unravel as she dissolved Aenah's barrier.

Kalen's sword slid out of his scabbard, runes flashing through the air. Fire streamed toward the Faceless, but she evaded it. Telemaine drew his own heavy sword, countering Kalen's blow.

"Is this what it has come down to, Kalen?" the king said, taunting him. "Do you now raise your hand against me, as your father did?"

"*You* betrayed *us*!" Kalen shouted.

Telemaine swung again, and Kalen's blade shattered. The Deathseeker retreated, and I saw faint cuts on his face and arms where the sword's fragments had sliced him. "Common steel versus royal metal. This is no contest, boy."

"Don't underestimate me, Uncle." Kalen sidestepped the next attack and lashed out with a leg sweep. The king stumbled, and Kalen rose to strike him on the arm, sending his sword sliding several feet away. Then he struck again at the center of the king's chest, sending the burly man flat on his back. Zoya snatched up the sword, tossing it to Kalen.

"Surrender, Aenah," Polaire said grimly, her and Althy's runes weaving around them. "Immediately."

"No."

The ground shuddered again, breaking apart underneath me and lifting me off my feet. The *aeshma* forced itself up from the soil, screeching, only a few feet from where Mykaela, Khalad, and Vanor stood.

"Move, Khalad!" Zoya yelled.

"A few more seconds," the forger insisted, his hand still through Vanor's chest. The *aeshma* yowled, and its spikes lengthened.

Khalad ripped his hand free, and the bright light of Mykaela's heartsglass illuminated the room. After years hidden away, its light seemed brighter than any asha's heartsglass I had ever seen.

But the ground shuddered again, and Khalad lost his footing. The silver heartsglass landed with a thud by Vanor's feet.

Mykaela staggered, and the *aeshma* attacked.

I tried to fight my way into the *aeshma*'s mind but couldn't; Aenah's hold on it was absolute. Kalen leaped forward, and I saw Polaire and Althy closing the distance to Mykaela, *Shield* runes forming around their friend.

King Vanor moved.

There was a sickening crunch.

Mykaela stared wordlessly at her former lover, impaled by one of the *aeshma*'s spikes. The royal noble's arm reached for her, and the silver heartsglass glittered in his hands. He smiled slowly—a strange look on the otherwise expressionless face, like he was in the process of relearning how.

"Vanor," Mykaela said softly.

He placed the heartsglass in her hands and, with a sigh, crumbled into ashes and dust, leaving only the *aeshma* and the spike behind. Furious at being deprived of a victim, the daeva lunged forward again.

Runes burst forth and surrounded the *aeshma*. The beast abandoned all attempts at assault and retreated, shrieking, as currents danced through its flesh. Mykaela stood in the center of that glowing storm, her heartsglass a beautiful display of unrepentant magic and light, scorching the walls of the tomb around

THE HEART FORGER   469

her with her fury. For a few moments, the *aeshma* lay under her thrall, enough for it to retreat. But soon, her strength left her, and Mykaela sank down, breathing hard.

"Welcome back," Zoya said, grabbing Mykaela. "Now let's get out of here before we literally have no more ground to stand on!"

We made it out of the tombs just in time—before the *aeshma* breached the catacombs' roof to take a swipe at the *azi*. The latter sent flames through the broken ceiling.

The *aeshma* hollered in response, a ball of spikes tumbling toward the daeva. I grabbed at the *azi*'s mind, registering its shock and pain as the two creatures collided. I tasted metal in my mouth as the *aeshma*'s spikes dug in. The *azi* breathed fire directly at the other beast; it detached from our hide and rolled away, its barbs black and charred.

"Assassins!" I heard King Telemaine scream at the soldiers. "Kill them!" I could hear the sounds of battle in the distance and realized that Alsron and Shadi were also attacking the city.

Althy extracted the moisture from the air, channeled *Water* and thick *Mud* into the soil surrounding the *aeshma*. The *aeshma* grunted when its spiked talons sank into the newly created quagmire. It struggled to raise itself but only managed to submerge itself deeper.

"The face is its most vulnerable," she called out. "Concentrate your attacks there!"

The *azi* swung its tail spike, striking hard across the beast's snout and tearing through flesh. The *aeshma* wailed in agony.

Polaire threw cutting *Wind* and *Fire* in Aenah's direction.

Earth, *Air*, and *Water* runes sprung up around Zoya, twisting themselves into a complicated knot to spew jets of acid. The Faceless called up walls of the dead even as Polaire's corrosive magic hissed and fizzled against the corpses. Althy sent more *Earth* runes burrowing deep, but Aenah avoided the sinkhole, her cadavers carrying her to safer ground. "Is that all you have?" she said mockingly.

Even trapped, the *aeshma* was still a deadly opponent. Its spikes lengthened to twice its size, and we all had to dance out of the way when it began attacking indiscriminately. A lone spike came whizzing in my direction, but a *Shield* rune from Kalen kept it from slicing into me.

Very few of the soldiers had taken up Telemaine's order, not wanting to get in between the two battling daeva. The half dozen who were courageous enough to do so were easily dispatched by Fox.

Mykaela ignored the danger, walking toward the *aeshma*, her face intent.

"Mykkie!" Polaire cried out. "Keep away!"

The *aeshma* hissed, turning its terrible gaze on the lone asha approaching it. Mykaela was close enough for the beast to swipe at her with an outstretched limb.

"*Stop.*" The asha raised her hand. The claw stopped in midair, as if hitting an invisible barrier. The *aeshma* reared back, and a quick brush against its thoughts told me it was confused, though still under Aenah's control.

"What are you doing?" the Faceless hissed. Her willpower

was extraordinary to retain her influence on the *aeshma* while fending off attacks by Polaire and Zoya.

I soon understood. Aenah was too firmly ingrained in the *aeshma*. To wrest control would take too much effort, too much time. But she was using minor spells to confuse and intimidate the daeva, which I had never thought to do before.

The *aeshma* hissed, runes of doubt and confusion coloring its mind. It stopped.

"Fight!" Aenah screamed.

Mykaela threw fear into its mind. It scrambled back, but the sand retained its hold. When the *aeshma* threw its head up and howled, exposing the fragile flesh of its underbelly, I called to the *azi* and we jumped.

Three rows of teeth tore into the daeva's face and neck, the *aeshma*'s screams cutting off when we found its jugular. The blood flowed more earnestly, and the *aeshma* struggled and twitched. I fought off the urge to throw up at the thick clotting texture of it in my mouth and held on grimly until the jerking stilled and the daeva grew slack in our grip. Its limbs, no longer fighting, slid out of the quicksand with a horrific sucking sound.

Panting, pleased, I turned to smile weakly at Mykaela. I drew my knife—and drove it toward her chest.

"Tea!" Fox shoved my mentor out of the way, taking my attack through his arm. Stunned, I opened my mouth and found that I couldn't speak. No sound came from my throat, even as my mind screamed.

"It's quite easy to slay a beast." Though she lost her daeva, Aenah was triumphant, having nailed a better prize. She clutched my protection stone in one hand. It glowed. "Can you do the same with your precious bone witch, Mykaela?"

"Let her go, Aenah."

I set my own knife against my throat, feeling the sharpness against my skin.

"Not quite yet," the Faceless purred, and the pressure against my neck increased. "Attempt to get inside my head, Mykaela, and I shall slit your precious ward's throat."

I could feel Aenah increasing her hold, using me as a gateway into the *azi*, who was already struggling, alarmed, as my thoughts crumbled away. I could feel its fear as the strings between us unraveled.

"Tea," Kalen said quietly. The *Heartshare* rune spun on his hand; he had always been a quick study.

He released the spell, and I felt it fill me up. The knife dropped from my hand, and Aenah's gloating expression changed to one of consternation as she clawed at my thoughts but found nothing as Kalen stole me away from her reach. *Come to me*, I heard, and then I was running, throwing myself into his arms.

That brief second was all it took. In her desperation, knowing that the tide of battle had turned against her, Aenah lashed out at the one other mind she still had control over. The *azi* screeched in pain, its three heads weaving in agony as the Faceless all but tore into its thoughts, brutal in her quest for dominance. The daeva thrashed wildly, and its tail lifted, the deadly spike whipping through the air straight at Mykaela.

One second was all it took. One second for Polaire's *Shield* runes to flicker to life, one second too late for Mykaela to delve into the *azi*'s mind to pacify its rage. One second for Aenah to beat her there, the *azi*'s thoughts disappearing into darkness, away from mine.

The daeva's tail pierced through Polaire's shield. Trembling, the dark-haired asha's spell wavered and disappeared, leaving her stock-still, eyes wide in surprise, as blood spread through the front of her shirt where the spike had torn through.

"No!" Mykaela sank to her knees as Polaire toppled, catching her best friend before she could hit the ground. Althy ran to them, heedless of the still-writhing *azi*. Under Kalen's control, I watched in dazed disbelief as the healer fell to her knees beside the unmoving Polaire, Mykaela's hands over the wound to staunch the flowing blood.

Aenah was panting, the exertion of controlling the *azi* sapping her strength, though she began to smile. Telemaine had snatched an underling's sword and held it against Khalad's throat, a warning not to intervene.

"So much for the vaunted...Polaire..." Aenah wheezed, still drunk on power.

"Tea," Fox whispered.

But I was moving, my mind working from someplace far away, my thoughts scattered into the void. It was a sensation not unfamiliar to me from back when I had taken in darkrot at Daanoris and watched Usij die. But this felt different; I was quiet, filled with the cold detachment of fury and a horrible eagerness.

Althy looked back at us, her own face tearstained, and slowly shook her head.

And then I could hear the sound of my mind snapping.

THE PRINCESS'S REGIMENT WAITED A couple of miles away, far enough to evoke a deceptive feeling of safety. I feared that the Heartforger and I would be regarded as prisoners of war, but Lord Fox had commanded the soldiers to treat us like honored guests.

Princess Inessa sprang to her feet, flinging her arms around her consort with a sob. "Why are they fighting?" She wept into his chest. "Where is Tea? Lady Mykaela?"

"Most of the elders have been blighted," he told her soberly, and she recoiled in shock. "If Mykaela and the others fall, we must be ready."

"If they fall..." she choked out, staring at him in horror.

"If I die, you and the empress are to return to Kion without delay. Take your honor guards and ride as hard as you can for the ships. I sent word for preparations to begin."

"No!" She clutched at his arms. "I won't leave you, Fox!"

"I have no choice, Inessa. But I will die in peace if your face is the last vision I see."

She cried harder and refused to let go. The bone witch's brother made no protest. The Heartforger paced the tent, but I remained seated, finding little reason to move. If Fox died, then it meant the Dark asha had fallen too and the battle was lost.

But an hour passed and then two. The sounds of battle faded, *and lightning no longer leaped across the horizon. The princess clung to her lover the whole time.*

The end did not come. Mistress Parmina approached us, but there was none of the spitfire arrogance she displayed in the Daanorian throne room. Her shoulders were slumped, as if in defeat. "The scouts have returned, Fox. It is done."

"Then Tea is alive." Hope returned to the man's face, and the princess broke into fresh happy tears.

"But not without a price," Mistress Parmina said. To my surprise, she lowered her head and, unabashedly, began to weep.

31

I DIDN'T KNOW WHAT TO DO. Hope had disappeared with the deadly swipe of that spiked tail that ended Polaire's life. My world had shrunk until there was nothing but her dead body, the sounds of Mykaela and Althy's crying, and both Fox and Kalen's voices in my head, asking, worrying. Tea. Tea. *Tea!*

Kalen's control faded; I took over. I could feel nothing but minds all around me: Mykaela and Althy's grief, Zoya and Khalad's horror, Fox's anger and hatred. And Kalen, anguished and stunned and loving.

But the heartbreaking, wrenching silence of Polaire's mind was the loudest noise of all.

From somewhere nearby, I watched myself scream, and the world screamed with me. The *azi* screamed at my anguish, and Aenah too screamed as I punched brutally into her mind. The Dark surrounded me, filling me in ways I had never imagined before, filling me to the brim until I overflowed with Darkness. I welcomed the power, desperate to feel more than the heartache I could not prevent.

I expected the sickeningly sweet darkrot, the anger and the rage, to slowly eat away at my mind. But with every new surge of power came only fervor and impatience, the realization that I still had room to take in more of it, and more, and *still* more. Sparks flew from my fingers as I traced more runes, lingering on their curves and hidden corners. I had too much of the Dark in me, too much for even the Faceless to counter, and I wrested control of the *azi* from her one last time.

I remembered my short foray into Usij's mind, remembered the atrocities I had seen committed there, and twisted those images so that to Aenah's mind, *she* was undergoing the knife and its pain and blood. The Faceless wriggled on the ground like she was live meat on a hook.

And still I saw more visions. I saw memories of burning and loss, the dead child she held in her arms while she screamed at the gods, pleading at first and then rejecting them completely. I watched the trail of bones and corpses she left behind her as she moved from Arhen-Kosho to Odalia to Kion and Yadosha. It amassed decades of cruelty and blood. I saw her wars against the asha of the Willows—battles fought as she raised daeva after daeva, only to be repelled by bone witches that came before me. I rifled through Aenah's mind, my desire to find her truth stronger than my revulsion for the bloodshed spinning through her thoughts.

Then the scenes changed. The asha no longer appeared as

adversaries but as collaborators. I saw Mistress Hestia, and my blood ran cold.

"They cannot know." They *were Mistress Clayve, Mistress Joliene, and Mistress Fatima—upstanding members of the association, all. Mistress Hestia held the Faceless's book in her hands.*

"Mykaela is too powerful," Mistress Hestia said. *"She shall be better off without her heartsglass. Best to keep her alive, at least till the next bone witch comes along."*

The vision faded, but my wrath grew.

Telemaine started forward, but Khalad was faster. He slammed an elbow into his father's stomach, and when the elder king grunted and lowered his blade, Khalad wrested it away, landing his father on the other end of its point.

"No!" Aenah begged. The images I inflicted were invisible to everyone else, but she suffered with them. Yet to see her twisting and writhing on the floor at her memories was not enough.

I wanted to kill her.

I wanted to do more than kill her.

Aenah raised her head, her eyes focused not on mine but on my heartsglass. A cross between a wail and a giggle rose in her throat. "It's…happening," she gasped. "It's…happening…oh…Tea…"

I did not want to hear her voice ever again. The woman's eyes widened as I forced my final *Compulsion* on her, fixing her mouth shut and rendering the rest of her immobile. Even without my influence, I could sense the *azi's* thirst mixed with our shared revulsion for the woman who had made our lives a living hell for so long.

The Faceless made a strangled, hacking noise as the *azi* moved toward her. I saw her eyes, wide with fright, and I *reveled* in her forthcoming destruction; I fed off her growing fear.

"Aughhk," the woman warbled through unmoving lips. In her head, I could feel her shrieking, shrieking, *shrieking*, and it was a splendid melody. "Aucgghk-ack-gauug—"

All three of the *azi*'s heads dove down toward the Faceless, *their* mouths open.

There was a loud, sickening crunch of bone.

King Telemaine gaped at the body that had once been his lover, still twitching as my pet consumed her. He backed away from me, but I did not waver. Even in the worst of my rage, a part of me knew that to kill him would mean my head. Whatever crimes he had committed, the darkrot was fierce inside me, warping my desires. My desire was grotesque and cruel, hollering for more blood, for more vengeance.

It was easy enough. I luxuriated in the king's fright. I allowed my magic to sink into every pore of him until his consciousness was steeped in my hatred.

"For the rest of your life, this is all you shall have of your lover: a vision of her as living carrion," I whispered to him. "You will relive this moment in your mind for the rest of your days, and it will be all that you shall remember. Your lust for power blinded you, causing immeasurable pain to those you should have protected. Now you shall watch with open eyes and see."

An agonized scream erupted from Telemaine; he clawed at his eyes. Khalad and Zoya rushed to his side, fighting to restrain him.

I left him there in a heap, removing my presence from the *azi*'s heads so it could enjoy its feast in peace, but I managed only a few steps before I was on the ground, struggling to breathe. Mykaela held the lifeless Polaire in her lap with Altaecia beside her, their faces washed in tears. Likh's legs had given way, his hands over his mouth. Zoya stared at me. In their gazes, I found shock and repulsion. And Fox—

Oh, the expression on my brother's face. I felt shame—not for killing Aenah and destroying Telemaine but for the way he looked at me, the fear rippling through him.

I reached out for Polaire, wove the *Resurrecting* rune. *I can bring her back*, I thought. *I am so filled and so alive with the Dark, I can do anything. She will return to nag me for my shortcomings and bully me into doing everything she wanted—*

But the asha did not move. My spell barreled into her twice and thrice and four times and seven and fourteen and twenty until I began screaming into her quiet mind to live, to *live, to live, damn you—*

"Tea," Kalen said hoarsely. "Stop. Please stop."

The right side of my body felt sticky and warm, and I began to shiver.

Kalen's arms circled me, the *Heartshare* rune flaring once more before his presence took over every inch of my being, warm and inviting—the only forgiveness in the room I could find. The darkrot melted away as I let go of the power for an emotion greater than hate and, sobbing, allowed the soothing murmur of his voice to carry me away into darkness.

*T*HERE WAS ONLY SILENCE BROKEN *in moments by the sounds of weeping.*

The monsters were dead; the creatures that had once been asha lay strewn in bloodied heaps around us, grotesque even in death with their stiffened limbs and gaping mouths. They retained their monstrous forms, their secret selves exposed for the world to see.

Some of the bone witch's daeva lay injured too. The aeshma's *spikes had retracted from its body to reveal graying fur. The* taurvi *still sang, though its legs were broken, half its face covered in blood. The* nanghait *was silent on the ground, its many eyes closed. Even the* azi, *the most powerful of the lot, was bleeding, one of its wings bent and bitten. The* zarich, indar, *and* akvan *were conscious and standing, though limping as they plodded back and forth between their brethren, their mournful cries loud in the stillness.*

The Dark asha sat on the ground, her face bathed in tears. Lady Mykaela lay in her arms, pale and silent. Blood covered her hua, *spilling on the floor around them. I could feel magic sizzling nearby and saw the bone witch's heartsglass beat in tandem with the injured woman's. Khalad and Kalen flanked Lady Tea, their hands pressed against Mykaela's side, trying in vain to stop the blood flow before it grew worse. Beside me, a low cry of pain rose from Fox. I have seen my share of dying people, and I knew with one look that there was no hope.*

"Why did you save me?" the Dark asha cried.

The golden-haired asha's eyes opened. They focused on her, and she smiled. "I have always tried to save you. It is…not so bad, child."

"You cannot die on me, Mykkie." The Dark asha had vanished, and in her place was a seventeen-year-old girl, frantic to save the life of the woman who had so profoundly shaped hers. "Everything I do, everything I have done, means nothing if you leave me!"

"I have been living on borrowed time for so long, Tea." A bloodied hand stroked the weeping girl's cheek. "When my hours are spent, I will feel no fear, no sorrow. I have lived on borrowed time, time that you have risked your life and heart for. I am at peace, Tea. Thank you."

"No!" The girl's heartsglass shone bright, black and light swirling together.

Lady Mykaela's smile was beautiful, though blood trickled from the corners of her mouth.

"No, Mykkie!" The bone witch clutched at her arms, and for a moment, I thought I saw a strange symbol burning between them. "Don't let go!"

"I am going to Vanor now and to Polaire. They have been waiting for me." The woman touched the girl's face one final time. "Be well, Tea," she whispered, and the light in her heartsglass went out.

The Dark asha's scream tore through the air. Her heartsglass glowed, for the first time more silver than dark, as she wove the air with desperate movements. The woman in her arms did not move.

The Dark asha tried again, forming the same gestures over and over. I could feel the heat of the spells, the desperation and smolder of the magic, but Lady Mykaela's eyes remained closed.

"Tea." Kalen took her hand, stilling her.

She turned to him, her eyes blazing. "Why? Why can't I raise her? I raised you! I raised you, and I can raise her!"

"Tea," the Deathseeker said again, and she fell silent. She collapsed onto his chest, her arms still clutching the fallen asha. She howled at the sky, a savage sound.

The Heartforger, tears streaming down his cheeks, knelt by the Dark asha's side.

Lord Fox sat beside Lady Tea, his hand finding hers. His other closed around Lady Mykaela's. They held her in their arms for the longest time—without moving, without speaking. The moon rose and the stars ascended, but the Dark asha and her two familiars remained.

"Tea," Kalen finally said again with great sorrow in his voice.

"A few minutes longer," the bone witch whispered. "Let me stay with her for a few minutes longer."

32

I COULD ORDER YOU TO ROT in prison for the rest of your natural days. That's what I should do as king. That's what the people would clamor for."

I agreed but kept my head bowed. In the hours after sanity returned and the darkrot faded, I had tried to undo the chaos I had wrought. But the damage to Telemaine was already done. The king was confined to his personal chambers, where no one but his sons and his physicians could enter. I had exorcised the demons in his mind that I had put there in my pride, but I could not take away the nightmares I had ingrained in his head. The rest of Odalia had been kept in the dark, but his healers could do little: the king had gone mad.

"This is treason. By law, I could order your death."

I said nothing in my defense. Prince Kance had every right to proclaim such a sentence. I could feel Fox and Kalen on either side of me, their presences always a comfort.

"Look at me, Tea."

I did. A part of me still rejoiced to see him awake and well, bearing no lingering effects of the sleeping illness. But Prince Kance no longer looked at me with kindness or affection. There was no more "Lady Tea" in a pleased voice. The green eyes staring back at me were those of a stranger's—*His Majesty's*, I corrected myself—not my friend. Kance ruled Odalia now, and I was to blame for that too.

"What do you say on your behalf, Tea?"

"I will accept any punishment you choose, Your Majesty." How could I sound so cold and informal? "My life is in your hands to do as you see fit."

"Kance." Kalen moved to stand beside me. "You know as well as I that Tea had no choice but to act as she did."

"It does not matter. She lifted her hand against the king."

"Your father killed his *own brother* to take the throne, Kance. *Both* his brothers. Even worse, he conspired with a Faceless to risk the kingdom in his quest for power. By your own logic, he too is guilty of treason."

"He was my father, Kalen!" Kance's shout echoed in the room. "He took you in when you lost your parents! He treated you like you were his own son! I looked to you as my own brother, and this is how you repay him?"

"Your father's mistress was responsible for summoning the very daeva that killed our mothers, Kance! Telemaine threw my father in prison when my father discovered the plot, and the king had the Faceless compel him to carry out their orders! The king allowed Aenah to poison you. He clawed his way to the throne on the bones of his own family, including yours. You owe him nothing!"

"Don't you think I know that? Whatever my father has done, I cannot allow people to besmirch his name. But how can I determine if he was in his right mind throughout all this, that the Faceless didn't compel him as well? Now we will never know! Whatever accusations have been made against him, he was a good father, Kalen!"

"He was a good father to one of us, yes," Khalad said from behind us.

"Even my own brother turns against me?" Prince Kance snapped.

The Heartforger shook his head. "I was never against you, though he tried to make it seem that way. He capitalized on your guilt for taking the throne. Father was good to *you*, Kance. He would have had you rule in my place, with or without my silver heartsglass."

"But why? There was no reason to prevent you from being king."

"Our father was enlightened in many ways, Kance, but he shared one thing in common with the intolerants of Drycht. You suspected as much the day you took sick."

Kance rubbed his temple. "Why didn't you tell me about this, Khalad? Surely you did not think that I shared in his prejudices?"

"Because it should never have been a problem to begin with. I had no obligation to tell anyone about my personal life if I chose not to. I confessed to Father in the hopes he would understand.

It is one thing to be treated well because he thinks you can do no wrong, Kance. It's another thing entirely when he decides you've outlived your usefulness."

"You can have the throne, Khalad. I never intended to take it from you."

"And that is exactly why I never told *you, Your Majesty*." Khalad grinned. "I would have made a horrible king. Father and I agreed on that much. To be the next Heartforger is all I want. I'll help people my way, and you'll help them yours. But please— forgive Tea. She has served you faithfully. Do not punish her for your father's crimes."

The young king's hands were trembling; for all his anger, he was finding my sentencing difficult, and my heart twisted, knowing what I had done to bring him such pain.

When he finally spoke, even his words shook. "Return to Odalia at your own peril, Dark asha. I do not wish to see your face in my kingdom for as long as I live, for any reason. Return here, and I'll wield the executioner's sword myself if I have to."

I nodded, struggling to hide my tears and failing miserably.

"Now leave." The new king's heartsglass glowed a bright red, fierier and more royal than I had ever seen any king's.

"You are being unfair, Kance," Kalen said.

"I am doing what must be done for the safety of my kingdom, Kalen. I do not need your approval."

"But you need Telemaine's. That's what you have always wanted but rarely gotten."

"Do not raise your voice to me, Kalen!"

"Barely even a week, Your Majesty, and already you sound so very much like your father. Has the crown always been this heavy?"

The two cousins locked gazes; Kance was angry and Kalen sad. But after several moments, the fury drained from the royal noble's face, and he turned away. "I have been asleep for so long that I no longer recognize my own friends upon waking. I release you from your vow to protect me, Kalen. I cannot ask that from you any longer, knowing what my father did to yours. Do whatever you wish. The same goes for you, Khalad."

"Then I shall stay here awhile longer," Khalad decided. Kance looked surprised. "I haven't been around as much as I should have, given my duties as the forger's apprentice. We have some catching up to do, Kance."

The king hesitated. "I would like that." Kance looked back at me again. "Go with the gods, Tea." There was not as much anger in his voice, but the regret in its timbre hit me harder. "May you one day put to rest the demons that still hold you."

·· ☼ ··

"Why didn't you defend yourself?" Fox asked me as we left the palace. "You know you had no choice in what happened."

"But I did. I shouldn't have raised a hand against Telemaine. Guilty or not, he was the king. Kance deserved every chance to hear the old king's deception from his own mouth, with his own words. I took that away from him." I closed my eyes. *If you had been stronger,* a voice inside me whispered, *if you had been better, then Telemaine would be sane and Polaire would need not be dead.* "Shouldn't you be with Inessa?"

"She understands."

"We have different lives to lead, and sharing a bond makes that much more difficult. I...I don't know what you want to do, but if we have an option to break our—"

"No!" My brother leaned forward and wrapped me in a fierce hug. "We need someone in our heads to tell us whenever we're being idiotic. It's the Pahlavi way."

I returned his embrace. "But we don't need to be in each other's heads *all* the time. The best thing you can do for me is to live the life *you* want, Fox, and I know that is with Princess Inessa. I'm fine. I've been exiled, but Kance isn't going to lop off my head."

He glared at me. "Are you reading my thoughts again?"

"A wise man once said: 'We need someone in our heads to tell us whenever we're being idiotic. It's the Pahlavi way.'"

Fox sighed. "I'll get the horses. Best to leave Kneave before Kance has second thoughts."

As my brother took his leave, Kalen said, "You're good at hiding things from him, despite your bond."

"How would you know that?" I asked.

"I've been with you long enough and can tell that Fox doesn't read heartsglass. Polaire's death wasn't your fault, Tea."

"Then whose fault was it? I brought these events to fruition. I killed Aenah. I drove the king mad. If I was responsible for those happenings, why can't I be responsible for anything else?"

"Tea." Kalen's hands were on my shoulders. He did not argue, he shared no words in my defense, but his eyes were soft and his heartsglass glowed several brilliant shades of white. *How strange it is*, I thought, *that Kalen knows my guilt, knows my culpability, and yet, it doesn't matter to him.*

"You cannot let your cousin dismiss you like that," I whispered. "You cannot let what I did affect your relationship with Kance."

"It doesn't matter. As soon as I learned that Telemaine was responsible for my mother's death and my father's imprisonment, I knew I could not stay here in this kingdom. We will mend our bridges one day."

He took my hand. "I am no longer of the prince's guard nor his protector. I have no position to speak of other than *Deathseeker* and nothing but the sword on my back. I...I am not sure how much use I can be to you."

"You really are a bumbass." I kissed his hands. "If it wasn't for me, you would not have lost favor with Kance, and I will always bear that burden."

"What are you planning, Tea?"

"The elder asha are complicit in all this intrigue. Vanor said they did not conspire with Aenah, but I saw them in her head, Kalen. They shared common goals—enough that the elder asha were willing to look the other way when it came to Mykkie's heartsglass. I hold them just as responsible for Polaire's death as..."

Saying her name provoked another fresh bout of tears. "I have to find out, Kalen, for my peace of mind. I want to know why the elders are keeping secrets from the other asha. I want to know why they wanted Mykaela's heartsglass to stay hidden. Whatever falsehoods Aenah said, in this I know she spoke the truth: the elder asha are not what they claim to be. You should return to Holsrath and…and mourn."

"Are you turning me away, Tea?" His fierceness broke my heart.

"I can't ask you to stay. You just lost your father…"

"I lost him a long time ago, Tea. I'll mourn in my own way, and it won't need to be at Holsrath."

"But there's something wrong with me, Kalen." I unfastened my cloak, letting the fabric fall down my shoulders. My heartsglass gleamed in the fading light. Amid the hues of silver were the telltale flecks of black swimming in and out of view.

"Aenah talked about black heartsglass, and I can feel it starting within me. I killed her so brutally…and even now, I feel no remorse. Kance was right. Fox was right. I am changing—and not for the better. I don't want anyone else to die." I stumbled over the words. "I don't want to lose you."

"You will never lose me, Tea." Kalen kissed me gently. "And your heartsglass is all the more reason for me to be by your side. Turn me away if you want to, but that will not stop me from following your lead."

"Promise me one thing," I said. In the days after Polaire's death and Telemaine's madness, I could feel the darkness swirling inside me grow, the urge to give in to the darkrot became more appealing than ever. I felt no guilt over Aenah's death, and even with Telemaine, my conscience was affected only because he was Kance's father.

But that darkness eased whenever Kalen was near. I knew I would not break his trust for even the sweetest of the Dark. I remembered the comfort of his heartsglass when I had lain injured in the gardens, his *Heartshare* warming me like no antidote could. "Don't let me become a monster like Aenah, Kalen."

"You aren't a monster, Tea."

Not when you are with me, I'm not. I closed my eyes and lifted my face so Kalen's lips could find mine. *With you by my side,* I thought, *I could never be a monster.*

*I*T WAS EARLY DAWN.

She watched the sun rise and the stars fade beyond her reach. Her daeva were gathered around her, like children devoted to their mother, and the Deathseeker was at her side. She had healed them with her blood and a touch, but she remained fractured and broken herself, the never-healing scars inside her soul bearing the names of friends long gone.

"You were right, Kalen," she whispered. "We should have run—as far as we could, for as long as we could. I thought I had nothing left to lose, but I keep being proven wrong, time and time again. Stupid. So stupid. I will not lose Khalad. I will not lose Fox. I will not lose any more of the friends I abandoned in Kion and Odalia. Let us finish this. I..."

The Dark asha's voice wavered. She took a deep, shuddering breath. When she spoke again, the steel in her voice had returned. "Let us finish this."

The daeva rose to their feet. I moved, but she stopped me. "You will not be going with us, Bard."

"Your promised me your story," I reminded her.

"My war is with Drycht, Bard." She smiled grimly at the stunned look on my face. "It would be dangerous enough for you to return there alone, even without a bone witch and her familiars as company. I have already given you part of my story in the pages you have received. The rest are here in these letters addressed to my brother. Stay with him; he still knows so little. It would ease my mind if you would enlighten him." The azi lowered its body to the ground, and the bone witch and her familiar climbed up.

"Tea!" Lord Fox and Princess Inessa ran toward us. "What are you doing?"

"I killed Aenah, and I have killed Usij. There is one last Faceless to attend to." She wore two heartsglass around her neck: her own, still black as night, Hollow Knife's heart, and Usij's, now Blade that Soars's. "And when Druj is dead, I shall complete shadowglass."

"Stay, Tea," the princess pleaded. "The asha are willing to talk. The emissaries of the other kingdoms are prepared to hear what you have to say. Isn't that what you wanted?"

The bone witch shook her head, her voice raw when she spoke. "The asha will not like what I have to say; the remaining elders would make sure of that, and their companions' deaths will only be laid at my door. Kings and emperors fear change. It's far too late for simple conversation now, Inessa. There is only one way to end this, and I will not risk any more of you."

"Any risk you take will be mine as well." Lord Fox sounded hoarse. "Or have you forgotten our bond?"

The Dark asha smiled at him. "Distill the juices of the First Harvest into a familiar's heart to take back what death had decreed," she quoted, her hand on the faint silver-like heartscase around her throat, and the man's eyes widened. "Do you remember? You should. You were angry at me once for even suggesting it."

"*You can't!*"

"*Can't I?*" *She raised a hand to the sky, fingers grasping at something invisible to my eyes. "What's one more lie to believe when I am just a scheming, murderous bone witch, constantly seeking stars beyond her reach? Most people reject the truth, Fox. Lies are sweet to the palate, but the truth is often spat out, bitter and rancid. Politeness and veracity have never walked hand in hand. But when I die, at least I shall die knowing my eyes were open, looking at all there was to see. And when that day comes, I will make sure you have no part to suffer in it."*

Her voice dropped, gentled. "The bard has my letters. It would do you good to read them. Be well, Fox. If we are doomed to give our lives for missions good and great, then at least let mine be for you."

"*No!*"

The azi *lifted off the ground, its wings spreading. All the daeva roared as one, and from the towering* nanghait *to the spike-ringed* aeshma *to the crooning* taurvi, *they moved to follow. None of the soldiers were mad enough to block their path.*

We could do little but watch, Sir Fox and I, as the beasts retreated into the distance. The breeze came as the last of them disappeared over the horizon; in it, I smelled, strangely enough, the faint salt of the sea. I looked down at the papers in my hands, the Dark asha's parting gift, pages I had yet to read. I have always known darkness, *she had written in the first line of the first letter.*

Lord Fox broke my reverie. "We break camp within the hour," he ordered. *"Tell the men we shall leave first for Kion and then to Drycht." And I knew the story was far from over.*

The World of the Bone Witch:
The Eight Kingdoms

ISTERA

- The coldest among the eight kingdoms
- Has gone to war with Tresea over the Heartsbane Islands in the past and still shares some animosity
- Separated from Tresea by the River of Peace

CAPITAL: Farsun

CURRENT RULER: King Rendorvik of House Petralta

TRESEA

- Composed of mostly dense woods and wide plains
- Population is concentrated mainly in cities, with small scatterings of villages throughout

CAPITAL: Highgaard

CURRENT RULER: Czar Kamulus of House Ambersturg

DAANORIS

- Mild to moderate weather, most-populated kingdom

CAPITAL: Santiang

CURRENT RULER: Emperor Shifang

YADOSHA CITY-STATES

- The whole continent was originally the kingdom of Yadosha, but infighting among the royal descendants soon splintered it into several warring states and shrunk their dominion into only its upper continent
- While each city-state maintains a high degree of independence, all share one main government to foster ties and maintain diplomatic missions
- Each city-state has a second minister to govern them; every seven years, a first minister is elected among the second ministers to represent Yadosha as a whole

CAPITAL: None

CURRENT RULER: First Minister Stefan

KION

- Once a part of Yadosha; many kingdoms conquered and fought over this land before Kion was able to achieve its independence through Vernasha of the Roses, a legendary asha
- A melting pot of culture and the main headquarters of the asha
- Smallest land among the kingdoms

CAPITAL: Ankyo

CURRENT RULER: Empress Alyx of House Imperial

ODALIA

- Composed of plains and forests
- Originally a part of the kingdom of Yadosha but was the first in the continent to rebel and break off into its own kingdom

CAPITAL: Kneave

CURRENT RULER: King Telemaine of House Odalia

ARHEN-KOSHO

- Large group of islands on the Swiftsea, near Odalia and Kion

CAPITAL: Hottenheim

CURRENT RULER: Queen Lynoria of House Imperial

DRYCHT

- Desert kingdom
- Also notable for its austere and extreme perspective generally held in contempt by most of the other kingdoms but tolerated for the runeberry cloth it provides
- Only the western continent of Drycht is heavily populated; the majority of the kingdom is made of sand

CAPITAL: Adra-al

CURRENT RULER: King Aadil of the Tavronoo clan

Acknowledgments

Writing is a solitary affair, but a book is a group effort rarely acknowledged. With that in mind, I would like to thank, as I always will, the lovely Sourcebooks team working to add coherency to my drafts—Annette, my lovely editor; Elizabeth; Alex; Kathryn; Gretchen; and everyone else. And always, always, my eternal gratitude to Becca.

Much thanks to my husband, Les, who has learned to interpret my inarticulate grunts and growls of frustration while I slave over chapters by cheerfully getting out of my way and attending to our other immediate concerns on his own until I emerge from my lair, wild-eyed and stubbled, signaling my return to sanity.

And also to Idris Elba. Because if you haven't thanked Idris Elba for anything yet, what have you been doing all this time?

About the Author

Rin Chupeco wrote obscure manuals for complicated computer programs, talked people out of their money at event shows, and did many other terrible things. She now writes about ghosts and fairy tales but is still sometime mistaken for a revenant.

She currently lives in the Philippines with her husband, their son, a hyperactive dog, and far too many cats. Find her at rinchupeco.com.